THE T
DEFENDER

EMMA JAYNE TAYLOR

This book is dedicated to those who continue to fight through the barriers of fear to succeed in their dreams!

PROLOGUE

Lights were shining in all directions and swords were shimmering with blinding sharpness. Gold faces moved in and out of view. Greys created mist shapes flowing through the light in snake-like movements.

Metal-against-metal clunked, with muffles of voices expressing effort.

Eagle calls echoed through the lights and shadows.

The light faded slightly to allow the view of golden helmets and silver swords moving so swiftly, creating smears of action. Blindingly bright - a golden helmet becomes clearer as focus zooms in. Gritted teeth just in sight - sweat and saliva is seen thrown violently into the air.

A familiar figure comes closer, grunting and moving with great effort. The silver glimmer of an inscribed sword moves through the air, cutting through the grey mist, allowing light to crack through.

The lights of white and gold become too bright to view and the battle is clearly over. Breaths of recovery and relief now fill the ears of everyone within the zone.

All that remains is mist dropping to the floor.

The view becomes clearer.

The master stands tall with his glimmering sword now resting by his side, yet gripped in readiness.

A tall lady of golds and oranges walks into view and a strikingly powerful voice leaves her, pulling everyone's attention.

'The time is coming. Be watchful my friends.'
The master and all of the golden-armoured fighters
congregate and lower their heads slightly to the tall lady
figure.
'Come to the table.' The powerful lady spoke again with
gentle encouragement.
The golden armour moved with tiresome bodies to a small
circular table, where many gathered in peace.

Tall people appeared from a distance, carrying large, golden
jars.
The armoured fighters congregated around a table and sat.
The jars were placed in front of them.
As they drank from them, their energy was replenished.
After a small few minutes, they stood and walked away with
great strength. The master remained in view and watched
the fighters move away.
The tall lady stood in the background, casting her voice
gently over to the master with a reminding sentence.
'The time will be soon.'
The master nodded in respectful acknowledgement.

The scene around them glimmered in light and peace.
Stones and rocks appeared to be alive and vibrant.

The master stood silently, placing his sword in his sheath.
Two very large, golden-striped tigers came from gaps in the
nearby shrubbery to sit either side of him. Their appearance

was of great pride and strength. The master stood with them as if normal daily practice.

The tall lady walked away, grinning broadly.

ONE

Kyle Parsons was a teenager who was just about to walk in on a surprise. It was a Wednesday and he was on his way home after another day of school. It hadn't been an easy day, as his History teacher had decided to keep him alert with various questions that pickled his brain. Thankfully Kyle's last lesson was Mathematics, which he enjoyed very much. His teacher was very encouraging, but it helped that she was a stunning looking lady with matching kindness.

Walking home was a fair distance, so by the time he arrives home he generally throws his shoes and jacket to the ground and heads for the sofa. On this particular day the sun was scorching, so his jacket sat comfortably over his arm and his walking slowed to a steadier pace.

Today was Kyle's birthday, but the secret remained within his own mind at school. He didn't want anyone knowing, as he hated any embarrassing attention. His one friend would have struggled with it too. They were both quiet and always wished to avoid any awkward situations. Kyle is picked on quite frequently, as he doesn't fit in with the majority of the school kids.
Kyle had a natural cuteness to him, with dark hair and brown eyes. He was of slim build with long legs that gave the impression of added length, despite being of average height. His intellect matched the high ranks, but his confidence was

low which didn't help when faced with school examinations. His lack of confidence shows at school, which unfortunately has been attracting some bullying. He knew he lacked confidence but simply put it down to his personality and that there could be no deliberate change. The problem with his lack of confidence is that it shows in his expressions and in posture. His face looks shy and fearful, while his shoulders typically hunch forward.

Kyle of course wasn't aware of the way he was portraying himself, but he knew people just simply recognised that he lacked confidence.

He was now walking close to home and walked up the thin pathway which brought him to the large front door. The handle was always stiff this time of year.

His parents had a very old-fashioned house. The main doors were of very thick wood with wrought iron features. It reminded him of a castle at times, as all of the doors, windows, walls and coves in every part of the house had that ancient feature. It wasn't the biggest house in the neighbourhood, but it gave the four of his brothers and his two parents, plenty of space.

He opened the door and walked in to an unusually quiet hallway. This time he looked about suspiciously as he decided to hang his jacket on the nearest wall hook and leave his shoes directly underneath. Something disturbingly quiet was occurring. Usually the house was a hive of activity and noise. He walked cautiously into the kitchen which was directly ahead. He wondered if everyone had gone out without being informed. Disappointment filled him, as they *usually* did family things together. It was too quiet, but he noticed the kitchen window had been left open, which he thought was a bit careless.

He gave up looking and decided to find the staircase that took him towards his bedroom. Getting changed into a pair of casual jeans and a light t-shirt, he felt he was a little more like the "cooler" group of boys he'd see locally. He decided to head downstairs to watch some television for distraction from the quietness. The door to the living room was closed tightly, which took a force to push open.

'SURPRISE!'
He opened the door to a group of familiar faces, all holding big grins.
Once his mind and heart had settled to the scene, he noticed the giggles in the room and his father calling him over to a large cake on a small table in front of him.
'Happy Birthday, Son.' He grabbed Kyle and gave him a hearty hug.
'Fourteen years old today! - Not long before you're saying goodbye to your school years. You're growing up fast!'
Kyle wasn't sure if he should feel elated or worried about leaving school, or about the age he had just turned. The thought of any kind of responsibility in life didn't seem a factor in his mind. Youth and dependence was most certainly a way of living at this point. At age fourteen, he was starting to notice the already-serious relationships taking off at school but he didn't tie it up with the future of having a

family and working long hours. The occasional thought was his dream girl, Karen – the only girl that his eyes lit up for. He always believed that it would manifest one day despite the many brief boyfriend encounters she was already having with her popularity.

Kyle realised his mind had slipped away, so brought it back to the room. He looked around and spotted his family members. His four brothers (who were only interested in their slice of cake soon to be administered); his mother who was already entertaining her sister and all of the cousins (which contained three teenage girls and one boy of 11); two of Dad's single male friends were in the room as well as a couple of people who Kyle didn't recognise.

Kyle began to wonder how they all managed to keep so quiet when he first arrived home. He didn't think too much on the situation however, as they all began to sing 'Happy Birthday' vibrantly. They then took turns patting him on the back or giving him a bear hug.

Kyle's brothers were varied in age. One was at 16 years and soon to leave school (Jack); the others being 13, named Paul; one at 11 named Geoff; and the other only 9 - named Carl (which proved difficult when the names Carl and Kyle sound very similar). Often the mother would call one and both Carl and Kyle would respond.

Paul and Geoff were very close as brothers it seemed, but Kyle was protective and loving of Carl. As they aged, attention on one another varied.

Jack (the oldest) seemed to hang out with other people his age and appeared keen to escape school in order to get to work. He often spoke of how his house was going to look and how his ideal design of furniture would be. He was keen to have parties organised for his popular friends. Although Jack loved all of his brothers, he kept his distance from them when he was with his friends, as if he was too "cool" to be associated with anyone younger or not up to his standards. No habits appeared to bother anyone however, as everyone was innocently growing up and observing things in their own way. The house was buzzing with life and energy.

Kyle enjoyed his moment of celebration and ate as much cake as he could manage. Everyone embraced the little party that had gathered with conversation and playfulness.

Jack walked up to Kyle and punched him on his upper arm in the way that he always did. It appeared to be his level of affection.

'So little bro, isn't it time you got yourself some gear and a new rep?'

Kyle gave a look that said 'huh?'

'You know...' Jack Continued, 'you need a new look if you're going to get any lady luck.'

Kyle felt a little insulted. At home he could truly be himself, so responded honestly.

'I can get any lady I like. I don't want someone to like me for my image.'

Jack stumbled for a moment over the wise reply.

'Ok, well let's say I wanna help you as a bro. I've seen the way you walk around at school. Others pick on you and you just let them. I get my mates coming over asking me if you're really my brother. They can't understand why you are, *like,* the opposite of me.'

Kyle felt the hair on his neck stand with offence. He didn't think the insult was appropriate at his own birthday party.

'Stuff you Jack.' He walked away and began to look for Carl. Jack followed swiftly behind and tugged his t-shirt to re-gain his attention.

'Ok, ok... Let's start again.' He breathed. 'How about I say I could make you cool and get all the girls to like you? Not entirely for you, but because it's killing me seeing you get pushed around. Maybe it could be your birthday present.'

Kyle still wasn't certain he wanted to listen, but felt that Jack was genuinely trying to help. Perhaps he could assist in moving the bullies away.

'If you're serious...'

Before Kyle could finish his sentence, Jack grabbed him by his upper arm and dragged him in a manly fashion to Jack's bedroom.

'Ok, look at this.' Jack pulled his clothes out of the cupboard, showing him the styles.

Kyle just watched on as Jack attempted to talk him through what works and how to wear clothes in a way that portrays the right image.

They spent hours in the bedroom going through the right look and how Kyle's new wardrobe could look. By the end of it, Kyle acquired some of Jack's hand-me-downs – some older jeans and school trousers.

They even went through the right walk and way to stand, along with better hair styles, giving Kyle a "trendier" look and feel.

Everyone celebrating Kyle's birthday downstairs appeared to continue with noisy chatter. It appeared that he wasn't necessarily required in the room for the party to continue. His mother occasionally popped her head into the bedroom to see what he was doing, but didn't disturb the two brothers, as it appeared to be a bonding time. It brought a smile to her face.

TWO

The following day came and Kyle felt a lot more confident about his day. He wore Jack's old school trousers, allowing them to fit in a way that Jack said looked a little more fashionable. His school shirt was a little baggy and portraying a more casual image. Kyle knew deep down that it was very shallow to follow fashion in order to gain popularity, but if it helped to avoid poor treatment then it may be worth a try.

Jack spotted him on the way out. 'Don't let yourself down now. Remember how I told you to stand and walk.'

Kyle had already forgotten about his taller way of standing.

'I bet you go back to walking like a plonker as soon as you get to school.'

'I won't!' He replied hard, but Jack had a teasing grin.

School time had arrived and Kyle already noticed people giving him second glances as he walked up through the main entrance towards the main doors of the school. He found his deliberate walking method felt rigid and uncomfortable, uncertain as if he would be able to hold his ground.

His first lesson was English literature. The others were talking between themselves, taking glances at Kyle. He felt uncomfortable, noticing the little ball he was making of himself, trying to hide.

Even his "dreamy" girl – Karen, took a look and managed to hold her eyes on him for longer than a few seconds. He felt

14

himself get uncomfortably hot. He knew his face would be bright red at this point, but he reached down to the side to pretend to look into his bag, perhaps to have them believe the blood had rushed to his head for that reason.

The class began...
'Ok everyone!' The teacher pulled their attention to the front. 'Let's continue where we left off with this book.' He pulled out the "Of Mice and Men" title and pointed to the front cover.
A gentle whisper of discontent went through the room.
'In fact, today I am pleased to tell you that we are going to watch the film up to the point that we have read up to - and compare the two.'
Kyle began to worry about his concentration levels as the occasional person continued to glance back at him as if he had something written on his head.
'All eyes to the front!' The teacher grew impatient to gain their full attention.
'I expect everyone to be able to make a lot of comparisons by the point it's paused.'
Everyone watched as the teacher fumbled with old technology in order to play one old video cassette.

A few hours had passed – a few lessons attended and eventually everyone seemed to acclimatise to Kyle's new image.

On the way home, a girl from his Business class rushed over to him.

'Kyle.' She went red. 'I noticed your hair today. It looks nice.'

He couldn't believe his ears.

'Thanks.' He didn't know how to respond to compliments since he wasn't accustomed to them.

Just as she continued on her intended route home, one of Kyle's usual bullies brushed past his shoulder – knocking his head enough for his black hair to dangle across the front of his face like an older rock star.

'Look at little Kyle trying to look all cool and sexy. You're still a pussy to me.'

He moved closer to Kyle and pushed his shoulder into his body so hard, that he ended up off balance, falling back onto his ruck sack full of books.

A group of boys stood still, all laughing in his direction.

'See! You're still a pussy weakling geek.'

Kyle looked up to see Jack looking on from a distance with a disappointed face.

The bully moved away, laughing mockingly.

Kyle stood, looking in all directions for people's reactions to the event. Everyone slowly moved away – some shaking their heads.

It wasn't until everyone was at home that Jack mentioned the incident.

The family sat around the dining room table, consuming a small meal of sandwiches and nibbles.

'You shouldn't let that guy push you about.' Jack spoke quietly to his brother.

Kyle grew angry. 'You shouldn't just watch him push me about. A little help would have been nice.'

Jack knew he would never win in an intellectual argument. At the end of the day, Jack was more of the sporting hero than the academic type.

'Show them that you're not afraid of them. Resist their pushing. I'll show you later.'

Kyle wondered why Jack wanted to help him after all of these years of humiliation. Why now? Why not at an earlier age? He remained suspicious, but at the same time recognised the attention he gained within one day of an appearance-adjustment.

The father looked up. 'What are you boys talking about over there? Let's get some smiles on our faces and enjoy some good grub.'

Their Dad was always looking to keep the atmosphere light at dinner times.

It was a quiet meal however, as everyone appeared to be absorbed in their own thoughts.

Later on, Kyle sat in his room looking at the overwhelming homework he had been set, wondering if he could get away with leaving some of it for another night.

His door opened very slightly. Jack's face appeared through the gap. 'What you doing?'

'Homework. It might be best to leave me alone.'

'Look I'm just trying to help you. I'm leaving school, so you need to take care of yourself now.'

Kyle frowned. 'I've always had to take care of myself.'

Jack looked guilty. 'Ok, maybe I should have paid more attention to what was going on. I'm a bit late, but I really noticed how you're letting your friends push you about lately.'

'They've always pushed me about. I wouldn't call them *friends* either.'

'Ah man. Well, maybe I was blind before. You got to understand that I can't look like I'm being uncool in front of my friends. That probably sounds really bad doesn't it?' Jack was attempting showing a soft side. 'Can I just show you how to move if someone tries to push you?'

Kyle was encouraged gently. 'I guess so.'

Jack gestured for him to climb to his feet.

They both stood and Jack got Kyle to push him while he stood still. It moved him slightly but the push didn't faze him. Then Jack showed Kyle how to twist his waist every time one arm came in to push one of his shoulders. If two arms pushed him, then he stepped back with one leg whilst raising his arms to block.

Kyle found himself enjoying the brotherly lessons and soon picked the moves up, wishing to know more.

'Maybe you should go to some kind of class and learn some fighting art.' Jack suggested. 'I'm limited, so can only show you what I know.'

'Can't you teach me a bunch of stuff?'

'Like I say, I don't really know that much. I just know enough to make people think I know how to defend myself. You see a lot of the time it's about being confident enough to make people think you're able to handle yourself. That's why you've got to relax your shoulders and not hunch.'

Jack moved Kyle's posture about again. 'You'll get it with practice.'

'Boys!' Mother was shouting from downstairs. "I need you all to come down here and help Dad get this heavy stuff out to the skip.'

'I guess that's all we can do for now.' Jack sounded frustrated at the interruption.

All of the boys had previously helped their father pull all of the old kitchen tiles from the walls and replace them with a modern set of tiles. It had taken a few weekends to do, but now the rubble from the old tiles needed moving out after they had arranged a skip to come.

Jack and Kyle looked disappointed with the disruption, but still made their way down to the kitchen.

Jack smiled. 'You need to do more of this stuff too. It'll get you stronger.'

19

Kyle secretly knew he was relatively strong, but he just didn't know how to use it effectively. It was like having a super power he didn't know how to utilise.

The following day Kyle walked to school, again being aware of his posture and enjoying the feeling of knowing a little more about standing up for himself. As the day went on, he noticed a few more looks from Karen. The unfortunate thing was that she was always in the company of the most popular people and very difficult to get anywhere near.
He was very surprised however when they all walked away from the cafeteria when lunch had been consumed. Karen deliberately ran over and brushed shoulders with Kyle, giving him a cheeky smile as she passed, continuing to run through one of the long corridors. He felt so much excitement fill his mind. His eyes almost bulged out of his head with the shock of his dream lady giving him attention.

Karen and Kyle shared the same Art group, which was a little bit more of a relaxed class. The students were allowed to chat as they worked. Karen decided to sit in Kyle's eye view this time and discretely look over occasionally. He felt uncomfortable for the entire hour of this class. Being sociable was now something he needed to look at, as he wasn't used to talking with anyone outside of his comfort zone. His best friend was someone he felt comfortable with, since he was one of the least popular people at school.

Kyle overheard Karen say something to her friend who sat next to her. It sounded as if she said that Kyle was looking "sweet".

The lesson was soon over - much to Kyle's relief! It was time to head for home, so he took the quickest route through the school gates to avoid any conflict from any of his bullies. Unfortunately someone had been waiting for him and managed to trip him up just as he turned the sharpest corner. Kyle's body leaped forward and he landed hard on his hands, instantly hurting his wrists. Before he had chance to figure out what had happened, he felt someone lift him up from his shirt collar. He tried to grip the person's hand to loosen the feeling of being strangled. As he attempted this, he heard a deep voice bellow into his ear.
'Keep away from her. You understand?'
He couldn't reply, but still managed to move his head slightly with a nod.
A noise of scuffling came from behind him and a familiar voice came to his ears.
'Get off him!'
Kyle managed to roll over onto his back, looking up to see his brother, Jack, pushing his bully to the ground. Jack reached down to help Kyle up. As Kyle reached to his feet, he looked over to see Karen looking directly at Jack from a distance. Her eyes were large and her mouth sat open with amazement. Kyle instantly knew that Jack would have caught her attention for being very much the hero.

Despite the fact Jack had saved him on this occasion, Kyle walked away feeling very sorry for himself. It wasn't easy being humiliated by one of Karen's admirers and then being second best to his brother.

Jack however ran after his brother. 'Kyle! I got your back man! Where are you going?'

Kyle continued with his head looking downward, walking in silence.

'Hey! Kyle!' Jack's running footsteps were heard.

'I saw you in trouble and helped this time.' It appeared he was seeking a response of gratitude.

Kyle slowed down and looked over, realising his errors.

'Sorry. Thanks for helping me.'

'Come on. Let's move on. I think we've really got to find a defence class for you.'

'It's not that... I was getting some looks from a girl I've fancied for years, but now she is looking at *you* because you saved me from getting my butt kicked. That bully made a fool of me big time.'

Jack looked back, noticing a cute girl staring at the two of them walking away.

'Argh. I'm sorry. I didn't realise. It might not be that bad.'

They both walked in silence until they arrived home. Kyle shook his wrists, hoping the pain of his fall would soon pass.

Jack looked on, not sure of the best words of comfort.

Everyone was at home again, all consumed in their own interests. Kyle was feeling quite fed-up with his humiliating times. He often thought about running off somewhere as they do in films, hoping to find someone who would take him on to provide him with all things for survival, giving him chance to recreate his life somewhere else. Of course things don't work out the same as they do in films, so he shook the idea from his mind. He did however think about going for a long bicycle ride just to clear his mind. After a few minutes he stood and decided to take action.

'Mum, I'm just off for a bike ride!'

There was a pause.

'Ok, well make sure you're back for dinner! Don't go off too far!'

Kyle was well on his cycle route, feeling active and full of energy, working up hills and through some country land too, trying to find adventure of some sort. He went out for what felt like hours. He thought he had better check the time, so pulled his small phone from his pocket to see it was beyond dinner time and that his mother had attempted to call him. Panicking, he changed direction and cycled as fast as he could towards home. He knew he would be at least half an hour, but he didn't think about returning his worried-parent's call. He just pushed through his cycling power to get a fast move home. The cycling made him feel alive again.

Once he arrived home all sweaty and muddy, his parents were extremely angry.

23

'I tried calling you several times! I did say to get back before dinner. When will you listen to me?'

His mother had a very deep red colour to her face. The rest of the siblings looked uncomfortable at the dinner table, having only just finished their meals.

Kyle could only hang his head low and wonder if they saved him a plate. His father looked at him with a stern face. 'You can get your dinner and then head upstairs for the rest of the day. You're staying in this weekend. It's important that you understand the reasons for rules in the house.'

Kyle began contemplating his father's words instantly and felt guilty for not keeping an eye on the time. He secretly felt better however after his energetic cycle ride.

THREE

Kyle didn't expect to feel so bored on the Saturday. Everyone sounded as if they were moving in and out of the front door with high energy and excitement, whilst he remained indoors feeling sorry for himself. He couldn't remember the last time he had upset his parents, as usually he was the introverted one in the house who stuck to the rules and usual routines.

His innocent cycle ride and loss of time had cost him his weekend. The worst for him was hearing his best friend arrive at the front door, to be turned away by his Dad, explaining that he was grounded.

He sat, playing games on his phone, feeling fed-up about things generally.

The contemplation of sneaking out entered his mind. He heard his mother and father discussing a trip to the local supermarket to get a monthly shop done. Kyle knew that would take the entire afternoon to complete, as he generally got dragged along to help push the shopping trolley and haul the bags into the car. His brothers were usually designated to empty the contents of the shopping bags into the appropriate cupboards.

He heard the car leave, which triggered him to go and see where his brothers were. The house felt empty, so he ran downstairs to grab his push bike with the idea to go for another bike ride. It would at least erase his boredom for the rest of the day. He felt too hyperactive to stay in the house for another minute. He pulled his bike outside and began to cycle in a safe direction, away from any usual routes his parents would take.

He peddled hard and fast down the road and took himself to a hidden path that brought him to some steps that he sometimes liked to rattle the bike down. He rumbled over the steps, downward and went through a deep puddle of mud, through a sandy path, taking him a few minutes through some wonderful green scenery. The ride made him feel alive and strong, so he pedalled harder through the rough ground of rubble and mud, through to some large trees. The branches on the ground were thick and long, allowing him to use them as jumping ramps for more fun.

He came to a section of ground where a group of older teenagers were smoking together and play-fighting in a collection of old leaves. Kyle wanted to stop and turn around, but he was going too fast, so the braking noise would draw attention to him. With one path and no alternative way through, he focussed forward and attempted to move faster, but one of them jumped out and attempted to grab the handle bars, even at great speed.

'No!' Kyle shouted as he pulled the brakes to avoid hitting the stranger.

It gave the boy a chance to grab the bike and shake Kyle off, onto the ground. He landed on surprisingly soft ground (much to his relief). The boy had taken ownership of the bike however, leaving Kyle panicking and shouting.

'Hey! I need my bike!'

The other boy looked on with deep, dark and heavy eyes. His hair was gelled back tightly, with one strand of hair falling over his face with the physical motions.

'Come and have a smoke.'

Kyle looked at them and felt himself shake inside. They must've been a couple or so years older than him. They were much taller and broader, so he knew he had no chance of winning any battle with them. Any means of escape would be difficult. Their leg strides would be much longer and their strength would be impossible to tackle.

Strangely, they all stared at him, waiting for a decision.

Kyle felt pressure to stay and comply with any request, even if he could fake something. It would be the only way to keep them sweet and possibly escape at a later minute.

The other boy handed a small item to him, which he nervously accepted.

'It's a smoke. Take a breath of it.'

Kyle wondered why they would bother with him. He only wanted to cycle past.

The face of the boy looked a little more intense.

'Come on! Smoke it!'

The pressure was on. For some reason, he had to please these strangers and smoke something he would never normally touch.

He moved his hand up, firstly thinking he would be sharing the saliva of a stranger.

The other boys moved to form a circle around him.

Tension grew and Kyle now wished he had stayed at home and visualised himself still sat on his bed, playing safely on his phone.

He placed the small rolled up paper to his lips and breathed inward, instantly coughing it back.

The older boys laughed. One of them hit another one the chest. 'He's just a 10-year-old.'

Kyle didn't feel insulted as he knew the group of boys were life-wasters. His only concern was to escape the situation.

'Take a proper breath!' The boy said again with intensity.

Kyle spoke up. 'It doesn't work for me.'

The boy walked up intensely close. 'Take another breath! Deeper this time!'

As Kyle was about to comply yet again, a rustle from a nearby bush was heard and the gang of boys looked "twitchy".

They all gathered their items and began to run off rather swiftly.

'Enjoy little boy! Don't waste it!' They shouted as they ran off.

Kyle turned to see a man, aged similar to his father approaching the area. Kyle hid the cigarette behind his back and dropped it to the ground discretely.

'Hey!' He shouted in a deep tone.

Kyle felt trouble again and reached for his bike, preparing to cycle for his life.

The man grabbed the saddle of the bike, just as Kyle was prepared to jump onto it.

Kyle's heart felt as if it was going to burst from his chest.

'What were you doing with those trouble makers?'

'Nothing, Sir. I was just cycling through here and they ganged up on me.'

The man looked into Kyle's eyes as if reading his mind.

'Ok, well you'd better scoot off, but don't stop for anyone you don't know. You don't want to get mixed up with those kinds of boys. They are always hiding around here, smoking things they shouldn't be smoking!'

'Okay Sir.' Kyle agreed politely and confidently jumped on his bike to finally escape the weird scene.

'Get out of here!' The man shouted aggressively.

He realised his lucky escape and cycled faster than he had ever cycled before, taking full control of his breathing.

His home was now within view and he pulled up into the front door fairly swiftly as if being chased by a ghost. As he moved inward, carrying his bike, he could hear Carl speaking with Jack in the kitchen, so he had-to go back outside and find his way through a pathway that would lead to a side door. Luckily he made it in with no trouble, placing his bike in its usual place. He made his way upstairs as quietly as he could.

'Oy! You're meant to stay in the house!' Jack's voice stunned Kyle, as he reached the top end of the stairs.

'I know. I just wanted to stretch my legs.'

Kyle noticed that Jack observed his muddy trousers and red face, but said nothing.

Sunday came extremely swiftly.

Kyle's parents felt guilty about the grounding, so encouraged him to be more sociable with the family for the day. His Mother began by sitting beside him on his bed.

'Kyle, I know it seems harsh keeping you inside for the weekend, but I just want you to know how serious I am about the rules we set. What I do for you now is for your safety. Most of us don't realise until we are parents ourselves. We always think our parents are harsh on us. Just because you're grounded, you don't need to stay in your room. We do miss you when you're not with the rest of us. I just want you to know that we truly do what we believe is right to bring our kids up.'

Kyle already knew the reasons and felt guilty for sneaking out without their knowing.

'It's OK Mum. I already realised that you must have worried.' He wanted to add more about losing track of time that day, but thought it would be best just to accept his faults.

She hugged him and agreed the end of the grounding.

The family went out for a nice meal together, forgetting one another's troubles.

FOUR

Monday came all too quickly and panic rose in Kyle's stomach, with the thought of having to face Karen and those who frequently make a fool of him. He threw his shirt on and looked at his hair in the mirror, redesigning it to Jack's suggested style. In his mind he decided it would be yet another opportunity for a fresh start.

Walking into the main school corridors, he noticed Karen in the near distance, looking through her locker whilst chatting with her friend, Kate.

He studied them as they spoke, admiring Karen's wonderful long and luscious hair which seemed to flow naturally with any of her movements. He imagined the silky feeling as he visualised his hand combing through her hair.

Just as he went deep into his thoughts, he noticed Kate nudging Karen, which caused her to turn directly to Kyle's dreamy stares. She flushed and instantly looked downwards, then swiftly looked back up to something in her locker. Kate looked as if she was making jokes. Kyle realised his obvious expression and quickly changed the direction of his eyes. He spotted one of his friends leaning against a wall, waiting for the first bell to direct him to his class.

'Mark!' Kyle shouted with relief.

His friend looked up and smiled to see a friendly face.

'Hi.'

'What class is first? I haven't even looked.'

'Geography... Boring.'

Kyle realised his favourite girl wouldn't be there. 'Darn.'
The bell rang almost at the same time as his words hit the air.
All of the students responded to the noise and closed lockers;
picked their bags up and moved in different directions.
Kyle was surprised to see a familiar face in the background.
It was Jack, waiting for him in an obvious place. 'Kyle!'
Jack waved him over. 'I need to see you quickly.'
He walked over, wondering what could possibly be so urgent.
'I've got a great idea on how to get your girl to fall in love
with you.'
'Oh yeah?' Kyle was trying to show some interest, but had
his reservations.
'Trust me. I've got a plan. It's gonna be great!' Jack gave him
a pat on the back and casually walked away.

Kyle thought Jack was behaving weirdly lately. Giving him
attention and trying to do nice things. They usually had a
distant relationship – but he didn't have time to think about
that now, as he had five minutes to get to his first class.
He reached the room and noticed all seats other than his
were occupied, but luckily the teacher hadn't arrived as yet.
Everyone was engrossed in conversation and laughter.
Mr. Sarcombe walked through the door only seconds after
Kyle's arrival, much to his relief.
'Good morning everyone!'
The class responded with a feeble and scattered 'Good
morning.'

'Ok, so no time to slack this time of year. We have some studying to do before our Mock exams. I'd like to go through any weak points that anyone would like to bring up.'

... And so the class continued, until the bell rang for the next subject in another room down the lengthy corridor. Luckily, many of the students followed one another to each class with its' new subject, as many of them would no longer have the navigation skills to find the locations.

The next lesson was Art and Kyle grew excited about seeing his 'eye candy' for an hour. He could attempt to give subtle looks at Karen again with the hope that she may accept a compliment.

As he walked through the wide and cold walkway, he noticed a group of boys form a restricting circle around him. Kyle stopped in his tracks and tried to study each face. It was like a telepathic language, causing the entire crowd of students on the same route to stop, leaving Kyle as the centre of attention. A boy that looked very familiar stood eyeball to eyeball with Kyle without warning.

'Whatchu trying to be cool for? Huh?'

Kyle was shocked and confused at the negative attention, suddenly mindful of needing his brother's help at that very moment.

He felt a finger prod his chest hard. 'What do you think you're playing at?'

Kyle was still confused about the situation.

Jack shouted through the rear of the crowd. 'Finish him Kyle!'

Instant fear hit him, as he wasn't sure why his brother's voice shouted violent instructions without the will to help. Previous promises of his assistance ran through his mind within a spit second. *This wasn't a method of help!*

The crowd that gathered - started shouting various words that didn't make any sense. The energy was building with tension, fear and aggression. Names and accusations were being thrown about with no meaning at all.

Kyle felt a bubble of bravery fill him. It was almost as if everyone's voice gave him a sudden burst of courage.

Perhaps it was the pressure to do something. Strangely, the pressure was working.

He visualised pushing the boy backward so hard that he would have no choice but to fall to the ground. He felt that bubble inside his mind so much that the strength in his body appeared to grow fiercely. His arms felt like coiled springs that suddenly decided to lift up and push the boy as powerfully backwards as possible. He pushed hard, with surprising force, causing the bully to lose his footing and fall on his bottom. The whole corridor of people grew silent... then seconds later a brewing of laughter filled the space, echoing through Kyle's ears extremely loudly. Fear hit him, with worry that his opponent may stand and attempt to fight again.

To his surprise, his enemy was so offended by the mass of laughter that he grabbed his feeble-looking school bag and stumbled in the opposite direction, pushing through gaps of the crowd, who pointed at him and insulted him.

A loud, mature voice shouted from the distance.

'What's going on here?'

Everyone looked nervous and scattered about trying to look for their original direction to class.

Kyle felt shocked and brave at the same time, trying to gather his thoughts, ready for his next lesson.

He looked behind him to see Jack give him the thumbs up before running back towards the class he was meant to be in. Then suspicion hit him. Why was Jack there for the event as if expecting it to happen? Either way, Kyle felt good about what he had managed to achieve. Never had he ever pushed anyone to the ground, looking strong in a crowd of many. A buzz of heroic feeling made him feel like dancing. He gulped, as if to swallow his emotions. Everyone had diverted to the normal course of the day as if the event hadn't even occurred. He managed to focus on going to his next class.

The art class was a dream come true! Karen looked directly into his eyes from the opposite side of the large table. Her lips opened with a bright white set of teeth smiling.

'You were great back there.'

The class was loud with chatter, but he heard her words very clearly, causing him to find a comfortable, thin smile in response.

He noticed her flush with embarrassment, much to his surprise. Knowing her shyness gave him added confidence. She had-to say what she thought however. 'You're quite a quiet guy aren't you?'

Kyle realised he probably hadn't even spoken to her as of yet.

'Well, I guess I'm more of a listener.' He almost stuttered, but managed to keep a clear and steady sentence much to his relief.

Strangely these were the only words they exchanged, but the glances continued throughout the lesson. He felt that his life was about to change for the better.

It was soon lunch time and people were paying Kyle much more attention. Some were walking past, patting his back, while others were throwing him brief compliments of his bravery.

He overheard people talking about the fight and how the great bully was pushed to the ground with one push.

Although he felt very excited about the positive attention, he also felt a little nervous about the consequences of this new bench mark of fighting ability that he secretly didn't have.

The day was enjoyed immensely however. He soaked up every moment.

The usual trek home began and Mark came running over with interest.

'Hi Kyle! You've had a great day then?'

He glanced over to see his happy friend's face.

'Well, yeah. I didn't enjoy the fight, but the rest of it was good.'

'Great! Well, may it long continue.'

Mark ran off towards his own street in high spirits.

It wasn't until Kyle was five minutes from home that he found himself on his own. Another shock was about to come his way. He caught his breath suddenly to a sharp jolt forward. He nearly fell to his knees, but he managed to keep upright and spin quickly to view another enemy. This time his shirt collar was gripped firmly, pulling him close to the familiar face he had made a fool of earlier. His victim earlier was now almost foaming at the mouth.

'You made a fool of me earlier. You're gonna pay!'

Kyle was trying to plan an escape in his head. This time a push wouldn't be enough to get him away. There was no crowd to run to his safety if necessary. He felt alone and in extreme fear.

He felt an internal crush, followed by intense sickness as he realised his enemy had lifted his knee to crush him between his legs. His breathing felt shallow as he crumbled into a ball on the pavement before him. Before he had chance to recover, he felt a sharp and powerful blow to the side of his face. It felt rough and sharp on his skin, which made him aware that it was a shoe connecting with his face. Sudden fear of death hit his mind and adrenaline pumped hard through his system.

He heard his enemy's voice again.

'No one messes with the Tye.'

His words sounded very childish even for Kyle's tender age of 14 years.

Kyle was too afraid to look up, as he remained crunched on the floor, awaiting another crush of pain.

It was quiet around him for a few minutes, which allowed his eyes to wander up the pavement, noticing no shoes in front of him. Lifting his head slightly, he noticed a figure running off down the road.

He was free. He breathed a huge sigh of relief. Just as he did, he noticed a car slowing on the road near him.

'Kyle?' His Dad's voice was instantly recognisable.

He lifted his head to the side, to show a nasty gash he didn't even realise he had. His Dad's face showed an expression of horror through a half-dropped car window, prompting him to open the door instantly and move swiftly to his assistance.

'What the hell happened here?'

Kyle didn't feel too bad at this point, particularly with the knowledge that life had rescued him again.

'I'm ok Dad.'

'How can you be ok? Look at the state of you!'

His voice certainly demonstrated concern.

It wasn't until they were on the way to the hospital that Kyle wondered how bad his face was looking.

Kyle felt his Dad was fussing over nothing until he looked down to see blood smothered over his shirt.

Four stitches to his cheek later told him how deep the cut would have been.

It wasn't until they were in the car on the way home that his Dad started asking the probing questions. The hospital staff only dragged the basic events from Kyle and offered to contact the police.

'What actually happened then Kyle? You've only told me and the doctor that some kid kicked you in the head unprovoked on the way home. Should we be calling the police do you think? Why are you so calm about things?'

Kyle realised how calm he must have appeared.

'Dad, I really am fine.' Although the image looking back at him in the passenger mirror said something completely different. His cheek had swollen quite considerably, even looking over the dressing that hid extremely accurate stitches.

'Don't just brush it off as nothing. What the hell happened?' His voice forced information from him.

'Ok. Well this guy was pushing me around at school and I made a fool of him in front of a few people. He was the bully though. I was just defending myself. I didn't expect anything else to happen after that.'

His Dad breathed out slowly but heavily.

'If any of my kids suffer, then so do I Kyle. I'm going to have to speak with your teacher.'

Kyle felt uncomfortable again, recognising his reputation may plummet if word got out.

'Ah no Dad, please... I've only just gotten a bit of respect at school after today. Please!'

His Dad recognised his plea. After a pause, he calmed his voice.

'Look... I had a time of bullying too. I get it. I realise it may cause some bother if anyone finds out about what happened this afternoon. Maybe we should call you in sick to hide that cut of yours for a while, then make some crazy story about you having an accident.'

'What kind of accident?' He worried about giving a ridiculous story.

'I'll think on. We have until the morning to make any call, ok? We just need an idea to get you some time away.'

Kyle managed to grin for the first time since the incident.

'Ok.'

Having his Dad's support comforted him. He couldn't remember being this close to him for a long time.

'Just remember we have your Mum to explain this to yet.'

'Yeah. I hope she doesn't get upset.'

'Ah, she's more likely to go on the hunt for this guy who hurt you.'

They both chuckled slightly, knowing how protective and strong she could be.

A memory came to him as they drove back home.

His mother had once rescued him from a couple of kids on a playground.

They were jumping on him and taking a couple of miniature toys from his pockets. Not only did his Mother drag the two kids away from him, but she went up to the parents and had a word with them about allowing such an event to happen.

Talking to them loudly and clearly about the lack of discipline taught. The biggest memory was of the parents simply standing there open-mouthed, uncertain of what to say or do in response. When she walked away they stared at her with white faces as if in shock, unable to move.

She always fought very sternly for her family where she felt it was morally right.

Kyle's Dad sometimes looked nervous about potentially having-to step in if words got out of hand.

The visual memories were interrupted when his father felt he needed to add further thought.

'This guy seems dangerous though Kyle, perhaps we should report him to the police. It would stop him from doing it again. We could potentially keep it quiet from the school.'

Kyle knew he was right.

Later on at home, his dad had a quiet word with their Mother in the kitchen before she had chance to take a glance at Kyle's face. The brothers could hear her slightly raised voice, but it was to be expected. She walked in to speak with all of them.

'So all of ya... We were thinking maybe a last-minute holiday may suit us all.'

The statement was in a tone that sounded more like a question.

Jack spoke up. 'You mean we are actually going to go on a holiday? Or just taking some time off?'

'Well your Dad and I discussed the fact that none of us have been away as a family for a couple of years now. Perhaps we could do with some time together, just having fun somewhere a bit sunny?'

Carl, Paul and Geoff instantly stood and jumped on the spot with excitement. The excitement among them made Kyle and Jack smile. The parents looked pleased with the response.

Their mother added 'We were thinking we'll explain to the teachers that we have won a holiday and taking everyone away. They may not like it, but I'll be telling them it's something we can't miss.'

'So where are we going to go?' Asked Jack.
Their Dad looked at them with a slight cringe. 'Well I suppose the best deal with a bit of sun and sand.'
'Yeah!' Geoff shouted with excitement again and continued to jump while everyone else found comfort in their seats.
'So is that a yes?' It was almost as if the parents wanted to see a bit more enthusiasm.
They all responded with a 'Yes!'
The father walked off, knowing he had to get onto the computer to find the best deal he could.

Kyle was relieved to know he didn't need to fake an illness to be away from school.
As he thought, he noticed Jack staring at him again.
'So I know that this guy you pushed came back to smash you up...'
Kyle felt charmed by the chosen words, but looked on to listen further.
'I was surprised. I thought you had the upper hand.'
Kyle's worst fear began to filter in. 'Did you set the fight up at school?'
'No, no! I spotted him and his friends moving around you in the corridor. I also noticed your fancy girl looking on, so watched over just in case you needed help, but hoped you could tackle him. I wanted you to look good for your girl.'
'So you would've jumped in if I was stuck?'

'Of course!' Jack seemed genuine.

'...And you didn't set the fight up?'

'No!' Jack was stern.

'Well, surely you can understand my question. You came to find me earlier just to tell me...'

Jack didn't allow him to finish his sentence. '...I was going to catch you later. I had a great idea about this friend of mine teaching me and you some skills. He's also really strong, so he was going to help us with some muscle-building tricks. He was planning on sorting out a day after school already. I was excited to tell you.'

Kyle felt guilty for suggesting the fight set-up at this point.

'Well that would be cool.'

Jack looked as if the excitement no longer resonated inside.

Kyle wanted to encourage him. 'We can still do it right?'

'Maybe. He is leaving school earlier than I am though. He doesn't need to finish the year. He's got a job to go into next week. The problem now is the holiday.'

'I'm sure we can find him when we come back.'

Jack really did look as if the spark for the idea had gone.

They all sat in silence now, listening to their parents going through various package holiday ideas.

Kyle noticed his mother giving him concerned looks from time-to-time, but he smiled back with convincing wellness.

FIVE

Before they knew it, the family were getting stressed about what they were going to take on their travels. The father sometimes wondered how he managed to take care of so many boys. He had a regular job but such a large family. He often thought *'five boys! What was I thinking?'*

The bags were all packed and the journey to the resort was soon over. The youngest boy cried most of the way during the flight. There was an unusual amount of turbulence which didn't help with the poor mother trying to keep the younger boys distracted from the fact they were a few thousand feet from the ground. At least the final coach trip to the resort left most of them sleeping on each other's shoulders.

As they reached their apartment, the fights began over who was sleeping where, but eventually the bags were thrown into their place, with clothes already picked for the evening time that remained (the local people had briefed the family on the best eating places).

They all dressed swiftly, ready for their evening meal. They walked around the resort in excitement, spotting the swimming pool – imagining the next few days of fun in there. With the sky now dusk and the pretty lights around the resort glowing in their eyes, they truly felt comfortable and excited about their sudden holiday. Even Kyle felt as if it was

a heavenly result (compared to his previous nightmare).
'Thank goodness for good parents' – he thought.
His Dad certainly wanted the trouble from home to be
behind them. It had brought stress to the entire home,
knowing that one of their family members had been badly
hurt. It certainly could have been worse, but still an
unpleasant situation that needed to be forgotten as quickly
as possible. The only reminder would be the stitches and
slight swelling to Kyle's face.
His Dad wondered if it was painful, but he didn't want to ask
as it was easier for them to attempt to forget about it.
As they walked through to the nearest restaurant within the
resort, they all spotted a sign:
KIDS EAT FREE.
'Super!' The Father said.
'I hope they don't charge double for the parents.' The
Mother jokingly commented.

The meal was more than they expected and the cost was
reasonable, which was a huge relief to the parents. All of the
brothers were already settled into the fresh environment.

Every day of the holiday was stress-free and very enjoyable.
The boys were the best of friends throughout. Smiles were
beaming on their faces.

The final day of the holiday came and everyone crammed
some time in and around the pool. The parents enjoyed

some drinks that they knew they wouldn't have freedom for once they got back to homely routines.

Before they knew it, they were all home and unloading their clothes into the wash basket.
The post blues were setting in, but they at least felt as if there was a bit of a fresh start in life again.
Jack had the tan he'd hoped for; Kyle felt refreshed and full of fresh opportunity, although a bit nervous about facing school after his previous incident. His stitches needed removing within a few days so he would still have to face the questions the others will throw at him.

The sun came up and shone brightly through the curtains in Kyle's room. He felt fairly nervous about the first day back at school. The holiday did break time up quite well.
He felt as if he had already dressed and prepared for school a million times in his life, despite the break. Another day came with buttoning up the same shirt buttons and shining his shoes in the same fashion. His Mother noticed his mood, as she caught sight of him in the bathroom.
'You've only got a couple of years of school left if you choose not to stay on longer... then you'll be looking back wishing you could do them all over again.'
Kyle looked over in surprise. 'I really doubt it. You parents always say that.'

'Because it's true. Wait until responsibility starts creeping in. Stress and worry come over things you never had to worry about before.'

He couldn't even grasp any of her concerns.

'Well, it can't be worse than being beaten up a few times.'

His mother came into the bathroom and wrapped an arm around him.

'I know. That certainly isn't nice. We will find a good self-defence class for you. In the meantime, try to ignore the bad ones and keep your distance.'

'It's not easy Mum, but I'll try.'

She held him tighter. 'Just walk home with one of your brothers. Jack ideally.'

'He'll be leaving school altogether soon.'

'Make the most of him for now. We'll find a class for you and get you started.'

Excitement grew slightly now, hearing of the plans. The trouble he had experienced at least drew his family closer. School didn't seem so bad in his mind now.

Before he knew it, Kyle was already on school grounds, moving between class subjects and juggling books between his hands.

During break-time, Kyle was walking towards the 'social hall', where most of the school pupils gather.

Karen came from behind and tapped him on his back, giving him a fright enough to spin his head quickly, yet almost ducking with the shock of someone suddenly behind him. She noticed his surprise. 'Sorry. I just wanted to say that I missed you when you were away.'

He felt her staring at his face, so thought he would make his story good while he had his opportunity.

'That's sweet. My family had a holiday. We won it in a competition.' He already felt a fool. Blood rushed to his face as he tried to hide his lie. He couldn't go into the reason for the stitches in his face. Sweat built under his shirt. The more he worried about the sweat showing, the hotter he seemed to feel.

He felt easier however when he accidentally caught glimpse of Karen's facial colour. She too grew red in the face, as if the room had suddenly gotten too hot for both of them. He grew slightly braver knowing she most likely felt the same.

'My face, erm... I had a fight on holiday. But you should see the other guy. I was lucky.'

He regretted his story already. It wasn't in his character to be in continual fights. The last thing he wanted was to give that impression. Instead of disgust, she demonstrated concern.

'How did you get into another fight?'

He realised the story was going to get deeper and best to keep it brief. His Dad always told him from a young age *'Son, if you're going to lie, lose the detail.'*

He continued. 'Well, erm, I was defending my little brother from this guy who was pushing him about by the pool.'

She looked impressed. 'You sure are getting very good at defending yourself lately.'

He grinned with the result of his lie, but knew he needed to demonstrate humility to keep her interested. His head dropped slightly with embarrassment. The sudden realisation that he was speaking with his most desired girl in the school hit him. Luckily, she saved the awkwardness.

'Ok, well I'm going to get back with my sista's.' She joked.

He smiled. 'Yeah, they'll be wondering where you are.'

She spun quickly in the other direction and gave out a little giggle as she walked quickly towards some girls who were occasionally looking in their direction out of nosey-ness.

He breathed a huge sigh whilst walking away in order to find one of his friends. A sudden worry that they may not be in the break room hit him. Being on his own didn't seem a cool thing to demonstrate at this point. He decided a loo visit would allow him time before the bell to the next class.

The day went smoothly overall and his walk home was safe, along with Jack who offered company. Jack had earlier discovered that Kyle's bully had been expelled from school whilst they were on holiday. Informing his brother brought about huge relief. Perhaps the holiday gave the opportunity to tidy things up.

When they reached the front door of their home, their mother opened it to greet them as if she'd been waiting excitedly for their return. She immediately directed her attention to Kyle, holding a small leaflet at his eye level.

'Hi, look what I found in the letter box today.' She produced a piece of paper.

They both moved in the entrance and tried to take their shoes off.

Kyle reached for the paper and had a glance. Jack managed to lean into its view.

'Mixed Martial Arts and Self Defence Classes'

He read the details, which mentioned classes in their local hall.

Jack spotted the words and grinned agreeably.

His mother looked at him. 'The classes start tonight. The convenience of this leaflet arriving is remarkable. Do you fancy heading down there a bit later? We have time to eat and let your food go down.'

He gulped at the spontaneity.

Jack looked worried. 'I think you still need some company on the streets, so I could walk with you. '

'Your brother's right. He could walk you to the door and collect you afterwards.'

'Ok.' Kyle decided he needed to bite the bullet.

Jack seemed very excited for him.

'That's so cool! At least we don't need my friend's help now. This will be so much better.'

Kyle smiled at Jack's display of care.

Things moved swiftly that afternoon. Their mother seemed focussed and determined to get Kyle to this new class.
There was time for food and talk over the dinner table. Jack and Kyle were throwing conversation around about how confidence will build if any kind of fighting style is taught to the human mind.
Kyle wasn't entirely convinced, but if it could help get bullies off his case, it would certainly improve his life.

Before Kyle knew it, he walked through the doors of their local hall, expecting a group of experienced fighters.
Jack said goodbye before Kyle had chance to walk through the lobby area. Kyle felt as if arriving home from school had spiralled into a wind tunnel, not allowing him time to adjust to the thought that he was about to embark on a Martial Arts lesson.

Everything seemed eerie. The hall lights were dim and there wasn't a soul to be seen. An old clock sat on the wall, with the wrong time completely. Maybe he was too early, or the details were incorrect. Kyle wondered if he should turn and head back, but then he remembered it would be safer to wait for Jack – even if he had to wait for the entire duration.
A slight wave of bravery came over him, so he decided to stand outside near the entrance to wait for any other participants.
Ten minutes... Twenty minutes... He pondered over the thought of leaving again and decided to stand outside the

main entrance and look across a green patch of land which the hall stood in the middle of.

There were some distant voices approaching gradually which made him wait awhile longer.

He suddenly felt his nerves kick in when he realised he may be seen as the 'newbie' of the class once people begin to arrive.

As the voices grew clearer, so did the view of some young men from around the back of the building. Much to Kyle's shock, there was instant recognition of the male ahead of the others. The greased backed hair of the person that he had recently encountered during his bike ride - suddenly reared his head, along with his recognisable friends. It was too late to hide now.

'Ah look who it is! I reckon you're following us. Looking for some more smokey smokey? I knew you liked it!'

Kyle couldn't believe his eyes and felt very nervous about what could potentially happen. He looked as far as he could for any other company, but he noticed he was on his own. Just as he pretended to ignore them and slowly move back into the hall entrance, the obvious leader of the pack moved swiftly forward and grabbed Kyle by the neck, tightly squeezing it with his apparently large hand. Kyle had time for a gasp before being paralysed by the strong grip. He felt as if his veins were expanding and soon to burst inside his head. Just as the enemy was about to follow up with another move, the others whispered fast words of warning to stop, which loosened the grip around Kyle's neck. Suddenly they all sprinted to get as far away from the area as possible. Kyle

52

was confused about the sudden release, although instantly relieved of course. He looked around to capture his own thoughts, noticing his body recovering swiftly from the attack.

Kyle couldn't see anyone else about that could have frightened his attackers off. He recovered quickly from the shock of the unexpected attack.

It was weird how no-one had turned up for the advertised class. He walked back into the hall and found a latch to lock himself in with, just until it was time to be collected by Jack. It was tiring being bullied for what seemed all of the time, so in some ways he was disappointed that the class didn't appear to exist.

As he looked around the hall, he felt fairly small but strangely comforted by his own company.

He pulled his phone from his pocket – he could phone Jack – he realised, but instead he decided to run around the hall as if instructing himself in his own, invented class. It felt liberating, encouraging him to set his mind free with more exercise. He ran in large circles, throwing his arms around as if he knew how to punch. At least he felt invigorated by the thought he was exercising in a fashion he imagined it would have been.

Checking the time again, he noticed he had ten minutes left of the expected lesson time.

He rolled on the floor, not caring about the hardness hurting his coccyx slightly.

'Nice work!'

Kyle was stunned by the deep voice that came from the corner of the hall unexpectedly.

He felt extremely self-conscious and embarrassed, knowing that someone would have seen him messing about, with his lack of skill.

Although it was quite unusual for a man to be in the corner of a hall amongst the shadows, Kyle didn't feel threatened by him. In fact he found himself feeling at ease about it, *assuming* it was an authorised adult.

'I'm just leaving now. I was here for a martial art lesson, but no-one showed up.'

There was silence for a few minutes followed by the man's deep voice speaking over a shuffle of bags, as if he was preparing for something that had been organised.

'Well, if was the mixed martial arts, then that was meant to be me, but I wasn't expecting anyone.'

Kyle instantly felt slightly annoyed. 'Well there was a leaflet, so new people could turn up!'

'I admire you for your courageous words, but the leaflet would have been very old.'

'But my Mum found it today and told me they were new classes.'

'Sorry kid.'

The conversation seemed to end there and the man's shadow appeared to be moving away.

'Hey! Can't you start a new lesson? How come you are here now?' He clutched at straws. 'I really need to learn something good. I'm always getting bullied.'

The man sounded as if he stopped in his tracks with the words.

'I've come to collect some kit I thought I had left here in the back cupboards. You seem like a nice kid. I'm sorry to let you down.'

Kyle felt disappointed. His body language demonstrated his acceptance of the situation.

A door click distracted both of them. Kyle glanced across to the main doors to see his brother's familiar figure.

The man pondered for a moment and studied Kyle's disappointment. After a strange, still moment of thought, the man spoke.

'It's dark in here now. You should go home. Maybe come back next week the same time and we'll have a chat ok?'

Kyle began to walk away, nodding his head slightly to demonstrate confirmation.

He opened the doors and went out into the dimming light.

'Was it good?' Were the first words excitingly leaving Jack's mouth. 'Where are the other students?... Did you find out how much it costs?'

Kyle thought for a second and decided on a cover story. Perhaps turning up next week could lead to the man deciding to teach him.

'Err, yeah... We didn't do much this time, but I might come back next week to give it another go.'

Jack looked a bit uncertain over Kyle's response. The lack of people leaving the hall completely confused him. He looked back a few times at the main entrance, eventually accepting that there would be no others departing.

Kyle lay in his bed that night, wondering what had happened that evening. He also started to feel a little bit miserable about all of the people drawn to attack him. Was he really that much of an easy target? He eventually went into a deep sleep, not noticing any other noises that the family were making with late night shuffling.

SIX

The following morning seemed full of high energy, with everyone rushing about and gently fighting for the bathroom. Kyle was ready to go, as if the sleep had rectified his worries and concerns completely. It was a new day full of new possibilities.

School was positively good today. Karen said hello to him passing through a corridor and glanced at him for a while. He wondered if she might still be in her relationship, as she was certainly showing him interest. The risk of asking her would be too great however, so he would have to wait to see if she threw the right words at him one day. He imagined the moment with a great empowered smile on his face whilst sitting in his English class.

'Wake up Kyle!' The teacher had a very loud voice after such a calm setting in the room.

He jumped in his seat and blinked a few times, realising his mind wasn't actually in the present.

Everyone looked at him nervously, as they knew how strict the English teacher could be. She made it very difficult for everyone if one person caused any aggravation. Luckily the teacher moved on and didn't mention any punishment. Kyle sighed in relief as the bell rang for the following lesson. He didn't escape fully however, as on his walk out, she called him to her desk. He panicked at the thought of a negative twist on the day.

'Now Kyle, I know you're a young lad, but please do pay attention in my class. It's going to be vital in the next couple of years for you. I'm only saying this for your own good.'
Kyle felt uncomfortable but responded lightly. 'Sorry Miss.'
'That's ok. Luckily I know the *real* you Kyle.'
He wasn't sure what she meant by that, but he was happy that she could see something that allowed her to forgive him.

It came to the part of the week where Kyle was due to face the empty hall again, to see if the mysterious instructor would offer any hope.
This week was the first week that he hadn't experienced a bullying incident, which felt pleasant and had been quite a relief. To top his week, his stitches had been removed and a thin slither of a scar remained.
The possibility of someone training him to defend himself gave comfort now. He craved the confidence of a useful skill.

Jack walked with him again to the local hall and left him by the door.
'Ok, so go straight in now.' Jack watched to ensure his safety.
Kyle really did begin to think that Jack was becoming more of a protective brother after years of brotherly mischievousness and teasing.
Despite his background thoughts, he aimed for the door and walked into the dark hall. This time he looked for signs of light switches. It seemed unnecessarily eerie with the dark

scene. However before he had chance to look any further than his first glance, the same voice hit his ears.

In some respect Kyle was shocked, but a great sense of excitement instantly filled him.

'You came!'

His stuttering voice returned. 'Err, err, yes.'

The man slowly walked with light and natural movements – like a silent ninja moving towards him, slowly revealing his silhouette from the opposite end of the hall. He still appeared mysterious – and almost a part of the shadows.

'So, you wish to learn a Martial Art you say? Why is it you wish to learn?' The man's voice landed gently, but with depth into Kyle's ears.

Jack didn't quite know how to summarise everything into a sentence, but something came out.

'I keep getting beaten up.' His words felt silly, but they were at least honest.

'So you wish to be able to fight back?'

'Yes.' His innocent answer wasn't prepared for the next response.

'You know I do not wish to advise someone of how to beat others up.'

'Oh, err... I mean, I am being bullied and keep getting hurt.'

'But you do wish to hurt them back?'

There seemed no sympathy for his sufferings.

'I guess I would look better if I could defend myself.'

'So you wish to look good in front of your friends?'

Kyle felt as if there was no right answer at this point.

'I, err, I am just tired of being pushed about and getting hurt.'

'You mean you are tired of your body being hurt? Or is it your ego that is being damaged?'

'Well, I suppose when I think about it, there is shame for not being able to stand up for myself.'

'So you wish for a braver character?'

Kyle was starting to get a bit frustrated.

'I was just hoping to find a Martial Arts class and learn to defend myself.'

The man sensed his negative tone.

'Ok.' The response was brief, but he walked closely now, revealing his facial features.

He was of olive skin and dark hair. His age was of middle years, with a solid-looking body, showing through lapels of a black Martial Art's suit. Kyle had a few thoughts fly through his mind. One being impressed with his stature; another recognising his intellect and wisdom; the other of intimidation by his close approach.

'You look worried. You give an impression of low self-esteem. Firstly you need to push those shoulders back.' Kyle felt a firm grip on his shoulders, pushing him upright. 'Your head needs to relax in this position.' He moved Kyle's head to face forward.

'Always have a confident posture. It also does wonders for your back. If you have a strong spine and foot position, then the rest of the body will fall in place. You only have one back, so look after it.' The man walked slowly back into slight darkness, making Kyle feel insecure about how the rest of the conversation would go.

'Confidence may not be inside you, but if you portray it, you can be less of a victim to others. Your mind will eventually believe that you are confident as well.'

'I – I understand.' Kyle felt silly again. 'My brother tried to show me this the other week.'

'Did you not listen to your brother?'

'Oh, yes. I did, I just let it slip I guess.'

'Well, if you need help, then advice must be followed and practice must be continual. Do you have dedication enough to learn new things?'

'Oh, of course. I suppose it was just because even though I tried all of those things I still got attacked.'

'It's about faith in yourself! You not only need to portray confidence, but you need to believe you are confident. The facial features will also give away your true feelings. You can stand tall and pretend to be confident, but to *believe it* will bring the right overall image of you.'

There was silence. Kyle wasn't sure if this was the beginning of a *real* lesson, but if it was, then all he could do at this point was to stand and listen.

'So, let's take another look at you.' He walked over again steadily, with a sense of power. 'Your eyes say it all. I see great fear in them.'

Kyle felt even more uncomfortable and self-conscious, but stood in silence, aware of his shoulders and head being in the right position.

'Hold yourself in the right posture, but with relaxation. No tension in the shoulders, no stiffness in the neck.' The man's

61

hands shook his shoulders gently, trying to relax them.
'Relax.'
It was difficult for him to relax, as all he could focus on was a stranger faulting his 'look'. The added discomfort was the fact that there was no discussion of training – and the hall remained dark!
The man looked down, only using his eyes.
'Ok, I'm going to move your feet.' He pushed Kyle's feet slightly further outward with his own feet.
Kyle thought this was even weirder.
'A good foundation is the most important thing you can have. A house with poor foundation will not last for many years; a tree will not stand in strong storms with poor roots.'
'I understand.' Kyle couldn't think of anything else to say.
'Ok, so you're looking better, but I need you to relax your eyelids just slightly, as if your eyes are really and truly relaxed. Close your mouth too... Perfect.'
Kyle now felt a little bit like laughing. He couldn't see himself holding the same position without something slipping back to old habits.
'Right, so remember all of that. I'm going to watch you now. Walk around the hall in a relaxed way. Keep the shoulders relaxed, with the head comfortably above, looking forward. Breathe through your nose and relax those eyelids.'
The man watched as Kyle walked awkwardly around the hall.
'Well... This is how you look.' The man walked around as if awkwardly balancing a heavy load of dinner plates on his head. 'You're all stiff and awkward. If you're worried about image – well, this will most certainly give you a bad image.'

Kyle laughed at the impression the man gave of him, but humour was not something this man was going to encourage. There was momentary silence again.

'Now think this: You don't care what people think. You have just walked tens of miles and your legs now need to preserve themselves with the most efficient way of walking...'

And so the man continued to criticise Kyle's posture and walking style.

He made Kyle walk and stand for some time, continually correcting any faults.

The man moved onto the subject of 'lightness' and 'fluidity.' It was important to teach Kyle how to feel and appear light; loose and fluid in his movements.

After what seemed to be a tedious amount of time concentrating on standing and walking with different concepts – there was a sudden knock at the main door, which made Kyle jump.

The man walked away, aiming for the far corner. 'I shall see you next week Kyle. Continue to move like that every day. It's your first line of defence in the street. So, until we meet again. This was your first lesson. It has begun.'

Kyle wondered why the man walked away. It seemed short and sharp in time, but after looking at his watch, he noticed that they had been in the hall for over an hour. With the sudden recognition of time, he realised it would be Jack at the door! To save him any worry, he ran over and pulled the door open.

'Why is it so dark in there?' Were Jack's observations upon glancing in.

'Oh, I was trying to find light switches, but the instructor seems ok with the way it is.'

'Weird.' Jack crumpled his nose up. 'What have you been learning?'

Kyle thought he would exaggerate his lesson.

'Erm, it was mostly punching in different ways.'

'Cool!' Jack put a strong arm around Kyle's shoulder and tugged him in. 'You'll soon be kicking' ass.'

Kyle nodded with a big grin, giving the impression of satisfaction. In his mind he was slightly disappointed, wondering if it was actually worth returning to. Walking and standing seemed too much of an unnecessary practice. He wanted to get straight to the *real* self-defence.

It wasn't until later when Kyle was in his room thinking, that he realised there was no mention of money for the lessons – or even if that was indeed a lesson. He also wondered if the man *really was* a Martial Arts instructor. The intrigue was enough however to make him wish to return.

It was another school day and Kyle was walking between classes, holding his books under his arm.

The Art class was upon him, which always excited him for seeing Karen. This time was different however. Her alleged boyfriend decided to sit with her at the large desk opposite Kyle. It certainly felt awkward for Kyle and he could see that Karen was trying to avoid eye contact. Kyle studied the looks of her boyfriend. He had sharp blonde hair that was gelled rigidly in place and quite sharp facial features. He certainly looked like the sporty type, with his shoulders and chest broad and strong. Weighing up another man wasn't a usual habit of Kyle's, but he couldn't help it on this occasion, with his continual desire to win the heart of Karen. She would always be his dream girl.

During the Art lesson, everyone usually continued on with their project with minimal interaction from the teacher. It gave people a chance to chat and work casually. On this occasion, Karen and her boyfriend were having an awkward conversation that didn't look too pleasant. Kyle tried to listen in whilst working, but only heard the odd word.

He heard one of Karen's sentences...

'But I don't want to be stuck to you like I haven't got any space at all.'

Her boyfriend was trying desperately and discretely to explain why he wanted to spend more time with her.

They didn't seem to understand one another, which made Kyle smile secretly inside – knowing their relationship wasn't perfect. He was shocked however when Karen's boyfriend suddenly laid eyes on him.

'Hey! Whatchu looking at ya little dweeb?!' His words were fairly loud, which made Kyle feel like sinking his head into his neck.

Luckily the class continued to converse with a reasonable volume enough not to pull all attention to the awkward moment. Kyle felt himself crumble, with the blood going to his head really quickly.

Karen looked concerned. 'Leave him alone. He's just innocently sat there.'

He stared at Kyle for what felt like eternity, but in reality it was a mere few seconds. The stare was most certainly a warning to him to mind his own business. Kyle didn't know where to put his eyes, but he tried to relax them to attempt to demonstrate a lack of interest in their business.

They continued to have their conversation a little quieter, leaving the awkward feeling around the desk.

Another boy next to Kyle reached over to him and whispered: 'Don't worry. They won't last the month.'

Kyle looked at his class mate. 'What do you mean?'

'I know you like her.' He whispered.

Kyle looked over at Karen to make sure nobody heard the comment.

'Ah, she is cute, but I have no chance anyway.'

The boy moved back to his work, leaving a comment in the air. 'I guess you won't with that attitude anyway.'

He didn't realise his eyes and actions were obvious to others, so thought he had better keep a low profile for a while and attempt to show disinterest.

The bell went for the end of the Art class and Karen's boyfriend decided to jump ahead of everyone to ensure he caught up with Kyle. They just made it to the other side of the classroom door, out of the teacher's view.

'Hey!' A strong hand pulled Kyle by his shoulder.

Kyle spun in shock, leaving him physically paralysed with fear.

'Stop nosing at me and my girl. I've seen you around. You come anywhere near her and I'll do you over.' He pressed down hard on Kyle's nose with one finger as he spoke.

The pushing on his nose brought about a fresh anger in Kyle.

'I'm not interested in your girl!' He pushed the boy's hand away, surprising himself with his bravery.

A new push from two solid hands knocked Kyle onto the ground. Luckily most of the class had left, only leaving one or two scattering by, avoiding any involvement. Those that caught Kyle's eye looked as if they'd seen it all before. It was at that moment that he realised he must have the reputation of a victim. It made him feel angry and helpless. There was no way he could get up and face this tough guy without knowing any decent fighting skills. Instead he decided to just sit there, against the wall behind the class door, holding his head in his hands. The teacher suddenly noticed his figure through the door's partial glass panels. It was the regular Art teacher, Mrs. Jamieson.

'Kyle, what are you doing sat on the floor?'

It was the obvious question, but he couldn't be bothered to answer. He just sat feeling humiliated and completely fed-up, wondering how she didn't notice the commotion earlier.

'Whatever it is we can talk about it and sort it out.'

There was distant chatter in the hall ahead, but he could sense that no-one appeared to be interested in the situation Kyle was in. His thought of caring about reputation had diminished at this moment.

He felt a kind hand on his shoulder. 'Come on, let's sit you up on a chair and talk about whatever is going on. You don't have to go to any other lesson for the day. I can see to that.' Kyle had no intention of going to any classes. All intention of usual routine went out of the window anyway.

Being weak and having matching weak friends was all he could think about now. He instantly thought it would be easier to quit school and perhaps see if he could begin work at a younger age.

All of these negative thoughts were ploughing through his mind.

The teacher wasn't giving up on him however. She grabbed his hand and pulled it gently to prompt him to stand. 'Come on Kyle. I promise we can talk about this privately and nothing will be said. You can be signed off sick for the rest of the day.'

Her gentle voice was so encouraging that he actually felt sorry for her for being in this awkward situation. He slowly rose to a standing position, but his head hung low in shame. The teacher showed him to a chair and closed the classroom door for privacy.

As she sat closely, she spoke gently, looking away to avoid face-to-face discomfort for him.

'Ok, let's sort this out. I heard a bang, but was late looking over. Did you fall over?'

'You must be blind miss. I was pushed by some jealous boyfriend. Pushed to the ground and humiliated... Again!'

'What do you mean "again"? Has this happened once before or many times before?' She ignored his criticism of her observation skills.

'Oh I have been pushed about a lot this year. I don't know what I can do to stop people thinking I'm a push over. I even started a Martial Arts class, but it's too weird to keep doing it.'

'Well that's a good start! It can bring confidence just doing something like that. How would you feel if we spoke to someone at the school who could help you a bit more? We have a councillor who can help.'

He felt it would be useless. 'I can't see how having more focus on me can help. It will just make it obvious that I'm a complete dweeb and someone who can't stand up for himself.'

'Ah, come on Kyle. Let's try to sort this out and face the situation. I'm not talking about fighting back, I'm just talking about perhaps finding a solution so that you don't have to keep putting up with this. Maybe I was meant to notice this so that I can help you. You certainly look like you could do with a bit of support right now.'

'I'm just a loser and all of my mates are the same. Someone taught me that like attracts like, which is what I think I do. We're all losers.'

'Oh dear. Look, you're just seeing things in a very negative way. We can look at things in a fresh light and find some way of resolving the situation.'

'I can't see any resolve.'

'There is always a way out of everything Kyle. It doesn't matter what happens in life, you never give up. If you get knocked down, you need to keep getting up. It's one of the biggest lessons we learn, even as adults. We all experience things for a reason. Maybe the reason here is to recognise that you are not happy with yourself right now and that you can find ways to improve things. It's good to recognise things and work well to fix it... Now, I'm not a fan of violence, but there is a boxing class that has been set up for kids who need to focus their attention on something positive, or need to build confidence. I would like to put your name forward for that and come along with you to settle you in, if you would like? Obviously I would need to discuss all of this with your parents.'

He looked over at her, realising she may have a good idea after all. The Martial Arts class wasn't moving fast enough for him, so it would be a better focus for him.

She noticed a little shine in his eyes. 'Ok, I think it could be a good start, but only if your parents agree. Right?'

He nodded as didn't want to appear like a child that suddenly grew excited after such a 'down' mood.

'Right, I shall have a word with your parents a bit later on, okay?'

'Sure.' He managed.

'Now I want you to promise that if the boxing becomes a possibility that you won't use it for revenge or anything nasty. It will just build your confidence and give you a self-defence skill. Promise me you'll remember that.'

70

Kyle nodded in agreement and they automatically shook hands as if agreeing on a business deal.

Kyle stood and walked away, assuming the conversation was over and that everything would be arranged promptly by the lady.
He took advantage of the emotional moment and headed straight home, knowing the lady would cover for him anyway.

As soon as he got home he raided the freezer for ice cream. No-one was home yet, so he took advantage of the nice food that was usually only available for occasional treats after their main meals. A little bit of stolen of ice cream wouldn't be noticed. It helped him feel better about the day. The thought of boxing in a new class of others who also needed focus in their lives – gave him so much inspiration at this time. Perhaps at last he would be able to keep bullies at bay.

By the time everyone in the family arrived home, he felt much happier. Jack looked at him as if he knew something was occurring. His Dad also gave him a glance, noticing his mixed expressions.

Everyone had settled in for the late afternoon and Dad picked up a phone call, whilst everyone else went about their ways, either watching television or playing some kind of electronic game.

Just as Kyle looked for something similar to do, his Dad came over to him.

'So, I spoke to a Mrs. Jamieson?'

It was almost as if he had asked a leading question.

'She said you're hoping to do boxing lessons to hopefully give you a little more self-confidence. Have you been having more issues at school, boy?'

'Ah no. I just got pushed today and I started thinking about everything as if it got too much. The teacher wanted to talk about helping me.'

'You know I'm always here. It gets a bit embarrassing when you hear these things from teachers. It's almost as if we aren't approachable. You know I am approachable right?'

'Oh yeah. It's only that it all happened there and then if you get what I mean?'

His Dad frowned. 'But it doesn't explain your happy features this afternoon.'

Kyle realised he had shielded his previous problems.

'That's because the Boxing class gave has given me some hope.'

'Ok. Well if that has cheered you up, then I am pleased about the decision. I agreed with your teacher, but not sure if it was an appropriate thing to suggest. I really don't know what made her think about fighting violence with violence. Either way, if it really does help you, then I'm ok with you to try it. If you get hurt though, I can't hide it from your mother.'

'Can't we tell Mum then?'

'She's always been against Boxing - I'll be honest.'

Kyle panicked. 'But she wanted me to do the martial arts. *You'll* let me do it right?'

'If it can be a secret between us then it could work. We will have to just say it is your martial arts class if you come home with bruises. Maybe say it's now twice a week... Let our secret slip though and it's both of our necks on the line. I have given your teacher my mobile number just in case she needs to call again - covering all bases.'

'Okay, I'll make sure it stays a secret.' Kyle smiled, although couldn't help wonder why it would be ok to do martial arts but not boxing.

It felt good to have a man-to-man chat and feel secretly supported. Between them they agreed it would be okay to do both the martial art classes and the boxing until one became favourable over the other.

SEVEN

The evening came when Kyle was meant to return to the hall for his martial arts class.

The hall was dark as per normal and it was almost threatening with an eerie feel to it.

'Good evening.' The man's voice gave him a small fright.

'Oh, hi.'

'So, you are here to learn more. Well done for continuing on despite things starting off a bit strangely.'

'Well, I...'

Before Kyle could finish any sentence or statement, the man spoke up again.

'I realise we haven't even been formally introduced. My name is Zane. I am from Jamaica originally, as my family emigrated there from Dallas, America. They expected Jamaica to be paradise, but after a few years they decided to come here, to settle into a country that would give me an education for a lesser cost. They didn't have enough money to give me an education elsewhere, but it worked out quite well.'

They both had a very brief moment of silence, which encouraged Zane to continue on.

'So, anyway, I realise things started off strangely and I have some explanations to give before you feel comfortable to continue coming... You see my style started in Jamaica when I was just three. I was taught by a very traditional Martial Arts Master of a mixed style. He learnt styles from Japan,

China, and Korea and put them altogether. He also went to America to study Kick Boxing. He always told me that he wanted no weakness, so he felt he had to study as many arts as possible. He had no name for his style, so just called it a Mixed Martial Art. He competed in many underground organised fights of which he always won. He was well respected in the underground world of Martial Arts. He said that the 'above-board' fights that created fame and extreme fortune were much safer. He didn't want fame and he wanted to test his art to the ultimate level. No safety nets as such. Does that make sense?'

Kyle felt he couldn't speak and that things had gone into a lot of depth in a short space of time.
He felt pressure to respond with something.
'I haven't done any kind of training as yet.'
It seemed very brief compared to his instructor's life story.

'You seem distracted Kyle. I am sorry for diving straight into criticism last week. I should explain that the lessons are very traditional to the ways of my Master. They may seem very odd, but they most certainly work.' He looked down into a bag at this point. 'Here, I brought you something. I realise it have taken a lot of courage to face your demons by starting these classes. This is an important gift that I want you to use. It is ancient and holds energy that will be very beneficial to you if you believe in it.'
Kyle was now curious and intrigued. He noticed Zane pulling a long cord from his bag.

'This is a necklace, but it is quite a manly one. If you believe in the power of energy it can bring you the strength of a man of great force.'

Kyle instantly disbelieved Zane. Hearing the words 'power' and 'force' felt like a childish piece of bate to keep him interested.

The man grinned, knowing Kyle wouldn't believe him instantaneously.

As Kyle reached his polite hand out to receive his gift, the item gently dropped into his palm.

To start with he didn't notice anything unusual, but after a couple of seconds he noticed the solidity of a stone and began to feel heat building. The heat gradually grew in intensity, causing Kyle to drop it to the floor. He shook his hand in pain, looking up at Zane with confusion.

'You must believe Kyle.'

The man reached down to collect the necklace and reached it out in offering to Kyle again.

This time Kyle took the item tentatively, prepared to feel the heat again, however it felt stone cold and continued to get so cold that he had-to drop it again.

'You need to believe in the magic and accept it Kyle. It's the only way this gift will accept you.'

He began to wonder what tricks this man had up his sleeve. He looked down at the nearby bag to see if there were any items that would heat or cool an object. It was ridiculous to think that he would have planned such a bizarre event.

Zane reached out again and offered the gift.

Kyle reached out to receive the gift and held it with slight belief. This time the temperature moved to slightly warm, followed by slightly cool, but it remained relatively steady. 'It is very powerful Kyle, trust me. You need to be very careful with it. Now that you have accepted one another's energy it will work positively for you.'

Kyle thought his words were completely bonkers, but the item was most certainly very intriguing now that he had felt the temperature changes and managed to control it.

'It works on your thoughts and energy. When you need power it will give it to you. When you need help with your emotions it will help you.'

Kyle was still speechless and concerned about what kind of weird situation he was in. At the end of the day he was still in a hall with a stranger with no other students, for a class that was meant to exist.

'I understand you must be having some strange thoughts at this moment, but let me demonstrate.'

Zane took the necklace away from Kyle and placed it back in his bag. 'You will have it back. I just want to bring it back to you gradually.'

Kyle was now wondering what the heck was going on. He even thought about making a dash to the door and finding the fastest sprint home.

Zane pulled a pair of boxing mitts from his bag and told Kyle to place them on his hands, while he removed a couple of focus pads for him to hit.

He showed him how to punch with power and technique with both hands. This took the best part of half an hour.

'Ok, so we haven't yet perfected the punch, but it doesn't matter with what I'm going to demonstrate. Firstly, I want you to punch this mitt with all of your power using the safety tips we've been through, okay?'

Kyle took note of the words then punched the mitt as hard as he could.

'Ok, now aim back here.' Zane directed him to an extra width behind the pad. 'In other words, punch through the pad as if your target is further back, over here.'

Kyle knew about having to punch through a target, as his dad once gave all of his kids a quick lesson in basic punching, but practicing this thoroughly was interesting.

He punched well - his fist now sinking deep into the pad, making a nice deep noise.

'Okay Kyle. Now forgive me for creating a bad vision in your mind, but really try to visualise the pad as a person who is bullying someone you care about. Now, in reality I wouldn't advise you to punch someone who is bullying someone, but just use this as a visual aid for now... So someone has hold of someone you care for and you need to hit them on this occasion, otherwise the person you care for will be seriously hurt.'

Kyle knew what kind of emotion he was trying to work out of him, so he stood for a moment to build the emotion in his mind and body. His fist sank deep into the pad, making Zane's arm move back a bit more than before. The pad sounded as if it was hit deep and harder.

A few seconds after the latest punch, Zane pulled the necklace back out of the bag and asked Kyle to wear it around his neck. Kyle gently took the necklace and it went over his head with plenty of length without having to untie it. He felt different temperatures yet again – emerging from his chest, where the Crystal now lay.

He felt a powerful surge fly through his body, as if he had a strong electrical current moving through every single vein and artery at the fastest rate of time.

'Punch it again, but build up the same emotions you had.' Kyle felt as if his eyes were going to bulge out of his sockets at this point.

Zane added more encouragement just before his punch. 'Put in the same energy as you did a minute ago - I liked that power.'

Kyle built great power in his mind, which transmitted to his shoulders and hips. He punched the mitt as hard as he could. Zane knew what to expect, but his arm still flew back fairly far, giving him a jarring pain to the shoulder. He hid the pain and took the mitt off. Kyle did notice the difference in Zane's arm jolt and wondered if the necklace really was the cause of the added power. He wasn't completely convinced, but the lesson on how to punch was certainly worth a visit.

'Well done... Lesson over... Take the necklace, but be careful with its power. Keep it only to yourself. It will only harm another, since it is now attuned to *your* energy only.'

Kyle frowned with weird thoughts and took the mitts from his hands, returning them gently into the hands of his Master.

'Thank you Kyle. Now it doesn't seem as if I have gone through very much today, but the foundation needs to be strong. You need to get used to the crystal, as you'll be amazed at how it can enhance your strength and energy. Just give it a little chance. Hopefully I shall see you next week.'

Kyle walked off gently. 'Okay.'

Just as he arrived at the main doors, Jack had arrived.

'Yo Bro!' Jack's words were a strange comfort to normality. 'Can you kick my ass yet?'

Kyle remained intellectually quiet, refraining from a silly response.

They walked home casually. Kyle was trying to remember how to walk with confidence whilst Jack jumped up and down the curb of the pavement, full of excess energy.

EIGHT

The following week came and it was time to have Kyle introduced to the new Boxing class. He felt so awkward about doing two fighting arts. A slight level of guilt filled him, seeing Zane's efforts in his mind. He reminded himself of the comparison opportunity.

There were five other boys at the class. Each one of them seemed to have some kind of emotional issue. One of them most certainly had an anger issue. It was obvious by his expressions and aggressive words. A couple of boys looked extremely shy and nervous. One of them looked frail and skinny, while another appeared large and muscular, yet very self-conscious. Kyle suddenly found a funny side to being there, but held his laughter inside and concentrated on the lesson. He had to remind himself of the reasons he was guided there in the first place.
The instructor was firm and fair, which was a good foundation for each person there.

A couple of types of punches were learnt in one lesson with no real delivery of technique. There was a lot of talk about using the gloves to protect the hands. It did appear very "on-the-surface", nevertheless it was fun and Kyle began speaking with one of the boys who shared the same school year as him. His name was Frank and he seemed a gentle soul. He had very little confidence and looked as frail as someone who hadn't eaten a square meal in months. It was weird that Kyle was noticing weaknesses in people he wouldn't normally notice.

The lesson had ended and everyone left without goodbyes, just a placement of all boxing gloves into the appropriate box followed by a walk through a main hall towards the main exit of the school.

Frank caught up with Kyle after leaving the building.

'Hey Kyle. Can I join you?'

Kyle was surprised but pleased.

'Of course.' They walked together.

'That one boy is mega angry. Did you notice? I hope we don't have to get in the ring with him.'

Kyle realised there may be a day of fighting in the boxing ring and visualised the angry boy being a challenge.

'Oh sugar. I hope he gets partnered with that big guy.'

'I'm afraid I might have made the wrong decision joining this class.' Frank looked white and sweaty.

'Ah it'll be ok. I'm sure the instructor will make sure we don't get hurt. We need to build our strength and confidence.'

'So why *is* that big guy and the angry guy there? They look like they can take care of themselves.'

'Oh. I don't know. I think the angry guy needs to learn to focus his anger on a sport. I don't know about the big guy. He's just big. Ha-ha!'

Frank was surprised about the laughter. 'You seem brave about it all.'

'Oh trust me I'm actually quite frightened. I hope we just do stuff with the pads.'

'Me too.' Frank looked ahead with a fearful face. 'Where do you live then?'

'Oh not far. I have to walk home. It's too close to catch the bus or anything.'

'Maybe I could walk with you, as far I can before my route.'

Kyle looked at him. 'Did you want to come over to mine for a bit? Then maybe my Dad will sort you a lift home?'

'He would do that?'

'I could ask him.'

It brought a smile to Frank's face.

It seemed Kyle had found a new friend. Someone who was a tad more nervous than himself, which actually helped him feel better about his own confidence levels. They went back to the house and ended up having to call Frank's parents to let them know that he would be staying over for a while. Their friendship had an instant 'click'. Kyle could share the same game entertainments and their conversations were as intellectual as he would naturally like. Frank kindly told him that he felt very comfortable with him.

It came to a time in the evening when Kyle's Father had to inform him that it was time for Frank to get off home. They said their goodbyes and the Father kindly gave Frank a lift back home.

During a moment of quietness, Kyle reached into his school bag to begin to prepare his books for the following day. In there he found the magical necklace that he had neglected since receiving it. As he pulled it out to view, it appeared to glimmer in the light as if extremely pleased that it had been rescued from hiding. He felt a strange sense of power from it, as if it had a life of its own.

He gently placed it over his head and allowed it to land gently over the centre of his chest. It glimmered with a strong mix of blue and green. Staring at the amazing colours relaxed him and he sat back against the headboard of his bed.

Kyle suddenly fell into a misty dream state. Fog swirled around his mind for what seemed like an eternity. Eventually a distant shadow formed of a man who appeared to be trying to give an important message. He was mysterious and dark, so it was difficult to see or hear what he was trying to say. It was if he was attempting to call him over. Kyle walked over to him and his hand was gently taken. They walked through very vibrant green fields, moving over to a strange, old brick structure that had no roof or solid structure. There were lots of entrances to it. Eagles flew through the same area from different angles, as if easy prey lived in the open centre. The Eagle's callings were getting louder and louder. Kyle could tell that a storm was coming, so he looked around, wondering where the shelter would be. One Eagle flew barely above his head, with such a loud squawking noise that it suddenly shocked him out of his dream state and woke him up! He lay in bed trying to figure out the difference between his dream state and being back in his physical mind. He realised he was most certainly fully awake now and noticed a little bit of light coming through the curtains. His focus moved to his alarm clock, saying that it was six thirty in the morning. He wondered if he had just the one dream throughout the entire night, as he could only remember the fog engulfing him at the very beginning. He felt strong and vibrant, ready for the day, but he could sense that the rest of the house was completely silent. It was very early for him, but he decided to slowly get out of bed and get ready for the day in a relaxed way. It was actually quite refreshing getting into the bathroom without a rushed battle of time between all of them, so he spent a relaxed time washing and dressing. The sound of his parents rising pushed him to finalise his hair preparation.

'Kyle?' His Dad was surprised to see him leaving the bathroom.

'Hi Dad.'

'You're up early.'

'Yeah, I think I dropped off early, so naturally woke up earlier than normal.'

His Dad still looked sleepy and walked into the bathroom after the brief conversation.

Before Kyle had time to think about anything he was already in his first class at school.

He noticed Karen was looking over at him as if with sympathy over the previous incident. Kyle was worried that she may have heard his words about not being interested in her during the brief battle with her boyfriend. Luckily her boyfriend wasn't in this particular lesson, so at least there was less tension for a while. He wanted to speak with her and it was almost as if she read his mind, as she decided to move desks in order to sit directly behind him. In this class the teacher was usually very meek and mild, allowing everyone to work at their own pace, so long as they were working on the set assignment. On this occasion the teacher seemed nervous about the students completing their latest assignment in good time. They were reading parts of a book and making notes about what they felt the deeper meaning of these sections were.

Karen tugged at his Kyle's shirt as he tried to behave cool and calm. He turned, pretending to be very casual about it.

'Oh, hi.'

He didn't want to seem overly excited, despite his heart racing twice as fast and sweat building on his forehead.

She leant closer over her desk.

'I'm really sorry about my boyfriend. He can be a complete...'

Before she could finish, she quickly had to stop, as the teacher shouted across the room, completely out of character. 'Right you all! I need this work doing before the end of the lesson, so no muttering.'

Karen felt as if the words were directed at her, so she urged herself to apologise.

'Sorry Miss.'

The teacher moved back behind her own desk to look her usual nervous character. Everyone knew the teacher should have perhaps been in a different profession, but she came across as keen to help young people despite her obvious fears.

Karen picked up the conversation more subtly, reaching over again with cautious movements.

'So, I am really sorry about him.' She continued.

Kyle took in a brave breath.

'It's ok. He didn't hurt me. I just tried to keep it peaceful.'

He felt Karen's pause of silence, hoping it was because she was thinking further. After a few moments she spoke again.

'Well you took it well. You could have fought back I know, but I'm pleased you didn't.'

He felt braver, thinking she had more faith in him than he did.

'Well I didn't want to get into a fight and be in serious trouble. Sometimes it's better to take the fall.'

She was surprised and gulped a brief amount of air. 'You're very kind Kyle. Sometimes I wish I was with someone like you. My guy can behave like an ape... all primitive and stuff.'

He grinned to himself, but also felt a bit unwanted with the words "*someone* like you".

'Well I'm here if you're ever single.' He couldn't believe those particular words had left his mouth.

She went quiet again, which made him feel very foolish for the words he had selected. Perhaps they were too arrogant. A minute had passed and still no response. He felt his eyes bulge with worry, so he ruined the brave comment with an attempt to correct himself...

'I'm sorry... That probably sounded arrogant. I mean, why would someone like you want to be with someone like me?' He felt ridiculous, as if trying to dig himself out of a very deep hole. The resistance to look behind him to see her expression was killing him.

The teacher suddenly spoke. 'That's enough moving around now Karen. The deadline doesn't leave much time for messing about.'

Kyle was stunned with the comment and turned his head to note that Karen had moved back to her usual seat. The worry was now about "when" she had moved and if she heard everything he'd embarrassed himself with. When he looked over at her she looked very settled at the desk. He prayed in his mind that the last heard words were before his mention of her "ever being single again."

She noticed him looking over and gave him a subtle wave with the base of her wrist sat on the desk with fear of being told off by the teacher. Kyle grinned knowing he was still on good terms with her.

Everyone's heads were now tilted downward as the teacher appeared unusually keen for everyone to complete their work.

The lesson had ended and they all walked out into the corridor. A couple of boys deliberately hit shoulders with Kyle in a rough and bullying way.

'You're scum Kyle-the-Style. Don't think you'll ever get someone like Kaz. You're low life.'

The words should have cut deep, but he had internal comfort after the conversation in class with Karen. He also didn't mind the new nickname "Kyle-the-Style."

Kyle ignored his bullies as he often did and walked through the corridor, bumping into Frank, who was walking towards a Library session.

'Hey! Good to see you Kyle!' Frank's eyes instantly lit up then continued with mention of his timetable. 'I'm going to the Library. Where's *your* next one?'

'Ah History. Why couldn't you be in my group Frank? I have weirdos in my groups.'

Frank's heart warmed. 'I wish we were in classes together too. I can only relate to one guy in most of my classes. He's ok I guess, but I can't really have much of a laugh.'

They both walked together until Kyle came across the door to his next lesson. Karen wasn't in this one, but there was a science class that she was due to be involved in afterwards. Luckily History was only half-an-hour long. He realised he must be either deeply in love with this girl, or have a very healthy obsession. The thoughts were crossing his mind. It was strange for him realising that she was the only girl he could ever be with. He hoped that she would fall for him one day, even if it took a few years for her to recognise it was him she was meant to be with.

There was a brief break period after the History lesson, which allowed everyone time to get hold of a nice drink or brief snack. Kyle and Frank found one another again when both of them were attempting to get hold of a hot chocolate from the canteen.
'Oh, I wasn't sure we'd catch each other.' Frank seemed happily surprised.
'Cool to see you at break time!'

They started having longer conversations about Boxing and how they needed it for confidence.

Frank told a story of how he and his sister were adopted, as his biological parents were arrested for something he never knew the full story of. Kyle realised how lucky he was to have a very kind and loving family. Although Frank and his sister were now very happy with their new family, Kyle was naturally sympathetic of the reasons for his confidence issues.
'So do you get bullied as well?' Frank suddenly asked.
'Um, Yeah.' Kyle felt embarrassed.
'Well you don't look like you should be. You're quite tall and you look strong. That should really put people off.'
'Oh, well thanks. I've been learning the art of perception. You know? How to look confident when you might not be inside? I am strong though, but don't know how to fight

back. I'm hoping the Boxing will help me to at least defend myself from the guys that push me around.'

'Why are other guys bullying you though?'

'Oh. I dunno. I seem to remember it starting a long time ago and I somehow attract it from loads of people. I guess I'm now only just starting to do something about it.'

'Ah!' Frank felt angry for him, but sympathetic at the same time.

'I have lack of confidence but I only get bullied in a mental, emotional way I suppose.'

Kyle was quite surprised, but felt bad about assuming he would be bullied physically.

'I guess all ways of bullying are nasty.'

Frank smiled. 'I'm pleased you understand. Some say I just need to get over it, but no-one knows why I lack confidence. I can't just reinvent myself.'

Kyle felt an uncomfortable heat in the middle of his chest. He clutched his chest and remembered it would be the crystal necklace that he left on. It left him wondering why it suddenly got hot again. A sudden panic that it would get burningly hot entered his mind and he began to sweat. Frank noticed.

'Hey, what's going on in your mind?'

'Oh it's ok. It's just something I'm getting used to.'

Frank frowned but continued on.

'I wanna be such a good boxer that people respect me.'

Kyle remembered something his Dad had said that he hadn't even practiced himself.

'My Dad said that if we want respect from others then we first need to find respect for ourselves.'

'I think I heard that before from some therapist I was forced to see. Thing is I don't know how to.'

Kyle sympathised. 'Me neither actually. I don't want to come across as arrogant. Surely people would hate that too.'

They both continued on with their conversation and enjoyed sharing their thoughts until they were due to head for their next lesson.   Even then, they could have naturally continued their natter quite easily.

Kyle thought he had better be the first to exchange goodbyes for now. 'I guess I'll catch you when we next bump into each other.'

Frank began to walk. 'I'll text you. Maybe you could come to mine and meet my adopted parents.'

'Yeah, that would be cool.'

Kyle waved as they both walked in different directions.

NINE

It was time for Jack to walk with Kyle again to the Martial
Art's lesson. Kyle wasn't sure how to feel about it, but
thought he would still play along to see how it pans out.
As soon as Jack dropped him at the door, Zane was waiting in
the shadows.
'Hello Kyle. How are you today?' He walked into a shimmer
of light, showing his solid frame.
He almost resembled a super hero or super human. Kyle felt
a sudden honour to train with such a model of a man, which
brought him to the ultimate question:
'I have been thinking. You haven't asked for any money and
my mum is expecting me to spend my pocket money on
these lessons. How much am I supposed to be paying you?'
The man grinned with a thin smile.
'Kyle this isn't for money. It gives me great satisfaction to
know that I am helping someone who gets pushed around. It
is also very good for me, as I haven't taught for a long time,
but knew there was a reason I needed to return to my hourly
slot at the hall.'
Kyle thought. 'But you must be paying to use the hall too?'
'I know the guy who rents the hall. He thinks I'm using it to
practice, but teaching another who needs the knowledge is
always a good test for *my* knowledge too.'
'Wow.' Kyle was humbled by this man.

93

'You do help me Kyle. You help me to help myself. Everyone needs a purpose.'

Kyle wanted to ask so many questions. He could only ever visualise that he was this dark shadow in a hall that hid out for hours. The questions on his tongue decided to stay there however, as he didn't want to overstep the mark.

'Come, let us train.'

Kyle walked into the main part of the hall with a feeling of gratitude.

'Last week we focused on power with the basic punch. We shall continue with that and then look at punching whilst defending. Then the plan is to look at defence from punches on the whole.'

'Cool.'

'Ok, let's get some discipline in here now. I think we should treat this as an ancient school and stick to the same rules.'

'Ok.' Kyle didn't know as of yet what he was talking about.

'I only want you to address me as Sir. When we start I shall give an instruction to go and an instruction to stop. Every time we stop or start, we give a respectful bow to one another. Ok?'

'Yes.'

'Now then, I don't want to sound like the typical army sergeant, but let's start with a "yes Sir".'

'Yes Sir.' Kyle smirked at the same time.

'Ok, here's the other thing. Not so much smiling in the lesson. It's about taking things seriously. There will be times for smiles and laughter later.'

Kyle dropped his mouth. 'Yes Sir.'
'That's better. Let's get cracking on with the lesson.'

They worked on basic punches again; then punches which
added movement to avoid a punch whilst throwing one.
Then there were movements to avoid punches as a whole.
Everything went swiftly, yet thoroughly. Kyle was sweating
and enjoying the level of training. It gave him a buzz, which
made him realise he will definitely be returning to this lesson
weekly.
Zane continued to push Kyle hard physically and mentally.
The defence was already becoming natural. The teaching
went deeper into reflexes and peripheral vision; watching
shoulders and body language; reading eyes generally. Kyle
found it extremely interesting.
The lesson grew very exciting and powerful, yet very fluid
and natural.
Before they knew it, the time was over, which was indicated
by a nervous-sounding knock at the main door.
'That will be your brother.' Zane confidently knew.
'Yes Sir.'
'Good man. Go home and practice. Come back next week
and I shall be able to test your interest in the amount of
practice time you've put in.'
'Yes Sir.' Kyle felt energised. He didn't care how cheesy the
"yes sirs" were.
'Ok... Little bow.' Zane reminded him.
They synchronised bowing and then stepped away from each
other like repelling magnets.

Kyle ran to the door and opened it energetically to Jack.

'Woo! Must've been a good lesson today then!'

'Yeah! It felt great.'

'So do you think you could kick my ass yet?' Jack pushed and pulled him to the side as they walked.

'Not yet Jack, but thinking maybe you should do something to catch up.' He joked.

The week as a whole was turning out well. School was peaceful, with only an occasional threatening glare from his usual bullies; Karen occasionally looked over at Kyle with a smile and subtle interest; Frank managed to meet up with him during most breaks which allowed them 'buddy' time. Things seemed to be looking up.

As time went on, the Boxing skills picked up and his Martial Art classes were growing increasingly interesting. He continued to wear the necklace, even during sleep. It appeared to glow during his times of being full of energy. Warmth in the necklace seemed to be felt with different emotions, although he hadn't quite fathomed it out. His instructor left it mysterious, other than his initial words. He wore it more out of loyalty for his Martial Arts instructor.

It came to a point in time where Kyle was due to move up to the next year at school. His exams went well and his teachers were pleased with his progress. As a reward to everyone doing so well, there was an end-of-year party planned. Most seemed excited, but Kyle was a little reserved about it, as he feared humiliation by his bullies. There were a few of them unfortunately.

At his latest Martial Art's class, his instructor spoke with him about the potential issues.

'You most likely have the skills to take them down at this point without having to hit them. Fear them no more as it is the past *thoughts and patterns* that you fear. What you need to realise is that you are in a different place *now*. You have had no attacks for a few weeks you say, so they must notice your change in confidence, even if it is at a subconscious level. Go with it. The past has truly gone. Your skills will come automatically if they attack you. Just use the minimal force so that people can witness your defence and not destroy you for injuring someone really badly. Remember now that some of your moves are deadly, so you need to be very careful. Only use those moves I taught you that are using the person's momentum against them – unless your life is at threat – then unfortunately you will need to consider the more lethal moves.

You are still a novice in the terms of the years you need to train to gain a high level, but even the less-skilled hand can cause severe injury or death. Your weapons are dangerous now, so be aware and attempt to avoid any situation in the first place. Be the "cooler" first... someone who will diffuse a fight, or just walk away. If you walk away be aware of any attacks from behind by the attacker.'

'Yes Sir.'

Zane noted a weak tone in his voice.

'No, I *really* need you to have heard all of that Kyle. It is important.'

'Yes Sir. I really do understand... minimal force; be aware; be the cooler; avoid and walk away first, but be ready for attacks from behind if they are really *that* bitter.'

'Good man. Now I need you to practice the moves we learnt tonight, ok?'

Zane always enforced the need to practice beyond the classes. He explained that one hour per week would not solidify the lesson. He needed to spare a little time per day, when he had the opportunity.

Kyle would sneak out into the garage and practice against imaginary opponents most days after school.

At first his parents would wonder where he was after a certain time, but they soon grew used to his new habits and knew they would find him in the garage ninety-nine-percent of the time.

Some of Kyle's brothers would often peep through the door leading from the house into the garage. Sometimes they would make it clear that they were spying by having a little chuckle at the door.

Although Kyle knew about their antics, nothing fazed him. His practice was good for his mind and body.

TEN

The school party was due on this particular evening and Kyle was stressing about what to wear. They often had non-uniform days, so he knew that most of his jeans and smart trousers had already been seen by his class mates and others. He couldn't believe what he was thinking when he decided to walk over to Jack's bedroom.

'Jack. I need your advice. You were good at telling me how to do things with my sense of style but now...'

'Hey you should knock before you come in!' Kyle didn't realise Jack was on a call from his mobile phone until he took the phone away from his ear.

'Oh.' Kyle was a bit shocked at the bad timing. He hoped he may get another opportunity before it grew too late in time. He looked at the clock and realised he had one hour left to get himself ready. Thoughts filled his mind of how inexperienced he was at big social events.

Many of his class mates were already declaring their nights out to pubs and clubs with fake identifications. He never knew if it was all false bragging, but the pressure was on to look as if he had a little bit of experience in the partying field. He wanted to go in there looking a little bit 'cool' if nothing else.

As he walked back into his room, Jack pushed him on his back.

'Just check before you barge in on me ok?'

'Sorry.' He paused, with a shock. 'Can you help me Jack? I really need your help. I've never snuck into a pub or anything before so I don't know what's cool or anything.' He felt like a child, using childish words and panic-breathing.

'Yo, Yo, chill! Let's see what kind of clothes you've got then.' Jack looked through his wardrobe and began with insults. 'Ah jeepers. Why don't you ask Mum for better things?' He made Kyle feel even worse.

'Ok, well let's not dwell on the crap, let's look at what we can put together here.' He pulled a few things out of the wardrobe and threw them all over the bed. Kyle wasn't sure if he should feel happy about being helped, or annoyed about his brother's insults. He hoped to focus on the task at hand.

'Ah man it feels like the pressure is on to look good. I bet the others will just turn up with smart jeans and a shirt.' Kyle added.

'Here you go... perfect for you.' He selected a few items and laid them out on the bed.

Jack pointed them out. 'So, you have these trousers... and I reckon you should wear this top, with this jacket. The top looks like it should hug your chest. I've noticed you've started growing in the pectoral area... Then the jacket looks like you're not trying to show it off. Subtle showing off... do you know what I mean? All looks cool together.'

'Eh?' Kyle focussed on the "pectoral" words and looked down at his chest, noticing that perhaps his chest muscles *had* grown very slightly over the last few months.

'I didn't even realise I had grown.'

'Well, it's only a bit, but that also comes with age, so don't start getting too big headed about it.'

Kyle was grinning with the pleasant surprise.

'It was gradual I suppose!'

'Okay, stop staring at yourself. Try it on and show me, then if it looks stupid I'll suggest something else.'

Jack was always good at being candid. He found a knack for just saying things as they were.

Kyle tried on the suggested clothes whilst staring at himself in the mirror. He hadn't realised that all of the training had begun to define his shape. It was all done without thought of muscle development. Thoughts as to why he had perhaps been avoided by the bullies lately came to mind. Either way he swiftly moved on to getting the clothes looking right.

Smart, dark coloured jeans were Jack's selected trousers; then a white V-neck top, finished with a dark cream jacket that hung nicely.

Jack walked in to see what the holdup was.

'You done it yet?' There was a pause as Jack inspected him.

'Oh yes. That'll impress the ladies. That's exactly how I dress if going to a club.'

'You go to a club?' Kyle felt alone on the party life.

'You're too young to know about that kind of thing.'

'Well, so are you!'

Jack looked a bit guilty. 'There's one that my friend runs. He keeps an extra eye on us and doesn't let us have alcohol, but he lets us stay there until it closes.'

'How do you hide that from Mum and Dad? They'll go mad!'

'I didn't want to have this conversation with you really to be honest. I shouldn't have let it slip. Please don't let anyone else in on this. I've helped you, so maybe you could keep this deal quiet?'

Kyle gulped, with a look of further interest.

Jack continued. 'Look, I've been watching your back and been there more lately, so please watch my back and don't let anyone know about my parties. Anyway I only do it when there are no risks of being caught out.'

Kyle wondered how that could be, as it was very hard to sneak in and out of the house.

He could see Kyle's brain attempting to calculate it.

Jack wanted to finalise the conversation.

'Look, when you can take care of yourself better and you look a little older, then I will tell you everything and maybe sneak you in some time. Until then, keep young and enjoy it.'

Kyle felt patronised but grateful at the same time.

'Thanks Jack.'

He trusted the selected clothing and finished it off with some polished, black shoes.

His Dad was waiting downstairs in preparation to give Kyle a lift. In fact, it looked as if he had been pacing.

'Are you ready? Your mum wants me to make sure you get a lift there and back.'

Kyle continued to make his way down the stairs.

'Uh, yes, I'm ready.'

They both left the house and walked to the car.

Sitting in the car seats and moving off the drive-way, his Dad gave him an unexpected speech.

'Hey Kyle, I hate these little talks, but I need to tell you my thoughts, just as my Dad did for me when I reached your age.'

Kyle thought *'oh, here we go'*. He cringed and thought the timing was poor with his more important worries over keeping reputation at the party.

'Ah Dad, I know all about that stuff.'

He looked over at Kyle in surprise. 'Oh I hope you don't know too much. It's something you need to be very careful of. We grow very tempted at the age you're at. I just don't want you to end up having to take care of a surprise family and ruin your youth. You still have so much more to enjoy before trapping yourself.'

'Oh Dad, don't worry I don't want to do anything like that until I'm married.'

His Dad was surprised yet again. 'Oh, ok. Well that's a good start.'

'It's not on my agenda, honest. I just want to get my confidence up and concentrate on all of this self-defence stuff. When I finish school I don't know what I'll do for work, but it would be good to make some money and get a car.'

His Dad breathed a sigh of relief.

'Phew. Your Mum reminded me of the fact it's around the time I need to speak with you about it, especially as you seem to be discovering your identity and growing up so fast.'

'Ha-ha! Don't worry Dad.' It made sense as to why his Dad was pacing to get out of the door swiftly.

'Just promise me you won't make any stupid mistakes. I don't want you to ruin your life.'

'I promise Dad.'

'Ok, well, we're nearly here. I'll park around the corner so you can keep your cool-ness.' He grinned.

'Ha-ha. Thanks Dad.'

They stopped and Kyle climbed out.

'Enjoy.'

Kyle walked up the school path and the crowds were coming in thick and fast. Everyone looked glammed up. He was surprised at how many were in the same year as him. Some of them he had never seen before. There were many pretty girls and a lot of confident young men. He tried to blend in whilst feeling a bit inferior. It did appear that he was at an age of change. Now he could see what his parents could be worried about. There were a lot of good looks and hormones flying around for sure.

The music was already blaring from the sport hall doors. People were walking in and out, looking for others and trying to settle into things. Kyle began to feel nervous about the whole event. He went with the flow of things, knowing to expect some loud music and dancing. The music excited him slightly, so the emotions were getting a little mixed.

'Kyle!' Frank's voice instantly brought comfort.

'Hi! How did you spot me?' Kyle turned his head to see him running towards him.

'I spotted you a mile off. You're tall. Ha-ha!'

Kyle never thought of himself as any taller than the majority of the others his age.

'Can I walk in with you?' Frank seemed to have a nervous wobble in his voice.

'Of course! It will help me too. I was afraid of walking into the hall looking like a loner.'

'Oh I think most of us are anyway, but we would be much cooler in company I guess. Ha!'

They both looked around at the pretty girls as they walked indoors. The hall was dark, with colourful spotlights filling sections of the floor. School teachers were spotted in the odd corner, trying to appear camouflaged against the walls. They couldn't hide themselves however, even if they had tried. It was to be expected of course.

A big sign at the opposite end to the entrance marked 'DRINKS'. Kyle noted it and walked over slowly, Frank in toe, trying to look cool and casual. Another boy ran over, clashing shoulders with Frank carelessly, making him feel even more uncomfortable.

'Hey, don't let them ruin it. I think it was an accident anyway.'

Frank pushed out a big breath and looked a bit more relaxed again. They both picked up a fizzy drink and walked back into the middle of the hall, wondering how the evening was going to pan out. People were still coming through the main doors and settling in. Some adults appeared to be putting things together as if rushing at the last minute.

'I really hope I at least get a kiss.' Frank looked around the hall with big eyes.

'Ha-ha! You're not getting one from me.'

'Ha-ha!' He took the joke well. 'Maybe you could help me. You could ask that girl over there if she'll dance with me later on.'

'Ah let's give it a bit of time. Let the party kick in and the people blend into the dance floor first.'

The two of them felt as if they were scheming already.

Frank could see what Kyle was dreaming about, so offered help.

'If Karen's boyfriend isn't about then I'll go and ask her for you.'

'I'm sure he'll be here. It would be a risk to lose his girl if he didn't come.'

'Well I heard he's off sick with a twisted ankle from football.'

Kyle felt a bit of excitement fill him.

'Ah, maybe there is a chance then!'

'Yeah, but I guess we have to be careful of his friends.'

'I wouldn't even really be able to recognise any of them. I don't know who he hangs out with. Do you?'

'Not really. I was thinking though – if Karen comes over to you then at least it was her choice and you didn't force your company on her.'

'True. We can try.'

It was like prompting the circumstance, as just as they spoke about Karen, they spotted her and her boyfriend coming through the main doors, looking a little nervous with the vast room and bright lights. The boyfriend had crutches, but still brushed up with a nice suit and his usual strongly-gelled hair.

'Ah man!' Frank showed disappointment for his friend.

'Oh it's ok. At least if he gets funny, he can't defend himself that well with his balance problem.'
'Ha-ha! Well hopefully we can have fun without them.'
Kyle still felt slightly disappointed.

The night went on and somehow things seemed relaxed. The music was very enjoyable and well selected. Everyone danced and soaked up the happiness. Frank gave Kyle a signal to ask the girl he had spotted earlier – to dance. Kyle instantly responded with a big grin. He walked over to the girl who was dancing with a couple of her friends. He felt as if he had broken their triangle-dance-structure.
'Excuse me?' All of them stopped as if a large pause button had been pressed. He then felt the pressure to keep calm under the embarrassing situation. He looked over at the girl with the pretty, curly, blonde hair.
'Erm, I know this is geeky, but my friend was wondering if you might have a dance with him when the next song starts.'
They all frowned at him, looking disgusted. The girl asked loudly, 'Which one is your friend?'
Frank noticed Kyle pointing over at him, looking all uncomfortable in his own company.
'Oh, erm I guess so.' She tried not to act interested. 'So long as there's no funny stuff.'
Kyle innocently didn't know what she meant by the 'funny stuff', but smiled. 'Great.'
Kyle swiftly walked away and gulped.
He quickly reached Frank's side.
'She said she will.'

Frank looked pleasantly surprised. 'Yes!'

'Hey, she's looking over. Play it like you're not bothered. Girls love the hard-to-get attitude.'

Frank changed his demeanour to a calmer and carefree image almost in an instant.

'Not too much. She's got to know you like her.

'Jeepers, this is complicated.'

'Ha-ha! Even I don't really know. Try it though.'

The song stopped and the start of the new track seemed to come quicker than they had to time to plan for!

The girl looked over and carefully walked awkwardly over. She walked straight up to Frank, giving Kyle the body language that told him to move out of the way. He promptly stepped back and placed his hands in his pockets.

It was a bit awkward for a while, standing around watching his friend with a partner. They started smiling and enjoying some humorous dancing. Kyle moved even further away before they had the chance to judge him for still being there. He moved over to a wall space, where some were already standing awkwardly watching on. The relief to see others feeling out of place was very helpful.

He accidentally caught the eye of Karen, who was dancing with a friend of hers. She looked very happy and contented, soaking up the music and moving liberally to it. Her friend was just as relaxed and enjoying herself just as much. He stared on when suddenly Karen's friend caught his eye. It startled him, so he quickly looked down to the floor, already too late to hide his actions. After only a few seconds, he sensed someone approaching him. A few seconds further

and he noticed Karen's friend stood right before him. Her
eyes met his quickly.

'Fancy a dance then?'

Kyle was completely blown away by the surprise question.

'Err, yeah… why not?'

She grabbed his hand confidently and brought him to Karen,
which confused him. He wasn't sure if her friend was helping
Karen, or if Karen was encouraging her friend.

Either way he didn't mind. Before he knew it, he was
dancing with two girls that encouraged him to have fun.

Karen reached in and shouted in his ear. 'I've wanted to
dance with you since I spotted you earlier.'

Kyle blushed and felt a sudden surge of heat rise to his chest
and head. He was instantly worried about her boyfriend.

Karen could see his thoughts.

'Don't worry, he's not here. He got fed-up with just sitting
around, so went off home. You can relax.'

He breathed relief with her words, but also wondered about
her loyalty to him. A smile filled his face. 'What if his friends
say I danced with you?'

'They'll be fine. We're close to breaking up anyway.'

It made Kyle's heart flutter to hear this news, but didn't ease
his mind with the witnessing friends. He realised he could be
seen as the person that steals the girl.

After a few songs, some improvised moves and some
occasional whispers between ears, Karen's friend grabbed
Kyle's hand again. 'Why don't we go and grab a drink?'

He felt shocked again. 'B – But what about your friend Karen?'

'Karen wants to go to the loo, so thought we could take a break.'

'Uh, ok.'

They walked to the drink area, with Kyle caught sight of Frank, who was still enjoying a dance with the girls. It pleased Kyle to see his friend having fun.

When they reached the area for drinks, they spoke briefly.

'So Karen really likes you but she's stuck with a difficult situation at the moment.'

'Oh. Well that's nice to hear. I have to confess that she is my dream girl. I wouldn't make a move unless she was single though. I don't want to be seen as the one who broke her relationship up.'

'Oh you wouldn't be seen as that. Almost everyone in our circle can see that it won't last much longer. Maybe just wait until they are well over and then make a move.'

'Maybe I should let her get over him first too?'

'Ah I wouldn't even worry about that. She's already over him.'

Kyle was shocked. He worried that he might be treated the same way, but he liked Karen enough to take the risk if the opportunity became available to him.

'You know my name right? ... I'm Francesca.'

'Oh, I think I knew that anyway.' He wasn't sure, therefore grateful for her information.

'So, do you think you could make a move on Karen tonight?'

'Ha-ha!' Kyle laughed in shock. 'I, erm – I think she should break it off with her boyfriend first.'

She looked disappointed.

'Jeremy? Ah. You know his name is Jeremy right? She can't stand him anymore. He treats her so badly and there's so much pressure for her to look amazing for him every day, like she has to be fake for him. She's fallen for you because you're so kind and brave. She was hoping for a kiss tonight.'

He wondered what the rush was.

'I just don't want to get into any kind of issues with anyone. I've already had a fight with her boyfriend... Err, Jeremy...whatever his name is.'

'Have you? I thought he just pushed you and you chose not to fight back. That's what she told me.'

'Well, yeah that's true. That's how crazy he can be. Imagine what he would do if I kissed her while they're still together.'

'Ok, well you shouldn't disappoint a lady if she wants something.' She gave him a side glance with her eyebrows raised.

He felt uncomfortable and pressured.

'I'll see how the night goes. If Jeremy comes back or anything, I've got to be careful.'

She pushed him from the side in excitement.

'Yes! That's awesome. I hope you do.' Francesca seemed a very lively and bubbly character.

He smiled but didn't know what else to say.

One of Francesca's friends came over suddenly.

'Hey, where's Karen?'

'Ah she's in the loo. I need her to hurry back so we can get back to the jiggin'.'

Kyle realised he may have a bigger group of girls to dance with.

'Oh right, I'll go see if I can find her in there.'

Her friend ran off to find her.

'I wonder why she's keen to dance with us again. We were all dancing together earlier but she went off with some other group. We thought perhaps she grew bored with us.'

'Oh right.' Kyle felt too mature to be involved in silly group rivalry.

They turned to get another drink, since the cups didn't seem to be filled up so high.

'Thirsty.' Kyle managed.

'So, Kyle...' Francesca decided to change the subject all together. 'What's with the necklace?'

He looked down, forgetting he continued to wear it, even at the dance event.

'Oh! I forgot about that. It is a gift from a teacher.'

'A teacher? You're not a teacher's pet are you?'

He crumbled at the thought.

'Uh, no! It is something my Martial Arts teacher gave me. He said it holds some kind of energy but I don't quite get it yet. I'm thinking if I keep wearing it, it may make more sense.'

'Freaky! So you do Martial Arts?'

'Yes. Not for very long though, so I'm not any kind of black belt or anything.'

'Ace. Me and my sister used to do Karate when we were growing up, but we stopped once my sister decided it wasn't cool anymore.'

'How could it not be cool?'

'Well, I think she started seeing some guy who wasn't a fan.' He thought quickly. 'I'm guessing he felt threatened by it, ''cause it sure is an awesome thing to learn.'

'You could be right there you know.'

Francesca put her cup down. 'I might go and see what Kaz is doing in there.'

'Oh, err that might be an idea.' The conversation felt awkward with them.

He wondered for a moment what having a sister would have been like.

Before Francesca had chance to walk away, the friend looking for Karen came running back, grabbing Kyle's hand.

'Quick! I think Karen has some problems!'

Kyle felt his heart sink into his socks and began to run with this girl, who was dragging him in every direction to avoid the groups of people in their way.

Kyle shouted. 'Why don't we tell one of the teachers?'

There was no reply, which didn't help with his sudden nerves of being involved in a situation.

His Dad came to the forefront of his mind. He panicked that if he had a problem, it may get back to him. Thoughts were flying everywhere in an instant. If someone were to catch his thoughts, the weight of them would be very heavy at this moment!

They ran over to the toilet areas. Luckily the Boy and Girl toilets were right next to each other, so it didn't look out of place for a boy to be outside of the doors.

At the end of the toilet corridor – shouting voices could be heard. They weren't distinctive, as the corridor was quite long.

'Quick Kyle, she's getting pushed about!'

He looked on and felt his adrenaline pump to maximum levels.

'Maybe we should get a teacher. Why did you get *me* here?'

'Stop being such a wimp! She needs your help!' Sincere panic was in her voice.

'Ok.' He managed the word, but wasn't happy with what he may have to face.

As they grew closer to the scene, Kyle could make out the gelled-hair of the boy shouting at Karen. He was now faced with the situation of Jeremy behaving quite aggressively with Karen.

'Oh no... .' Kyle was beginning to curse in his mind with panic, knowing Karen's so-called boyfriend was extremely tough.

He walked toward the scene even though his mind was telling him so desperately to turn around and go for help.

Karen looked over, which made her boyfriend look over. He was holding onto Karen's arms, shouting obscured words at her. Kyle knew he was in trouble now that he was spotted for potentially interfering.

Karen shouted over. 'Leave it guys. I can handle this. It's our issue.'

Her friend responded. 'But I saw him push you to the ground Kaz. You need to get away from him.'

'No! Get away!' Karen warned. 'I can handle it!'

'Yeah! Get lost you divs.' Her boyfriend turned to insult Kyle and anyone with him. 'Can't you see this is private?'

Kyle felt his blood boil now and felt he should do something. Her boyfriend was still holding onto her arms quite tightly, not allowing her to move.

Kyle spoke out, trying to sound brave, deliberately projecting his voice forward. 'Could you just loosen your grip on her? Maybe talk like adults? Then we promise we can relax and leave you to it.'

Her boyfriend grew red, with enlarged eyes.

'What?! Now you're getting involved, let's get you over here little Kyle!' He hobbled towards him - his injured ankle evident, gripping his fists with obvious intent to harm.

Kyle knew he had to prepare for the worst. He stepped back to allow a slight side-on stance. He ignored what felt like an internal shake, making him feel weaker than he would prefer.

Her boyfriend, Jeremy, hobbled over, not getting anywhere too quickly, allowing Kyle to think of some defence moves, whilst shouting.

'I don't want any trouble! I thought you went home!'

'I came back when I heard you were dancing with my girl. You've had it now matey.' He walked over with a push, using his entire bodyweight.

Kyle stepped back quickly whilst pulling one of Jeremy's arms forward, encouraging him to fall forward to the ground, not able to rescue himself with his injured ankle – he placed both palms on the floor and pushed himself back up slowly.

Kyle was tempted to attack him while he was vulnerable, but he stood strong and loose, prepared for another attack.

Karen shouted in the back ground.

'Just leave it Jeremy!'

It didn't stop him though. Jeremy decided to go for a rugby tackle, which Kyle had prepared for as predicted move. He was hoping he wouldn't, as the grip Kyle had prepared in his mind was potentially dangerous. Thoughts of Zane came through, remembering not to use 'death moves' on anyone who isn't threatening his life. If he messed this evening up, then who knows if he'd ever be permitted outside the house ever again.

Kyle automatically went for a good grip under one of Jeremy's arms and his neck, forcing Jeremy to release the tackle-grip reasonably quick. Kyle let the grip go completely with fear of going too far. He realised it gave Jeremy an opportunity to stand and unleash another attack, forcing Kyle into another automatic thought. He grabbed Jeremy's clothing and threw a front knee into his solar plexus, crumbling him into a ball of pain. He shuffled back slightly and surprisingly tried to stand to attack Kyle again. Kyle couldn't believe the pain tolerance of Jeremy, but didn't want to hurt him anymore. Knowing he had full control of the situation, a wave of confidence took Kyle by surprise. An unusual wave of warmth consumed his chest, bringing a welcomed level of strength. He threw a front kick into

Jeremy's midsection, causing him to shift back and fall into a ball on the floor, where he gasped for air.

The fight was assumed over and Karen came running up to Kyle, flinging her arms around him. Kyle attempted to keep his eyes on Jeremy, looking over Karen's shoulder. He realised he must have felt tense with adrenaline. It was difficult for him to calm down, but Karen's tears eventually brought him back to an even keel. Jeremy wasn't going to get up, but he was breathing and occasionally looking up from all-fours with anger. That gave Kyle the signal he needed – knowing of Jeremy's strength to recover.

The three of them grabbed one another and ran swiftly back to the hall area.

One of the teachers looked at them with suspicion and began walking over.

'Uh oh.' Karen noticed the approach. 'Act cool. Nothing happened.'

'Everything ok with you guys?' The man asked.

Much to their relief the teacher was demonstrating concern rather than heavy investigation.

'Yeah, we just tried a funny dance. We need to get our breath back.' Karen was quick with a weird response and a silly looking smile on her face.

They all looked at one another and began to chuckle, which thankfully added belief to her story. The teacher walked away gradually with a look of part belief, part confusion.

'That was close.' Kyle whispered, trying to get his heart to calm down, but he was still extremely high on adrenaline levels.

Karen grabbed his hands. 'You're shaking.' She noted.

'Ah it'll fade. I'm used to it.' He was referring to his bullying times, but realised that Karen may have taken it as perhaps that he always got into fights.

Luckily Karen didn't respond negatively.

Karen's two friends had caught up with one another, leaving all of them speaking about the incident for a while. It was difficult trying to appear normal in a disco when they all felt a bit shocked.

Karen had explained how Jeremy returned to keep her away from Kyle after receiving a message from one of his friends. It escalated into forcing her to into an aggressive kiss. When she tried to get away they ended up having an argument about every little partner issue and it grew heated. She tried to escape the situation, but Jeremy forcefully held her there. Every time she attempted to get away, he pushed her closer to the wall and gripped her arms tighter. It was getting rougher as they battled, with one push landing Karen on the hard floor. Jeremy's hand forced her swiftly to her feet to continue the argument.

The situation felt as if it was escalating, leaving her feeling trapped. She truly wanted to resolve things herself and tried to avoid others even noticing the scene.

She thanked Kyle again with extremely gratifying hugs.

Much to Kyle's surprise, the rest of the night was so amazingly magical. He danced with the girls and Frank eventually joined the group, with his new-found girlfriend. Time flew so fast and before they knew it the slow music hit their ears, pressurising a 'partner dance.' Kyle took courage and held Karen for the tunes. Frank suddenly found new courage and also leaped in to offer his new girl a slow dance. She obliged much to his relief. The night was such a happy affair for the two boys.

That night Kyle couldn't sleep for hours, tossing and turning with high levels of energy, worrying about how much he might have hurt Jeremy. He could have been in trouble somewhere on his own with no help. Thoughts of severe health issues for Jeremy plagued Kyle. He tried to think that it was deserved pain, but his conscience was eating him up. He eventually dropped off into a deep sleep, but even his dreams were unsettling and disturbing for him.

ELEVEN

It was a Saturday morning and Kyle went off with one of his brothers, Paul to kick a ball around in the local park. It was sunny and warm and there was plenty of energy to be rid of. Paul was reasonably close to Kyle in age, so it was nice when they could do things together. Paul was a quiet brother who seemed to crack on with life without making any scenes. He always appreciated bonding time with Kyle. They usually had fun times when they were together.
Kyle felt especially happy as of late, as he had succeeded in winning the woman of his dreams and appearing a hero. Word of this had spread and the brothers were all proud to be associated with Kyle.

As they were kicking the ball around, they were talking about it. Kyle was speaking of his horrors at the time and how he had to overcome weak legs and shaking hands with the adrenaline pumping through him. He spoke of how the heroic image was good, but how he would prefer to avoid any such events from occurring again. An underlying fear of any come-back sat deep beneath the heroic thoughts as a reminder of the need to remain humble and watchful.

As they shared their thoughts, Kyle spotted a familiar group of boys approaching from the distance. He recognised them almost instantly. They were the few he previously bumped into when out cycling, as well as the recent strangling outside of the hall. The one with the heavy-gelled hair appeared to lead the group, occasionally looking back and laughing at some comments. Kyle had a funny thought about people with heavy-gelled hair lately. The theme was interesting - Jeremy and then *this* leader-of-the-pack. His funny thoughts stopped quickly after studying the crowd growing closer.

Kyle advised Paul to move back towards the path to link a quick escape home before they got any closer. Paul wasn't fazed, but only because he was naïve to the growing circumstances. Kyle pressed for them to move further back.

'Come on! I don't think I could tackle a load of guys.'

Paul studied the crowd of boys walking closer from the near distance.

'Who are they? They might be normal people.'

Kyle wanted to warn him.

'They are trouble.'

Paul was so slow in his reaction to Kyle's words that it was too late to move away swiftly.   They both noted the eye connection and change of body language from the boy at the front. He was certainly going to pay them a direct visit.

'Ah sugar.' Kyle whispered. 'They're bigger than us.'

Paul looked calm. 'They may not do anything, just be cool.'

The dark haired boy came over in a short space of time, as if their walking had multiplied in speed.

'It's the geeky boy!' He shouted as he kicked their football in arrogance. 'I've been wanting to catch up with you for ages.'

Kyle looked uncomfortable.

121

Paul wasn't sure what was happening but he was confident enough to stand strong.

Their ball went to a house garden, a short distance from the piece of land they were playing on.

'Oh no, sorry about your ball. I thought I would save you from making a fool of yourself. Shameful footwork.'

Paul piped up some foolish words. 'He could kick your ass with his feet.'

Kyle felt the sensation of his heart dropping into his shoes. This would be another fight he didn't want! He prayed in his mind for no trouble.

'I want no trouble. I can't fight.' Kyle attempted to save himself.

The trouble maker looked at Kyle directly in the eye with invasion of personal distance.

'I remember strangling your little neck and you didn't do anything to save your own life. Who are you anyway? I keep seeing you about like a little frightened mouse. Why are you always in my way?'

Kyle wasn't sure how to respond to avoid further provocation. He frowned, not understanding the logic of this guy's mind.

The other boys stood with their hands in their pockets, looking at the two of them.

Paul now began to understand the danger and felt extremely nervous and looked around the nearby houses for any escape routes. One of the other boys noticed his thoughts and walked over to him, pushing him on his shoulder. 'What's your trouble boy? What are you, about ten years old?'

Kyle looked over with panic. His adrenaline was now pumping throughout his body, but his mind not knowing how to react.

'What do you want from us?' Kyle thought he should ask the most obvious question.

'What do we want from you? Just to kick your weedy bodies away from our zone. You're ruining the street rep.' He said aggressively as he added a point into the middle of Kyle's chest with his sharp finger.

Strangely, Kyle felt the finger press directly onto the crystal of the necklace he forgot he was wearing. He suddenly became aware of extreme warmth, which filled his chest. He stood back in a panic, as it formed a very unusual sensation. The warmth spread into his shoulders and down his arms, making him feel extraordinarily big and strong. So much so that he had to look down to check he hadn't suddenly grown into an odd shape. He felt as if his veins had filled with a surge of energy that he had absolutely no control of. His enemies laughed on, assuming the poke in the chest was enough to cause a fearful reaction. The immediate bully laughed really loudly. Paul stood in the background feeling extremely worried for his brother and uncertain of what to do. In an instinctive move, Paul moved in and tried to push the lead enemy from the side. It certainly caused an unsteady wobble, but the instant reaction to the push brought chaos to the two groups. The group of bullies turned their attention to Paul, being much younger and milder than Kyle.

Kyle noticed the change of energy in the group and realised he needed to focus on the situation despite his strange internal occurrences. His brother was about to be attacked by older boys, who were bigger and stronger. Kyle noticed his eyesight had adjusted, with extreme focus on the enemies, as if looking through an old fashioned telescope, yet with a heightened technology, with extreme clarity. Seeing a hand reach for Paul by the group's leader, Kyle moved in and kicked the enemy's leg from behind, causing him to crumble swiftly onto his knees. He knew there would be no damage to the leg, but enough power to the hinge joint of the knee which brought him to the floor. Just as his hands reached for the ground, Kyle added a pushing kick to the shoulder, causing the enemy to fall on his side, jerking his neck slightly with the sudden force of direction.

Kyle's voice suddenly came through without thought. 'Stay down!'

Paul and the other group members all looked at Kyle instantaneously with fear and compliance. The leader of the group remained on the floor, looking up at Kyle with a wide-eyed frown.

Paul wanted to shout words of praise for his brother, but thought it was best to move closer to Kyle, with the hope that the fight may be over.

The others stared with confusion as Kyle encouraged his brother to move backwards, whilst pointing a finger at the group to keep back.

Paul and Kyle walked backwards - and relatively swiftly until they realised they weren't going to be chased by the group.

They continued to look at them, but didn't move a muscle as they moved away. They managed to reach an area where they were out of view from the group and they certainly didn't want them to see where they lived, so a small diversion was made in order to confuse them, just in case they were watching.

Paul finally felt the courage to speak. 'Wow! You were so tough!'

Kyle was still a bit confused about the feelings he had experienced during that time. 'I think it was the adrenaline going through my body.'

'Oh yes. The type that makes you fight or run away.'

'Exactly it,' Kyle left it at that as he felt his body gradually return to its normal strength.

They arrived home and Paul grew so excited about telling the brave story that he ran over to their father, spilling words that were uncontrollably fast. Kyle gave a cringing smile and went to get a drink from the kitchen. He discretely worried about the possibility of their father disapproving of the situation. His Dad *did* visit him in the kitchen and spoke about what had happened.

'Kyle, I heard all about it. I'm pleased you were able to defend yourself and your brother. Tell me what these boys look like. They shouldn't be roaming around causing such problems.'

This was a question Kyle wasn't expecting.

'Oh, well I think there were about four of them. The guy that seems to be the leader uses a lot of hair gel.'

'Not the best description Kyle.' His father chuckled under his breath. 'How old are they? Do they have any defining features? Like an extraordinary sized nose; Big ears? Or tattoos? Anything that would help me identify them?'
Kyle worried about what his Dad was planning on doing with the information.
'Erm, all I can remember is that they are slightly older than me and one of them has really heavy gel in his hair. It's dark hair with a style that looks like it won't move, even with very strong wind. You would know what I meant if you saw him. He is the instigator, the leader of the group I think. He seems to do all the talking.'
His Dad sighed. 'Okay Kyle. I'm sure I'll recognise them if I look for the leader perhaps.'
'What you going to do Dad?'
'Don't worry boy. I will only sort them out if I come across them. See if I can figure out if I know any of their parents. They shouldn't be going around picking fights. If Paul was on his own he could have been hurt badly. I don't agree with these gangs that are just looking for trouble. I'm pleased you've been going for lessons to take care of yourself. It's really turning you into a young man.'
Kyle smiled.
'Me too actually... I feel like a different person.'
'Well, just one thing I must say... It's always best to avoid a fight best you can. Someone will always get hurt somehow.'
'I know Dad. I did try my best to avoid it. I didn't hurt anyone badly. I just knocked the leader over onto soft grass. That was enough to frighten them all.'

The conversation died, but he could see that his father was proud and it made him smile inside.

Kyle was surprised to note that his adrenaline and worries had cleared relatively quickly on this occasion. He did however wonder if it was healthy to acclimatise to such horrible situations.

Everyone settled into the rest of the day and enjoyed each other's company.

TWELVE

The weekend had passed very quickly, with peaceful events within the family home. They were all forcing themselves out of bed and preparing their appearances for the day very slowly.

This was Kyle's last week before a nice long school holiday break. Upon return he would be heading for the next school year. Jack was due to finish school all together at the end of this week, so he was beginning to plan for his next venture. He craved work so that he could earn money and create an independent life for himself. As they were all getting ready in their own space, Jack wanted to tell Kyle of a secret plan. He walked into his room and closed the door behind him.

'Kyle?'

Jack was standing right at the door, looking mischievous, making Kyle feel uncomfortable.

'Yeah?' Kyle asked with a discrete volume of voice.

'My mates are having a party at one of their houses on Friday. They said you and Paul should come. Their parents are on holiday and you might want to meet Scott's younger sister. She's hot.'

Kyle wasn't particularly interested. 'I don't even know a Scott - and don't want to cheat on Karen. Surely Paul is too young.'

Jack frowned.

'Look, Kyle. You and Karen aren't going out with each other. You just danced at one little party. That doesn't mean you're stuck on each other. Meet this girl. Scott reckons she looks at you all the time. I think you'll really like her.'

'I don't want another girl. I love Karen.'

'Love? Are you mad? You're fourteen! You've got to date lots of girls before you fall in love.'

'All I can think about is Karen. Don't ruin it for me.'

Jack paused. 'Ok, look... You and Paul should come to the party. It'll be fun. You can meet all of my mates. I'll tell Dad we're all going over to Scott's. He doesn't have to know it's a party. Please? You need to get some experience of these things for your clubbing days.'

Kyle raised one eyebrow.

'So do you. You're only sixteen.'

'Ah come on man. Live life on the edge.'

There was silence for a moment as a few little thoughts went around Kyle's head - thoughts such as improving his popularity by being with older boys and getting a taste of slightly grown-up parties.

'Ok, ok. Maybe just to keep you happy, but as I say - I think Paul might be a bit too young to tag along.'

Kyle continued to get ready as if the conversation wasn't even occurring.

'Cool. Alright then, we'll leave Paul out of it. I'll come and get you on Friday.' He opened the door happily and left without a further word as if receiving a gift and going off to play with it.

They were all ready for their day at almost the same time, which frequently happened within their household, as if they were all synchronised. Paul and Kyle left to walk to school together. The others were only a few minutes behind in their leaving times.

Kyle felt there was a strange atmosphere at school today. It felt calmer. Frank came to find him again during one of the period breaks. They were due to go to their boxing class that day after school times. Frank wanted to make sure he wasn't going alone.
'You coming after school?'
'Yeah, of course!'
'That's cool then. If you didn't go, I don't think I would go.'
'Why not?'
'I'm scared of going on my own.'
'Ah well, don't worry, I'll be there.'
They both walked together through corridors, talking as they aimed for the social hall of the school.
Kyle recognised a hobbling figure in the near distance, walking towards the same destination. Jeremy was walking awkwardly with his injury, without any crutch aids. In a surprise glance, Jeremy turned his head to notice Kyle's presence too. They both glared at each other in silence.
'Hopefully he won't bother you again.' Frank whispered, noticing them looking at one another.
'I hope not. I think I had a lucky moment that night. He might have been drunk or something.'

'If he was, he hasn't forgotten what happened. Look at him - he's keeping his distance for a change.'

Jeremy walked through to the canteen area, trying to hide his face now. Just that one action confirmed his friend's words and gave Kyle a sense of victory.

'That's awesome. He can't even look at me.'

'Ha-Ha! You'll soon be the popular guy at school and I'll be lucky to have your protection.'

'Ah, I'm not too fussy about being popular. I just want people to stop pushing me around. At least boxing gives us both the edge.'

'Yeah, but you don't just do boxing. It's obvious you have a bit more skill.'

Kyle smiled. 'I'm so pleased I started learning this stuff. Imagine how smashed up I'd be after all these things happening?'

Just as they were enjoying a sense of pride, a heavy shadow seemed to hit them from the side.

A couple of Jeremy's recognisable friends hovered over Kyle and Frank with great power and confidence. Adrenaline hit Kyle hard and the shock seemed to make him instantly weak with fear.

One of them grabbed Kyle's clothes by the shoulder. 'You think you're some kind of tough guy, but wait 'til Jeremy is back on form. You had a head start this time with his injury. He's gonna kill you!'

Frank was so frightened he felt heat and sweat consume his body, making him feel as if he was going to explode in fear.

Kyle remained silent, attempting to hold an emotionless expression.

Jeremy's friend looked down with deep eyes and a hardened frown.

'You sure are a pussy. Picking on an injured man isn't right. We should kick your ass right now.'

At that precise moment, their Science teacher walked through and looked over at the group, causing the boys to move back with innocent expressions. The teacher noted the false pretence and walked over confidently.

'All okay here boys?'

'Yes Sir.' The enemies said loud and clearly.

'Ok, well maybe we should all start moving to our lessons. There's only a minute left before the bell.'

'Yes Sir', said one of Jeremy's friends.

The teacher moved slowly into the canteen, looking back on occasion to ensure their movements and continual peace.

Kyle felt relief for the teacher's protection on this occasion. His Dad's words hit his mind, reminding him of avoiding fights where possible. He couldn't possibly go home with further rumours.

One of Jeremy's friends looked back at Kyle, grabbing a final opportunity to make a statement with a warning glare.

'Saved again pussy. We'll have our moment.' He pushed Kyle slightly sideways as he spoke, with precision timing to avoid the teacher's final head-turn.

They walked off, leaving the two boys feeling intense discomfort.

'Ah no!' Frank was red in the face and shaking slightly.

'Don't worry, they're just trying to frighten us.'

'Well it worked for me.'

'Jeremy will be frightened when he's on his own. He's all cocky when his friends are around.'

Frank knew those were true words and nodded, trying to calm his nerves.

They stood with slightly shaky legs. Kyle noticed his friend was even worse than him.

'Try not to show it or they'll know they have won.'

Frank shook his hands as if he was drip drying them from a wash.

'Ok. I'm fine, don't worry.'

'Boxing will do us good tonight right?'

'Yeah.'

They both walked in the direction of their next lesson.

'I must admit, I'm sick of this feeling Frank. I'm sick of being bullied.'

Frank looked unable to give comfort or advice. 'I know. I don't know what to do.'

A vision hit Kyle's eyes suddenly! A holographic image instantly stood in front of him, stopping all of his movements completely as if confronted by a brick wall. The necklace around his neck grew extremely hot and he felt himself drop to his knees in shock.

The hologram was the perfect image of Zane standing and looking directly at him. Kyle froze and found himself completely transfixed on the three dimensional image of his instructor before his eyes. He knew this wasn't a normal thing to see, particularly at school, but his mind was too shocked to focus on hiding this vision. Words hit his mind, as if he received a message deep within his ear, beyond his physical ability to hear. It was the strangest experience of his life.

The words hit him hard:
'Anger is a sign of strength and the desire to change something, however allow it to pass swiftly, as to hold onto anger will not serve you wisely. An angry fighter is a foolish fighter. A good fighter has an open and calm mind.'

Just as soon as the words hit his mind and the image shocked his eyes – it had all disappeared.
He found a muffled voice trying to gain his attention.
'Kyle! Kyle!'
He looked around him, noticing the normal view of school corridors and clinical white walls. Frank's legs were in view, reminding Kyle of his knelt position. He stood and looked over at his friend's concerned expression.
Taking a breath, he managed to speak.
'It's okay. Sorry, I didn't mean to do that.'
Frank was confused and concerned. 'What happened? You looked as if you fell but you were staring at something!'
Kyle looked for a rational explanation, mostly to comfort his friend.
'I'm okay. I think I just got so angry that I had to calm myself down.'
Frank relaxed his breath. 'Maybe you should see the school nurse just in case.'

'Na, I'm fine. Perfectly fine.'
Kyle knew he was fine, but couldn't explain the occurrence.
He shook his head. Frank took a closer look at Kyle's face.
Both of them attempted to reset their minds with great
effort. The school bell confirmed the need to be at the next
lesson without further excuse. It rang with an unusual drone
in Kyle's ears.

Mrs. Jamieson happened to walk through the same corridor,
accidentally meeting up with the two boys.
'Oh hello!'
'Hi Mrs Jamieson.' Kyle hid his face in embarrassment.
'How are the boxing classes going? Are you sticking with
them?'
The teacher was looking at Kyle as if studying his general
behaviour.
'Yes Miss.'
'Well, are you enjoying them?'
'Yes Miss.'
'That's good. Well, if you still need any help just come and
see me. You know where I am.'
'Ok, thanks Miss.'
The teacher noticed the two boys were looking
uncomfortable in her presence, so she just tapped Kyle on
the shoulder and walked away with a friendly smile.
They both gave time for Mrs Jamieson to move away from
any "hearing zone" before speaking further.
'Do you think she could tell we were nervous?' Frank
whispered as they began walking in the right direction again.

'I hope not.' Kyle felt as if their behaviour was transparent.

Kyle couldn't wait for his day to end, so that he could crawl into bed and sleep the day away, almost as if praying for a "reset". The bonus was at least noticing that the teachers appeared to be about in full force today, keeping a close eye on things.

The boxing class (at the end of the school day) went extremely well however and he felt better about himself after the session.
Even Frank looked much happier. The two of them were fresh and invigorated, despite looking red-faced and sweaty. They both walked back to Kyle's house, chatting and enjoying their friendship. Frank reminded Kyle of his invitation to meet his parents very soon.

The buzz from exercise gave Kyle a zest for life again.

As he showered later that evening, he looked down at the crystal necklace. He noticed it was glowing strangely. It pulsated as if it was very much alive.
He then remembered the vision of Zane that had frightened him and looked back down at the crystal, wondering if it had some kind of communication.
He realised life was becoming very different.

THIRTEEN

Later in the week, it was time for Kyle to head to his Martial Arts class.

He arrived as per normal – in the dark shadows of the hall, waiting for his still-mysterious instructor to attend. As usual, Zane came through to the main hall from a back room at the end corner. It always felt mysterious, but in a positively good way. He knew he was safe right from day one.

'Kyle! Nice to see you again! Have you been practicing since last week?'

'Yes, I have Sir.'

'Ok, well let's do some pad work and see how you are progressing with your speed.'

Zane pulled a large bag near and removed some padding.

'Sir, I have a question if you don't mind?'

Zane stopped his movements and gave Kyle his full attention, with a tilted head.

'Erm... well, the necklace. I have been wearing it the whole time. I just wondered what it is exactly. It gets hot sometimes and does strange things that scare me.'

Zane expected the question and felt he was long overdue an explanation.

'Oh yes. I am sorry for not explaining far earlier. I wanted you to have time to connect energies... Firstly, it cannot harm you. It works *for* you at the times you need it. It works directly with your emotions.'

Kyle felt a little more comforted. 'Oh okay. How does it work though?'

Zane smiled. 'Well, it is a very powerful crystal that works with energy. Energy is within us, without us and connects everyone and everything. Crystals hold energy and they can work with our energy.'

He could see confusion on Kyle's face.

'Don't worry about it too much. I will teach you more as time goes on. The most important thing to remember is that it works with you and that it is a good thing. Just go with it and don't try to fight against it. The important thing to do is relax and know it is like a friend.'

'A friend?' A smile and frown came together.

'It does sound very odd doesn't it? Nobody tells us when we are younger that everything is about energy. Energy works together and we can affect one another with it, including all nature. We are all conditioned in this modern world to believe that everything is solid and that we are all pretty much machines. All of this technology - and we forget that we are all nature and that nature has a cycle of life. I will go into a bit more detail each time you digest a bit more information in each lesson.'

Kyle looked a bit confused.

'So everything I know so far has all been a lie?'

'Well not everything, but some things. It's no-one's fault. We are controlled by the big powers – people who have money to consider. I'm guessing your parents wouldn't even know what lies beneath what we see with our eyes.

The big bosses of countries – or those who think they are - don't want humans to work against them and they don't want to have a nation full of confusion and fear. The land would be in chaos if it went too far into what I would call the *truth*. We all have to be conditioned by our education, which is followed through with work, to make money and keep particular systems working. We are distracted that way in order to make money for ourselves, but also for the big leaders and our economy. Television and all of the latest gadgets are hoped to be big distractions as well. The bottom line is that life is beyond that. It is very magical if you look for it. That's what brings spice to this life. Without connection to the reality of life, we encourage bad things such as sadness and a feeling of being lost.'

Kyle looked a bit dumbfounded. Zane knew it was time to move on to the training.

'Let's get you warmed up now. Don't worry about any of this information for now though, just go with what you feel. That's the best thing you can do.'

'Yes Sir.' Kyle tried to consume the new ideas quickly, but had to shake them from his mind temporarily in order to move onto the task at hand.

Zane worked on trying to get Kyle to feel a build-up of energy within his solar plexus before putting powerful moves into his training. It was a good training session generally for both of them. Zane noticed good progress, whilst Kyle focussed on putting every effort in.

At the end of the training session, Kyle was wet through with sweat.

'Great effort young man. If you're tired after a session it shows how much effort you have put in. One great quote in life is – 'what you put in, you get out'. It is so very true. If you sit back and wait for everything to come to you it generally won't happen. If you put lots of effort into life and what you wish to achieve, you will succeed. Even if you have to keep trying and trying. What we learn from our failures is most powerful, so don't see failure as the end. Persistence is ultimately the cause of succeeding. See "failures" as the beginning of change. We can take them and work on things some more, but knowing more and perhaps adjusting for the next attempt.'

The words were quickly understood this time, but Kyle suddenly had the vision of Zane in the school corridor fly back into his memory!

Zane noticed his changed expression. Kyle threw the memory from his mind with fear that his instructor may think he was behaving strangely.

Kyle felt honoured by the words. 'Thank you. No one ever seems to give advice like you.'

'Everything happens for a reason. I know you were meant to meet me and learn from me.'

Excitement grew within Kyle. Zane could feel his energy build.

'Ok, Kyle. I shall see you next week. Continue to practice. It will help you to progress well. As I say – do not be afraid of failure, it is how we learn.'

They both bowed mildly at one another then moved in opposite directions.

Jack didn't escort him to the hall and back on this occasion. There was a natural belief that things felt safer now and that Kyle could at the very least – defend himself fairly well as of late.

He certainly felt a lot more confident about himself after this later lesson. It was almost as if someone had injected something brave into him all of a sudden, as it certainly felt instant.

Gratitude filled him as he remembered the difficult situations faced in recent times. With the ability to defend himself, he would at least have more confidence.

It was now Friday at school and Karen was watching Kyle walk through the corridor towards their Art lesson which was just about to start. She noticed the way he was walking and found herself drawn towards him. They queued together at the front door of the class. She smirked at him.

'You look so tall today. I don't know what it is.'

Kyle felt the blood rush to his cheeks.

'Oh right. Ha-ha.'

He glanced at others in the queue and spotted her previous boyfriend's face, so suddenly tried to look less interested.

Karen noticed his adjusted expression and knew what he was thinking. 'Don't worry about him. He learnt his lesson and he is a chicken when he hasn't got his tough mates with him.'

He turned to face her with a smile. 'Hey thanks. I just don't want any more problems. Things are quite peaceful at the moment.'

'He'll leave you well alone. I want to sit next to you today if you don't mind?'

He felt weak at the knees now.

'Are you sure that's such a good idea? Surely that would provoke some problems.'

'Ah no, he knows I have no interest in him anymore.'

'You don't know what guys are like though. You know? I guess we are very protective and possessive.'

'He doesn't own me. It's all over between us. We're past history.'

Kyle didn't feel easy about her idea, as nice as it would be to have her by his side. Jeremy's friends were a threat to him and he didn't fancy any fighting.

Mrs Jamieson was already in the classroom and walked up to put her head around the door.

'Right! Come on in. Find your seats quickly!'

The queue moved forward in a hurried fashion.

Kyle tried to watch the movements of Jeremy and noticed he had already considered his seating position, as he picked a seat that was at the opposite end of the room. It certainly gave slight relief to his mind.

Karen whispered in his ear as they moved.

'You see? He is showing that he doesn't want to be near me.'

'Must feel horrible for you.'

'It's horrible that I can't get him to go to a different class, but I guess time will heal.'

'Very wise words. Maybe in our new year he will be somewhere completely different.'

'Well, hopefully he picks the opposite subjects just to avoid us. Ha-Ha!'

Mrs Jamieson shouted out to the remaining few.

'Come on! I haven't got all day! We have a lot to cover today!'

Kyle and Karen faced forward and moved faster. The teacher caught glance of them and smiled discretely. They moved in and sat together, which felt extremely unreal for Kyle. It was most certainly a dream come true. There he was sat with the girl of his dreams.

The class was fairly intense today, as Mrs. Jamieson wanted to go through some historical art. They were expected to pay added attention due to a written test at the end, which she claimed was forced on her by the big bosses. It was certainly different to their usual Art lesson, which was normally extremely casual. The room was usually filled with relaxed chatter and art work scattered all over the tables. The tables themselves were evidence of the usual behaviour. Spots of paint and different mediums randomly marked over the robust wooden tops. It always looked dry enough to lean on. Kyle and Karen were struggling to focus on the lesson with their new found excitement between them. Karen was also very excited about the prospects of some happy company with Kyle, expecting them to get on famously well for a long time. She sat dreaming of a happy family home in some country setting, with two little children running around some fresh green fields. Kyle was simply visualising a possible kiss before the day was out.

As the paperwork for the lesson was distributed around the class, the teacher briefly focussed on Kyle, leaning over to whisper in his ear. 'Try to concentrate on this lesson.'

He felt intensely embarrassed that she would have noticed his behaviour and perhaps even what he had been thinking about. Karen didn't pick up on the words of Mrs. Jamieson and was already looking at the paperwork they'd be learning from.

Kyle noticed a glance from Jeremy while the class settled into things. It wasn't the nasty glance he would have expected, but it still made him feel reasonably uncomfortable.

The lesson needed focus, as the delivery of the information wasn't provided in an exciting way. Students were finding it difficult to absorb the information, with some almost drifting to sleep in their hands. The teacher tried extremely hard to keep their attention.

Time moved forward and the test papers were now distributed. The teacher noted the start time and set everyone their targets. Everyone hung their heads in concentration, trying to remember the details of the classwork.

As they continued to work through the test papers, Kyle felt an extreme heat come from his chest area. He recognised that it was his necklace heating up. It was almost too hot to bear. He felt himself begin to sweat and knew that he had to hide his face. His cheeks were beetroot red now and he tried to undo his school tie and top button of his shirt.

Mrs. Jamieson looked at the clock on the wall and decided to stop the class.
'Right everyone! Put your pens down!'
The instant clatter of all pens hitting the table fell into the room.
The teacher came over to Kyle's side first, noting his red face as she walked along, collecting everyone's papers.
Kyle began to slip into a day dream that he didn't seem to have any control over.
His mind was suddenly in one of the school corridors. An image of himself holding Karen's hand was a comfort to him. The hall appeared to turn a deep red and he felt a sharp attack hit hard into his back. As he spun himself around swiftly, he spotted Jeremy holding a baseball bat. He was moving his arm backwards to prepare to swing the bat towards Kyle's head. As the bat began to move through the air, Kyle stepped forwards, getting into Jeremy's chest area. He moved his arm upward, over one of Jeremy's shoulders and swept his legs behind. Jeremy fell back onto the floor hard, luckily lifting his head up to avoid it hitting the ground. The fall winded him badly. As he lay flat, Kyle placed a foot on Jeremy's chest, saying 'Let that be the final warning.' As he felt the words leave his mouth in his powerful day-dream, he jolted back into the real world, where he sat in the

145

classroom, sweating profusely. Everyone stared at him, with the occasional person making a quiet comment.

'Kyle?' Mrs. Jamieson was concerned. 'I shall see you at the end of class.'

He panicked, wondering what he might have done whilst in his almost sleep-like state. The crystal felt cooler now, much to his relief.

The teacher walked on, continually picking up each student's papers.

Karen looked over at him and spoke softly. 'Did you fall asleep?'

Kyle looked back in embarrassment. 'I think I might have done. Did I say anything?'

'Nearly! You grunted something, but more of a funny noise like you just woke up.'

He felt relief that he didn't do anything too drastic. Students have been known to fall asleep briefly during his school days thankfully.

People continued with their normal thoughts and focussed on the lesson finishing.

Before their thoughts had chance to get impatient, the teacher announced that they could go to their breaks a little earlier than usually scheduled. Kyle remembered that he had to go up to the teacher. Karen looked at him.

'Shall I wait for you outside?'

'If you want to.'

They both picked up their bags and stood, looking into each other's eyes, as if pausing to take an opportunity to stare.

'Kyle! I would like to make this quick!' Mrs. Jamieson had a definite frown on her face.

He looked awkward and made his way over, leaving Karen to walk cautiously to the door.

Karen overheard a few words about Kyle not giving full attention to the class, followed by Kyle's words of apologies. It seemed a couple of minute's worth of conversation before he walked to the door to find Karen kindly waiting there.

'Phew. Thanks for being here.'

Karen smiled. 'That was quick.'

'Yeah. I knew she would think I was deliberately sleeping, but I don't really know what happened.'

'Ah, it's over now. Let's get a milkshake.'

Kyle couldn't express his own worry for what had happened, but didn't feel as if anyone would understand, so decided to ignore the concern for now and brush it off as an imaginative moment.

They both grinned at one another, noting the mischievousness in each other's eyes. Noting their isolation from everyone else, they shuffled swiftly through the corridors, chuckling to themselves, gradually coming to the company of others.

A couple of teachers grunted towards them to slow down, but together they appeared relentless and reckless. They continued to shuffle with a half-run speed. 'What can they do?' Karen said rebelliously.

Kyle realised he was working his way *away* from being the nervous, unpopular boy – to becoming someone recognisable, particularly being with the most beautiful girl

147

he could ever imagine being with. He knew people were looking at him differently and he loved his new reputation. As he thought on about how wonderful things were going, they suddenly realised they were running the wrong way, so turned to run through the correct corridor, chuckling more so between themselves.

The great humour washed away in an instance when they spotted Jeremy standing close to where they needed to get to. He stood there with intent, knowing they were due to arrive in that particular zone of the school.

The wind was taken from Karen's mouth and Kyle instantly felt extremely uncomfortable.

One of Jeremy's arms sat comfortably behind him, bringing it slowly forward to reveal a small baseball bat. It looked like a child-sized bat, but made of strong, solid wood. Kyle gestured Karen to move behind him. Everything then appeared to move in slow motion. A sudden flashback hit Kyle's mind. He realised his brief 'daydream' had reality to it. Jeremy was most certainly holding the bat that he had seen in his dream or vision. His mind grew confident now, knowing his foresight was a preparation for this event. He now expected them to walk closer to one another. It felt a little like an old cowboy shoot-out as the movement began. Jeremy had his slight limp from his injury, but looked in solid form. Kyle had a momentary feeling of fear, but remembered he would be able to defend himself well.

Karen was murmuring some warning words, but they fell on deaf and unfocussed ears, as the two enemies moved closer to one another. No words were exchanged between the two

148

boys, but the motives were extremely clear. Jeremy suddenly went into 'war zone' mode and charged forward with a grizzly and nasty expression. He meant business and Kyle was prepared to face the challenge. A blurry image of an adult body slowly formed around the corner headed for their direction, but before they had time to register the event, Jeremy threw the most powerful bat swing towards Kyle's head. Kyle's thoughts moved swiftly through him, as if he had plenty of time to determine the best form of defence. Everything appeared to be moving in slow motion. He moved inward, close into Jez's chest area, causing the baseball arm to wrap around the back of Kyle's neck and almost behind Jez's own neck. Whilst all wrapped up, Kyle decided to follow his vision and place his foot behind Jeremy and add a nasty throw to the ground. It was certainly a harsh landing for Jeremy, taking the wind from him. He looked paralysed on the floor. At this point, the adult in the background had witnessed most of the event and ran over, shouting for them to stop immediately. He ran over and reached down to Jeremy to ensure he was okay. Kyle stood over Jeremy without a word. Karen was partly pleased but horrified by the event.

Jeremy caught his breath and was able to move into a sitting position on the floor. The teacher was clearly happier about the situation, but turned to Kyle.

'Get to the headmaster's office right away. I will be seeing both of you there immediately!' He turned then to Jeremy, inspecting him visually for any physical trauma. 'Get up and make your way to join us.'

Kyle walked back to Karen and gripped her hand intensely, both of them shaking slightly with shock. They whispered to one another whilst walking.

'You've got to go to the headmaster now?' Her voice was trembling.

The only worry Kyle had was the consequences.

'Yeah, if my Dad hears of this I'm in big trouble.'

'But it wasn't your fault.'

'I hope they see that it was Jeremy carrying the weapon.'

Sure enough the Head Master's office gave good judgement and Jeremy was deemed the instigator. Kyle was however warned to avoid fights. He didn't feel as if he was verbally able to defend himself.

It was later rumoured that Jeremy's parents were invited to the school for a discussion over his recent violence. He had been suspended for a short term as a result. It certainly encouraged some gossiping around the school.

FOURTEEN

Things began to settle again generally with Kyle. He couldn't help but feel disorientated about the bizarre occurrences that were unveiling themselves. The crystal seemed to be his friend after all. He began to realise the visual warnings and the helpful sensations and experiences. Over time he practiced working with it, by recognising the warmth it produced when he needed help, or grew fearful or angry. It felt cool when he was calm or happy. He just felt nervous about any visions that may occur unpredictably. The awkward times in classrooms that could potentially get him into further trouble. He hoped to gain control over what he noted as the 'daydreams'.

Life appeared to be much better, although a new twist on everything he ever knew. The difficult part was feeling as if he was unable to discuss his experiences with anyone other than Zane. Even then, they would usually proceed straight into the physical training of each lesson.

Friday came and Kyle had forgotten that Jack was going to take him out to his friend's party. He felt uncomfortable about it and would have preferred to have stayed at home. Jack however, was excited and had waited for Kyle to arrive home so that he could prepare him for the night.

'Broza!' It was the new nickname Jack was using lately it seemed.

Kyle looked at him in surprise, noticing his excited expression as soon as he entered the hallway of the house after a busy day at school.

'I've been waiting for you. I want to make sure you're ready for the evening. I've told Mum and Dad we're out. We're all covered, but it's just you and me, so I really need you to come with me. No letting me down.'

Kyle looked at him with a one-sided smile. 'I said I'd come.' His tone was low.

Jack reached out for his shoulder, holding it solidly, behaving relative to a television gangster.

'You'll love it once we get in the house.' He looked about to make sure the parents weren't near-by. 'Let me help you pick your gear.'

'I can pick my own clothes really Jack.' He sounded slightly condescending.

'Jeepers, you're acting all confident lately. I really hope it stays that way.' After touching Kyle's shoulder, he couldn't help make a further comment.

'The only thing I would now say is it wouldn't hurt to stack some muscle on them arms.'

Kyle frowned whilst throwing his school bag on the floor. 'I don't need big muscles. I'm strong without having to show it. The element of surprise is good. If people will think I'm a weak person then they'll be shocked when I can handle myself.'

Jack grinned. 'I'm impressed. You're getting mature and confident quickly. You don't look weak, but I thought you might want a bit of arm muscle that's all.'

Kyle made his way upstairs with Jack following only a couple of seconds behind.

They both relaxed a little more and decided to get ready together. They changed their clothes and compared styles, ensuring each other's confidence. Kyle felt better knowing it was an equal comparison this time. Times were certainly changing.

It was time to make their way to the party. As they approached Jack's friend's house, they heard the bass of the music bellowing out into the street. Kyle was throwing himself into the scene without much desire, but more so to please his brother.

They reached the door to Scott's house, hearing the sound of crowds talking and laughing. The music grew to a heart-pounding volume. Kyle felt nervous about his first official 'big person' party. He'd only experienced the family, school and close-friend gatherings on occasion up to this point, so it was a different scene. Trying to appear calm, he kept his head up and attempted an expression that was almost cold. He couldn't show his nervousness or insecurities. Jack could see through his 'mask' but encouraged it.

'You'll be fine. It's all about just going with the flow, having a laugh and just relaxing. We need to aim directly for the drinks first. Once you have a bottle or can in your hand you'll feel part of the group. Just keep your thoughts light and talk to anyone about anything. Mingling with anyone is the key.'

Kyle's nervousness elevated slightly.

'Like I say, don't worry, just go with the flow and relax.'

They both took deep breaths and walked into a very noisy house, full of welcoming smiles.

As they walked in, the young men initially welcomed Jack and left Kyle feeling a bit of a loner, but soon enough he was involved in conversations that made him feel more comfortable. Before he knew it, he was part of a group that spoke very maturely about not wanting to rush into drinking alcohol. They spoke of horrific experiences where friends had been admitted to hospital – not only for over drinking, but also for injuries incurred from miss-haps or incorrectly thinking they were invincible. The subject made Kyle feel nervous about drinking as a whole.

They all moved to the outdoors area not too long into the evening, so that Jack's friend, Scott, could show everyone his outdoor pool and Jacuzzi. Kyle and Jack were impressed until it was suggested that they get into the water with their underwear at some point during the night. Scott, being a tall and sporty young man, had a fearless tendency to show his body to everyone whilst performing any thinkable stunt to impress his friends. Not everyone wanted to share the same interest, but he could be very encouraging.

A few drinks later and some of the more relaxed people were splashing in the warm pool and enjoying a bubbling, hot Jacuzzi. Kyle felt as if he suddenly had a bird's eye view of everything and felt prompted to look around to notice everyone's actions around him. One group of boys were playing a drunken game with the spirit 'shots' and getting themselves completely intoxicated. Some were laughing so hard at each other's conversations whilst standing, holding their drinks. One male and female had decided to roll on a carpet floor, tickling each other and giggling like small children. The ones in the Jacuzzi were quite calm and drinking from a bottle that was being passed around the circle of people.

Is this really fun? Kyle couldn't help think it was such a waste of their youth. Then he wondered if he was the only boring person and should perhaps drink more. He realised he was stood in a new circle of people who weren't really talking much, just drinking liberally. One person was rocking backwards and forwards quite a lot but still managing to keep on his feet.

Jack suddenly came up behind him and patted him hard on his back.

'Hey! Let me introduce you to the girl.'

Kyle cringed. 'Oh no. You know how I feel about Karen.'

'Just put on an at... I mean 'act'.'

Kyle noticed his inability to speak normally. His eyes were very glazed over.

'How are we going to get back home in your state? I didn't choose to be the responsible one.'

Jack frowned. 'We're staying! Now get that stuff in you. You obviously haven't had enough.'

Kyle felt pressure to fall in line with everyone else. His brother looked disappointed.

He took several sips and it was almost as if he could feel the alcohol burn through his chest and cause his legs to ache.

'I don't like what it's doing to me.' Kyle admitted.

Jack looked as if he was going in and out of 'focus', like an adjusting camera lens.

'Once you get past the discomfort you'll be flying. Keep going bro, or I'll get you playing some crazy drinking games to speed you up.'

Kyle worried about potentially sleeping on the floor and politely took some more sips. Thoughts were going through his mind about what he was doing to his body and how long it would take to leave his system.

Jack could see his thoughts.

'Don't worry. Everything you're experiencing is totally the same as everyone else with their first time.'

'Can you tell it's my first time?' He grew even more self-conscious.

'Only because you're my brother. No one else cares. Look around!'

He took Jack's advice and had another view of the scene around him. Everyone was most certainly in their own little world. It encouraged him to try some more. Gulping more of his drink gradually made him feel easier.

Jack then disappeared for what seemed like a lifetime, leaving Kyle to focus completely on his drinking until he wasn't noticing how much was going down into his system. Time passed by and he continued his self-inflictive drunken mission. He felt invigorated and full of invincible energy. Within his mind he had a brief vision of his Dad killing him for drinking at such a young age.

Jack was suddenly back in front of Kyle's eyes, gently encouraging a young lady along with him. She had beautiful locks of blonde hair and freckles perfectly placed around her face. Her eyes were so young and vibrant. They were large pools of green with almost yellow specks flickering within them. Jack spoke up, as they both gazed into each other's eyes. 'So I found this beauty Kyle. She said she noticed you and wants to meet you.'

Kyle wanted to speak but no words could leave his mouth. It wasn't purely over her beauty. His confidence had risen but his mouth didn't seem to want to catch up. He reached out for her hand and she cupped it automatically. Kyle and the girl walked off out into the garden, standing near the Jacuzzi, where the odd splash of water hit them without a care in the world. Kyle realised he was behaving completely out of character.

'Did you want to sit down?' He tried to focus on being polite at the very least.

'Ok.'

They both sat in unison.

No words were exchanged, but Kyle reached out and stroked her neck as if she were a tame cat that had decided to be his friend. She seemed to relax with it and landed her lips directly on his, as if nature had intended this magnetised action to take place.

It was almost as if they had fallen on to each other's faces, as neither of them were able to put any deliberate action into the kiss. Kyle felt comfortable and "floaty".

The girl seemed to go with the flow. She had obviously drunk enough to be in a similar state.

They both removed their heads to be in seated positions, just gazing towards the Jacuzzi.

There was a sudden hot sensation coming from Kyle's chest now, waking him from his inebriated state. He sat boldly upright and wondered what was happening to him. Adrenaline pumped through his body but he didn't know why. He suddenly had an image of his brother sinking deep into the Jacuzzi, losing his breath. Kyle jumped up and bolted with sprinting speed, over to the Jacuzzi to see everyone continuing on as if zombies. Kyle was now extremely sober with clarity and heightened senses. He noticed a shadowy figure under the water, with someone else's leg about to rest on top of it. Kyle shouted and jumped in, startling everyone slightly, despite their drunken conditions. He managed not to land on anyone else, whilst reaching down and pulling a black piece of clothing directly upward. Recognising the dead-weight figure in his hands, Jack appeared unconscious, his chin leaning on his chest. Kyle had lifted him with one arm without even thinking about it. He instantly realised his next required move, so carried him with both arms now, onto the grass beside the Jacuzzi. Others began to rush around, looking concerned, also appearing to sober up considerably. Kyle placed him on his side, trying to encourage any water to leave his mouth, shouting for Jack to regain consciousness. Others gasped, with some girls screaming in panic. It was as if everyone had suddenly awoken from their drunken states. Some tried to intervene with their ideas and knowledge.

'Get back!' Kyle shouted, as he noticed some water trickling from Jack's mouth.

He then decided he needed to do the basic First Aid. Just as he was about to check for breathing, Jack coughed in a frightening way and moved himself on to all fours in order to correct his breathing. He gulped in deep breaths for a few moments, regaining his consciousness.

Kyle and many others gasped in relief at his sudden recoil back into life. Many appeared to walk back to their original places and start the whole drinking process again. Kyle was still in a mild state of shock. 'Jack. Can you breathe? What happened?'

Jack managed to get his breath enough to talk now.

'Jee. I don't actually know. Maybe we should creep home now.'

Kyle was quite happy to leave, but didn't know if there should be a hospital visit first.

Jack appeared to read his mind again.

'Don't worry. I'm fine. I must have just slipped under the water for a few seconds.' He clutched his own chest for personal comfort. 'Maybe this was a bad idea anyway. I thought *you* would be the one in trouble.'

Kyle was going to argue about why he would bring him along to a party if he expected his younger brother to get into some kind of trouble, but he realised he was most probably getting his comeuppance anyway, so decided not to speak of it anymore.

They both crept out of the party zone and walked home in a calm and remorseful manner. Their wet clothes clung to them, looking shiny and wrinkled.

It was fairly dark outside, but not dark enough to cover up their dishevelled appearances.

Kyle suddenly realised their conditions about four hundred meters from home. 'Ah no, we can't go in smelling of alcohol and being all wet!'

Jack appeared care-free, but listened and tried to think of a solution as they slowed their walking pace. 'I know they are out for dinner tonight, but don't know what times.'

A sudden realisation hit Jack at this point, distracting his thoughts about sneaking into the home.

'Hey, how did you know I had fallen into the water? Were you watching me constantly or something?'

Kyle hadn't thought about it too much with all of the emotions he had experienced all in one hit.

'I don't really know. I must have noticed it when I was drunk but then it made me completely sober when I went into action, so not sure what state I was in when I saw you.'

'Ah, well I think I was only gone for a split second. It was like as soon as my lights went out, they came back on. They came on when you got me on the ground. Weird experience.'

Jack felt a big sense of guilt fill him.

'I should never have gotten you to drink. You're too young. We're badly influenced by some people. Never lose your wise head brother.'

Kyle continued to walk without responding, making Jack feel even worse about dragging his younger brother into such a situation.

'Really though, Kyle, we are both too young to drink like that.'

Kyle realised the seriousness of his brother's words, especially when using his *real* name in a sentence. Perhaps he was genuinely remorseful.

He felt he needed to comfort him.

'I guess we were lucky this time. A lesson, hey!'

They both looked ahead to the drive-way to notice no sight of the family car. With great faith, they were able to get into the house with no sign of their parents. They rushed their showers and enjoyed a pile of random food that they were able to raid from the fridge. They decided it would be clever to fill the washing machine with their wet clothes along with some other clothes that needed cleaning, to make it appear as if they were doing some useful chores. To their surprise they had plenty of time and decided to go to bed for an early night sleep.

Their parents and other brothers returned home fairly late in the evening. Their mother walked around the house to perceive all as a normal home.

The night was calm and all the family enjoyed a restful sleep.

FIFTEEN

All of the brothers were spending a lot of time at home with the long summer holiday now in play. With boredom already kicking in - Kyle found plenty of time to sit and ponder. He sat on a comfortable chair in the sitting room, relaxing with thoughts naturally flowing. Life felt very different for him lately, moving from being the invisible, yet bullied kid – to being recognisable for a bit of heroism and popularity.
He thought of the new view of life being about 'energy'; and a crystal that allegedly guides him. All of this was beginning to make him feel nervous, as his perception of the world was becoming very different. He felt very secretive over his new life, but it was certainly a favourable time compared to a few months ago.

Then he thought hard about everything leading up to this day. The recent party sprung to mind. He regretted the momentary drunkenness at the party that brought a kiss to a stranger. He prayed the information would never get to Karen.

It seemed Jack too was contemplating a few things in his life. He had now finished school completely and was sat nearby, attempting to confirm his future plans. A career path was already laid out for him, but he wanted to be certain of his direction.

The television blared blindly at the young men thinking.

The younger brothers were playing an invented game on the floor, without a care of life's circumstances.

Time flew by and it was soon evening. Kyle's Mixed Martial Arts class was now due. He grew slightly nervous as he hadn't practiced recently.
He felt uninspired to attend his lesson, but he knew that if he didn't, there was a risk that his instructor may not see him as a loyal student. Thoughts of all of his bullied days made him a little bit more grateful for the effort his instructor had kindly offered. The big reminder prompted him to get his gear on. He slowly stood and brushed his clothes as if preparing for a smart event. His brothers noted his movements for a few seconds and then turned back to their own thoughts and actions. As he changed into training clothes, he looked down at the necklace, wondering if Zane had always given such gifts to his students. It was always a weird part to the lessons, but wearing it continually was a promise he kept. The necklace always seemed to change in colour slightly and upon close inspection there appeared to be a small Far Eastern inscription, which somehow blended in so well that it was almost impossible to see. Going inward with his thoughts, he decided he needed to focus on what his evening would entail. Kyle knew he'd feel better about everything once he got to his lesson.

When he arrived at the hall, Zane came from his usual shadow-cornered section. He appeared very focussed, so Kyle instantly picked the same mood in order to match the feeling of the room.

'Did you feel that Kyle?' Zane asked with a very deep and meaningful voice.

Kyle didn't know how to respond however, as he didn't understand the question. Zane comforted him with the answer.

'You matched my feeling. That is what energy is all about. You felt my energy and decided to match it.'

Kyle was surprised at the words but went along with it, giving an understanding nod.

'Today, we shall be focussing on energy in a powerful way, testing what you can pull in and push out.'

Kyle didn't understand the meaning of his words and wondered if he should have decided not to come after all.

'Do not fear young Kyle. Not everything I say will make sense until we approach things stage by stage.'

It was almost as if Zane was reading his mind, creating worry about thoughts that might be heard.

They both prepared physically for the lesson. A brief warm-up began and Zane picked the intensity up to a hard work-out, bringing sweat and determination to their bodies and minds.

Zane managed to speak clearly despite their hard efforts.

'Now do you feel the energy changing to a more vibrant feeling?'

Kyle nodded, continuing to move and control his laboured breathing.

They recapped some moves when Zane suddenly stopped the lesson.

'Are you using boxing techniques?'

Kyle felt his blood rush to his feet and Zane picked up on the panic.

'Look, I picked you for a reason Kyle. I need your loyalty, as this is the style you need for your purpose.'

Following those words, the hall felt uncomfortable and quiet. Even the heavy breathing seemed polite. Kyle almost stopped the exercise and left out of pure shame, but knew he had to continue to see how this new information would affect things.

Zane shocked himself with the automatic words that left his mouth. He didn't want to frighten his student away from the lessons. There was silence for a few moments. Zane then realised he had to hope they could continue. It was almost as if they understood one another's thoughts again.

'Ok, Kyle let's move on. Today I brought with me a stand-alone punch bag. It's heavy, as the base is full of sand. We need it heavy for the power we're going to put in, so get your gloves on and we'll make a plan to get started. Don't be too long though, as I don't want your heart and lungs to slow down otherwise we'll have to warm up all over again.'

Kyle wasn't sure where to put his thoughts after his boxing moves were "rumbled". He tried to throw his distracted mind into focus swiftly to attempt to hide his thoughts. His gloves were on before Zane could get the right position of the bag ready.

'Ok,' Zane gave the impression of calm. 'Let's get you closer.'
They lined up with the punching bag.

'Right Kyle, this is where things need to be felt. Like the energy we have been changing through this lesson so far. We consciously changed the feel of the hall with our initial meeting. We lifted the energy up with our warm up, then yet again with a tougher work out. I want you to feel energised and excited for this section of our training.' He paused. 'Visualise this... You have a powerful colour of your choice, filling the top of your head. It fills you with power and strength. Then you have another colour filling you from the top of your head and consuming your body. This second colour reminds you of your correct technique in order to keep the power strong whilst keeping your joints protected. You are protected within and without. Now go back to your first powerful colour and allow that to completely consume you. It is making you feel so powerful and strong.' Zane raised his deep and powerful voice now, more and more as he spoke on. 'Your power is building. You feel it growing within your solar plexus, like a coiled spring that is so tight. Hold that spring and place it in your right arm. You are going to line up with your left arm with a short, sharp jab. Then you are going to hold that coiled up energy from your right arm so tight until you release it with full force and energy behind it.'

Zane did a demonstration. He did a very short, sharp jabbing punch with his left fist and followed through with an almighty

166

powerful punch with his right arm. The standing punch-bag slid across the hall floor with great speed and wobbled at its halting position.

Kyle stood in astonishment, as it was the first time he had seen his instructor perform anything that proved his force. They both walked up to the punch bag's new position.

'Your turn now. I want you to keep that feeling of intense energy. Keep that coiled up power feeling and when you release your punches, just let yourself go completely, putting your hips into it and breathing outward with it.'

Kyle felt pressured, as he would naturally expect a much lower level of performance compared to Zane's ability.

Zane ensured the punch bag was in position and told Kyle to focus and concentrate.

As Kyle focussed and allowed the energy to build up inside, he felt intense heat in his chest. He remembered that sensation from previous events, so decided to go with it. He felt the intensity of the energy build up and threw his left arm in very quickly before releasing his pent up power from the right arm, which pushed through with his body. His fists felt invincible and his mind focussed. He put everything together perfectly as instructed.

It wasn't until his mind calmed to a level of focus that he processed his actions. The punch bag had moved about the same distance as Zane had forced it to go. His instructor was extremely happy and wasn't shy of demonstrating it.

'Yes! That is what it's all about!' Zane looked down at the necklace that settled in Kyle's chest area, over the top of his clothing. Kyle wondered if he was talking about the punch or the crystal.

The crystal colour had changed to a deep blue, but the most prominent feature was the markings he had previously noticed on the crystal - They had erupted into a prominent bright white colour within the blue.

'Power! That's what the crystal has programmed itself to do in this instance. That is what the symbol represents. It's working with your energy. That is the sign we've been hoping for.'

Kyle couldn't help but wonder why he used the word "we".

'So, the crystal needs a lot more explanation, right?' Zane had a slightly worried look on his face.

Kyle nodded with nervousness.

'Well, look at how you punched that heavy bag. The base is filled high with sand, so it's really heavy. You're a young lad with a lot of promise and hope. If I say that everything in our lives is already pre-programmed and that we were meant to meet, would you believe me?'

Kyle wasn't sure, so shrugged his shoulders with a slight doubt.

'This world we live in isn't a real world. This is just where we practice things in order to advance in our real world.'

Kyle wondered if he should run away and call for his Dad. He began to feel as if things were getting too bizarre and above his head. He stopped to notice Zane's face however and it looked a lot clearer to him than it ever had. Upon a closer inspection, Zane had many deep scars, yet a very rugged handsomeness at the same time. His eyes suddenly looked very wise and caring all at the same time.

'There is someone I would like you to meet.'

As soon as Zane had completed his sentence, another figure appeared from the dark corner of the room, as if they had been hiding in a back room for the first twenty minutes of the session. Kyle didn't feel threatened however.

'This is Clara. She is one of our great guides within our real world. She wanted to come and meet you for herself.'

Kyle was completely baffled by the new circumstances, but went along with it as if he was living in a surreal situation. He reminded himself that the lesson was only for a temporary time. Knowing he could leave at any time gave him great comfort.

The very slim, tall, elegant figure came closer. She held a gentle, yet large hand out towards Kyle. He caught a glimpse of her size and shape. She was most certainly over six foot, with everything so perfectly slender and proportioned. As Kyle reached his hand out to meet hers, he noticed the colours of her clothing. They were mainly oranges and yellows that flowed around her like the most perfectly relaxed dress that hung, yet clung so gently. The yellows seemed to blend into golds in some areas. Her clothes appeared more striking to the eyes than anything else at this time. That was – until she spoke!

Her voice was as soothing as silk to the ears. Kyle felt weak at the knees as if the vibration of her voice gently vibrated every part of him. He wondered if he was just love struck or if she brought the same feeling to everyone she met.

169

'I've heard a lot about you young Kyle.'

He just stared, finding her eyes with his. It took a while to realise that her eyes were very different to the type he was used to seeing on a day-to-day basis. They were almost orange and gold combined, but with blueish pupils in the middle. Kyle glanced at the nearest window to see if it was the sun shining directly on her, but there was no logical explanation. Although this situation was extremely odd, he felt very comfortable as if drawn into the most beautiful painting.

He noticed that the hand still holding his was more of a gentle warmth as opposed to a solid touch. The warmth went through him and brought relaxation to his entire body, despite the training he had just completed. Although he was standing still, he felt intensely energised. He looked down at a bright light on his chest, realising the crystal had changed colour to the most emerald green. The symbol had changed shape slightly too. He was too taken by this lady's presence to stop and analyse this however.

After a few moments he realised that he had not responded with any words. Zane moved closer and spoke with a much calmer voice than Kyle was used to.

'This is one of our great leaders of the real world. She is a calming and loving influence that holds many of the good ones together in peace.' He briefly looked over at her, almost for permission to continue. 'I am Clara's protector. There is always a battle between right and wrong, love and hate. Even within ourselves Kyle.'

Kyle was still feeling relaxed, but a bit confused about the evening lesson this had become. He was extremely excited to meet such an amazing lady, but he didn't know how to react.

Clara turned to Zane and nodded gently, then smiled down at Kyle before slowly moving backwards. She walked back to the end of the hall and disappeared into the shadows.

Kyle couldn't understand her sudden departure and wondered if she was going to return. He looked about and realised the hall lights had never been on during any training session and that there was always quite a lot of darkness in the hall, however everything appeared clear. The sudden realisation of that made him wonder about how weird the whole situation was. Zane watched Kyle's eyes as he noted the dark corners and the lady disappearing gradually.

'As I said Kyle, this isn't our real world.'

Kyle frowned with frustration and naturally began to speak up.

'So, what is this all about then? I thought I was here for Martial Art training.'

'That is a perfectly good response. You *are* here for the training. I need to explain a lot to you. I want to start by saying that you have already learnt a lot today. All I want you to do is take away what you have learnt with the energy manipulation and how you were able to punch that bag to the other side of the room with such force. I want you to practice that safely in your own time. Just remember how amazing your ability is and know that it will become stronger and more vibrant with each positive thought. One thing I must say is that you must never hit another person the way you hit that bag tonight.'

Kyle was confused again.

'So what have I learnt this for if I can't use it during life threatening times?'

'It's also natural of you to ask that. Only ever use that power in life threatening situations, but it is potentially a deadly move. That is how serious it all is. I would like to discuss that further when we meet again.' He noticed doubt in Kyle's eyes.

'Trust me Kyle. It is worth continuing this training. You have the talent I have been looking for, for many years. You have a great purpose whether you believe it or not.' He noted Kyle's expression again. 'Let's leave it there for today. I know it's only been...' He looked at his watch. 'Thirty minutes exactly, but next time we can talk more. You have experienced quite a lot this evening and I need you to absorb the level of power you have mastered today. Just please use it very wisely and safely. Save any questions for next time. Get them all in your head and write them down. We can then go through anything you wish next time.'

'Ok.' Kyle didn't know what else to say. Everything felt extremely strange.

They both parted company and Kyle took a slow walk home, taking time to ponder over what had happened. He wondered if anyone else experienced such strange happenings in their lives. It was difficult to know if he should discuss the occurrences with his father.

He decided to take some time out to consider the training - perhaps making up an excuse not to attend for a couple of weeks.

He reached home and walked up to his bedroom, removing the necklace and placing it on his windowsill. His thoughts were frustrated and he began seeking a simple, normal situation for a while.

SIXTEEN

Several weeks had passed and Kyle hadn't attended the lessons with Zane. His crystal sat on the windowsill looking cold and empty. Kyle was due to return to school for his new year in a short few days and he had already decided not to attend the boxing lessons either.

His summer had been filled with visits from friends, family meals and entertainment. He felt as if he was returning to normal life and preferred to remain that way.

On this particular day, Kyle began attempting to get in touch with Karen. Text messages flew back and forth with suggestions to meet. The final decision was to meet at a local park closer to Karen's home. It had been quite a few weeks of not seeing one another and Kyle was growing concerned about their "relationship".

Kyle prepared himself and left the house on his push bike. He pedalled aggressively, enjoying the speed he picked up on the road. The streets were unusually quiet, giving more enjoyment.

Kyle reached his destination swiftly, almost without a sweat. He dropped his bike on the nice soft grass and paced to prepare for Karen's arrival.

He spotted her walking swiftly towards him with a delicately flowing dress. He smiled and reduced her distance by walking to meet her. They hugged deeply, feeling like long lost lovers. A brief kiss on their lips confirmed their happiness to reunite.

'So, where is your necklace?' Karen was observing the missing item around his neck.

He was shocked at her initial words. At school it was easily hidden beneath the sharp shirt collar and often worn sweater.

'Well, it kind of got on my nerves a bit.'

She looked strangely shocked, but swiftly changed the subject.

'So how come we didn't get to meet earlier? You always seem busy.'

Kyle grew guilty. 'I guess I've been sucked into family life.'

Karen didn't appear to like the answer.

'Well, I think we should see each other more often, otherwise we're just together during school break times. That's not exactly a relationship.'

Kyle realised his inexperience in such things and nodded.

'Yeah, I agree. I have been thinking about you a lot though.'

He reached in and gave her another gentle kiss on the cheek, hoping it would resolve her concerns.

Karen grinned in comfort.

'So, maybe we should head somewhere. What time do you need to get home by?'

It was nice to hear she considered his family with return deadline times.

'They normally expect me home for the evening meal. My mum tends to text me to find out what I'm doing.' He looked at her frown and returned the question. 'Err, so what time do you need to be back for.'

'Well I have a strict father. He has only given me a couple of hours. I thought we could make the most of it and do something super fun.'

Kyle tried to analyse the words "super fun".

She hugged him tight.

'I was thinking the shopping centre. I want to show you off to everyone.'

Kyle tried to contain his excitement. It was the first time a girl thought so much of him.

'Well, of course, I'm happy to go shopping.'

She jumped childishly. 'Great! Let's go.'

He looked back at his bike. She noticed his thoughts.

'Did you bring a lock?'

'Hmm, no. I guess I was just trying to save time getting here, so rushed without thinking.'

Karen realised the solution. 'You could just leave it in our back garden. You can't get into the garden without unlocking our gate.'

'Perfect.' He worried about bumping into the strict father however.

They walked over to the house, which was literally two minutes away. Kyle noted a large car on the long driveway, which brought them to a double sized garage and a side-gate on the far right hand side. She unlocked it with a small key amongst her house key set. The gate opened to a large,

green-filled garden and a wooden summer house at the far
end.   Everything looked huge and vibrant.
Karen caught his eyes.
'My Dad is an Entrepreneur. I never really know much as
he's always working. My Step Mother is always at home just
enjoying everything he has. I try to keep away from her. She
seems to be his spy. He sets the rules and she watches me.'
Kyle was shocked at her parental situation.
'Wow. Do you have any brothers or sisters?'
She looked down.
'I don't. I know you have some brothers.'
'Yeah. Our family seems quite big. I have my two parents.'
'You're lucky to have a good family.'
'Well, I guess so.'
'I have all this space and stuff but I learnt a long time ago that
stuff doesn't make you happy.'
Kyle felt sorry for her and wrapped an arm around her
shoulder, encouraging her to move away from the garden.
'Let's go and do that shopping thing.'
Karen smiled and knew he was being kind.
Kyle realised her popularity at school didn't portray the
perfect life as many perceived it to be.
He was beginning to realise that life wasn't all that it seemed.
The necklace came to his mind for a moment. He wondered
if perhaps the lessons from it weren't too far from similar
theories in what he thought of as normal life.
Thinking deeply about people and perceptions, Karen pushed
him as they were walking along.
He looked at her, stunned.

'I'm talking to you and you're not really listening.'

Kyle refocussed his mind.

'Oh I'm really sorry, I was just thinking about something.'

Karen looked slightly disappointed.

He realised he had been thinking for some time, as they had already reached the central part of the town. Thankfully Karen spotted a market place that had a stall of her favourite style of shoes. She pulled Kyle swiftly over to look, bringing her a beaming smile. He panicked over not having any money. The sudden realisation of what the future would hold if he couldn't afford to treat his lady hit his mind. Thoughts of her father re-emerged in his mind. The thought of his money and work status would be very difficult to match.

Karen admired a few pairs of shoes but walked away without expectancy, much to Kyle's relief!

He was surprised at some of his own thoughts. Some that he would never have expected to have to think about at such a tender age.

'Hey, why the serious face?' Karen seemed to notice his every expression.

'Oh I was just thinking.'

'Maybe you should do less thinking. It would be nice to have you here with me right now.'

Kyle realised she was right. 'I'm really sorry.'

Karen grinned as she spotted a small group of people from the same school year. 'Finally, some people I can show you off to.'

Kyle panicked, thinking about all of the bullies he'd encountered in recent times. He prayed they would be some of the nicer students as not to ruin their day. These thoughts made him realise his confidence was still not matching his new reputation.

As they approached the fellow school acquaintances, Kyle felt himself sweating. He automatically reached for the crystal that would normally have rested on his chest. His immediate realisation of it not being with him was that of horror. His disregard for such a powerful comfort now seemed careless.

Karen ran over to a couple of the girls and grew excited about her new company. She spoke in a slightly high pitched voice and looked back at Kyle several times as if bragging about her day out with him. They all giggled intermittently, leaving Kyle feeling uncomfortable. He grew close to the group and stood with his hands firmly in his pockets. Luckily there was another young man within the group who also looked slightly uneasy about this new interaction. He exchanged a friendly nodding 'hello' gesture toward Kyle, which made things feel a little more relaxed between them. The girls continued to giggle between themselves for a few moments. Kyle wondered why he had agreed to spend time with his girlfriend only to be completely ignored. His thoughts became private moans within his head.

After what felt like a long time, Karen finally pulled away from the group and linked one of her arms to one of Kyle's, signalling their departure.

'See ya later!' She confidently pulled Kyle along just as his mother used to as a younger child.

The other girls appeared to shout 'Bye' in unison and continued to walk in their group, moving in their original direction.

Kyle and Karen continued to walk with linked arms, which felt nice for both of them.

'Sorry about that. They were my best friends in last year's home group. I don't see them much.' Karen sounded mature with her explanation.

'No issue. I didn't really know what to say to anyone.'

'You did look a bit nervous. I did my best to be quick.'

Kyle felt embarrassed about his obvious expressions.

'I didn't want it to show.'

'Ha! Well I like reading about psychology and seem to understand everyone's behaviours. Sounds boring but it's really clever too.'

'Wow. There's a lot more to you than meets the eye.'

Karen smiled and walked with what felt like a very light skip. He could feel her excitement and still couldn't believe he was holding onto his dream girl.

Before the couple knew of it, the two hours of time had passed. Karen was shocked upon noticing the time and looked as if she was in extreme panic.

'My Gosh. Dad's going to kill me.'

'I thought he would be at work anyway.'

'Yeah, but don't forget my Step Mother is very much like the old fairy tale with the wicked witch. She reports everything back to my father.'

Kyle thought it was an over-dramatic reaction, but just the same he encouraged them to run back towards her home. As they rushed, Karen gave him instructions on how to get into the rear garden to collect his bike without her assistance.

Luckily Karen approached her front door only ten minutes after her set deadline time. She unlocked the door as silently as possible and crept in, hoping to pretend to have been there for a while. They didn't risk words or any goodbye kisses, as Kyle could feel the tension in the air. He reached down to his chest again, forgetting the absence of the crystal. He cursed in a whisper under his breath. It was becoming clear that he missed the comfort of the crystal.

Kyle crept into the back garden to collect his bike. As he crept through the beautiful sight, he was very aware of his silent tiptoe action. The bike was within easy reach, but his ears were distracted by a haunting voice, stopping him in his tracks. Upon analysing it in his mind, he realised it was a lady shouting with intense anger from within the house. It became obvious that Karen was being reprimanded for arriving home late. With fear of being seen and making matters worse, he intensified his caution and moved swiftly to obtain his bike. He was able to leave the garden and cycle away without being noticed. The ride home was highly intense. He pushed the pedals as hard as he could, as if being chased by an aggressor.

As he calmed his intensity, he thought sympathetically of Karen, realising her genuine reasons for concern to be home punctually. Gratitude of a loving and caring family filled his mind as the same time.

As he calmed to settle into a refreshing drink at home, he heard his phone receive a text message. It was from Karen's number:

'Grounded until first day of school. Do not contact.'

Kyle felt nervous about the situation, wondering if he should inform anyone of the harsh parenting of his girlfriend. He didn't want to respond to the text anyway as it could quite easily be Karen's Step Mother sending the message.

With helplessness he decided there was nothing really that could be done. All he could hope for was to see her during school time, which was soon approaching anyway. In the meantime he prayed in his mind for her safety.

He paced around the house nervously for a little while, but eventually submitted to the fact that worry was a waste of time. His family were all occupied with various activities, so he decided to vacate to his bedroom where he could get a bit of time to himself. He looked over at the windowsill only to see the cold and empty looking crystal. It had been a while since he wore it and guilt began to fill him over the lessons he deliberately missed.

He reached over and gently picked the necklace up. The crystal instantly lit up like an extremely bright, blue lightbulb.

182

At first Kyle was shocked and almost jumped at the sudden change, but managed not to drop it with the surprise.

He looked at it again, more intensely this time. He was beginning to realise that he was giving it life - a life force for the crystal. He placed it back on the windowsill to compare any differences and the light slowly began to fade. He lifted it again and the blue light shone so brightly.

This began to amaze him. Testing it in this way was more revolutionary than having worn it for a length of time.

He held it for a while then slowly attached it around his neck again. The crystal naturally hung around the sternum and began to change colour again. Many colours went through it to begin with, almost as if it was programming itself. It was amazing for him to watch. It appeared alien-like. He touched it and flickers of blue shone outward.

'Wow'. He spoke to himself in amazement.

He studied it further to see if he could identify any small entry points or batteries. To find something explanatory would certainly help his attempt to understand it.

There was nothing explainable however. The item was completely smooth, with a transparent appearance. The colours were settling to a combination of greens and blues now. The feeling of it was cool and comforting, encouraging him to continue to wear it.

'What was I thinking?' He whispered to himself, whilst deciding he was a fool for leaving such a magical item lying around with no function.

It was evident that Zane was correct. The crystal did work with his energy. Although he didn't understand the energy connection completely, he certainly *felt* it. It was almost as if there was no need for explanation, as it was a natural connection.

He suddenly knew he had to go and find Zane. Feeling brave, he decided to go over to the hall on his own to see if he might be there at such a random time. It was wrong to neglect what was changing him for the better. His life was becoming magical – and he suddenly saw the best in this fact.

He ran with all of his might, feeling part guilt, part desperation and part wonderful about his personal recognition.

The hall grew near after a few minutes of running. Sweat poured delicately from his forehead.

The doors were near and he approached with great hope. He pushed them gently at first then noticed the partial opening allowing him to get into the hall. Much to his relief, he felt it was safe and empty enough to look around the dark hall. It was as weird as it always was – slightly dark but perfectly clear to the eyes. This was a strange contradiction which brought him to look for the light switches. Strangely he couldn't find any despite searching very hard. After walking around the hall for what seemed a long time, he decided it might be best to return when the lesson time would normally occur.

A slight disappointment hit him and as he looked down at the crystal, the colour changed to a slight cream colour.

'Interesting.' He whispered with interest.

Just as he allowed the full word to leave his mouth, a figure caught the corner of his eyes. He moved his head to look at the image full on. At the same time he thought about his escape route. The doors were now behind him.

The image before his eyes was very hazy. He began moving backwards, whilst facing forwards. It was a slow and gentle movement to gain a direct run to the door. Just as Kyle was beginning to recognise the figure as a dark, hazy patch of fog, a powerful swing of a silver sword came from nowhere, swiping through the fog swiftly and with great force and intent.

Kyle stepped back and was beginning to prepare for his sprint out to safety.

'Kyle!' The familiar voice of Zane hit his ears hard.

He stood in shock, instantly wondering if his instructor was deliberately trying to frighten him.

Kyle stood in shock and fear, ready to run for his life, yet something still made him wish to see what this scene was all about.

Zane's figure moved forward, a large silver sword held downward by his side.

'You returned?'

'Well, I...' Kyle felt extremely speechless.

'I knew I needed to be patient with you Kyle, just as you need to be with me.'

Kyle still stood in shock, since there was still no explanation for the sword action or the unusual fog.

Zane realised from Kyle's expressions that he needed some comforting words.

'Oh, I realise this must look a little odd, but I am often training here, keeping an eye on things. Again, so much to tell you and teach you, but I shall only continue when I know I have your full loyalty.'

Kyle frowned but relaxed his shoulders slightly realising Zane wasn't there to harm him.

'Okay Kyle. I guess you caught me looking a little odd. I was keeping on top of things in here. I have to look after this hall. It's a long story.'

Kyle assumed he was the manager of the hall who just so happened to know and practice martial arts.

'Again, I shall tell you everything when I know you're back to the training one hundred percent.'

Kyle swallowed and began to speak with a little more courage.

'I have kind of discovered that I need this. The crystal works with me so I think I am obliged. I think the crystal needs me and I need the crystal.'

Zane smiled. 'Aha! I see you have had time to think everything through.'

There was a brief and awkward silence before Zane spoke again.

'It takes a moment to leave a moment, to discover a moment.'

Kyle's brain switched off with confusion.

'Don't worry – I am just basically saying that you needed to take time out to think about everything and appreciate what you were missing. The lucky thing here is that I expected it. I just didn't know how long it would take. I wasn't going to give up on you, as I knew you'd return to realise you cannot give up on me, or at least the circumstances. Your purpose will always pull you back on to the right track.'

Kyle was relieved to hear he was welcomed back, however still remained confused about a few things.

'The truth is I cannot expect you to take in too much all too quickly. You just need to go with the flow and know this.' Zane paused. 'Excuse me a moment, I shall be right back.' He walked back into the corner of the hall for a short time and returned without the sword.
Kyle automatically assumed he had returned it to a safe location.
Zane continued. 'Okay, so let's have a little chat first then decide on our future training.'
Kyle agreed with a small nod.
'So do you have any questions that have popped into your head just at this particular moment?'
Kyle looked down in embarrassment.
'Yes. What is this purpose you talk about?'
Zane grinned. 'Ah well that is something I should summarise for now, as it will be revealed to you gradually anyway.' He took a breath as if preparing for a huge speech.
'You see, I come from a world which is parallel to yours. This hall was created for the good of this parallel world I speak of. I will explain more of that later. What I intend to say at this point is that in my world - which also mixes with your world – I created a leaflet to advertise the martial arts classes, but I

placed an intention on it which was quite powerful.' He looked at Kyle as if to inspect him before he continued. Zane knew that what he was saying would come across as "crazy", but tried to keep everything light.

'The leaflet would reach the person who would be the correct person who could adapt to our relevant training. The training for the correct person is needed in order to save the parallel world and equally – the Earthly life as well. You see we are all in great danger of becoming consumed by a great darkness of which we need to defeat before it becomes too late.'

Kyle was listening but the words didn't seem to lock into his mind. He studied Zane's features for a moment. His face looked slightly shadowed by the hall, but with a continual studied stare, his features were slightly faded. It was almost like viewing a face on a television with a poor signal.

Kyle took a deep gulp and realised Zane was speaking of something beyond "normal life." With this realisation, he thought of the crystal and how "magical" that was proving to be and began to make vague connections to the idea of "unexplainable things".

Kyle suddenly grew extra excited but nervous. 'So things are not what they seem?'

Zane remained silent to allow thoughts to settle.

Kyle recollected the memory of the appropriate leaflet at the needed time.

'So, I am a chosen one?'

'Yes. The leaflet was created by something you humans may term as magic, but it is purely energy that manifests into reality. It was sent to find the chosen one. I had complete knowledge that the leaflet would find its way to the correct person. I knew that once the person found the leaflet - they would find their way to me. Once I was found, I would be able to train the "chosen one" up in order to be using the correct level of good energy to defeat the threatening darkness.'

Kyle looked into Zane's eyes, noticing his genuine expressions. If he was lying then he was extremely good at it.

Zane wanted to ensure Kyle was comforted.

'Take all the time you need to calculate this and understand where you want to go from here. You may not wish to see me again if this is all too frightening or strange for you. I will completely understand... although, obviously I would prefer you to continue with our training as this is your great purpose. We cannot force anything on you. Everything in this life is created by "choice". You have the choice to walk away and call me mad, or to pursue this task and experience it with your own mind.'

Kyle imagined how anyone else listening to Zane's "story" would just walk away and label him as insane. Thoughts of leaving flew around his head, but he knew somehow that all of the mystery was starting to make more sense.

Zane looked nervous as he continued:

'Now that you know this, you are free to make your own decisions. You can walk away and forget any of this happened. You can put it down as some kind of maniac playing silly games... Or, Kyle, you can choose to pursue this purpose and fulfil your destiny.'

Kyle frowned and felt as if everything was a bit over dramatic.

Zane spoke further:

'The truth is that in this life and the parallel life that exists – we work on feelings. If it feels right then work with me; if it feels wrong, then walk away. Go with your feelings. They are much more powerful than the decisions you make in your mind.'

Kyle was slowly adapting to the strange things that were gradually unfolding with this conversation.

'I did miss the crystal. It did feel part of me. Is that an example of feelings?'

Zane beamed a great smile. 'You are right! The crystal was created for you. It is actually going to give you the ability to function in the parallel world. The energy is much greater there, so the function of the crystal is to work with you and bring you great strength for the true person you are.'

Kyle felt well informed by Zane, however still bewildered by the entire situation. Thoughts of his parents and what their reaction would be became a concern.

'What about my parents though?'

Zane looked down with care.

'You only need to be in this other world at times when you are due to train. On Earth, the time-set system is different. You can feel as if you've been over there for hours, yet return to the Earthly realms and realise it would have only been a mere ten minutes.'

This really confused things for Kyle.

'Okay.' Zane knew this would be difficult to digest. 'Let's just take one thing at a time. There is so much to learn. In the meantime we need to train you well on this side of life. I need to teach you the amazing possibilities now that you have really found the connection between yourself and your crystal friend. There is much to learn, but trust me - you will pick it up very swiftly. How about we take one step at a time and continue with our training each week? If at any point you feel this is not for you, then you can walk away and put it all down to strange occurrences... Now then, what do you think? May we begin with our training on our usual training day and evening? I need you to learn patience in our training however, as there is much to learn and it mustn't be carelessly rushed.'

Kyle decided to be spontaneous. After some moments or recollection, he realised he could trust Zane. After all – if Zane was any kind of strange maniac – he would have done something criminal by now. In truth, he has only ever learnt martial arts with him. He decided that if Zane was simply full of wild imagination, then at least he was receiving free training. His mind relaxed and decided to go with the flow.

'Yes, let's do this! Next week?'

Zane smiled again. 'Fantastic. Now it is entirely up to you if you want to continue with the boxing. The only reason I am concerned is if you train elsewhere and you end up accidentally putting in too much force. I don't want you to harm anyone. I need to know you have control of your power, but that it needs extreme levels of caution.'

191

Kyle thought he understood his reasoning.

'I'll give up the boxing class then.'

'There's no need to, but I will leave that up to you Kyle. I'm just saying that your punching will become extremely powerful. You won't believe me now, but you will see in time. With me I can teach you in a controlled environment, but with another you need to be very mindful. The only reason is literally to ensure you are safe with yourself and others. I can incorporate boxing with our training anyway, as it all interlinks... In fact with the different fighting arts, they all interlink somewhere, even if it is a mental or energy link. This is just as our two worlds. They interlink, however, very powerfully. Is this making sense so far?'

Kyle nodded but felt as if his eyes were slightly crossed with the excess information. He decided in his own mind that boxing would most likely need to be dropped in order to focus on the one thing.

'I must remind you of your need to be patient.'

'Ok Sir.' Kyle decided to open up about his feelings a little bit more. 'I do feel a bit lost and frustrated that I can't really talk to anyone else about all of this. It's a bit like holding a really big secret. No one would believe me.'

'Kyle, it is important to keep this between you and I. I'm really sorry about that. You will meet others from my world, so you will not feel alone or lost about it all. It is a huge responsibility I know, but just remember that those with a human mind will analyse you. Doctors would diagnose you to have a mind that is unwell if you tell them of our experiences. Please know that you have an extremely well mind and that no matter what anyone says or believes, you will know our world exists, as you will see it with your own eyes.'

Kyle grew nervous again and began to have doubts.

'So I have to keep this a secret basically.'

'Yes Kyle. You have already seen the power of the crystal by your experiences. You know that these things have happened. That way you know that you are not imagining these things. If another person has not experienced such things then they will not believe it. It is the same with everything you will learn as time here moves forward.'

The words were beginning to make sense.

'I suppose I haven't spoken to anyone about the meaning of the crystal. I've already been able to keep that a secret. It's as if I already know how people would think if I told them the truth about it. They would think I'm bonkers.'

'That's very true Kyle. It's fantastic that you know the difference between what people would know as "normal" and allegedly "imaginary". Thankfully at your age, others may brush your ideas off as imaginary, but some parents would be concerned about their children if their imagination appeared to go a bit too far. Do you know what I'm trying to say?'

'I do.' Kyle felt as if the conversation between the two of them built a stronger friendship bond.

They both stood in thought for a few moments.

Zane realised he needed to speak up. 'Okay, so let's start the *real* training next week. We haven't finished with the basic level of martial arts yet. That is the first thing we need to

193

work into your subconscious mind so that it all comes automatically to you.'

Kyle still stood in silence but acknowledged the words.

'Okay Kyle. Next week... same time, same place?'

'Yes... Okay. I'll be here.'

'Great Kyle. Between now and then just observe how the crystal works with you. It will work mostly with feelings, but observe how it works with your physical actions, your emotions, senses and your thoughts. Okay?'

'Okay.'

Zane looked at him firmly.

Kyle realised his reasons for the firm look and responded as he did during the previous lessons.

'Yes Sir!'

'Okay!' Zane began to turn away and walk back into the usual corner of the hall which was now creating curiosity in Kyle's mind. He wondered what was at that section of the hall. At this particular point however he found he needed to leave. It was comforting to know that he was permitted to return however.

He left the hall feeling a lot happier than he was when he made his way there. His thoughts then moved to Karen, hoping she was safe. It was surprising for him to feel happy about returning to school just to see her again.

SEVENTEEN

The fresh week of school came around extremely quickly. The first shock for most of the brothers was the fact that they had grown slightly taller during the summer holiday. The shirts felt tight, with some looking shorter than before. Their mother ran around attempting to reassure them all that they did still fit. She admitted the forgetfulness of replacing the school uniforms before the new school year. Luckily they were all passable.

Jack was due to start a fresh chapter in life with a new career in just a couple of days' time. He appeared focussed mostly on obtaining his first car and somewhere to live to give him his independence. His father was attempting to remind him of his youth and advised him to slow down and focus on the work ahead. Jack didn't appear to listen to anyone else's advice as he sat in the lounge, drinking a cup of coffee. Everyone else raced around him. He felt slightly odd about not being part of the morning programme.

The father of the family drove off to work, leaving the boys with their usual walk to the school gates.
Kyle felt weird about Jack not tagging along with them. Times were slowly beginning to change and he needed to adapt swiftly.

On the walk to school, Frank identified Kyle from a distance and ran over to him.

'Hi!'

Kyle was happy to see the familiar face.

'Hello!'

'I didn't see you much over the holidays. We went to stay with my grandparents for most of it.'

'Oh right. Where are they?'

'They live over in Malta.'

Kyle couldn't even visualise having relations overseas.

They both walked into the main school hall. Teachers were handing out informative papers and directing them to their assembly points. Today would be strange for them, as new classes were appointed and their final two years loomed ahead of them.

Everyone studied the paperwork, which also had a list of which classes they were in, along with their class mate names. They followed the teacher's instructions and fell into queues that brought them to their newly constructed classes.

Before they knew it, everyone had fallen into a structure of home groups and class timetables. The home group teachers were making sure everyone was well informed.

The most amazing discovery was for Kyle to know that Frank was now in his home group and some of his lessons. He noted that Karen had selected Art and Geography. Two subjects that he would get to see her in. Throughout the morning he was unable to locate any view of her. Worries filled his mind as the first day grew, since there was no sign of her anywhere so far.

Frank and Kyle were close throughout the day, sharing breaks and some classes together.

Frank was beginning to notice Kyle's concerns during the final break of the day before their last run of lessons.

Kyle sat there and suddenly heard a voice in his mind that sounded just like Frank's.

'Pardon?' Kyle asked politely.

Frank looked over at him.

'Uh? Oh, I didn't say anything.'

'Oh, sorry. Ha-Ha. Funny when that happens.'

Kyle chuckled under his breath.

Confusion struck when it happened for the second time however.

'Bet he's still looking for Karen.'

'Pardon?' Kyle turned to Frank again.

Frank looked equally confused.

'You must be hearing someone else over the way.'

Kyle frowned. 'Oh sorry, it really sounds like your voice.'

They both sat in silence, looking over at everyone around them, trying to figure out who Kyle could hear.

'Maybe it's someone to the other side of him.'

Kyle heard Frank's voice again.

'I heard you say that.'

'What?' Frank asked extremely confused.

'I heard you say that it might be someone on the other side of me.'

Frank spoke too quickly. 'I didn't say that with my mouth - I *thought* those words.'

Both boys were shocked over what was occurring with their minds, wondering if it might be possible that Kyle had heard Frank's thoughts.

'**Surely not.**'

'That's what I thought.' As soon as Kyle allowed the words to leave his mouth, he shot up to stand.

Frank sat with nervousness, looking up at him.

'Did you do the same thing again?'

Kyle panicked. 'I think I heard your thoughts!'

Frank's eyes opened wide.

'It can't be. Someone must be playing a trick on us.'

They both looked about and noticed everyone appeared engrossed in their own conversations and actions.

Kyle looked at Frank as if staring into his mind.

'**Uh oh.**'

'Oh no! Did you just think that?'

'Think what?'

'Like worrying thoughts?'

Frank looked over at him with a worried look.

'What's going on here?'

Kyle looked up the corridor and began to walk swiftly towards it.

'Kyle?' Frank grew worried. He viewed Kyle running up the corridor as if trying to run away from his own ghost.

'Kyle!' He ran after him – other students staring on at the sudden drama.

Kyle ran up the corridors and up the nearest stairwell he could find. He was really scared and didn't know how to cope with it all.

Frank struggled to keep up. His breathing grew so heavy that he had to stop and walk to catch his breath again.

Kyle had reached the top floor of the school and began now running through different corridors, almost tripping over someone's carelessly laid school bag. He re-paced his run and kept going until he found another stair case taking him down to the ground level once again. His breathing didn't seem to be affected much by his violent running. It seemed impossible to "outrun" himself. With that realisation he slowed his pace to a fast walk and looked around for some comfort in familiar surroundings. His mind was settling a bit more and finding logical explanations for his experience.

'Kyle!' Frank spotted him from a distance.

They walked toward one another until they grew close enough to speak.

'Frank, what is going on with me?' His arms hung by his side with the impression of failure.

Frank grew concerned. 'I don't know mate. Maybe it was just super hearing.'

Kyle wanted to know.

'Okay, think something deliberate now... Please.'

Frank didn't want to frighten Kyle anymore, but also felt the need to confirm their fears.

There was silence followed by a brief sentence.

'Oh sugar.'

'Argh!' Kyle let out a panic, with an expression to follow. 'It just can't be. My parents will think I'm totally crazy!'
Frank quickly grabbed Kyle's upper arms with a tight grip, attempting to calm his friend.
'What did you hear Kyle?'
'I hear you say *"oh sugar"*.'
Frank felt his heart sink with fear and confusion, realising that this was all becoming frighteningly real. He tried to turn their combined fears into something useful.
'Okay Kyle. Let's think of this in a good way. You might be able to hear people's thoughts, which could bring you a lot of power. Just imagine knowing what the teachers are thinking. Maybe you could hone your skill to do some amazing things!'
Kyle began to calm slightly. It helped knowing that things may be more useful once fear is alleviated slightly. He wondered if he could calm his thoughts completely given the sudden shock.
Frank noticed that Kyle wasn't out of breath from all of the running and that there was no sign of sweat on his forehead.
'Err, are you sure you aren't some kind of superhero anyway?'
Kyle looked at Frank with dark and lost eyes.
'I really don't know.'
Frank was surprised to hear the answer and worried to see the hollow look in his eyes.

They both stood in silence for a few moments, looking around as if something or someone might come along to comfort them.

The bell rang for them to make their way to the next lesson. It rang through their ears with sudden realisation of the present circumstances they were in.

Frank brought some logic to both of them again.

'I think we just need to behave normally and go to class.'

Kyle found it hard just to string a sentence together.

'I don't know if I can concentrate.'

'Well maybe think of it as a test of what you can actually hear.'

Kyle realised Frank may have a useful tip. He looked at his friend, realising he had great supportive wisdom.

Frank could imagine his thoughts through his obvious expressions.

'Come on...' Frank encouraged. 'We don't need this situation to create another situation.'

'What do you mean?'

'I mean we need to continue as normal, otherwise we'll get into trouble for not going to class.... Then all of this will cause a visit to the head teacher and it'll probably get to our parents...'

Kyle knew he was right. He had to get his mind clear and focussed to continue as normal.

'Let's focus on normality. Okay?'

Kyle now wondered where Frank was gathering his wisdom from.

They both moved wearily toward their next lesson.

Kyle felt very nervous about how he might react if things become even more complicated.

Frank looked at Kyle, as if to check for sanity as they both walked into the same lesson, seeking a free table.

The teacher had a stern expression, waiting for everyone to find their places. He spoke to the class, hoping to create instant fear.

'I am Mr. Bates. It's a simple name, so I don't expect you to forget it. If you are likely to, then write it down now.' His features remained hard and cold. 'Now in this subject we are here to work hard and get good results. I have no time for deliberate slackers, so if I see little or no effort with one person – the entire class will need to work harder. Get it? You will be working with the weakest link.'

Some students nodded in agreement, but there were no voices brave enough to speak out.

Kyle felt unusually comforted by the strict authority, as if it was his only level of comfort.

The teacher looked over at Kyle and Frank, noticing their discomforting, pale features. Kyle didn't enjoy the intensity of the look and tried to look down at the desk. A new, harder voice slipped into his mind.

'Oh no. Two nervous characters.'

Kyle looked up with a defensive frown, realising he was hearing the teacher's thoughts!

He felt extremely nervous again, but pinned himself to the chair, by gripping the sides underneath.

After some seconds, Kyle realised the teacher was insulting himself and Frank. He felt his chest warming. Realisation that the crystal was reacting to his feelings, he quickly worked to calm his mind to avoid looking any worse.

Any further discomfort would certainly become obvious. The teacher scanned across the room at other faces before continuing.

Kyle leant toward Frank with a whisper.

'How dare he judge us personally.'

Frank tried to hide his response, by discretely whispering without moving lips.

'I don't think he was talking about us.'

Kyle couldn't understand Frank's ignorance.

The teacher looked over at the pair again.

'So, you think it's okay to interrupt me in your introductory lesson do you?' He began walking aggressively toward Kyle and Frank.

Kyle felt his legs growing weak with fear.

A red faced Mr. Bates grew close within seconds.

'I wouldn't have thought two frightened little boys would interrupt my class so quickly!'

They both sat in silence with heat creeping up through their bodies.

'This will show the class who's boss. Picking on two little weaklings.'

Kyle grew with a mixture of fear and anger when he noticed the teacher hadn't moved his mouth. Mr. Bates' thoughts were being heard. Kyle felt his blood boil and spoke suddenly as if possessed!

He couldn't believe his own actions...

'Don't think you can pick on us, thinking we are weak targets! We are not! You can surely expect me to speak to my parents about your inappropriate aggression.'

Mr. Bates stood back in shock.

'Argh! What the heck? I've got to gain control… Gain control!'

Kyle grew a confident smile, whilst Frank wanted to tuck his own head deep into his shoulders.

The teacher moved cautiously back to the front of the class, viewing everyone.

'Right everybody! This young man…' He pointed to Kyle directly '…Thinks he can back chat a teacher. My first words told you all of what happens to the class if one person slacks in any shape or from. So, we will be starting with some homework this evening. This needs to be ready by tomorrow's lesson. Let this be a message to you all! You misbehave in my class and I will demonstrate the punishment required to keep you all in check!'

'Ah man. I hope that frightens them. Damn kids.'

Kyle panicked with the realisation he had been connecting with his thoughts yet again. He began to understand that the teacher was actually acting out of fear and hate for his job. These were the actions of a resentful person.

Kyle spoke up yet again, even surprising himself!

'Err, Mr. Bates?'

'Oh crap, not this guy again.'

Kyle grinned at hearing the thought.

'Look, I'm really sorry about what I said. I was nervously reacting.'

'What is this guy up to?'

He heard the thought. 'Seriously Sir, I really didn't mean to say anything at all.'

The entire class looked amongst one another.

Mr. Bates didn't want to appear a fool, or a weakling.

'Well young man. Since you apologised, perhaps you should go and explain what has just happened to the principle, while the rest of us continue with our class. It will be up to you to catch up in your own time this evening.' He paused with a foolish expression. 'Well, go on. You know where the office is.'

Kyle stood and left the room, leaving the rest of the class shocked at the occurrences.

As he left, he could hear Mr. Bates continue with the lesson. Kyle walked slowly toward the principal's office, wondering how he was going to approach the subject. As he walked he also wondered how he could suddenly hear thoughts and why it wasn't everyone's thoughts all at the same time. The crystal around his neck suddenly gave a bright white glow. It shone directly through his shirt. He grabbed his chest to attempt to hide it. It suddenly dawned on him that the crystal had everything to do with his sudden abilities. He spoke quietly to the crystal.

'Why are you confusing my life? It's already hard just growing up as a normal boy.'

'Kyle?'

He heard the familiar voice of Mrs. Jamieson and instantly worried about what her thoughts may be.

She appeared to rush over, catching up with his walking.

'Why aren't you in class?'

Kyle realised his absence from a lesson may appear odd.

'I'm - erm... going to see the Head Master.'

She walked alongside him. 'What for?'

'Back-chatting a new teacher.'

He heard a big sigh come from Mrs. Jamieson.

'Kyle, what's going on? You can tell me as we walk.'

He sent her a sideways glance, feeling comfortable about having a bit of company.

He paused for a few moments, then found a way of explaining the situation briefly.

'You see... This new teacher was kind of picking on Frank and I just because we looked nervous. He was using us to demonstrate his power. Picking on us basically. Then I stood up for myself and told him I'd be speaking to my parents.'

Mrs. Jamieson took a breath.

'Oh Kyle. You need to understand that teachers are humans as well. It is best just to humour us. You know? In other words, just go with the flow.'

Kyle grinned with understanding.

'Yeah I know. I guess I just got defensive when I knew what he was doing.'

'Kyle you're very clever. Just use it for your studies and not to psycho-analyse the teachers. That way your focus is on the learning and not on the behaviours of others. Don't waste your time worrying about things that don't deserve your time.'

Kyle knew she was right, but he couldn't explain the complications of his new abilities.

Mrs. Jamieson decided to assist in the current situation.

'Look, I'll go and speak with the headmaster and explain the situation. It might get me into trouble but then save you a whole lot of unwanted trouble.'

Kyle felt better about the situation almost instantly. He grew slightly braver inside and attempted to see if he could hear her thoughts. The harder he tried, the stranger he looked. Nothing came through however.

Mrs. Jamieson looked at him oddly as he twisted and turned his head as if imitating a dog listening to his owner.

Kyle suddenly realised how his actions were appearing so quickly responded.

'Thank you so much Mrs. Jamieson. You are so supportive.'

'Well I wouldn't normally do this kind of thing, but because I've been monitoring you for some time, I know you haven't had things easy. Just please don't back-chat any teachers anymore, okay?'

Kyle nodded with a knowing grin, encouraging Mrs. Jamieson to go and speak to the headmaster. She spoke as she walked away from him. 'Just get yourself prepared for your next class.'

'Yes Ma'am.'

Kyle moved over to a seat in a student social room, wondering what to do with a few moments of time. He looked down at his crystal and decided he would need to speak with Zane sooner rather than later. He couldn't continue with such life shocking surprises if there were more to come. He longed for support and guidance.

Just as those thoughts hit his mind, a crackle of static noise came to his ears, followed by a sudden image in front of him. Luckily no one else was around at this point, so the privacy was a bonus.

Kyle felt he couldn't take any more surprises and gulped his own breath.

He recognised the figure coming into view. A strong holographic image of Zane stood in front of him!

Kyle looked in all directions to ensure he had complete privacy.

'Zane?' He whispered.

'Yes Kyle. I can be called whenever you need me.'

Kyle wondered if his day was actually a vivid dream he needed to slap himself out of.

'So the crystal has been teaching you the art of hearing people's minds?'

'Yes! So it *is* the crystal?'

'It is... just enjoy it Kyle. There is nothing to fear. Go with it...'

Kyle didn't feel this was enough to comfort such profound experiences.

A noise broke out from the corridor leading to the social room, forcing the image of Zane to crackle and disperse. He disappeared as quickly as he had appeared.

'Zane?' Kyle reached out, hoping he would return.

A tall, older student casually entered the same room, catching eye contact with Kyle.

They nodded acknowledgment to one another.

Kyle realised he needed to readjust his mind to the reality of his school day.

The short break he had gave him an opportunity to catch his breath and regain composure.
The bell rang and within a short minute, Frank ran down towards him as if he instantly knew his exact location.
'Kyle!' He was breathless. 'Did you get into serious trouble?'
Kyle grinned with confidence. 'It's okay. I was saved by another teacher. They dealt with it. I've just been sat here.'
Frank looked instantly relieved and sat next to him.
'I can't wait to go home.'
They both sat in silence for a moment, then a large crowd of students came towards them, chattering amongst themselves.
A few passed Kyle's shoulder and patted it. Random class mates passed congratulatory remarks such as 'Brave move.'
And 'Thanks Man.'
Kyle sat confused.
Frank explained.
'The rest of the lesson was really easy. The teacher told us to read one chapter and then finish. He said he wasn't in the mood to teach after you left. Everyone sat chatting and reading. The teacher looked like he didn't care.'
Kyle smiled. 'Ha-ha! Well I never thought trouble would bring me popularity.'
They both felt better, but the underlying thoughts of the strange events remained in both Kyle and Frank's minds.

Thankfully, the rest of the day went smoothly and resulted in non-eventful lessons. Kyle made a conscious decision to ignore any voices that may appear in his mind. It seemed that his decision actually stopped anything unusual from happening.

EIGHTEEN

Days passed and all was calm and quiet in Kyle's world. He looked back and decided that whatever was happening had to be something useful for him. In truth he realised that experiences were only enhancing for him and that perhaps these experiences would just improve all of his senses and abilities. Perhaps his friend was correct about the superhero capabilities. Excitement filled him as he accepted these thoughts during a walk to Karen's house. He realised he hadn't seen her throughout their new week and wondered if she was on holiday or even struck by illness. It was important for him to pay Karen a visit.

The house looked lifeless from the outside, as if everyone had moved out. He approached the door and pressed the bell button. An old man slowly opened the door, looking nervous about the unexpected visitor.
'Oh hi. I was just hoping to see Karen?'
The man grunted and looked at Kyle with beady eyes.
'Ah, they've gone away for some time. I'm just house-sitting. Shall I leave a message?' His voice was weak and high pitched.
Kyle half grinned and half frowned.
'Ur, do you know when they'll be back?'
He grunted again as if his voice only worked for a minute at a time. 'I'm not sure. I just do as I'm told.'

There was a moment of silence.

'Okay, well don't worry. I'll just wait for her to return to school.'

The door slowly closed with effort as older man pushed it to. He wouldn't have been able to slam it even if he wanted to. Kyle stepped backwards, followed by a spin to face his return home. He wished he'd cycled to save the return walk. It was the night of his Martial Art's training, so he didn't have much free time anyway. He couldn't wait to ask all of the questions that had built up in his mind. He hoped for some explanation of the week's events. He desperately craved comfort from someone who would know the answers.

The lesson time came and Kyle arrived early at the hall, so he attempted to do his own warm up to avoid a look of awkwardness.

Zane came from his usual corner.

'Well, hello! You are nice and early. I feel we have a lot to cover tonight.'

Kyle raised his eyebrows.

'Yes, Sir.'

'Well, how are you then?'

This opened the window of opportunity however Kyle didn't know where to start with his questions.

Zane could see the jumble of thoughts bubbling up.

'Okay Kyle, so let's start with any questions you'd like to ask.'

Kyle felt that Zane should know what the questions would be. He remembered that Zane *should* be able to read his mind, but recognised he still needed to physically voice the questions.

'Oh, yes, well…..as you know – I, erm, had a weird experience this week where I could hear people's thoughts.'

Zane gave a knowing nod.

'Well, you see it frightened me. I don't know if I want to have that ability. I don't know how to stop it from happening.'

Zane tilted his head as he often did.

'This is normal for you now. Your senses are going to enhance. The crystal is making you aware of your enhanced abilities now.'

Kyle began to feel some relief with the brief explanation. Zane could see his feelings change and smiled.

'There is a lot of adjustment to make and I'm sorry that things have started without any warning. I was hoping it would come with training, but the crystal is obviously starting things without me. There is a lot that needs to be said.'

Kyle looked extremely interested.

'Thing is Kyle, I preferred to do things gradually so that you don't get completely freaked out, but I may as well give you a brief summary so that you're prepared.' He grunted to prepare for more.

'So, the crystal will connect you to the energies within this world and the parallel world. When the crystal connects with your energy and the energy around you, you will be able to connect to other people's thoughts and feelings. Because it was a matter of finding you and training you, I wasn't sure what abilities would pop up and when.'

Kyle grew slightly excited. 'So it's true. I will be a little bit like a superhero.' He cringed after hearing his own words. They sounded slightly childish.

'Well in this world you will certainly appear to be, but you will be an equal in the parallel world of which I speak of.'

A broader smile formed on Kyle's face. Zane could feel his excitement.

'Okay Kyle. At this point I need to let you know that this is a great responsibility and cannot be taken as an element of pure fun. Okay, we will need you to experiment and play, but we don't want you to get a big head and begin to get out of control. The biggest thing you don't want is attention drawn to yourself. The trouble with that is getting dragged to some experimental lab for tests, leaving you imprisoned with scientific experiments.'

Kyle realised some of the implications of some of the enhanced abilities.

'You are young Kyle, so you have developed enough to understand how a normal man would live on Earth. This is when we can train you, as then you are still at a point where change is more adaptable. When adulthood is reached, routines become part of nature, even more-so. Comforts and desires for a steady and simple life can come into play. We need you before you become that way. You are going to enhance your life here on Earth.'

'Right.' He confirmed his understanding.

'Okay. So now that you understand that... I shall tell you that you can and will be able to hear people's thoughts, see people within and without – almost like x-ray vison. You will develop traits of various animals and creatures, such as be able to breathe under water like a fish, or fight with the clarity of a large tiger. This may sound odd, but it is because you are not as solid as you think you are in appearance. You are formed by many microscopic cells. These cells can be manipulated simply by thought.'

Kyle panicked. 'Oh no! So, I won't change into some kind of creature while I'm at school will I? It was hard enough trying to get used to hearing people's thoughts.'

Zane spotted the sweat on Kyle's forehead, but chuckled at his words. The small laughter brought some lightness to the room.

'Okay Kyle, the trick is not to think about it. I plan to train you to tap into different abilities. You should only use these skills as and when they are needed. Some you can practice – and since listening to other's thoughts may be useful, I can't see any harm in practicing that one a little, but not too much yet.'

Kyle relaxed a little bit.

'Now this idea may sound a little far-fetched, as if I haven't already reached beyond the so-called physical boundaries... You may, with a lot of training, be able to change colour and fade into various backgrounds. In other words – camouflage yourself. You can also make yourself a lot lighter, to the point where you may rise, or float. You will also be able to communicate with any life, such as animals, plants or insects... You will eventually be able to manipulate people's thoughts. You may also be able to leave your entire body and travel as your energy-self. This is very useful – a bit like the invisible man.'

Where Kyle was originally worried about his own mind, he was now beginning to wonder about Zane's sanity.

Laughter hit the hall with a loud booming echo.

Zane's laughter seemed to come from all angles.

'I found your thought funny. I'm sorry. Just so you know that I am not mad. I simply come from the parallel world and have brought with me a crystal to enhance your abilities in order to exist in this Earth as well as in our parallel world. If you allow me, I shall take you for a visit to this other world so that you can see I am not mad.'

Kyle felt nervous about everything Zane had said becoming a reality.

'There is one thing I must tell you about which is the most important thing you can do in order to have an element of control in all of this.'

Kyle looked at Zane with genuine interest.

'You can turn the crystal on to *standby* if you don't wish for it to interfere with your life at certain times. For example, putting it to stand-by mode when at school or at a family event.'

'How Sir?' He desperately wanted answers.

'You lay the palm of your hand over the crystal and say the word CALM, nice and calmly.'

'That would switch it off?'

'To stand-by, Kyle. You can't switch it off. Energy never dies. It's a bit like the television... When you turn it off with the remote control, but it's not switched off at the plug, so the remote control can still switch the full power back on at any time.' He paused to allow the thoughts to sink in. 'That is another elaborate lesson. Now, when you need the crystal to be full of life and need it to be working with you, then hold the palm of your hand over the crystal and speak the word IGNITE. At least then by being able to control the power, it can give you a break when needed.' Zane smiled to give comfort. 'Just be prepared for any surprise abilities the crystal may give you when it is ignited.'

Kyle grew nervous but excited at the same time.

'Don't worry, you will never be in any danger here on the Earth plane, as the crystal enhances you and protects you. It may be best if we keep all of this between us though Kyle. Remember the dangers of others knowing of your unusual abilities?'

Zane placed a hand on Kyle's shoulder.

'The crystal understands you more than you know. It will work with you to demonstrate things. For example, the hearing of people's thoughts kicked in without warning – perhaps because you doubted anything I told you about the parallel world. It needs to start showing you your new abilities.'

Kyle didn't want Zane to know his thoughts on the possibility of this "parallel world" being imaginary, but the crystal most certainly was demonstrating much truth to Zane's claims. If Zane was reading Kyle's thoughts, then he was certainly being polite and continuing on kindly.

'Let's start training you gently so that you can get to grips with all of this.'

Kyle grinned yet felt as if he was already in an unusual world that he didn't understand.

'We need to get your martial arts skills up to a high level firstly.'

Both Kyle and Zane moved into a mind zone where they were able to practice some physical skills. The lesson moved swiftly, with sweat pouring from the effort Kyle was giving. Zane was pleased with the results from the teaching.

NINETEEN

Weeks had passed and Kyle was progressing well at school and training hard in his martial art lessons.

Frank had spent a lot of spare time with Kyle. They found themselves cycling for miles, looking for imaginative adventures. They bonded well as friends.

They practiced boxing techniques together almost every time they met. It seemed to bring more confidence to both of them. Frank had reluctantly accepted Kyle's decision to leave the boxing lesson and focus on the martial arts instead.

Kyle was playing safe with the crystal and had kept it on 'stand-by' mode for the entire duration since the enlightenment of control came about. Zane was aware of Kyle's current preference to keep a normal life for the meantime, as it would be a gradual confidence build-up this way. He preferred a slow adjustment.

Weeks turned into months and Kyle was growing fast – Not only physically, but in confidence and skill. He spent many evenings before sleep, pondering over the 'parallel world' and how the crystal would gradually change his outlook on life.

A birthday came and went - and at 15 now, he felt bigger than all of his brothers, despite all of their growth spurts – (even his older brother, Jack!).

The crystal was looking slightly smaller, as it sat on his continually-growing chest.

A weekend arrived where Kyle had no plans or visitors, allowing everything around him to pause. He took a breath and realised how occupied he had been over the last few months. He stood from his bed and walked over to the mirror, taking time to notice his sharper hairstyle and slightly-changing features. He looked down at his feet, remembering his recent shoe size change. He pushed his chest out, admiring his developing shape and size, wondering how much more he would grow.

He walked casually over to his phone and began flicking through pictures. A picture of Karen came to view and he admired her beauty, wondering where she had disappeared to. All of his spare time had been so consumed that he hadn't stopped to figure out where she was. He realised how he missed the wonderful emotions he experienced when he was around her. It was helpless attempting to find her as no-one appeared to know of her whereabouts. Perhaps she was too much of a distraction to him anyway. His thoughts were putting positive tilts together.

He looked down at the crystal and decided to live a little more daringly. It was time to put some theories of Zane's together.

The house felt quiet, so he decided to walk downstairs and out into the rear garden. He looked through the windows from the outside to ensure nobody was about to watch him - and then walked slowly over to the most distant part of the garden, dropping his right arm to allow the palm of his hand to sit over the crystal which lay comfortably on his chest. 'Ignite!' His voice was strong.

He felt his hand being pushed away so powerfully as if a strong, intense wind had blown into his palm.

Although the current event held his attention, he quickly moved around to view the house, ensuring there was nobody watching him. With no faces looking through any windows, he began to wonder if everyone had gone out for the day. He continued now, looking at the crystal and being aware of his senses. As he looked out into the garden from the kitchen window, he noticed a small cat jumping up on to the perimeter fence. For some reason the cat gave him a small fright. He caught his breath and walked over to offer a pampering hand. The cat was very friendly with beautiful orange-tinged eyes. She accepted Kyle's gentle stroking and raised her tail with encouragement.

A sudden shadow came over them like a heavy cloud moving swiftly over the sky. The cat crouched low and prepared her paws for movement. Kyle dipped his head slightly and looked up to see a very large bird flying low and swiftly over them. He tried to identify the type of bird as swiftly as it flew over, but it all happened so swiftly. He heard the familiar calling of an Eagle and followed his ears and eyes to find a big beautiful bird perched on a strong tree branch looking in Kyle's direction. He stared at the Eagle for a while, admiring its size and obvious power. The Eagle appeared to be aware of the admiration and acknowledged with proud head movements.

Kyle suddenly realised how unusual it was to have such a bird of prey in the residential area and wondered if it was lost. Just at that moment the bird flew up and away, out of sight, leaving the attention now on the cat who was staring up at him innocently. He reached out to pamper her again and she enjoyed the attention.

The crystal suddenly felt warmer and upon inspection, it appeared brighter again. He remembered his original intention of experimenting with the crystal before the distraction of the animals. Just at that thought, he heard a sweet and gentle voice hit just inside his right ear.

'We *are* part of your experiment.'

Kyle jumped and looked about for his mother or a nosey neighbour. Instead all he could see was the cat staring directly into his eyes. He shook his mind and massaged the cat's neck, wondering if he was imagining things. He inspected the cat thoroughly. She was a beautiful black, shiny-furred cat with a pretty little pink nose.

'It's all very real you know? Energy communication.'

Kyle felt as if he had jumped out of his skin with the same voice communication coming clearly into his head again.

The cat looked into his eyes.

'Animals communicate too... Not just with our tones or body language, but with what humans define as "reading minds". We don't need science to give it labels. It's all natural to us. Humans used to be able to do it too, but they have mostly forgotten and only use their physical voices it seems.'

He clutched his forehead, letting go of the cat's neck - wondering if he was in a confusing dream.

He looked down at the crystal and noticed its strong glow. 'We are at your command. Just ask for our help any time.' Kyle looked down at the cat and wondered how he could ever request the help of a small domesticated cat. 'It's all a matter of perception.' The gentle voice hit his ear again.

The feeling of a sudden powerful wind pushed him backwards by a few steps, allowing an amazing spectacle before his eyes. The black cat appeared to have enlarged itself to be a great panther! Kyle crouched in fear of attack, trying his best to remain still.

'Do not fear.' She stepped forward with elegant, proud steps.

Kyle couldn't relax however. This was the weirdest, most threatening experience of all!

'I sense your fear Kyle. You need to calm yourself. I promise I am not here to harm you.'

He thought of the manipulative snake from old mythical tales and began to breathe faster from sheer panic. His instinct was to run into the house now, but he still wasn't convinced that all of his family members were out. It would be the oddest thing to run from a panther in his back garden.

The panther walked towards him and moved downward into a relaxed lying down position. Her head slowly relaxed on the grass in front of him. He now began to calm. As strange as all of this was, he was now able to reach out and stroke the large cat on her head. He recognised the same beautiful eyes.

'Well done Kyle.' The voice was still just as gentle. 'I am your friend.'

The whole scene was very surreal. For a few moments he still wanted to desperately escape the scene, as his fear would naturally wish him to run away, but he held on. 'Well done Kyle.' The panther was purring loudly with comfort. She decided that he had experienced enough stress, so allowed herself to shrink back into her regular, domesticated black cat. Kyle stood and stepped back. 'As I said Kyle. It's all a matter of perception.'

He stood confused and frozen in the same position.

The beautiful little cat looked at Kyle for a moment, then spun to jump over the nearest fence to head back to her original place.

Kyle felt a bit lost as he wasn't sure what to do with himself after such bizarre circumstances. The Eagle appeared to return over the immediate skies and settled nearby again. Kyle froze, wondering if this would be another strange occurrence. The brightest light shone from the Eagle, as if a white sun had consumed everything in view. It looked as if the white light had exploded outward, hitting Kyle's eyes so hard that he lost all sense of everything. All he saw now was white. After what seemed only a few seconds, he woke on the grass and found himself feeling totally relaxed and completely rejuvenated. He opened his weary eyes to see that everything appeared to be "the norm" again.

A familiar voice bellowed out into the garden.

'Kyle! Your dinner is ready. You've been lying about long enough!'

The words confused him. His Dad's voice didn't sound as if he was very happy with him.

He looked down at the crystal, which still shone a bright glow. Kyle thought it may be best to switch the crystal to the standby mode. He sat up and placed his palm over the crystal, whispering the word "calm". It was obvious that the crystal had faded to a very faint light almost instantly.

'Kyle! Stop messing about and get inside!' His Dad's voice shocked Kyle again.

He forced himself to stand up and walk back toward the back entrance of the house. His mother stood over the usual row of hot plates.

'We've been waiting for you.' His mother didn't sound too happy either.

Kyle decided to expose his innocence.

'How long have I been in the garden for then?'

Jack walked into the kitchen and answered on behalf of their parents. 'You've been there for a few hours. We thought you were practicing sleeping in the wild.'

He was confused and his expressions demonstrated it.

'Nobody came to check I was okay? It's not something I would normally do.'

Jack grinned. 'You've been doing lots of things you wouldn't normally do lately.'

Kyle grew concerned. 'Like what?'

The others looked at one another, but the father spoke out diplomatically, sounding a lot more relaxed.

'Well you've been preoccupied and seem quite secretive, but we know it's part of you growing up, so don't listen to your brother. He did similar things at your age.'

Kyle frowned, knowing what his family thought he might be doing privately.

'I've just been chilling in the garden! How can a tonne of stuff come from that?'

They all grinned at one another.

'What?' Kyle knew they would form their own ideas no matter what he said. He suddenly remembered the vivid words from the cat... About everything being a matter of perception. Even if it had been a dream, the words were proving to be right on every level.

During the meal, Jack grinned mischievously throughout. Kyle was extremely grateful for the control of the crystal. At least he didn't have to worry about further events when it sat in stand-by mode. It was quite relaxing to know his family assumed he was going through normal life changes.

He began to wonder why Zane hadn't instructed him on the control of the crystal when he first acquired it.

At this point it didn't matter too much however as he felt amazingly relaxed at this moment in time. Perhaps the sleep in the garden would explain the events. Kyle hoped the animal situation was one big, vivid dream.

TWENTY

The week was moving swiftly again and nothing strange had happened leading up to his next lesson with Zane, although he still had plenty of questions. The crystal remained in the 'standby' position through fear of anything strange happening at the most awkward times. Knowing that his family was aware of his "different" behaviour, he decided to stick to his regular routines and actions for a while.

As he walked over to the hall for his weekly lesson, Karen came to his thoughts and he concluded that he would have to do some further investigation into her disappearance. He had been too relaxed about her absence with all of his recent distractions. No matter what comforting thoughts he put into his mind - something just wasn't right.

He came to the hall a little earlier than normal and expected to entertain himself with his own warm-up. As he entered the hall, he couldn't hide his eyes from the scene that was so astonishing.
Zane appeared to be fighting against a black fog that moved like the wind. It moved through the air like a dragon would in a mystical movie. Zane was trying to slice through the fog with his sword, but it didn't seem to have any effect on the fog-like substance. Although there was no logic to what Kyle was witnessing, he wondered why he would use a sword against what looked like air!

As the sword went through the fog, it appeared to glisten however. Uncertain how Zane presented an unusual scene, Kyle witnessed a white cloak swinging from the back of Zane to consume the fog and drag it to the ground. As the cloak sat on top of the moving fog, Zane finalised his battle with a stabbing action, striking down into the strange enemy's existence. The tip of the blade sank slightly into the wooden floor and the cloak flattened. The fog had disappeared completely somehow.

Zane caught his breath and retained his vision downward for a few moments before looking directly at Kyle with a forehead of sweat.

The awkwardness of the unexplainable event hit the hall hard. They both remained still and in complete silence.

Zane stood tiredly and managed to catch his breath, pulling the sword from the floor and replacing it into the sheath that sat to the side of his belt. Without a word, Zane opened the palm of his hand toward the white cloak. Like a vacuum cleaner, the cloak lifted up and appeared to get sucked into the palm of Zane's hand. Kyle was completely bemused and like many times before, he turned his feet to face the door, with the temptation to run and escape. This time his temptation was stronger than ever. Kyle looked at his instructor's face with no word between them as yet. He knew Zane would be predicting his next move. Before either of them spoke, Kyle ran toward the hall door, almost tripping over his own feet.

Zane didn't know what to say or do, but attempted to shout for him not to run. His words didn't make sense and ended in a garbled rush.

Kyle managed to run out into the dusk air, however falling on to the first clump of grass. A familiar dark figure moved over the top of Kyle and perched on the ground. The Eagle had flown to his side, making Kyle want to jump up and continue to run. He wondered if he was in yet another vivid dream but it was all too real. The Eagle once again – seemed to disappear into a white ball of light, which emanated outward, causing Kyle to go into a deep sleep.

Moments later, Kyle slowly found his eyes opening to the hall's dusk light.

'Aha. I'm pleased you've made it back to us.' Zane leant over him.

Kyle woke up feeling most relaxed and calm again, wondering what had happened.

'I have a lot to explain again don't I?'

Kyle nodded cautiously as he sat up to notice his relaxed surroundings.

'Okay, well let's not do the physical training tonight. I need to go through a few things to update you.'

Kyle realised he was sat on a thin mattress on the hall floor and Zane was sat on a large cushion.

'So, firstly – you didn't faint. You are healed every time something shocks you. This protects you mentally, emotionally, energy-wise and physically. Have you seen the great Eagle? He calms and heals you whenever it's necessary.'

Kyle remained surprisingly calm whilst hearing the words.

'The Eagle is real?'

'The Eagle is real, but he comes from the world you haven't seen yet.'

Kyle continued to sit, leaning back on his arms, shifting his eyes to the left and right, wondering if all of the craziness was worth his time.

'This will be a large shift in what you see as "normal" in your life Kyle. You will become braver in time. I can understand your desire to run away.'

Kyle swallowed hard.

'I don't know if I'm the one you are looking for.' Doubt hit him intensely.

'Kyle you *are* the one we have been looking for. There is absolutely no doubt about it. You are so worthy. It is hard to see your ability in this limited body and mind. You will see the difference when I show you the parallel world of which I primarily come from. The training on the Earthly realm is always the toughest to learn by, but the most rewarding.'

Kyle felt slightly confused (as he often did when hearing Zane's explanations), but mentally, he stayed strong.

'This can all be over once you've completed a task you've been selected for. You can have what you call your "normal" life back.'

Kyle smiled bravely.

'How long do you think it will take?' He regretted the words as soon as they left his mouth. Memories of how he actually missed the curiosity of the works of the crystal came flooding back. 'I'm sorry. I think I like the mystery of it all. It's just quite a frightening thing – all of this.'

Zane did his usual head-tilting.

'I'm sorry you have been given such a task, but I can reassure you that it will be very rewarding for you one day.'

Kyle smiled with a bit more meaning. 'I know I should feel excited about being of some importance.'

'Kyle, everyone is just as important as everyone else. You are the one who is specific for this task however. Everyone has their different talents and abilities and yours are specifically tuned into the needs of the world you have not yet seen. Your task is great, but your underlying need to do this is also great. You don't know this yet, but the future is already written for you.'

Kyle grew more excited about the circumstances, however he suddenly became aware of time and wondered how long he had been away from home.

'Don't worry Kyle. We have almost a full hour to go as of yet. Healing time happens within a flash when it comes to Earthly time. You were early to the lesson and your healing was very swift. Your recovery is very quick. I'm certain you should be feeling very calm and brave right now.'

Kyle paid attention to his feelings.

'Yes. It's true. I am feeling exactly like that.'

Zane smiled. 'Then that is wonderful. Everything is going exactly as it should be.'

They both sat in silence for a moment, allowing Kyle to conjure up some questions upon realising what had just occurred.

'You say time is shorter on Earth when the parallel world stuff happens, but when the Eagle came to heal me the first time – my family said I was asleep on the garden for hours!'

'Ah yes. That is because the Eagle is very aware of everything around your life's circumstances. The Eagle knew that you needed to appear that way in order not to be seen doing anything unusual. If you were seen to be resting in the garden for a few hours, then the Eagle was protecting you from getting caught - so to speak.'

'Caught talking to the animals in the garden?'

'Well, if that's what you were doing, then the Eagle would have selected a good time to heal you from the shock of suddenly being able to speak to the animals, but also concealing the fact if your family was nearby.'

'Oh. So there was a risk of being seen acting weirdly with a huge Black Panther I suppose.'

Zane chuckled slightly under his breath.

'You get the idea...'

Kyle collected his thoughts and wanted to know more about the most recent occurrences.

'Erm, so what in the world was that Grey mist thing you were fighting?' He looked at Zane, noticing no sign of stress or fear considering the circumstances.

Zane took a breath.

'I'm not sure I want to show you the next move just yet as you have been through quite a lot today and received the healing specifically for today's events already.'

Kyle wondered what he meant by the words "next move".

Zane continued. 'How about you get a good night sleep tonight and return when you can tomorrow, then I shall show you something that will make much more sense to you.'

Kyle took a deep breath.

'Okay. What shall I tell my parents? How long will it take?'

'Well, I would tell them you are headed to an extended lesson. If you want me to draft up a quick letter I don't mind if it brings comfort to your parents.'

Kyle thought a letter was a bit over the top.

'Ah no, it'll be fine. How long should I tell them it will take though?'

Zane thought for a few moments.

'Well how about you go home in a minute and tell them we couldn't do a full lesson tonight as something popped up with me. Maybe tell them I have organised an alternative lesson for tomorrow evening?'

'Okay great!'

Things felt much happier between the two of them. Things were beginning to feel exciting.

Zane felt he needed to ask an appropriate question before they concluded tonight's lesson.

'So, tell me something. Have you experienced less trouble at school recently?'

Kyle thought for a moment and realised his life had been smooth and filled with much more fun for a while now.

'Well yes. I think I've changed a bit too.'

'You've been taking time out to grow and be human for a while, which is just great.'

Kyle realised the truth in Zane's words. Things had certainly been ticking over nicely recently.

Kyle smiled and started to move towards the hall door. He stood, recognising his new-found strength and bravery.

'Well done Kyle. You're ready for the next stage. Go home and relax. Head back here tomorrow at our usual time if your parents allow. I'll be here anyway.'

'Practicing with your sword?' Kyle innocently asked.

Zane grinned, not wanting to worry him before the next lesson.

'Yes, just practicing.'

There was a new handshake between them and a great surge of energy that built with the closer friendship that appeared to form.

They both knew something was different as they headed towards their own direction.

Kyle found his walk home refreshing, despite all of the very unusual circumstances yet again. He wondered how anyone else would cope with such strange adventures.

TWENTY ONE

Kyle found himself feeling nervous as he walked from home toward the following lesson that he and Zane had planned. He wondered how brave he would be expected to be. As his school day had been completely uneventful, he had plenty of time to think and ponder. Half of his thoughts were wondering about the whereabouts of Karen. It had been quite a long time since her disappearance. He hadn't been counting the weeks, but it certainly seemed a long time.

Just as he was about to reach the hall door, Zane pushed the door open to greet him.
'I thought I would change my introduction methods.' He smiled thinly.
Kyle felt more welcome.
'So what were you thinking about along the way? It looked like a deep thought.'
Kyle remembered Zane's abilities to read his mind, so spoke honestly.
'Well, there's this girl I really like and we've been seeing each other quite often up until quite a few weeks ago. She seems to have gone missing and I don't know what to do.'
Zane loosened his smile.
'Oh, yes I can feel your concerns. Perhaps I can help in some way. I will send out some seekers.'
Kyle wondered what he meant.

'I shall elaborate…' Zane continued. 'Just as the Eagle comes about at the right time to heal you, there are other animals and creatures that could help to find someone. A little bit like sending a dog to find someone's scent.'

Kyle wasn't sure.

'Okay Kyle, let's talk about that next time should she still be missing. Unless of course you feel she is in any great danger?'

'I don't know, it all just seems a bit odd. An old man at her house said she just went away for a while.'

'Oh, okay, so a family member perhaps?'

'It seems that way.'

'Hmm. Well, I guess we can look into it a bit later… In the meantime, how do you feel about seeing something magical?'

Kyle knew the moment was coming but gritted his teeth to face his fear.

Zane reached for his shoulder and cupped his hand to sit there comfortably.

'Don't worry. It is a wonderful thing to see. You will love it! Right now I need us both to remove our shoes. It's the best way to feel everything.'

Kyle didn't understand the reasoning, but had trusted Zane for quite a long time now, so simply followed his request. He felt a surge of calm fill him as if the magic had already begun.

'Let us start with some explanation as I go along.' Zane began, encouraging Kyle to follow him toward the back of the hall.

'There is a door that I have been entering the hall through. This is where I would like to begin.'

Kyle wondered if Zane's definition of "Magic" may be very different to his.

Zane could tell that Kyle wouldn't expect a normal situation but still hoped to give him a big surprise.

They reached the rear doors of the hall together, and Zane walked into a kitchen that looked untouched. Kyle followed him in and kept his mind calm.

'So, Kyle, I need you to know that not everything is what it seems. Are you ready to see something different from what you are used to?'

'Yes.' There was no time for hesitation, since he was just expecting something strange in the kitchen like some fresh cupcakes!

Zane raised his right hand and rubbed his hand over what looked like an invisible door. It reminded him of a mime artist performing in the street, with white gloves, acting out pretend glass windows and doors.

As Zane moved, small glimmers of light flickered around the edges of his hand.

'Do you see the light Kyle?'

He nodded his response, waiting for something else to occur. It was right to expect another event, as what happened before his eyes appeared impossible.

Zane appeared to conjure up a large golden key. It appeared to be made of transparent light, forming the shape, but not forming a complete, solid shape. Within a few seconds, the golden key appeared to become a normal-looking key. It reduced in size to be small enough to fit in Kyle's palm. It was almost as if it was made for him, as Zane handed it over to him to hold.

At first he was afraid that it may have been hot, but as it dropped into his hand he felt the smooth, cool metal sitting comfortably.

'So...' Zane started again. 'I need you to unlock this door for me.'

Kyle looked to see nothing in front of them. His thoughts were obvious, but Zane stood silently and began to raise his finger to point to a glass-looking door that slowly formed in-front of their eyes. Kyle couldn't understand how the door formed suddenly but looked curiously for a key hole.

As the door appeared to be pure glass, without any frames – he couldn't figure out how it could be unlocked.

He looked for a minute or two, wondering if it needed to manifest some more in order to form a keyhole.

Zane pointed again to a part which appeared 'blank'.

Kyle moved his hand slowly forward with the key clenched between his fingers. He noticed a slight shaking.

Zane picked up on his fear.

'It's okay Kyle. It's a beautiful scene. You'll see.'

Kyle reached forward more courageously and placed the key into an almost-invisible hole. The key appeared to have a force of its own. It moved anticlockwise and made a powerful clunking noise.

The apparent glass door appeared to open away from them.

Kyle felt a gentle tug from the back of his neck. Concerned, he looked down to see the crystal was lifting itself forward, as if magnetised by the door's movement. Kyle looked at Zane for comfort. A return smile worked perfectly.

Kyle focussed forward and couldn't believe the scene set before him. Colours began to form before his eyes. Golds and oranges began to swirl. Zane continued to look at Kyle with a smile.

Kyle's heart was beating swiftly with excitement yet couldn't help fearing the unknown. The silence felt slightly uncomfortable and Zane sensed it.

'It's all okay. Do you see the magic?'

They both stood looking onward.

Kyle swallowed and tried to keep a stead voice.

'I do. Is it *just* magic?'

'It's the parallel world Kyle, but it is a magical place. You will love it. Okay, so now follow me and keep close by my side. I will be a tour guide. We will be back here before you know it. It's just to show you *my* world.'

With no expectations, Kyle followed Zane's slow footsteps forward.

Kyle looked around him. The colours of gold and orange were blending into browns and creams. He felt as if they were walking into a blend of perfect coffee swirls. There was a lovely sense of relaxation and sweetness to it all.

Kyle's feet felt as if they were walking on silky coolness. He looked down briefly to notice a swirly golden floor that had the design of marble to it. Greens and blues were forming just above the ground. All of the colours were much more vibrant to Kyle's naked eyes. The colours alone were enough astonishment. As the colours swirled, they began to form shapes, which were manifesting into the image of amazing trees and flowers. The appearance of the plant life surrounded the golden path, which remained throughout the journey so far. Zane was leading with confidence. His back appeared very straight. His body was lean. Kyle began to study the back of him for a moment. He appeared vibrant in this light. His form was very solid and strong. The colour of his training clothes appeared to glow like an illuminous light. His hair was very black and youthful. His observations caused Zane to turn to observe Kyle briefly. It made Kyle curious about his own appearance. He looked down at his chest, noting a more settled crystal upon his chest. The skin of his chest appeared to have a slight glow about it. He lifted his hands to view, noticing the skin was very youthful and almost illuminous. His training trousers were extremely white. Every part of him appeared to have a vibrant and youthful glow shining through.

He looked ahead again and noted a trickling of water to the left of the path. The water was so sparkly and seemed to be just as much 'alive' as he was. It trickled similarly to a small canal that didn't appear to go very far. He looked back down at the golden path and somehow knew that it was carrying him, even though he was the one doing the walking. Everything felt alive and vibrant.

As they both continued to walk, a couple of beautiful birds flew over their heads, flaunting their wings. The flying was effortless – a light gliding. Their wings were of oranges, browns and gold. Expressions on their faces were proud and strong. As they flew majestically overhead, Kyle noticed the sky was a perfect blue. Even the sky appeared very much alive with an amazing sparkle to it. The odd leaf glided gently through the air, appearing to be alive as well.

Kyle began to wonder where he was. The place felt so calm and amazingly beautiful, but the worry of going too far into a place he knew nothing about, began to fill him.

Zane instantly picked up on Kyle's feelings. He stopped and gently knelt before him.

'There is no need to worry Kyle. I will have you back in the usual hall for the usual time. I am in full control here and you are safe where we are.'

Kyle stood in surprise at Zane's sudden words. He waited for Zane to explain further.

'In this world your thoughts will be much more prominent. They echo outwardly. Master your thoughts here and they will be even more useful when back in the Earthly ways.'

Kyle took heed but didn't quite understand fully.

'Don't worry...' Zane continued to speak as he stood upright and began moving deeper into his familiar world.

They walked to an open space, which mostly comprised of beautiful, handcrafted dwellings. The little houses looked similar to home-made huts, but they were so well made that they caused Kyle to admire their beauty. Kyle looked about the area and picked up on the odd tree; plenty of soft-looking emerald green grass; a beautiful blue lake with the same sparkle to the previously viewed of water; plants that appeared to have an abundance of very bright and pretty fruits dangling from them; The odd hand-made tool lying on the ground, unusually sparkling.

Very tall people began to appear from the huts as if the sound of their arrival caused curiosity. They walked closer to Kyle and Zane.

'Don't worry Kyle, they are our friends in this place.'

Kyle had no worry to tackle at the present time, but took note of Zane's words anyway.

The people walked effortlessly over objects that appeared to be rocks and small trickles of water. As they grew closer, Kyle noted their flowing robes of such varying colours. One person was wearing a beautiful array of reds and purples. Their hair draped over the reds with a tinge of orange and brown.

Another wore green, flowing robes which blended gently into emeralds and other very 'rich' shades.

Kyle's mouth must have been gaping open, as a gasp of air made him gulp back into his normal bodily feelings.

The tall people were now reaching out to Zane with friendly hugs and some kind arm tapping. Large smiles were exchanged, but words appeared too quiet for Kyle to hear.

The people appeared to encourage Zane to follow them into the openings of their huts, Zane gave a knowing glance to Kyle, encouraging them to follow.

Kyle was feeling nervous now. Zane must have known the worry would arrive, as Kyle remembered his words from only a short moment ago. He reminded himself that all was safe.

They walked on to the most amazingly soft green grass.

Kyle's feet felt so tingly and wonderful. The golden path

grew more distant and Kyle strangely felt himself miss the feeling of safety associated with it.

Zane smiled back to note Kyle's obvious feelings.

Everyone congregated around what appeared to be a large, round table with unidentifiable scribe throughout a fixed golden plate. Kyle only took a brief glance, trying to fit into the environment best he could.

The table sat surrounded by several soft stools on which they all slowly sat down on.

As they all sat, Kyle realised how small he appeared amongst the group of very tall people. Zane appeared taller than he would normally look as he almost blended in with their heights. The table now looked unusually large too. The stools on which they sat were as large as an average sized coffee table at home, however felt as soft as a pillow-full of feathers. Kyle felt them with his hands to attempt to fathom out how they appeared hard yet felt so soft but no matter what, couldn't figure it out.

They all sat silently around the table, allowing another tall person to arrive with what looked like a tray of drinks.

Kyle decided he was correct, as large glasses of fluid were left in front of each person.

Zane looked over at Kyle, who encouraged him to gently drink.

They all took sips and slowly appeared to turn their attention to Kyle more so than anyone else at the table. He couldn't understand the focus on himself, so looked down to notice a bright golden glow shining from his chest, spreading to cover his entire body. He shone outwardly, brighter than any glow he had seen so far in this new place. Everyone looked at him in awe.

Zane smiled again. 'Kyle, the drink shows our inner truth. It has exposed you as the one who has been chosen for our wonderful world. You are here to save us all.'

Kyle felt amazed, but pressured at the same time.

The tall people began to stand and gather around Kyle, all laying a hand on a section of his head and shoulders. A super strong surge of energy went through him, making him feel amazingly powerful. He wasn't sure if he wanted to bounce around or run through the grass to release the huge surge of energy he was feeling.

'Okay Kyle, absorb the power. We are all here to help you. We are your team of helpers. You are the chosen one, but the missing part in our set. You complete us. We are all one together.'

Kyle felt amazing, fresh and new. He felt beyond the usual youthfulness he had always felt up to now. At this moment in time he felt he could run to the top of the highest mountain and jump from the top to land powerfully and safely at the bottom. The vision went through his mind.

The tall people stood back as if they had completed a planned task.

They all nodded at one another, expecting Zane to stand.

'Come Kyle. We have completed our first visit. It is time to leave.'

Kyle frowned with disappointment. He had never felt so wonderful, comfortable and vibrant. The sudden expectation to leave, now felt untimely.

'Don't grow addicted to this world. Resist the urge to remain here, as your home is currently upon Earth.'

Kyle realised how "at home" he felt at this particular place, but shook his head at this reality.

The tall people all watched on with amazement and respect as Kyle and Zane slowly stepped back, aiming to leave. Zane offered a kind wave of goodbye, sending some words out toward them. The words were again - too quiet and muffled for Kyle to understand.

They both walked effortlessly toward the golden path which strangely appeared to draw them in like an old friend.

Birds with golden wings flew over, seemingly attracted to the pair and wishing to protect and guide them. At least that was the feeling Kyle had as they flew so closely.

Kyle used the time it took to walk back, to take in some of the sights. He was able to focus on the beauty a lot more. The trees didn't look like the same trees he was used to seeing. They were unusually vibrant and appeared to have leaves with what he could only relate to as veins. The "veins" seemed to have a golden light moving through them, as the equivalent of blood moving through a human's veins would look.

The sky glimmered as if it held stars during the daytime. The apparent stars were plentiful and very much alive in the bright blue sky. Kyle studied the sky some more, knowing that the golden path was guiding his feet safely and securely.

As he studied the sky from all angles, he noted some distant moon-shapes in a faded white light. Another planet-like image stood at a further distance away, portraying an image similar to that of the pictorial images of Jupiter. Everything seemed very familiar but also very different. Kyle couldn't understand his feelings either. He felt at home - so calm, happy and peaceful. His intrigue was enough to desire a few more hours in this place.

Zane was a footstep ahead and still looked even more 'alive' than he normally did.

As they walked, Zane suddenly slowed to place a strong hand around Kyle's upper arm.

Kyle felt a slight panic for a few seconds as they both walked through what felt like a fresh layer of clear gel. It was as if walking through a thin layer of cold hair gel, which was as tall and wide as a building wall.

Before he had chance to think about it all too much, he suddenly found himself feeling heavy and rigid. He looked down to notice the floor was now a dark wooden colour. His feet were now feeling the full weight of his body and the awareness of everything felt almost limited. He looked up to see Zane inspecting him intensely. Their eyes connected.

'Are you with me Kyle?'

There was a confused pause.

'I am.' Kyle replied with a tone that meant the opposite.

'You're back in the room now. I need you to look around and recognise it, but take your time.'

Kyle suddenly realised the familiar surroundings - the kitchen walls and dull light.

Zane appeared as he usually did – slightly mysterious and rugged.

'I see.' Kyle was now feeling almost back to normal.

Zane grinned. 'I can see you getting back to normality again.

Kyle continued to look around and move his body. Wiggling his toes and fingers made him literally begin to feel human again.

Zane raised his eyebrows. 'The only part I thought you might struggle with is the return through the door. It's always a very odd sensation. It's also hard to feel your usual sensations again for a few moments.'

Kyle suddenly remembered the wonderful feelings experienced at the other side of the magical door.

'Wow!'

Zane grinned.

'I know. It's an amazing place isn't it?'

'Yes.'

'Okay, so now I want you to remove the key from the door. Do you remember placing it in there and turning it in the beginning?'

He looked behind him to see the glass door with the large, golden key sticking through the clear section that would be holding it in position.

'Oh yes.'

'Take your time Kyle. I know you'll be disillusioned for a while. It's a magical world. Don't forget how important it is to remain here however – in this world. You'll have plenty of time to visit there. Unfortunately it isn't all sunshine and rainbows over there, just as here there is a bit of good and bad.'

It sounded as if Zane was deliberately attempting to put Kyle off returning.

'Okay Kyle, I need you to remove the key and place it in the palm of my hand. We will go back in next week if you are up to it.'

Kyle grew excited about the thought. The feelings from being in the parallel world were just so amazing.

'I wish I came from there too.'

Zane had a worried look on his face.

'You will have plenty of opportunities to go over. Please just remain grounded here. The next time I will show you the reasons we need your help.'

Kyle grew nervous at the fresh words. He had forgotten that there was a particular task pending.

Zane threw a look toward him that reminded him of the key within the door. He reached out and took the key easily from the blank-looking hole and placed it in Zane's outreached hand. With a mixture of dissolving and a vacuum sucking – the key appeared to disappear into the palm of his hand.

Kyle was intrigued yet again.

Zane spoke just as soon as the key disappeared.

'So, I am the gate-keeper. I protect particular parts between our two worlds.'

'Wow.' Kyle couldn't find any other words.

'So next time you will see more. Gently, gently does it.'

Excitement grew again with slightly more comforting words.

It was encouraging to know that he was being treated so gently and well. Respect away from home wasn't something he *always* had.

Zane reached up to one of the cupboards and collected a cup, filling it with some water from the tap.

'A good reason to have a kitchen just the other side of this door... Having a drink is a good way to ground you.'

Kyle took the cup and drank as if he hadn't had any fluids for many an hour.

Zane wanted to ensure Kyle was completely re-centred.

'Okay Kyle, so I need you to look about and notice how it's a bit darker here now. It would now be the end of your lesson really. I need to make sure you're familiar with your surroundings and ready to return to normality.'

Kyle complied and studied the entire surroundings, wriggling his toes and realising how he had settled into what was normal yet again.

'Right, you look great. One final thing is this... you are now sworn to complete secrecy. If you speak about anything of the other world, you will end up being labelled as unwell, disillusioned or mentally disturbed. I'm uncertain of the exact diagnosis doctors may give, but there would most definitely be concerns for your health and wellbeing. It's just something others will not accept. It also cannot be proven, since I am the only gatekeeper, so please don't put yourself in any tricky situations. I remember mentioning this briefly before.'

'Okay. I understand.'

Zane studied him for sincerity.

'I do understand Sir.'

'Excellent Kyle. Now, do you have any questions before we part company?'

A vision of Zane fighting the dark cloud appeared in his mind. Zane realised there would be very valid questions following those circumstances.

'Sir, I would love to know why you were fighting against a grey fog or cloud.'

Zane looked a little ashamed for not having explained earlier.

'Sorry Kyle, that was meant to be part of today's lesson. The trouble I have with being the master of the door and the key is that occasionally I time it wrong with my return. Or perhaps the others time it correctly.'

'I don't understand Sir.'

'Well, you see, as I say – not everything is sunshine and rainbows. There is also bad within *our* world. Sometimes upon my entry or return, one of the bad energies manages to creep through. If they do, then I have to prevent it from getting any further.'

Kyle worried for a moment, trying to imagine what would happen if Zane couldn't contain them.

'Don't worry Kyle, I've actually been doing this for a very long time. Some of them have gone beyond me and I've been through the streets trying to collect them with discretion.'

'How can you do that kind of thing without being seen?'

'As I said recently Kyle - once you're trained, you can manipulate yourself to become invisible to others.'

'Oh yes.'

Zane seemed to study Kyle's expressions again.

'I mean, yes Sir.'

Zane had no intention of encouraging the 'Sir' part on that occasion however it didn't go without appreciation.

'Can you see why we have to go through a lot of training now that you've experienced my world?'

'Oh, yes Sir. I realise I don't know what I'm doing with it all now.'

'Well, you know more than you realise at this stage, but we need to go through so much more.'

Kyle briefly wondered about how he would find enough time to fit everything in, on top of school work.

'Oh Kyle, don't worry, as this will only be on your actual training nights. Just one evening a week will be sufficient. There may be the odd thing happen between things, but remember you can keep your crystal on standby whenever you're at school or studying. You have full control of how much or how little time you wish to spend upon the training.'

Kyle had a flashback of a dream he had before everything became a little bit too weird. Fogs and Eagles and mystery all returned to his memory.

Zane, as always, noticed his thoughts.

'Everything that has happened so far has been happening as and when it is meant to happen.'

Kyle smiled to know Zane always had an answer to queries without having to ask.

'Okay now Kyle. It's time for you to head home. If you have any worries or concerns, then please just pop back here and call my name.'

'Yes Sir.'

They both turned to leave one another in the same way they often did.

Zane looked back however with a thought of concern, hoping Kyle could continue to handle the change of perceptions.

'Kyle!' Zane shouted.

He turned. 'Yes Sir?'

'Don't forget that all of this is only for a temporary time. You will have your normal life back soon.'

'Okay Sir!' Kyle shouted with a downward tone as if disappointed slightly.

It changed Zane's worry to that of slight joy, knowing Kyle may actually be enjoying his experiences.

They both walked towards their own direction, with the sound of the hall doors swinging closed.

TWENTY TWO

The following week was beginning to be exciting. One small niggling worry remained with Kyle – and that was of Karen's whereabouts, so he decided he would go to the house after school on the Monday.

He took the direction of walking toward the home just as soon as the final bell sounded. Frank looked concerned as he spotted his friend running off the premises with no final words.

With Kyle's long legs, he found the path to her home relatively quickly, hoping he would still make it to his own home not too far off his usual time.

The house seemed quiet from the outside, with no vehicle on the driveway. His hopes were already diminishing.

His knock on the door left an echo in his eardrums. He suspected his senses were heightened because of his slight nervousness.

To his surprise, a young lady opened the door, looking very familiar.

'Karen!' Kyle shouted with excitement.

'Shush.' Karen looked extremely nervous and frightened.

Upon inspection, Karen looked quite unkempt. Behind her house door she appeared to have weak and limp looking hair and skin that didn't even look washed.

Kyle lowered his voice. 'Can you talk?'

Her eyes looked to the furthest right point of the house.

'If anyone knows you are here, I will be murdered.'

He considered her words as exaggeration, but then
wondered if she spoke with some truth.

'Well how can I ever see you again? Why aren't you at
school?'

She paused and took a deep breath.

'My Step Mother is in the garden so there is a chance she
could come back in at any point. Meet me at the park in ten
minutes. If I'm not there after waiting for about fifteen, then
just go home.'

Before Kyle had chance to speak again, Karen closed the door
fairly swiftly, allowing for a deep 'click'.

He grew concerned, but at the same time felt a little bit
excited at the possibility of seeing her again.

Kyle had managed to get to the park he knew Karen spoke of,
within five minutes and sat on the grass with anticipation.

A few other young students had walked by, taking a brief
look at his location, obviously looking out of place.

He looked down at his watch, noticing a shadow covering his
arm suddenly. Expecting someone to give him some grief, he
looked up to see Karen looking down at him. He stood in
surprise and excitement, grabbing her tightly with a strong
hug.

'Where have you been?'

Karen looked as if she had been crying.

'My Dad has moved away to work for a few months. He said
it's to pay for a tonne of bills to keep our big house.

My Step Mum decided that studying would continue at
home. She hates that I live a life with make-up, jewellery and

perfect hair. She won't let me go back Kyle.' Her eyes welled up again.

'What? Well surely the school has something to say?' He kept his arms around her, but leant back to see her face.

'I don't know how it works, but she thinks it's all about image and getting pregnant at a young age. She was a teacher a few years ago, so she probably has this weird idea about female students.'

'That's crazy!'

'I know, but she won't let me out for longer than a reason to go to the shop, or do her a silly favour. I swear my Dad doesn't even know what she is like when he is away. He thinks she is all sugar coated and sweet. She acts so differently when he's home.'

'How long is he away for?'

'I think he has about four more months to go.'

'Jeepers. How can I see you? I miss you and I've been so worried.'

'She won't let me use my phone or the house phone. She seems to want to keep me trapped in the house.'

Kyle looked up to the sky in search of an answer to the problem.

'There must be something we can do. I'm going to speak with my parents.'

'No Kyle. Just wait for my Dad to come home, then I will try and talk to him in private.'

He thought on for a moment, wondering why she wouldn't accept help.

'Surely you can tell your Dad about this somehow?' He looked into her sad eyes. 'Can I see you sometimes? Like this?'

She looked downward. 'I don't know how. She is too clever and will notice the patterns. She beats me if she thinks I've done something that's not part of her plan.'

Kyle was now stunned and horrified.

'This isn't right. I know you don't want me to, but I will speak with my parents.'

'No Kyle. Please!' She shouted and cried heavily.

He looked on and cuddled her close to him again.

'Okay, okay.'

With tears, she managed a few little words. 'I need you to promise.'

'Okay. I promise.' He thought about his recent situation as well. It was tempting to tell her about the strange, new world that he visited.

'I need to go now.' Her eyes filled with fresh tears, as older ones trickled down her cheeks.

'Please help me keep in touch with you somehow.' Kyle sounded devastated.

Karen reached into a blouse pocket and pulled out a small piece of paper.

'Read this when I've gone.'

Just as soon as she handed the paper over, she moved away and walked as if slipping into the sunset.

Kyle's arms hung by his side like a lost little boy and watched her delicate body walking swiftly away.

He studied her until she was no longer in sight.
The only remaining part of her was held gently in his hand.
He lifted the note to read it.

You are the only person I can trust. Please do not say anything to anyone about us meeting up. I am hoping that when my Dad comes back we will be able to meet up again, so please be patient with me.
  – Kaz.

Kyle wondered if Karen was just giving into the situation and not looking for a resolve.
Clearing his mind with a few minutes of swift walking toward home, he decided he would need to find a way of helping her between his training and school times.

TWENTY THREE

Time was passing swiftly and over the weeks, Kyle was picking up new skills extremely quickly. Zane was looking impressed, as most of the kicks were mastered; many self-defence tactics were becoming automatic and a variety of strikes and punches were just naturally flowing with great power.

People at school were recognising Kyle's growth and confidence, gaining him respect and peace.

Kyle came to another martial arts lesson which built up so much sweat and shaking muscles. Zane decided that the remaining ten minutes deserved some rest.

'Let's walk up and down the hall Kyle to just have a cool down and chat.'

They both walked simultaneously length-ways up and down the hall, taking time to catch their breath.

'So, you've come so far now and progressing so swiftly all of the time. I don't know if you've noticed, but you're also really growing physically and mentally.'

Kyle spoke through a slightly strained breath.

'I have Sir.'

'Okay, good. Well, you are a natural. That is why the leaflet went to you as we were all looking for the same thing at the same time. You needed help with your bullying situation around the same time we were seeking the person chosen to help our world.'

Kyle took the words in easily. He was growing used to the way things were becoming.

'I'm also noting your ability to deal with things emotionally. Don't forget that I'm here for you as a friend as well as an instructor.'

'Thank you.' He glanced over at Zane.

'There is something else I need to add. I just want you to know that the crystal also opens up your energy consumption, which means you are receiving so much information without even knowing. There is a lot of stuff in your memory box. Or should I say – your subconscious. This basically means that the crystal downloads a lot of information into your mind. It mostly occurs when you're resting.'

Kyle wasn't surprised at hearing of this.

Zane was studying him as they walked, ensuring they were cooling down well and that the information was acceptable. They walked for a moment, just breathing and pacing.

Zane broke the silence again.

'I just want you to know that you are doing really well.   We will be working on some transitional stuff after today. I also need to introduce you to an extension of yourself.'

Kyle looked over with one eyebrow raised.

'I shan't tell you what it is until next week.' Zane smiled with the offer of suspense.

Kyle was certainly becoming very composed about himself. Maturity and strength was most certainly becoming very obvious. Zane was impressed and hoped that he could continue on the positive road.

'When you pick up something new and nerve-wracking, I have a useful tip for you.'

They both walked with their heads looking forward.

'When you feel fear and need some comfort – turn to your crystal when it is active. Hold on to it and ask in your mind for comfort. In fact, now that I am telling you this, it is important for you to know that you can actually ask your crystal for *anything*. Any emotional need; any skill requirement within its ability... All you need to do is ask and it will open up to you.'

Kyle was now fully recovered and slowed his walk down to a very slow pace. He turned to Zane.

'So, the crystal holds the ability to do anything with me?'

'Yes, but only things that are within the nature you know. All enhanced strengths of the ones you already have; emotional comforts and enhanced abilities. I've spoken of other abilities it brings. I must say that the abilities are enhanced intensely when we are within the other world. The reason I am telling you all of this is to encourage you to experiment now to get to grips with everything you are capable of doing. We'll go through some stuff as well, so that you can feel comfortable with certain elements. You'll always be safe as the crystal will know when to stop something or when your energy is ready to return to how it should be.'

Kyle felt relaxed. 'Thanks for all of this.'

Zane was freshly surprised by the response.

Kyle noticed his instructor's expression.

'I know you're working hard to get me trained up well and I'm very grateful. I know it is helping me in every walk of life.'

Zane was again surprised. 'You're growing up fast. Don't rush yourself. Remember to have some fun with all of this. Okay? Don't lose your youth.'

Zane signalled for them both to sit on the hall floor.

'Kyle, we have a lot to cover yet. When you get private time please practice, but try to have plenty of fun between things. Have a play with the crystal abilities. Whatever you do though – don't hurt anyone or expose your enhanced abilities. Do you understand what I mean by that?'

Kyle smiled. 'It's probably the least cryptic thing you've said for a long time.'

'Wow.' Zane was surprised by his intellectual answer. He held his voice for a moment. 'I need to know how well your school work is going though. You mustn't neglect your future.'

Kyle looked surprised this time. 'I guess it's going well. I'm not struggling anyway.'

Zane smiled. 'That's good. It's very important to do well. You may have an advantage over others, simply because you will be able to absorb and retain information more easily.'

A disappointed face responded. 'You mean I'm cheating by having the crystal enhance my abilities?'

'Well, not cheating. It is just enhancing you completely, but you're the one doing the work.' Zane had hoped his answer was acceptable.

Kyle looked satisfied. 'Oh, okay. Thanks.'

Zane felt relief and decided to swiftly change the subject. 'So, remember to practice some of these fighting skills at home. It will make your one hour here become many hours. As the old fashioned saying goes - Practice Makes Perfect.'

Kyle cringed at the quote. This made him realise how much he had changed. His confidence was coming through in different ways.

Zane recognised his thoughts. 'Go with it Kyle. I am recognising your change and you are beginning to feel it. I just ask one favour... Please don't let it change you for the worse.'

Kyle didn't understand how such a thing could occur. He looked over with a gentle frown.

'Well, you see with immense power comes responsibility. Some powerful people have chosen the wrong path – one which comes with harm to others. You have been selected due to your amazing, natural abilities.'

Kyle thought about the potential arrogance which could come along with such strengths.

'I promise to do my best to remain good. If I slip, then please point it out to me. I will always respect you as my master.'

Zane raised his eyebrows. 'Well that is fantastic. Thank you Kyle.'

This raised the levels of excitement in Kyle for a moment. He realised his power was intense and that he could potentially become a threat to many people. He looked over at Zane and wondered if he could even be a threat to *him*.

Zane knew his thoughts and smiled to himself, relieved to know he would always hold a greater wisdom and that Kyle would occasionally have such thoughts.

'Okay Kyle, well I hope you have fun at home, as for now we need to head off on our own way.   Next week then, same day and time?'

'Yes Sir!' Kyle looked directly into his eyes.

Again, Zane was impressed. Everything was working perfectly and there was great hope for the future.

TWENTY FOUR

It was a Friday night and everyone seemed to be sucked into their own little world within the family home. The television was blaring in the background. Brothers were entertaining themselves with books or handheld game consoles. Kyle was contemplating some gentle training in the garden, whilst Jack was preparing to head over to a friend's house. The parents were studying something together on the home computer. Kyle noticed Jack was paying particular attention to his looks – more so than normal. It was becoming increasingly obvious that Jack was going to be in the company of a female. Kyle wanted to follow his brother to his "friend's" house out of curiosity. During his contemplation of secret spying, he wondered if he could experiment with the crystal. Zane's mention of the ability to travel in an invisible way was a risky thought when there was a possibility of him being caught. He decided to casually leave the room and walk up to his bedroom. Once there, he looked down at his crystal and wondered how any of the 'magic' worked. He held his hand over the warm feeling of the crystal and spoke. 'Activate.' The crystal appeared to light up the entire room, despite the full light of the day filling the space. He looked down to see the ultra, bright blue light on his chest and wondered how nobody else ever noticed this unusual light when in company. Somehow, thankfully people only noticed it as a simple necklace.

Footsteps came down the corridor and a body barged into Kyle's room.

'What you doing?' His Dad came barging in without warning. Kyle whispered 'Calm' whilst swiftly placing his hand over the crystal. He turned to face his Dad.

'Oh nothing Dad. I'm just thinking about reading or something.'

'Are you messing with lights or a torch?'

Kyle remained convincingly calm. 'Oh no, I was just messing with the sun and a mirror for a second.'

'Hmm. The hall looked as if a light was shining from your room. I can't remember buying you anything ultra-bright like that.'

'Oh, ha! Maybe I'm just blindingly bright!' Kyle bluffed any ideas off with humour.

Thankfully his Dad changed the subject.

'Are you wanting pizza tonight? Your mum doesn't fancy cooking.'

Kyle was relieved to hear the change in conversation.

'Oh, yeah. Great!'

His Dad looked as if he was seeing directly through Kyle's fake excitement over pizza.

'Okay son. When it comes in I'll give you a shout.'

'Thanks Dad.'

The door closed behind his Dad and Kyle was stood alone, looking down on the crystal again.

He whispered 'activate'.

The crystal lit up again, but only through the cracks of his fingers as he tried to cover the brightness.

In a low voice he spoke. 'Could you maybe turn the brightness down so we get some privacy?'

The crystal light dimmed down instantly. Kyle raised his eyebrows with instant surprise.

'Wow.' He whispered.

'Okay. Can you switch my super hearing on?'

The first instant voice he heard was Jack's. He was speaking to himself in the mirror.

'Like this? Na... Like this? Argh, I guess I have to wash and style it all over again.'

Kyle walked out of his room and leant over the stairs to see Jack looking in the mirror at his hair, constantly pulling at fine pieces and getting frustrated.

'Argh. I'll just damn well wash it again.'

Kyle grinned to himself as he watched on.

Another voice came crashing into his head however. This time it was the recognisable female voice.

'Even resting for the evening – I still have to make the darn call. Where's the number... He can't even get me the number.' His mother walked into the hall to pick up the landline and make a call.

'I suppose I've got to decide what kind of pizza we're all going to have... Joint account? It should come from his account!'

His mother's thoughts were much harder than he ever expected.

The brother's voices were creeping into his head in small amounts.

Jack had decided to wash his hair. His thoughts were grumbled ones all the way through the traumatic event of fresh water.

His Dad's voice hit the air hard. 'Can we have drinks too honey?'

Kyle's mum was already on the phone, ordering in a random fashion, seemingly ignoring the drink request.

Kyle quickly held the crystal. 'Calm.'

He took a deep breath and enjoyed some silence for a moment. It wasn't pleasant hearing such miserable thoughts from his own family members. Perhaps privacy existed for a reason. Some false politeness brings comfort to one another.

With his normal hearing, he caught the sound of Jack blow-drying his hair to yet another style.

Kyle caught his breath and looked down at his crystal again. 'Activate.' He whispered.

'I guess this is all part of the practice that Zane wants me to get used to... so... Crystal, could you make me invisible?'

He felt an unusual sensation fill him, but he wasn't sure if it was his imagination. Walking gingerly to his mirror, he still caught sight of his usual self.

'Hmm,' His arms dropped in disappointment.

He heard footsteps coming toward his room again.

'Kyle?' Jack's voice filled his room. 'Can I use some of that aftershave you've got? Mine smells weird.'

Before Kyle had chance to speak, Jack walked in and sighed, moved over to his toiletries and helped himself to items.

His room was instantly filled with the strong haze of male perfumes.

Kyle began to cough slightly with the strength of it all.

'Oh sorry bro, I didn't know you were in here.'

Jack turned, sliding his eyes left to right.

'You can't see me?' Kyle realised that was the stupidest thing to say. Zane's words of warning hit his mind instantly. He can't expose these enhanced abilities.

'What the heck man? You're too old for hide and seek.'

Jack obviously couldn't see Kyle and walked out of the room. His stomping feet hit the stairs hard all of the way to the bottom.

Kyle looked at himself in the mirror again and nothing had changed. He wasn't certain on his visibility so thought he'd put it to the test delicately.

The stairs were taken silently all of the way to the bottom. He spotted everyone in the lounge. Jack was finalising pacing up and down, looking at the clock. The others were very distracted in their own thoughts.

Kyle walked over to his parents and waved a hand over the computer screen that they were staring at intensely. He expected them to tell him to stop messing about, but nothing was said at this moment. He kept a hand there for at least two minutes without a word from either of them.

Kyle's heart rate grew fast with excitement. He walked over to the old-fashioned clock on the wall that Jack was watching on and off every few seconds. Kyle moved one of the clock hands with his finger just as Jack was staring.

'Err, the clock is doing strange things Dad.' Jack frowned with confusion.

There was no reply to Jack's statement. Kyle moved the clock hand back to the correct time. He then promptly ran upstairs quietly with an over-excited feeling of opportunity. He jumped on the bed and bounced a few times.

'Crystal, please make me completely visible again.'

He felt a wave of strangeness fill him again, yet he knew his request was fulfilled.

'Okay.' Kyle was planning a few things in his mind. The first event would be to follow Jack.

It was only a few minutes later and Kyle was in his 'invisible' mode, sat in the back of a car with Jack. Kyle's heart raced with concern that something could go wrong at any point. He hoped the fear wouldn't let out any visible sweat, or fearful noises. Then of course he wasn't sure if there was a time limit on the ability.

Jack's friend was slightly older and had recently acquired his driver's licence. It appeared that some of them were heading out for the evening. They were talking freely over other people's mishaps and girls that they had an eye for. Kyle had managed to creep into the car swiftly while Jack held the door open to say hello for a minute.

The driving was aggressive, with obvious signs of showing off. There were chances taken with corners and crossings.

It was difficult to remain still in the back seat with all of the violent movement. Everyone else looked relaxed as if this driving behaviour was normal.

They reached a large building where a lot of people stood outside, apparently queueing.

Everyone left the car, slamming the doors quickly, leaving Kyle uncertain of his next move.

He watched their direction and quietly opened his door, closing it gently behind him. Looking about, he noticed there were many others heading in the same direction as Jack and his two other friends. Music came from the large building. It was all very loud and appeared to be an exciting event.

He caught up with Jack and stood near him. Kyle noticed no recognition from anyone, so felt comfortable knowing he was still invisible much to his relief.

The queue reached a couple of large men allowing people entry a few at a time.

As Kyle grew closer he realised this was a night club. He looked over at Jack and took note of him fumbling through some cards for identification. Kyle moved in to take a sneaky look at the one card he settled on. As he moved back from the sneaky view, a sudden realisation of the madness of being invisible hit him.

How on Earth could he become invisible? It seemed a silly situation. The thoughts moved around his head, recognising his new ability as difficult to conceive. He looked at his hands and feet, knowing everything was still visible to his own eyes. Everything was in perfect tact.

He looked up at the queue of people and realised Jack had disappeared from the group.

'Argh!' Kyle accidentally shouted, creating some head movements to see no one in the direction of the sound. He moved forward and moved around the back of the people controlling the entrants. He felt grateful for not having to deal with the heavy-set individuals in the security uniforms. Moving with stealth (despite being invisible) – he managed to get through the crowds and move into the club itself.

The music blared and the lights spun vibrantly, creating such an enjoyable venue. The energy felt wonderful to Kyle.

He walked in with less attention on finding Jack. Young ladies were dressed provocatively and the young men were most certainly behaving like cockerels. Kyle smiled, knowing he would be part of this kind of crowd in only a few short years. Thoughts of collecting knowledge and views of protocol were now seen as an advantage to fitting in when the time came. Perhaps he could observe for a short while to study how this event would work.

He walked in, trying to avoid everyone's shoulders for fear of causing confusion. He overheard some conversations – many sounded naïve or arrogant. The music blared with a heavy base, causing excitement in his chest. This was an exciting atmosphere. He decided to stay for a while.

He walked in and out of group conversations, chuckling to himself at the invasion.

As the night moved on, so he noticed people becoming more intoxicated. The drinks flowed steady with some, but foolishly fast with others. The security staff were busy at times, controlling misbehaviour. There were times when Kyle had to swiftly avoid a silly cat fight.

With such a pleasant beginning to the evening – Kyle was disappointed with the way many were starting to behave. It was becoming less enjoyable to watch.

He spotted Jack with his friends, drinking very colourful drinks and dancing very flirtatiously with young ladies. There didn't appear to be any reluctance from those they were trying to impress.

Kyle was impressed with his brother's dance moves. He began to mimic them since there would be no chance of embarrassment. Only a few minutes in and Kyle decided he'd mastered his obvious dance routine.

'Hmm,' Kyle knew he wouldn't be heard over the loud music and decided it may be time for him to leave and head home before his parents worried about his whereabouts. He would often nip over to a friend's house as of late, but knew there would be a natural curfew of some kind that wasn't always spoken of. A slow walk through a heavy crowd brought him to the main exit where people were still queuing to get in. He had grown desperate to gain some fresh air and space by this time. He looked at a large clock on a building and noticed it had become very late very quickly. An instant panic hit him. He had no mode of transport to get home! Thoughts flew around his head of running home, but he wasn't sure about his location. It was eleven thirty, which meant he was unlikely to be able to catch a bus home – even if he could find one. Worries of his parents hunting the residential area to find him became visions of horror in his mind.

He moved around the back of the building, hoping it would give him peace and quiet in order to think. Instead, a scene of young men overcrowding a lady came into sight.

'Oh no.' He whispered under his breath.

The men were trying to pull her in for close contact and forced kisses. The young lady was clearly uncomfortable. Kyle wondered why she would be on her own. No other female company was anywhere in sight. The whole scene looked confusing, as if they weren't aware of their behaviour. Kyle decided to intervene.

'Hey guys! Leave her alone!' His voice barely touched their ears. They continued to tug the poor young lady around the group of men.

Kyle drew a deeper breath. 'Oy! Leave the lady alone!'

One of the young men turned to face him, but turned back to the "game".

The words didn't seem to hit them, so he walked closer and pushed one of them to the side. 'Get off her!'

The man spun his head and hit one of the other young men. 'What? You think she's yours?'

The victim fell sideways on to his arm. His wrist was instantly injured, so he gripped the pain and remained on the concrete; growing annoyed about the attack.

Kyle decided to push the same man. 'I said... Leave her alone!'

The man looked over and then down on the ground, confused about who or what had pushed him. He decided to kick the man on the ground. 'Just stay down there you useless...'

Before the man had time to curse and battle again, Kyle gave a forceful push, knowing it would topple him over on to the ground. Kyle had already spotted his weak stance, so decided it was time for him to join his 'friend' on the floor. There were two other young men, still forcing a tight grip and kiss on the poor young lady. Kyle moved in close and felt their pure aggression. The atmosphere felt very wrong. He looked into the eyes of the young lady and noticed they were extremely glazed. Questions were moving around his mind about her attack. He gripped her arm very tightly and spun her to face a completely different angle. One of the men attempted to grip her around the waist, but his arms were too slow. Kyle pulled the lady away and forced her into a staggered run, away from the scene. The remaining young men were left grumbling and cursing her, hoping she would return. It was a very odd scene, as if the men were cursed by a Zombie virus. Neither of them attempted to chase or follow her.

Kyle continued to force the lady along, with her legs half-running in a weak and wobbly fashion. Her mind was most certainly not in a coherent state. He stared at her face as the body struggled to keep up with the pulling. Once they had reached a quiet and green part of the area, he sat her down and spoke to her quietly.

'Can I look into your purse to see where you live?'

The lady turned her head to look into open space. Kyle forgot he was invisible, so reached down to his crystal and requested visibility. Within an instant he came into view, just as a hologram would be projected with one switch of a button.

A slurred voice came to him. 'I am so dr-r-runk.'

Kyle smiled. 'I know. Those guys were taking advantage of that. Can I at least get you home safely?'

The lady had a very small bag resting on her shoulder. She gripped this and pulled it to her front side for view. Kyle realised her fingers couldn't even find the clasp to open it.

'Here, let me.' Kyle reached into her bag to find a couple of cards sitting at the bottom.

The darkness allowed enough light to recognise her driving licence. This reminded him of his very youthful age by comparison. He realised he shouldn't even be in this scene. Shaking thoughts from his head, he looked at the address.

'So where is this road?' He pointed to her card.

She tried to focus her eyes into his.

'Jus-st a ten minute walk.'

'Can you show me the way?'

Following the question, he realised the lady couldn't even get back up on to her feet.

Kyle sat next to her for a few moments, trying to figure out how he would get her home. The next question would be to figure out how he would reach his *own* home.

Thoughts of crystal uses went through his mind.

He wondered if he could call upon something as a form of transport. He held the crystal and wondered about asking about something such as a horse. Before he thought beyond that, a large brown horse came walking up to the front of them. Kyle scuttled back with his feet, falling back on the

275

grass. He didn't think the scene was real, but the horse neighed and remained in the same spot waiting.

Kyle stood, his heart racing. He walked over to the steady animal and touched the side of the horse's chest, encouraging another neigh.

He felt around the horse, as if to confirm it was a real animal. As he felt from the chest up towards the neck and head, he noticed a camouflaged set of reigns ready to be used.

'Okaaaay!' Kyle spoke with a disbelieving tone.

The young lady looked up without any shock or surprise in her blurred expression.

Kyle noticed her completely oblivious mind, so told her what he was doing, as he carefully encouraged her to climb up carefully on to the horse. He wasn't sure what this situation would bring, but thought it was worth a leap of faith given the coincidence.

The young lady sat comfortably on the horse with Kyle supporting her by sitting behind her. His next move was unknown to him.

'Okay, erm. So maybe point to where you live?' He gently coaxed the lady into remaining conscious. He attempted to support her by her waist to have focus on where they were. 'I know you're in there somewhere, so point the way.'

She managed to point in a direction, which encouraged Kyle to begin their journey somehow.

He thought of the many cowboy films he'd watched and automatically tapped his heels into the horse in a gentle way. The horse appeared to lift *his or her* head gently and move forward.

'Woo.' Kyle was surprised.

He wasn't sure if the lady's pointing had any logic or sense to it. He hoped she had some recognition of their route. The horse trotted gently, working through some minor groups of people, who looked up with disbelief. Kyle didn't care, but concentrated on the hope of getting the lady home. He chuckled to himself, thinking this would be a bit of a comedy knight in shining armour situation. They worked their way down some dark, shimmering streets that were full of residential homes. The roads were silent with it being so late – much to Kyle's relief.

The young lady selected a particular doorway, so Kyle pulled on the reigns and asked if it was her home. She nodded, but didn't seem to be one hundred percent sure. He climbed off anyway and pulled the lady down into his arms, attempting to stand her up. She could barely hold her head up at this point, but she was certainly comfortable with the situation.

'Do you have a key?' He asked, hoping not to knock on a stranger's door unnecessarily.

She fumbled around to find her bag again. He gripped it for her and attempted to find a key with his fingers. A metal object touched his fingers, so he pulled the item out. Thankfully this was a key. The next test was worrying.

'Is this definitely your house?'

'No.' She said firmly.

'What?' Kyle was disgusted that she had brought him to a house that wasn't hers.

'It's my parent's.' Her words appeared to be less slurred.

He gave a slight chuckle at her reply and felt happier knowing they were at the right place. At least this wasn't just some maze run. Hopefully not anyway!

He decided to gently and quietly coax the key into the keyhole.

Much to his amazement it went in perfectly!

He turned the key as quietly as possible and the door unlocked.

'Thank God!' He muttered under his breath. 'You're home!'

The young lady didn't seem phased at all with the circumstances. He held her and walked her into the home quietly, hoping some wild dog wouldn't come along and bite into his flesh. They didn't switch any lights on, but the remaining natural light was just enough to identify the sitting room with cosy-looking sofas. He knew he would soon be free of this situation. Her home brought such comfort. He moved the lady on to one of the sofas, where she instantly curled up into a sleeping position and fell soundly asleep.

Kyle began to worry about her health, but she seemed young and healthy.

He quietly stepped away once her heavy breathing made him aware she had fallen into a deep sleep.

Everything was very quiet and silent, so Kyle tiptoed carefully out of the house and closed the door perfectly noise-free behind him, dropping the key back through the letter box.

The horse stood care-free in the middle of the road, waiting to be ridden again. Kyle breathed to calm himself of the weird circumstances. He walked over and placed his hand on his chest again. 'Thank you.'

He climbed up to attempt to find a route back toward his own home. The horse trotted quietly and gently up to a main road, finding a useful sign. This truly was a useful sign, as his area was clearly marked, guiding him back to familiar roads. He guided the horse with a good sense of direction.

Kyle had never ventured beyond his known neighbourhood on his own. A road around the corner from his own street had appeared, making him relax.

He stopped the horse. 'I can take it from here. We'd better not go down together just in case my parents are keeping an eye out.'

The horse stopped, still focussing forward.

Kyle climbed down carefully and thanked the horse many times in a whisper.

He turned to view the street leading to the distant corner. As he spun back to thank the horse again, he noticed the animal had disappeared. He looked frantically in all directions, hoping to get one more glimpse, but the horse had definitely disappeared. A white fleck of light fell from mid-air down to his feet, like a miniature shooting star. It dispersed however, just as soon as Kyle had spotted it.

Kyle saw this as a sign of the horse going back to where he or she had come from. He smiled and felt grateful, but then turned his thoughts to those of sneaking into the family home. For a moment, despite such unusual occurrences – he had forgotten about the crystal 'uses'.

The crystal warmed his chest, pulling his attention to it.

'Oh yes.'

He held the crystal and asked for his hearing abilities to be enhanced. The ability certainly came within an instance. He heard people's chatter within their homes. Some bangs and scrapes were hurting his ears.

He attempted to focus his hearing on his home. The closer he got, the clearer he heard gentle conversations. His mother and father were obviously having a pleasant chat. Their voices were from the upper half of the home. Kyle reached deeply into his pocket and pulled out a small key. He was able to silently open the front door and creep into the kitchen, placing an act of innocence on him should anyone come to see him there. On one of the worktop spaces sat remnants of a pizza. Kyle had completely forgotten about the meal plans and worried that his parents will be angry with him the next time they speak. He ate the cold pizza pieces and enjoyed the flavours that hit his tongue. It wasn't until this moment that he realised how hungry he was.

The house was quiet other than the conversation upstairs. This kept Kyle comfortable, knowing everyone was tucked up in bed, relaxed or asleep - everyone other than Jack of course! Kyle's eventful night reminded him of how he could remain patient about the night clubs and parties that were yet to come into his life. This evening wasn't something that was encouraging him into such a lifestyle, but he knew it would be enjoyable perhaps when the right age came about. He moved upstairs and rested on a cold pillow, finding the sensation through his head very enjoyable. He requested his enhanced abilities to be 'at ease' and for the crystal to be on standby. A good sleep and restful night was much needed. Before he knew it, his head was drifting into a deep sleep.

TWENTY FIVE

Karen was sat in her father's lounge, longing for some freedom. Her Step Mother was in the kitchen cooking up a soup for the evening meal. Karen knew the basics of life were well taken care of by her, but it didn't bring the freedom and happiness of a young teenager. The frustration was beginning to build, particularly as she knew of people waiting for her in the big wide world. She wasn't particularly sure if her father knew the full extent of her situation, but she didn't have any privacy in order to have the much-needed conversation. There was no contact number given and her Step Mother wanted to keep full control. Karen wasn't entirely sure as to whether this situation was created out of love and protection to extreme levels, or out of control and nastiness. The problem Karen discovered was that she wasn't approachable and never *appeared* to be kind or caring in any form. The food wasn't an issue, as it was plentiful.

Karen found a small mirror and caught sight of her pale complexion. She knew it wasn't healthy to stay indoors and remain relatively inactive. Thoughts of escape were flying around her head. It was difficult to calculate something that wouldn't involve local police or worry to her father. This was the ultimate thing that kept her in this situation. Her father was very much loved and cared for. He was more of a gentle soul, who knew he had to work hard for his family. Karen knew it wasn't an easy decision to work away for several months.

She decided that her frustration was so extremely high on this particular evening that she would find the ultimate plan to have a secret discussion with her father.
There was a usual routine of dinner followed by a private catch-up call between her Step Mother and father.
The rest of the evening would always be a bit of studying, followed by a bath or shower and then bed - a frustrating restriction to adhere to every day without variety.

Karen watched for the phone call and noted the phone going down. This particular evening - the call appeared to be brief, but pleasant.
Karen made an excuse to go upstairs.
'Do you mind if I start preparing for bed early? I'm really sleepy tonight. I think I read too much.'
Her Step Mother listened and observed her face to make sure she was telling the truth. Karen noticed her eyes were very deep and dark. Her skin was always slightly flushed and very taught - her hair was always scraped tightly into a pony tail.
These features were looking hard into Karen's eyes, making her feel extremely uncomfortable.
'I suppose it wouldn't do you any harm - so long as you're up nice and early in the morning.' Her words were hard and heartless.

Karen nodded and stood with a slight backward tilt to attempt to avoid her continuing stare.

She moved sideways to gain space between them and made her way through the room and up towards the staircase. Looking back, her Step-Mother wasn't offering any goodnight wishes. In fact she appeared to be polishing a small table just below knee height.

Karen didn't know whether to feel upset or happy about the lack of care and attention. She forgot her feelings for the moment and walked upstairs with a reasonable speed. It was now important to make all of the usual noises to avoid any thoughts of suspicious behaviour. She continued as she would normally before bed – and even walked in an obvious manner to her bed to ensure the subtle noises of the floor boards were made. Once she knew she was convincing enough, she crept back out of her room and into the room where the second landline sat. It was heart-pounding to know she was attempting to deceive her Step Mother. Luckily the television was on downstairs, giving her some distraction.

Karen tip-toed with amazing quietness to the other room and managed to reach the chair (placed directly next to the phone). She picked up the head piece and pressed the re-dial button, praying it would connect to the right number. A ring tone hit her ear loudly, making her panic slightly about the noise. The television still bellowed, helping her to remain calm knowing that she remained safe.

'Hello?' Her father's voice was instantly recognisable.

'Dad?' She whispered.

'Karen?'

'Dad, I need to have a quick chat.'

'Is there something wrong?'

'Well, I need you to believe me when I tell you something.' Her hand cupped around her mouth and the mouth piece, hoping to conceal the noise.

'Karen, I thought you were at afterschool classes at this time.'

She grew confused. 'No Dad, she keeps me away from school all together. I'm not allowed out of the house.' There was a silent pause.

'Oh come on Karen, I know you don't get on with her too well, but you need you to try. It's only temporary – you know that. Time will fly by so fast that I'll be home before you know it. This could bring such great things for me if you just allow me to do well without having any worries about my girl.'

Karen felt guilty at this point. Perhaps he truly didn't know the full story, but this work seemed to be very important.

'Sorry Dad. You're right. I guess I just miss you.'

He breathed a calming breath.

'That's my girl. When you're not in afterschool events then you know you can call me around this time right?'

'Thanks Dad, but please don't tell her I called you. She won't be happy I borrowed the phone without permission.'

'Oh, well, okay honey, but I'll tell her tomorrow that it's okay for you to call me when you feel like it. So long as it's not during the day... unless it's very urgent.'

'Okay Dad.'

'You know I love you right?'

'Yeah. I love you too Dad.'

'Speak to you soon.'

They both exchanged goodbyes and Karen was able to silently place the phone back onto its charger.

Just as she stood, her Step Mother walked in with her arms folded.

Karen felt as if her heart had stopped and her feet had cemented to the floor.

'I thought you were going to bed!'

Karen attempted to breathe normally.

'I am. It was just a quick thing.'

'I told you no contact with anyone until your father returns.'

Karen frowned with confusion. Her fear then suddenly turned to rage.

'Why are you keeping me like a prisoner?' She shouted bravely for the first time.

'This isn't prison. This is what I call SPOILT. You have everything exactly where you want it.'

'What?' Karen didn't mean it as a one-worded question. Her frown grew deeper.

Her Step Mother walked closer with intent.

Karen slipped to the side and ran past her like a mouse would escape a stalking cat.

'Get back here at once!'

Karen knew this would change everything and didn't want to remain in the house for a minute longer. Her breathing was heavy but she ran without recognising the adrenaline pumping through her.

She ran down the stairs and out of the front door, leaving it wide open.

Her Step Mother shouted for her to 'Get Back!'

Karen had however slipped through the darkened light into familiar streets. Running barefooted, she felt the concrete as painful as it was numbing.

Her first thought was to find Kyle's home. She knew it by sight and hoped her memory was correct.

Looking back there was no evidence of being followed, so she slowed her pace and tried to regain her normal breath.

Thought of survival hadn't even entered her head. Escapism was her only option.

She found Kyle's home and then took a few yards back to hide under some bushes surrounded by large trees. This would be her perfect hiding place for the rest of the night. She knew from television programmes that she would have to be missing for something like twenty-four hours if the police were involved, so the first night would be fine.

As she tried to find a soft and comfortable piece of ground, a beautiful cat crawled over, rubbing around her legs.

She stroked it gently and they both ended up cuddling in together on the ground. Karen felt strangely comforted by the cat and managed to fall asleep, despite the intense stress of the situation.

TWENTY SIX

Kyle was rolling in his duvet restlessly, whilst hoping his eyes would open to match his body's desire to get up for the day. School wasn't something he wanted to face since his Sunday was so relaxing and recuperating.

The strange events of the other night were shaken from his mind with the normal occurrences of his family. He even escaped the expected disciplinary of missing the pizza meal much to his surprise.

He dropped one leg over the edge of his bed and allowed the rest of his body to follow through to the point of a lazy stand. His mother walked around the hall, shouting to remind everyone of the time – and how much they had to do to get ready to leave. Jack's voice was in the background, bragging about how he was already up and ready.

Kyle heard the fumble of everyone getting up and about, but still didn't hurry. He knew he could be ready within twenty minutes without any hassle.

They all stumbled around, getting ready in their own familiar ways. Most of the brothers timed their leaving in a synchronising manner and clambered around the shoes to grab their own pairs.

The door opened and Kyle wasn't as excited about rushing down the street as the rest of them. Jack watched them all from the front window, knowing he would only be a few minutes behind them, as he was due to start his new job today a little bit later than the school hours.

Kyle barely walked five minutes and thought his crystal had been activated on its own. Whispers of his name called and he continually covered his crystal with his palm, using the 'calm' instruction.

'Kyle!' The voice grew stronger.

It shocked him slightly and caused him to turn toward the voice, but nobody was there.

An even deeper fright hit him when he saw Karen coming out into the open from a few shrubs and plants.

'Karen?' He stopped completely in his tracks and looked at her - all scraggly-haired and pale-skinned.

'What the heck?' Kyle didn't have any polite words at this moment.

'Sorry Kyle. I had to get away from my Step Mother. She was going to kill me.'

'Oh man... Surely she wouldn't *actually* kill you?'

'Well if not a quick one - then a slow death from being in that prison. Will you help me? I need somewhere to hide.'

He looked back into the distance, where he could see the family car still sat on the driveway.

Thinking quickly, he thought of a temporary fix.

'Uh, we will find a way.' Kyle held her around her shoulders and tried his best to comfort her emotions.

He could see tears of relief forming heavily, about to drop down onto her cheeks. They walked together, looking about for any onlookers.

Soon reaching the family home, Kyle told her to now move behind him and stick close.

He coaxed her to the back garden, bringing back memories of sneaking into *her* father's back garden not all that long ago. They had to pause by sitting on the ground underneath the first window.

'We need to wait until we can hear the car leaving, then I know everyone has left the house. I'm certain Jack is scrounging a lift with my Dad.'

Karen acknowledged with a look.

As soon as they crouched down they heard the car leave the drive.

'That was quick!' Kyle stood and peered through the back window. 'Okay, let's go in.'

They both went in through the back door, unlocked by Kyle. The house certainly felt empty.

'Hello?' Kyle shouted, just to be certain, preparing to use an excuse of needing the toilet.

There was no answer.

'Phew.' He walked over to the fridge and pulled out a milky drink and handed it to Karen.

'Ah thank you.' She opened it and gulped it down within no time.

They both stood, easing into their own thoughts.

'So what are we going to do with this situation then?' Kyle always wanted to know of any plans to prepare for the consequences.

She wiped her mouth with her already-dirty sleeve.

'I don't know. Last night I spoke to my Dad on the phone and she found out. I felt as if she was going to kill me. I've been trapped in that house for a long time now and just can't live like that anymore.'

'You spoke to your Dad? What did he say?'

'He thought I was being dramatic about his wife. He just won't believe me. He did think I was going to some kind of after-school thing though. I think that's why he hasn't spoken to me for ages. That means she's been lying to him.'

'Won't your Dad worry about you when he gets back? When is he actually getting back?'

'I'm not sure. I know he's got a few more months to go yet.'

'So where can we hide you before he gets back? I'm sure the police will be involved soon.'

'Well, when I woke this morning, I had chance to think. If you could get me into school, then I could talk to one of the teachers and explain everything. They would know who to call. I'm sure they're trained for that.'

'Good idea. Do you want me to talk to my parents about you staying here?'

She looked up at Kyle with a longing expression. 'That would be really nice.'

'Okay! Let's get to school.'

'Oh, do you mind if I have a shower and borrow some of your mum's make-up?'

Kyle smiled. 'Err, yes. I guess that would make sense. Don't be too long though. We need to make it before the classes start... I guess before my parents get a call because of me not turning up too.'

Karen smiled and kissed Kyle's cheek, then ran upstairs as if she knew exactly where everything was.

Kyle was pleased to see her happiness return.

He grew excited about a better future now that she managed to escape her prison.

Within what seemed like only a few minutes, Karen came downstairs looking fresh and amazing. She had managed to straighten and wipe her clothes down somehow to look relatively fresh.

'Wow!' Kyle gripped her hand and moved her to the front door. 'Let's go!'

As they opened the front door, a black cat came to greet them.

'Oh, hello friend.' Karen reached down to give some loving strokes.

'This is my new cat friend. She kept me comforted last night.'

Kyle recognised the black, shiny coat and the bright eyes that looked up at them.

'I think I know this cat too.' Kyle added. 'She is a *great* cat.'

Kyle didn't have too much time to think about the coincidence of this situation, but felt gratitude for the cat's kindness. They both made a big fuss of their little friend for a few moments, then realised their small amount of time to get to school.

They both made it to school just as the assembly had begun, giving them time to find a teacher.

A lady teacher was coming towards them.

She appeared stern and sharp-featured, aiming directly for the two of them.

'Why are you not in assembly?' Her voice was hard yet obviously curious.

Karen answered her perfectly.

'I have been absent for a few weeks Ma'am and I need to have a very serious chat with someone, please.'

The lady dropped her features, allowing a softer approach.

'What is it you need to talk about?'

'It might take some time Ma'am.'

Karen was now sat, talking privately inside an office while Kyle waited patiently outside, wondering why he hadn't been questioned about his classroom attendance.

He looked down at his crystal and placed his hand over it, whispering. 'Ignite.'

He thought about the hearing ability and suddenly voices were bouncing about his ears.

He heard part of the conversation within the office.

'... Well he would need to obtain permission from his parents. We would also need to know that you are in safe accommodation in the meantime... I need to speak with the principle and take it all from there. You will need to remain here though until we know exactly what to do in these circumstances.'

Kyle knew there would be some child protection service involved, but he wouldn't have known where to begin without the link of the teacher.

TWENTY SEVEN

Kyle was now adjusting to even newer circumstances. After many talks with various people – Kyle not fully knowing who was who – it eventually tapered down to Karen sleeping in *his* room. He was happy camping in the study. A pull-out bed was always tucked in there for visitors.

His parents had agreed that it would be okay to help Karen out given the circumstances. A gentleman accompanying a police officer had been discussing things with Karen and Kyle's parents over the last few days.

Kyle had missed some training evenings to help Karen settle in, but Zane was fully informed and understandably patient. Apparently, Karen's Step-Mother had been informed of Karen's safety but not her whereabouts. There was a rumour of police investigation, but nobody knew the full story.

It was also possible to get in touch with Karen's father, although he didn't appear to be in any hurry to return. Kyle could see sorrow in his own father's eyes as he heard more and more of the story. Despite everything that was going on, Karen appeared to be happy and contented with her current situation.

Kyle's mother spent time talking to her in the kitchen at cooking times. They appeared to be getting on really well.

After some settling time, Kyle was able to walk to school with Karen every week-day and ensure she reached every class.

They grew to know each other very well. They spoke of how they could save money to live with one another once it was legally right – and even of going into business together somehow once they knew how.

Kyle's parents watched them closely, ensuring all remained innocent.

Several weeks had gone by and everything seemed to be ticking over with the same daily routines... That is, until a gentleman showed up at the door accompanied by a police officer.

Kyle's father called for Karen and a meeting was held in the family lounge.

Kyle, of course listened in from the hall door.

The gentleman was in fact Karen's father. He had returned to sell his family home. He had purchased a smaller home and just waiting for procedures to be completed before moving. He had picked up his old job, taking on less responsibility. It turned out that once Karen's father had been contacted and informed of events – he returned immediately, instructing his wife to leave and find a place with one of her own family members. It wasn't long then before Karen's father sold the big house surprisingly quickly, to take on less expense. His intention was to rebuild the father-daughter relationship and provide a stable, loving home.

Kyle thought he should feel happy to hear of the news, but instead jealousy hit him hard. It was almost as if he owned Karen and that nobody else could take her away. There were so many things he wanted to say... things such as it being too late to waltz in and make amends.

Kyle remained in the hallway, hearing Karen cry happy tears of reunion. He stood, feeling the pain of losing a life partner to someone with even more meaning to her. It was going to be a very hard adjustment.

'Kyle?' His mother spotted him leaning against the wall, thinking he had complete privacy.

He spun his head to see her concern.

'Sorry Mum. I have to know what's going on.'

She walked over and gave a warm and loving hug, knowing his thoughts.

'It's not going to stop you from seeing one another. It will be good to have normal space between you two. She needs her Dad just the same as you need us. You are both so young and need to learn about so many things yet...'

Kyle felt comfortable in her arms. He knew she was right and began to think a bit more about how young he actually was. Having his mother's arms around him, made him think about everything he had been through lately.

The day had moved so swiftly and before anyone had time to think, there were greater numbers at the dinner table all having a lavish meal. Karen, her father and all of Kyle's family had arranged to eat together. It allowed things to feel a little more stable about Karen and her father. Kyle began to feel happy about the circumstances. It would be better to have some healthy routine back in his life.

At the end of the meal Karen found time to speak with Kyle privately while the others sat in the lounge together.

'Thank you for saving me. Your family have protected me.' Kyle smiled broadly, realising the value of the events. She looked at him in the eyes before continuing. 'At least I know that the courage to run away was the right thing to do. I have my Dad back.'

'You're right. It was a very brave thing to do. It made big changes happen. I mean... your Dad is single now. You won't be trapped like a prisoner anymore.'

She smiled and summarised his sentence. 'Yes - Big changes.'

'So I hope your Dad won't be too protective. I still want to see you.'

'Don't be silly. I'll be at school and I'll have my normal freedom. My Dad is great.'

They both smiled and gave each other a loving hug.

Kyle's mother popped her head around the corner to spot them.

'Erm, Kyle... Karen's Dad wants to go home now.'

They both turned to look at her with expressions of guilt, dropping their arms from one another.

'I'm not stopping you from hugging.' She chuckled. 'It just means you have about two minutes to say goodnight.'

She popped her head back into the lounge and there were words of gratitude and departure just long enough for Kyle and Karen to give one another a glance of knowing one another's thoughts. They hugged once more and heard the clamber of people rising.

Everyone met in the hall, giving hugs of goodbyes like life-long family members.

As the door closed, the family dispersed to their preferred space and continued with life as if nothing unusual had occurred.

Kyle went upstairs to shower and prepare for an early night. He sensed his mother was keeping a subtle eye on him.

It wasn't long before the household had settled into the darkness and silence of the night.

Kyle had drifted into a vivid dream.

The grey mist seemed familiar to him. The sound of an Eagle flew overhead, circling – with a sense of protection as opposed to a predator attack.

Kyle knew he was safe, but felt on edge, about to partake in a battle. Through the mist he saw a tall, thin figure becoming more prominent. At first this figure was almost black, but with a little more light and a break through the mist – it became more of a light grey. He reached down to feel a sword attached to some form of elaborate belt.

A rumble sounded behind him, like a storm of heavy hooves. He wasn't sure of his enemy, so decided to use his senses and feelings – going with whatever situation arose.

The tall, thin figure grew closer – some colour now emerging - oranges and reds on flowing cloth. The heavy hooves came in closer. Kyle tensed and felt the need to crouch slightly, preparing to draw his sword.

The figure's breath was heard as a deep outlet.

The face of the figure came into sight - an elegant face, with deep, but clear eyes.

The heavy, multiple hooves now came in close, slowing to a pace as if arriving at their destination. Kyle spun to see large animals all standing in front of him. These animals were familiar to him. He viewed their features to be big, powerful bull-type bodies, but much bigger than any he had seen before. Their heads were more like images of the great Mammoth, but their eyes appeared to be full of great wisdom. Kyle found himself calm with them, as they stood, looking as if they came to meet him.

A great, but calm feminine voice came from the opposite direction. It was the figure that had grown close to him without his realisation.

'We are here to say that it is time.'

Kyle was understanding but equally unsure. He looked into her eyes and recognised the orange tinge.

'You know me as Clara. I am the great leader who seeks your assistance.'

He stood back in slight surprise.

'This will feel like home for you once you step in again. You have been given the lesson of great courage from another and now it is time for you to take that leap for a much greater purpose.'

Kyle found himself thinking of Karen at this point... The lesson of great courage was associated with her latest occurrences. The large figure of Clara was smiling with knowledge of his reference.

'That is correct Kyle. You have seen great courage as an example. Now it is time to use yours with a leap of faith. As you have now seen – courage brings great change. The courage and change will help so many others that you will see, and receive so much love.'

Kyle swallowed. Everything felt so real in this dream. He felt in complete control.

Clara looked down at his hand. He realised the grip remained on the sword, so swiftly released it, but stepped back to only offer a side-on view of him.

'Are you here to take me into the other world?' Kyle felt as if his voice echoed into the mist.

Clara gave a friendly expression.

'I cannot take you there - everything in this life is a choice.'

'It really is my purpose?' Thoughts of Zane entered his mind.

'You are the chosen one Kyle, but you always have a choice. The greatest thing, is that it is a large sacrifice of love for all.'

Despite the option given, the pressure was felt.

He looked into her eyes to attempt to study the orange glistening, but before he had chance to pick up any detail, a bright light flashed as if a camera flash had directly hit his own eyes. As the flash blinded him, he heard the Eagle cry loudly, causing him to wake-up suddenly.

He breathed heavily and had sweat running over his eyebrows. He managed to control himself and bring his mind back to the scene of his bedroom. The sound of complete silence comforted him, bringing him enough bravery to scan his room for normality.

There was a slight snoring sound coming from his parent's room, comforting him more so. He felt as if he had been screaming aloud, so reached over to clutch a glass of water he had left on the side. He gulped the water with much gratification. Upon recalling the dream, he realised it wasn't worth all of the sweat and adrenalin reaction. It appeared to be a relatively nice dream.

After only a few minutes his body had returned to complete calm and he was able to drift off into a deep and comfortable sleep.

TWENTY EIGHT

The following day, Kyle made his excuses to leave home and ran as if his life depended on it. He puffed his way to the training hall. It was important to rectify his time away from Zane and complete what was set out for him to do.

He entered the hall, knowing Zane would be there – and sure enough he was sat with his legs crossed looking forward, slightly immersed in the shadows. He spoke first:

'I have been expecting you.'

'I'm so sorry. Things have happened and I...'

'Do not apologise Kyle. All of everything has happened exactly as it was supposed to. You practiced the uses of the crystal and you have witnessed some brave circumstances.'

Kyle frowned with his deep breathing.

'You know everything?'

'Of course. I can see everything from our world.'

Kyle shook his head. 'So I have *no* privacy?'

Zane smiled and stood.

'One day you will understand. One comforting thing to know is that I have been looking out for your safety, as well as your young lady friend's. Didn't you realise after the connection with our lovely cat friend?'

Kyle frowned, followed by a grin with the coincidental situation with the black cat.

'I did wonder if the cat had a hand in any of Karen's situation.'

Zane smiled. 'Know that you are protected here by your animal friends. That is how important you are to us.'

'Wow!' Kyle was surprised at how vital he was to this situation.

'Right now we have bigger fish to fry.'

Kyle realised Zane was in control of this conversation, so held his mouth to listen to what the day held.

'Today we need to begin with something greater. I have a present for you.' Zane looked relatively excited. 'Close your eyes.'

Kyle complied.

'Hold both of your hands together at shoulder width.' Zane seemed very specific.

Kyle's hands both showed, palms facing upwards. He felt something solid landing across both hands and automatically opened his eyes without instruction.

'Wow!' He viewed a traditional-looking sword in a marked sheath. 'Is this for me? Is this for me to keep?'

Zane grinned. 'It is, but you must keep it here for safety reasons.'

'Oh yes, I would totally understand that.'

'First we must show you how to use it. I have decided that the crystal will work hard for you today – if you have time to stay for a while?'

'Oh yes. I am here for the day. It's a day of freedom for me. I had a dream last night that made me realise how much I need this.'

Zane nodded knowingly.

'Let's get you trained up. First of all there will be a moment of meditation. I need something to occur for you before we get moving.' He motioned for them both to sit cross-legged on the floor, facing one another.

They followed some breathing techniques, which relaxed the atmosphere. Zane then explained that he too held a crystal and that the energy was going to connect with Kyle's crystal in order to transfer some energy. A glow came from Zane's chest and hit Kyle's crystal – giving a soothing warmth. Kyle seemed to disappear into a state of sleep, with strange images flying around his mind, not too dis-similar to his dreams – and just as jumbled as some of them could be. This experience soon ended with a jolting return to his normal sitting state.

'Are you back in the room Kyle?'

Zane was staring calmly in his direction.

He looked directly at Zane, noticing his rugged features.

'I'm here. Did I fall asleep?'

'Not exactly... It will all make sense in a moment. I just need you to slowly move your fingers, toes, legs and arms and then slowly stand when you feel steady.'

Kyle couldn't understand the gentle treatment as he felt tremendous, but he complied with the instructions just as a matter of trust.

Zane offered a normal training belt and showed him how the sword would sit comfortably through the 'wrapping'.

'Now then...' Zane started. 'The sword is an extension of you. It's part of you. The energy which you share with the crystal is also shared with the sword. Now keep a distance from me and follow my moves.'

Kyle copied the sword removal from the sheath and placing it back correctly. After some time they were practicing various cuts, followed by cuts and movement. Kyle followed for hours – the time passing comfortably.

Kyle then learnt some attacks, defence and moves he never thought were possible. He was swinging the sword in all directions, following Zane's every movement with perfection. There was a time where Kyle practiced trained movements followed by improvised movements where imagined attacks or defence techniques would have occurred.

After several hours, Zane asked for him to place the sword in the sheath.

He looked at Kyle with great pride.

'Well done. You've come so far. Did you notice how much information you were able to consume and put into practical form within a short space of time?' He looked up at the small windows of the hall before giving Kyle a chance to respond.

'Look through the little windows. I think it's time for you to go home.'

Kyle looked up to notice the sky had turned into darkness, yet their eyes had adjusted to the hall so gradually.

'We've been doing this all day?'

'I guess we have, but look at what you have learnt! The reason for the meditation and the two crystals connecting was to transfer knowledge. This is a bit like a download of information from mind-to-mind or body-to-body. That is how you were able to use the sword so naturally... You already have the knowledge inside of you. It just needed to be come out.'

Kyle grinned with excitement but slight confusion.

'Now, don't forget that this whole thing takes a lot of courage and the training will take a lot of the fear away from future fighting situations. So the harder we train, the easier everything will be later on. This is your nature - to fight for love. This may sound strange, but this is what it is all about.'

Kyle was taken back to his dream but remained silent.

'I shall see you when you are able to come again. Generally, I will expect to see you during our usual lesson time to avoid getting you into trouble by your parents. I don't want them to think you're constantly training, as it isn't a healthy balance. We can't have anything stop you from training. Your parents need to be happy with what you're doing.'

'I understand Sir.'

Zane was happy to hear the respect between the two of them continuing.

The swords were taken by Zane and the two wished one another a pleasant evening.

'I need to show you how to manipulate the existence of the sword, but that is for another lesson.'

There was promise of so much more to learn.

When Kyle relaxed within the comforts of his own room that evening, he couldn't help replay the image of Zane connecting the two crystals for transference of energy and knowledge from one to the other. He looked down at the crystal, playing with it between his fingers, wondering what else this compacted item could do. As he looked down, the crystal shone various calm colours within it.

He relaxed whilst looking into it, finding himself falling into some form of meditation. As he drifted, he saw images fall into his mind. Some were of animals passing through rural spaces, while some were unrecognisable figures that moved through open grassland. All of it seemed relaxing and dream-like. Kyle slowly fell into a deep sleep and woke the following morning – fully clothed, on top of his bed clothes. He rose slowly, brushing the creases out of his clothing.

The rest of the family still slept, allowing him time to move freely around the home. He decided that perhaps he should have a shower and change his clothing, no matter how convenient it was to wake up pretty much prepared. He smelt his armpits to confirm the need, chuckling to himself. Half-asleep, he tiptoed downstairs first to drink some milk from the refrigerator.

As he drank, he felt he was being watched from the kitchen window. He looked out to see a large bird sat on the fence opposite, from across the garden. The bird was the Eagle that appeared to follow him from time-to-time. He knew now that the Eagle was his "healer", so he looked down at his body, as if checking himself over for any harm. His body appeared completely fine, so he looked out of the window again only to notice that the bird was no longer there. He shook his head and wondered if the Eagle was also used as some kind of protector or spy. Either way, he had soon forgotten the moment when he heard movement from one of the rooms upstairs.

It reminded him of his desire to shower before the house became an influx of mad, rushing family energy.
He ran to the bathroom and completed his morning cleanliness routine in good time. The sound of everyone rising for the day came when he was already finished.

Today was a school day and everything was falling back into routine. Jack was now in full flow with his new working life, but always left with his parents to acquire a lift.
Kyle noticed everyone rushing around him while he sat eating an easy breakfast.

The day had begun and before it was known, everyone was at school or the workplace.
It was a warm, dry day and Kyle was due a sporting afternoon with his Physical Education class. The track-n-field event was about to begin. Everyone was lined up in size order for sprints and longer distances. Kyle found he had won every event he was placed in. There didn't appear to be any effort required. His breathing was effortless, strong and healthy.
The main teacher noticed his potential and called him over.
He held him gently on the shoulder.
'You're a natural runner. What race do you enjoy most?'
Kyle didn't expect a fuss, but complied with an honest answer.
'I love the one hundred meter sprint.'
The teacher looked down at him with one raised eyebrow, reminding Kyle of some cowboy character.

'So, do you mind if I ask your name? I don't remember you in any sports team.'

Kyle felt probed. 'Err, my name is Kyle, Sir.'

'Kyle huh? Okay Kyle. Do you mind if I time your one hundred meter sprint then?' His lanky arms and long bony fingers pointed to the starting mark.

Kyle didn't answer but walked over to the starting line to begin his run.

The teacher had his stop watch in hand and counted down from five.

'Ready? Five... Four... Three... Two... One... Go!'

Kyle pushed off with stealth and left most of the students watching the scene. His legs pushed hard and stretched the long pace with a comfortable finish. He cooled down with a slower sprint to return to the teacher, who looked on with a frown.

'Okay Kyle, well you hit the fourteen second mark, but I'll be honest – I don't think you put any effort in. I want to see you put everything into your run. Imagine you're being chased by an aggressive dog that has no control over it.'

Kyle just collected his normal breathing efforts and started walking towards the start-line again. He looked over at his teacher and then held his chest, feeling the crystal heating up. A thought crossed his mind. This was an experiment that could be quite useful for everyone. The teacher can see his potential, while Kyle could test the crystal's abilities further. He whispered under his breath 'Activate... running ability.'

The teacher counted down slowly, giving Kyle a concerned look for holding his chest. Kyle gave him a convincing glance

309

that all was okay. At the shout of 'Go', Kyle darted off. He realised he was running too fast for normal ability, so paced himself to appear more realistic. Panic hit him at how fast he could actually move with the help of the crystal. It was too late to avoid any attention as a result of the speed... He had already reached a couple of meters away from the finish mark with what felt like a two second run. He felt ridiculous as he faked a few more seconds over the line. Kyle was just as surprised as every other onlooker. He casually ran back towards the teacher, who stood with a wide open mouth. Kyle grew concerned about what he had just exposed to a few witnesses. He panicked about going against his promise to Zane. The words stating he wouldn't uncover his enhanced abilities through fear of becoming some kind of experimental laboratory case.

'How stupid of me!' Kyle whispered regretfully.

The teacher caught his breath.

'Kyle? That is the right name you gave right?'

'Yes Sir.' Kyle nervously placed his hands on his hips, attempting to hide his nerves.

'Err, well... Kyle. Your speed was only seven seconds. You do realise that is faster than any sprinter recorded so far? In fact I think the world record stands at 9.58 seconds.'

Kyle gulped with fear.

'That can't be right Sir. Do you want to double check? I could do it again.'

'Erm. Kyle, let me go and get a witness to this, but when we do it again, promise you'll run with the same effort. Don't change it, otherwise people will think I'm crazy!'

Kyle attempted to appear normal. 'Okay Sir.'
Kyle looked about and noticed a few eyes on him. There
were groups of students standing around, looking interested
in the circumstances. One of the young men typically wanted
to make things feel uncomfortable by shouting over.
'Hey Kyle! Maybe your lanky legs have some kind of use
after all!'
Some of the surrounding students stood around with
chuckles, but most looked on with genuine interest.

The time waiting around seemed extremely long, making
Kyle feel like an awkward celebrity. He considered leaving,
but knew that would make things worse. His heart continued
to pound hard behind his ribcage, realising his major error.
He visualised himself in an experimental room with scientists
and doctors tying him up to machines and keeping him
isolated.
'Ah man, what have I done?' He whispered further regret
under his breath.

After what seemed like most of a lesson time, two teachers
emerged from a hall door and walked over to the pupils.
A more domineering teacher spoke.
'Okay everyone, please put up with us for just a couple of
minutes then we'll resume some relay races. So get
yourselves warmed up!'
The students looked a little nervy and walked about
performing unusual warm-up exercises.

Both teachers were tall and thin, obviously the athletic type, who must have had their peak times, but kept themselves fit. One of them retained the one slightly raised eyebrow, while the other appeared very solid, but with floppy blonde hair that didn't appear to match his personality.

The blonde haired teacher had an extremely 'booming' deep voice, which certainly made every student comply without question.

Kyle felt slightly nervous about being watched by two unusual leaders. He realised his last run was one without much consideration for his situation. He wanted to do well but didn't want the dangerous attention. With a bit of thought he wondered if he could change his speed by counting the seconds as he went along.

The start-line was by his feet and the two teachers were muttering their plans for timing and getting the race started. Before he knew it, they were counting down the seconds again and shouted 'Go!'

Kyle took off too fast, so made his stride long, but his pace a little steadier. He counted in his head. One... Two... Three.... It was difficult to guess the exact second timing, so all he could do was hope. During the sprint he had time to wish he had just disappeared off home to avoid this pressure he had accidentally put himself under.

He hit the finish line, hoping it was around the thirteen or fourteen second mark. Looking back at the two stern teachers – one with his blonde hair slightly blowing in the breeze and the other with his raised eyebrow – Kyle couldn't help but chuckle at the scene, taking some of his worry away.

'Well done Kyle!' The blonde gentleman shouted. 'I timed that to be exactly eleven seconds!'

Kyle felt his legs turn weak with his poor time measurement. The teacher continued to shout.

'That is only a small amount over the world record! I don't know if Mr. Barkley calculated the previous run correctly, but even if he didn't, this is amazing!'

Kyle crumbled with disappointment, but at least discovered the name of their new physical education teacher.

'Hey! Why are you looking so disappointed? This is a fantastic discovery for our school. We can win every single sprint race with you on the team – and we can train you to be faster and stronger. You'll be a world champion before you know it.' The teacher paused. 'What am I saying here? You are already at world championship levels. I think we need to find out who we need to get in touch with.'

Kyle walked up to the rest of the students, attempting to mingle in and hide, but they all stood around him – looking with star-struck eyes.

He had-to figure out a way of escapism from this accidental situation. He thought about playing a clever game, such as a fake injury next time he ran. Despite his thoughts, he was temporarily rescued by the school bell ringing loudly.

The teacher shouted for everyone to run to their next class. Kyle decided to stick to the crowd's pace. He felt all eyes on him the entire journey back up to the main building.

For the rest of the school day he felt like some kind of mini-celebrity. His fellow students were tapping him on his back or shoulder, making positive comments.

Even Karen had word of the news, making them a more popular pair to be associated with.

TWENTY NINE

Kyle had been keeping his head down at school, continually avoiding any other preventable errors. Everything else he was capable of needed to remain under control. He reminded himself of the need to keep the crystal on 'standby' when at school and to avoid any further temptations. In his mind he decided the use of the crystal would be to cheat in life. It was best used for the purpose of which Zane wanted – in *his* world. Practice of the abilities would remain during private time.

As time continued on - Athletics at school was postponed thankfully due to adverse weather conditions. Kyle calculated future excuses in his mind in preparation to demonstrate 'normal running speeds'.

Weeks had passed and Kyle managed to keep things on a level with everything in his life, other than his excelled training with Zane. His instructor continually recognised his student's improvements and Kyle humbly accepted that he was most certainly more able than he could ever imagine. He secretly trained in his bedroom and in the back garden when everyone was away for a few hours.
Despite all of the training and 'normal' behaviour at school, Kyle was enjoying life.

Karen appeared to have settled with her new situation. Her father had purchased a smaller home that was even closer in location. He occasionally came over for a drink and chat with Kyle's parents. Everyone appeared to be in a settled situation. All was wonderful.

Kyle was due to see Zane for what was described as the most exciting lesson to date.

The bait of this drew him to the lesson nice and early, finding Zane rubbing his hands, waiting to get started.

Kyle raised an eyebrow, reminding him of his sports teacher. The lesson began.

'So Kyle, I have something new to teach you, just as I promised you and teased you with from the last lesson.'

Kyle wasn't convinced that he would be surprised given everything he had experienced so far in his new topsy-turvy life. He stood in silence, but with respect, waiting to hear more.

'I need to get you punching first, then striking forward with an open palm. We will go from there.'

Kyle nodded with slight intrigue, but moved with the pace of the lesson.

He punched the pads that Zane held up for him. They moved onto more powerful punches, exaggerating the bodyweight moving in with the punches. They then moved onto strikes with the palms, which were just as powerful and less painful to the hands. Kyle was enjoying the power of it all, as they enhanced things by activating the crystal.

Zane encouraged a moment of rest after sweat began to pour into Kyle's eyes. He had worked him hard with positive encouragement.

'Okay Kyle, so the next thing is all about visualisation with power behind it.' He paused and demonstrated.

'Right, so you see that apple over there on top of the hall stage?'

Kyle creased his eyes up to focus.

'Oh yes, Sir.'

'Okay, well, watch this.'

Zane took a deep breath and prepared to throw a punch. Kyle watched him intensely.

Zane allowed every bit of power he had to extend forward with his fist, whilst blowing out hard. Kyle noticed his focus was extreme, but most interesting of all was seeing the apple move backwards by at least an inch.

They moved closer to the apple to inspect the amount of movement.

'Okay, so it moved slightly. Perhaps I should make a mark.'

Zane found some paper and a pen, marking the spot of the apple this time. He stood back in the same area of the hall before preparing for another punch.

There was a few meters between the apple on the stage and the middle of the hall, which was where he was standing. Kyle was very interested in the concept of all of this.

Zane completed the same punch with a matching level of power. They then both walked over for the inspection of movement. The apple had shifted back by approximately two inches.

'How does that work?' Kyle's eyebrows were showing confusion.

'Okay, so it's all about energy and intention. So what you do is activate the crystal for the level of energy to rise. Then you do a normal punch, but *intend* to push the apple backwards. It's a bit like your normal power punch, where you aim for further behind the target. Aim for further behind the apple. Use your visualisation for this. What I mean is, really believe you are punching with the intention to punch through the apple. Does that make any sense?'

Kyle was excited at his potential ability.

'Yes!'

'Okay, now let's give it a try. It may take a few goes.'

Kyle practiced, using all of the instruction and the copy of the demonstration. The apple didn't move at all for the first few goes. After several attempts, he finally managed to move the apple by approximately one centimetre. This was exciting enough for both of them to celebrate with joy of such an achievement.

'Great Kyle! This is an amazing achievement, especially for the other world. This will be much enhanced over there. We need to pay another visit.'

Kyle grew excited.

'When are we going over again?'

'Well, there is much more you need to know. Would you be brave enough to watch a battle, no matter what happens? We will remain invisible to it, so cannot be harmed. I don't want to expose you to negativity or danger, but I just need to show you who we will be working with and how it works over there. At the moment there are lots of mini battles going on. We expect one large one to occur in the near future, so we need you to be ready. Remember you are the chosen one, but if there is at any time anything you don't want to face as I offer it – please do be honest with me. If I asked your father he would most certainly not allow you to view a battle scene!'

Kyle remained excited.

'I really wish to see it. Although I am a little bit apprehensive about seeing anyone get hurt.'

'Injury and discontinuation of life is different over there. There is no blood or wound. The life force is literally an energy. There is no body of which is of solid structure as our eyes perceive over here. In fact *we* aren't actually solid on Earth, but our eyes see us as solid.'

Kyle remembered some of Zane's original lessons explaining things similarly.

'So there is no horror as such?'

'No, there is no horror, just the dark clouded energy that you need to know about. The dark coloured energy works on fear, so you need to practice a "no fear" state of mind. This will be our next lesson.'

'Can we train more often?'

Zane wasn't surprised.

'I think it's good to digest things between lessons. It would be too much to go through things too quickly.'

Zane could see Kyle would have preferred another answer, but saw his acceptance.

'Okay Sir.' There was a positive agreement. Kyle understood and wasn't one for sulking.

'Now then, this lesson is a tricky one to practice. I'd rather you didn't go around doing this without supervision. Let's keep the distance punching to the hall for now. Okay?'

'Okay.' Kyle could understand why.

'Don't forget your incredible journey. Keep happy about having such an amazing purpose.'

Just as those words were spoken, there was a crackling noise working itself around the hall. Zane paused in what he was saying and looked around him as if waiting for something to happen.

The cracks were like loud static noises as if something was manifesting. Sure enough, a colour formed a shape right in front of Kyle's eyes. He stepped back nervously.

Zane noticed his worry.

'It's okay Kyle. You'll see. Everything is perfectly safe.'

Green and pink shapes formed and became more solid to them. The shape became a solid form of a head and shoulders, followed by the complete trunk of a person. The legs were slowly forming but weren't as clear.

Kyle stared on, reminding himself to remain calm and think bravely.

The figure was definitely becoming a tall human figure. The pink and green fuzzy colours remained – but the facial features came to view. After a few minutes of Kyle and Zane standing completely still, the figure formed perfectly to show bright flowing clothing and long hair.

'Clara.' Zane confirmed.

Kyle looked at Zane and then back at the figure.

'Hello Zane.' The figure's voice was like velvet to the ears again.

Kyle moved his eyes, but kept every other part of him very still. Turning to him, Clara spoke gently.

'Hello Kyle. I just wanted to express my gratitude as a leader of our world. You are training so hard and doing very well; practicing everything so dedicatedly. I wanted to say thank you for continuing with all of this training. We owe you our lives. At least we shall owe you our lives. Not only our world, but also the Earth, as they are interlinked.'

Kyle heard the words and found himself gazing into her beautiful orange coloured eyes.

He found that he couldn't speak. He didn't seem capable of saying anything – and if he did there wouldn't be anything good enough to say. Or so it seemed.

Clara – now fully formed as if she had just 'dropped' into the room, turned to Zane.

'Thank you for your training and for your loyalty to Kyle and the rest of us.'

Zane spoke without hesitation.

'That is perfectly fine Clara. Thank you for your gratification.'

Kyle felt as if he was melting into a strange feeling within the hall. He stared at Clara, wondering how all of this could even "be".

As he stared, he wondered if there was anything else to be said or done. Her face began to fade again, as with all of her clothing. The pinks and greens were taking over, leaving the solid forms to disintegrate from Kyle's eyes. The colours faded and suddenly the air was clear. Zane and Kyle stood in silence for a moment, as if waiting for confirmation.

Zane looked over at Kyle.

'I hope that wasn't too much. I didn't expect a visit otherwise I would have given you advanced warning.'

'A visit?' Kyle was white with shock.

'It's okay Kyle. Let's go and grab a cup of tea from the kitchen and have a chat and relax.'

Kyle felt his feet were heavy but he managed to follow his instructor to the other side of the hall, hoping there weren't going to be any other surprises.

Kyle sat on a stool drinking some tea, while Zane gently explained the way Clara was able to manifest anywhere at any time.

'She is good at forming an image of herself. It is like being invisible in one spot and then making yourself become visible slowly. A bit like how you can now make yourself invisible using the crystal.'

Kyle nodded and listened.

Zane monitored Kyle continually. He didn't want him to suffer any trauma or fear.

'Normally your Eagle would come to your aid with a spot of healing, but in my mind I asked for him to allow me time with you.'

'You asked *him*?'

'Well, we can communicate in energy. I sensed he was about to appear in the hall, but I thought it may be better to chat to you thoroughly about it all instead.'

'Okay.'

Zane grew concerned over Kyle's unusual ability to cope with the information.

'I'm okay. I should be used to all of this strange stuff by now.' Kyle realised he may have been careless with his words. 'I mean, I'm sorry. I didn't mean...'

'It's okay Kyle. I know it's all strange stuff to you. It's not as strange once you get to understand both worlds and how they interlink. Once you see the meaning of it all, it all makes sense.'

Kyle frowned and smiled at the same time.

They sat in silence for a few moments.

'Well I'm okay Sir. I think maybe I should head home before my parents start worrying.' Kyle was honest about feeling comfortable about things again and Zane could sense it.

'Yes. I can see now that you're okay. Let's continue next week.' Zane stood during the words and encouraged movement through the hall toward the exit doors.

They both did their respectful goodbyes and parted company.

THIRTY

Zane sat at the large table, waiting for others to arrive. Clara moved near and sat opposite him, looking directly into his eyes. A connection ran between them and they telepathically spoke.

Others walked to the table – all holding tall glasses and offering one each to Zane and Clara. The glasses already held the gold-coloured fluid to about half-level. The stools around the table filled with the guests. As they all sat mutually, they all drank simultaneously. The gold drink filled them, creating an aura of gold around them all, individually, then shining outwardly and connecting with one another's auras. They all looked very relaxed and comfortable.

Clara spoke in her very comforting voice:

'We are now replenished. Our energy is again ready to take on further battle. Remember everyone, to keep yourselves protected.'

They all nodded without word and stood, bowing with gratitude before walking off back towards a large hut in the near distance.

Clara and Zane remained seated. They spoke openly this time.

'So, Zane, how is the young man getting on with training? I feel that he is growing in strength and knowledge.'

'You are right. He is almost ready. There are a few more things to show him. He also needs to come here again a little more often.'

'Yes, well remember not to be conspicuous with him. He still needs to be kept out of sight until the time is right.'

'I know Clara. Please don't worry. I am keeping him under my wing completely. He is mastering the crystal's ways quickly. I'm certain it will not be long now.'

'Well done Zane. You have done well in finding him and then training him with care.'

'There was no other way. He is gold to us.'

Clara nodded in agreement.

'So how are things looking here? Are we keeping on top of things?'

'The battle is growing greater. As you know – we have been expecting the little one to become the greatest one. I just hope Kyle will be ready when the time is near.'

Clara looked about as if she was sniffing for a scent.

'I honestly don't feel we have long Zane. The dark energy is growing. Prepare the young man for the worst case scenario.'

'I shall Clara.' Zane's calm feeling felt a little cracked.

They both stood.

Just as they did, others were rushing over with glimmering sliver swords. One of the tall characters shouted:

'This one is a little close!'

Clara sensed the trouble. Her outline began to fade, followed by a gradual dispersing of her solid appearance.

Zane noticed her slow departure and looked to the others, drawing a sword from his belt.

He turned to his left to notice a dark fog of deep voices moving swiftly towards them.

Zane's team ran forward with great force, moving directly into the expected battle. Once again the glimmering silver moved through the dark energy. Zane moved in to fight among them with no mercy. He couldn't help but become impatient with the battles now. They were increasingly tiresome considering the land was filled with peace and love not so long ago.

THIRTY ONE

Kyle and his family were enjoying a nice evening in with a movie and nibbles. Karen unexpectedly visited and joined in with the evening comforts. Kyle sat with his arm around her comfortably.

It was an extremely enjoyable evening, leading to a pleasant walk to Karen's father's house, allowing them some private conversation and holding hands. A gentle kiss goodbye gave Kyle a pleasant, thoughtful walk back home. It was still difficult to believe he was actually *with* Karen.

He arrived home, going straight to his bed and drifted into a deep sleep.

A dream came to him that made him sweat. He was fighting all of his bullies, one by one, using his sword. His sword felt heavy and almost impossible to lift. He managed to cut them as they came at him, but it didn't feel nice at all. The effort to hurt them, but not wanting to hurt them that way seemed to be a difficult contradiction. The feelings he had were those of frustration, resistance but necessity.

He continued to fight the bullies as they came in one by one. In the distance he spotted Zane coming up to them. Kyle felt comforted by this, but as he grew close, another person who wasn't recognised, caught Zane by surprise and plunged a sword deeply into his back, almost pushing all the way through. Kyle looked on in horror at the scene. Zane fell to the floor.

Kyle woke up with his heart racing! Sweat poured over his face and needed wiping before it dripped into his eyes. The dream was so vivid that it was initially difficult to tell the difference from his present reality. He reached over to switch a little side light on, as he needed time to calm down and re-focus. He caught sight of his alarm clock and noted it was four o'clock in the morning. The comfort of more sleep ahead allowed him to calm down almost instantly. He couldn't help wonder about the reason for such a harsh dream, but then he remembered the harder times. It wasn't all that long ago that he had too many bullies and not enough friends. He allowed the reasoning of this as his mind dealing with the past and mixing it up with the present.
He drifted off into another deep sleep, thankfully without any worrying dreams.

As the week moved into the weekend, things were moving normally, but Kyle couldn't help occasionally wondering about the dream. The sight of Zane being attacked really played on his mind. It distracted him at times during study lessons or when he had the opportunity to think too much.

The weekend was quiet and uneventful, so on the Sunday he made his excuses before heading out. His parents were used to their boys heading off for several hours at a time, but did their best to retain their responsibility of knowing their whereabouts.

He decided to take a walk over to the training hall to see if Zane happened to be there. As he walked, he tried to call him with his thoughts. Sure enough, as he arrived he spotted the shape of Zane walking up to the main doors and opening one of them to greet Kyle.

Kyle spoke first.

'I wanted to come and see you. I was worried.'

Zane frowned. 'What was your worry?'

Kyle studied his instructor for any wounds.

'I dreamt you were badly injured!'

Zane looked on with a smile. 'I do occasionally have injuries during battle, but so far I've managed them. Please don't worry. You are probably picking up on some reality of the battles, but I am fine.'

There was silence for a moment or two.

'Do you have time for a spot of training? Or are you busy today?'

Kyle's heart fluttered with excitement. He smiled with a nod, which made him realise how much he actually loved training.

'Come on through then. This is a great time to train.'

Kyle retained his excitement, but felt himself grow slightly nervous.

Zane enticed him through to the kitchen and opened his palm to offer the recognisable, large golden key.

Kyle realised the forthcoming event and held his breath nervously.

He took the key and placed it in the shimmering key lock that became more visible than the previous occasion. The door opened with bright lights shining into their eyes. Zane walked in, looking back to entice Kyle forward.

They both walked into the bright light. Kyle looked back to see that the door had sealed behind them. Although it was transparent, the appearance of the kitchen didn't seem as solid.

'Come on.' Zane needed his full attention on what lay ahead. They walked forward on the memorable golden path, with the vibrant and brightly coloured landscape either side.

'Place your attention on how much lighter you feel for a moment.'

Kyle noticed how wonderfully light he felt, despite his feet walking firmly on the ground. He felt wonderful and strangely liberated.

'Now, as you walk, pick up your pace slightly and attempt to jump, but as you do so - visualise it. Press your chest forward and push your arms back. Imagine you are launching yourself forward, perhaps like a ballerina.'

Kyle was a little confused about the request, but began to think about the movement before executing it.

He picked up the walking pace to a gentle jog, passing Zane's position ahead. He launched forward with the jump, pushing his chest forward and leaving his arms behind. Somehow his body remained upright when his feet left the ground. His body felt extremely light as it moved through the cool feeling air. He expected to land heavily on his feet, so pushed one leg forward to prepare. The time from the ground however was surprising him.

'That's it!' Zane shouted in his direction.

Kyle waited for his foot to land but a few seconds had passed before he felt his body slowly moving downward.

'Bring your arms slightly forward now and prepare one foot as you go down.'

Kyle began to wonder about gravity and if this was all scientifically explainable.

He moved his arms and felt himself gently drop onto his foot, propelling him forward into a bit of a running pace.

'Well done!' Zane shouted from the background with a satisfied tone.

Kyle slowed his pace to a walk and looked back.

'How does that work?'

Zane then jumped with extreme height and distance, landing himself by the side of Kyle.

'You see we are a lot lighter here. Earth is a place where our particles are heavy. Scientists obviously label this with "gravity".'

Kyle didn't feel as if he could speak. Once again he was surprised beyond expectation.

'This is just the beginning Kyle, but if you remember that you are as light as a feather here then that is a great start. Let's practice the jumping for a while. Do the same thing a few times and have some fun with it. Just learn to relax and literally go with the flow.'

Kyle enjoyed the idea of some light jumps, so got to it straight away, feeling like a younger person than he was just jumping through the air. He fell in love with the feeling of freedom, so continued to run and jump through the air as if he was semi-flying.

After what felt like a few hours of just pure fun for Kyle, Zane intervened.

'Okay Kyle, well done, you've grasped the light jumping. You have good control over it which I was hoping for. Let's walk for a moment.'

They continued on the never-ending golden path for a moment, until a large tree appeared very close to the edge. He stopped Kyle asking him to look at the tree.

'Okay, so this tree appears to be purely solid right?'

Kyle agreed with a nod.

Zane reached to touch the bark, looking very tenderly towards it. A golden light came from within the tree and appeared to soak into Zane's hand. The golden light moved into his hand and reached up into his forearm. Before the light reached his elbow, he pulled away. This was interesting enough for Kyle, but then Zane reached for the bark again and began the process of the light working through his hand, this time gently pushing his hand through the bark. His hand went through the tree bark, as if the tree was a hologram.

'You see everything as solid but it isn't.' Zane spoke as he gently moved his forearm deeper into the tree. 'Here you can use and manipulate energy in many different ways. You have witnessed me taking energy from the tree-life and now you are seeing me becoming part of the tree.'

Kyle looked confused.

Zane removed his hand and allowed it to sit on the bark now, as if leaning on the tree. Kyle then witnessed a white light leaving the palm of Zane's hand and filling part of the tree. Kyle frowned.

'So, now you are witnessing me giving the tree some energy. I am the tree and the tree is me. We can give or take energy, or mix energy up. At the same time we are still individual beings.'

Kyle was intrigued.

Zane continued. 'There is mostly love in this world, but the bad energy is trying to destroy our peace. I know that this tree is full of love and peace and that it would willingly fill me with energy if I was depleted of it.'

Kyle thought for a moment.

'A bit like battery power?'

Zane was impressed with his association.

'Yes! Perfect! We are all made up of energy. There are times when our batteries need recharging. I'm sure you've heard this from your parents perhaps? You won't need it so much when you're younger, as you should still be full of energy. When Earthly minds and bodies work so hard, then they need to be replenished.

Kyle frowned. 'So we are the same on Earth with our energy?'

'Yes, we are always energy, whether here or on Earth. The only difference is that our body on Earth appears solid and heavy. It is deceiving however, as we can still manipulate energy whether here or there. It's less obvious on Earth. It is much easier here as it is pure energy. Things may seem confusing at the moment, but there is still a lot to learn.'

Kyle was still a little bit confused. 'Okay.'

'Right Kyle, so now we are going to work on visualisation. This tree is okay for us to practice on as it is pure love and works well with us.'

Kyle raised his eyebrows with further interest.

'Now imagine this tree is completely empty.'

Kyle tried to visualise the image.

'Okay Kyle, a little more... I need to know you have this idea before we move on. Really visualise that this tree is like a hologram. You can see it, but it's completely transparent.'

Kyle imagined the tree as a ghost tree since that was his closest thought to Zane's suggestions.

'Okay Kyle, now watch this.'

Zane stepped back, then rolled into a ball and threw himself forward in a roll. He rolled through the tree, as if it wasn't there! He rolled until he stopped himself with one foot, allowing him to stand.

'Now *you* try this, but using the same visualisation – knowing it will do the same thing.'

Kyle grew nervous and allowed his mind to doubt this ability.

'Kyle, this only works with belief and visualisation. We are serious creators of reality here. The tree is always here, but in your mind it is transparent, so it is so easy to move through it.'

Kyle took some deep breaths and stepped forward, leaning down in preparation. He looked to the floor to see if anything on the ground would hurt him. The thought of smacking hard into tree bark put him off the idea, so looked back up at Zane with doubt.

'I can't... I don't think I can.'

'You see, your thoughts dictate everything. Just as you are able to win a sprinting race – you can either believe you can win it, or you can believe you will fail. Your body will be listening to what you are expecting. Know that you can do it and know that this tree isn't actually what your eyes are seeing.'

Kyle gulped and tried to calm his mind.

'I just don't think...'

Zane walked to him and placed a hand on his shoulder. Kyle felt extreme warmth and calm from his hand.

'Just relax Kyle. Just remember how much you have learnt and achieved that you didn't think you could do. Look back and realise how everything you've experienced has manifested so amazingly.

Kyle wasn't sure of his entire meaning, but the calm that came through him was effective enough to ease his mind. He automatically rolled forward into a ball and found himself moving forward with no hazards. He stepped up and looked back on the tree and Zane standing on the other side.

'Woohoo!' Kyle jumped up elated.

'You did it!' Zane smiled with relief. 'Did you feel anything as you rolled forward?'

Kyle tried to recall the brief experience in feelings.

'Erm, it just felt smooth and light.'

Zane knew there was a lot more to learn going by his answer.

'It's okay Kyle. You did well and everything else will come in time. Let's walk further.'

They walked down the path to find a variety of rocks and stones with amazing colours. Zane stopped Kyle to allow him to admire them.

'You see that each stone or rock is very different from one another, but they are classed as a stone or rock generally?'

'Yes?' Kyle knew more was coming.

'Well pick a few up one by one and make a pile on the pathway. I'll explain why when it is done.'

Kyle went along with the request and picked the rocks and stones until Zane appeared to be happy. A mini wall sat on the pathway. The colours shimmered in the light.

'So we are the same as rocks and stones. There are a few of us in different shapes and sizes; different colours and weights. They also hold energy. Everything does. Now we are going to try something else. I need you to stand back over here with me.'

Kyle wondered what they could possibly do with some stones and rocks.

'Okay so, now we are going to do what we were practicing last time. You remember the apple on the stage in the hall? Well, we are going to do the same thing with the rocks and stones. Let's see how good your visualisation is *here*.' Zane paused. 'I shall demonstrate for you.'

They stood about a meter away from the pile and focussed ahead. He pushed all of the power of his punch into the lump of stones and rocks like a ball of air flying towards them. He added a loud outward breath. Kyle was surprised to see almost the entire pile of stones and rock fall back and onto the pathway, glimmering as they landed.

'Wow!' Kyle couldn't control how impressed he felt.

'You can do just as well. Try it using the same methods we used before.' Zane walked over to the rubble and placed them into a similar-looking pile.

Kyle felt excited about the pending attempt, but retained an amount of uncertainty.

'You can do it easily Kyle – just as we practiced okay?'

Kyle noticed his instructor's faith, so hoped to prove his ability.

He took a breath and moved into a strong stance.

Throwing the movement, he pushed all of the power he could possibly envision forward, towards the pile.

To his surprise he knocked most of the rocks and stones over, onto the ground.

'Wow!' Kyle was again impressed with the entire event.

'Just as predicted.' Zane grinned with contentment.

'Now then, just as we did with the tree, let's go and feel the energy of the individual items.'

They both walked over. Kyle copied the actions of his Master. Zane demonstrated the energy that he pushes in with his mind, then the reverse where he could obtain energy by allowing it to enter his hand and arm. Kyle attempted to do the same, but it took quite some time for him to grasp this time.

They were there for what felt like quite a while, but Kyle was enjoying every moment of it. He began to experience some feeling of warmth coming from the larger rocks and attempted to visualise pushing some energy back into them.

They moved along the path now with Zane looking focussed on what they were going to do next.

There were some inexplicable noises in the background, which made Zane crouch down and encourage Kyle to do the same.

'We need to move into some secure place. Follow me.'

Kyle wondered what this part was all about, but moved along with his master to what seemed to be a very rural spot. The grass was lush green and the bushes and trees sparkled with a vibrant emerald colour.

The noises became clearer to Kyle's ears and Zane advised that they remain silent until instructed.

Between some blades of grass and leaves from the surrounding bushes and trees, Kyle could see mists of dark and light greys swirling around. A glance at Zane suggested a hint of fear. Kyle hoped this was another one of his lessons. Sounds of metal on metal came to their ears, causing a rush of adrenaline to move through Kyle's body – at least that was how the sensation felt.

A voice came echoing through the air.

Kyle recognised some of the words.

'We sense... he is here... find him...'

Zane moved uncomfortably, shuffling closer to Kyle.

Other voices shifted through the air, most unidentifiable.

Kyle looked over to see Zane staring forward, obviously observing with intensity. A voice grew closer to them.

'I sense him!'

Zane gulped and looked over at Kyle with a look of worry.

Just as a feeling of intensity hit them both, Zane reached over

338

to grab his own belt. As he touched the belt, the formation of a handle grew before Kyle's eyes. The handle grew into a longer one, which formed a golden edge. Under the golden edge, a long silver piece of metal came to view. Kyle suddenly recognised this as a sword which Zane appeared to have created from nowhere - with his hand.

Kyle was about to ask him how he performed such a thing, when Zane prepared to leap. A few noises of groans and screams left a sudden silence. Zane looked through the gaps and relaxed his legs, knowing he no longer needed to leap. He reached down to his sword and held it long enough to allow it to disintegrate before Kyle's eyes.

Zane looked and sensed everything around him and began to speak gently. 'It's okay now. All is okay.'

A recognisable voice spoke out, obviously being aware of Zane's presence. 'It is clear!'

Zane motioned for Kyle to stand cautiously and walk with him gently back out into the open.

A male presence stood with great valour - an obvious warrior with great power. His clothing was loose and flowing gently in the wind. He held a golden helmet under one arm.

Zane and Kyle walked over to him with quiet footsteps.

The warrior noted their approach. 'We are clear. It was close.'

Zane moved with an honourable bow.

'Thank you Clazadon. They must be sensing his presence.'

The warrior looked at Kyle.

'I could feel his power too. It may be best to return when we know they sleep.'

Zane nodded. The warrior walked slowly away from them, clenching his sword tight against his hip.

Kyle looked over at Zane for questions.

'I know. There is a need to explain. But now we must leave here. We have spent longer time here than planned.' He noted to turn and face the golden path back to the opening to the hall.

They both walked, arriving swiftly to the entrance door. Zane prepared him for the heavy feeling at the other side of the door as they walked through the portal. Kyle remembered the sensations, but fought against them to rush the recovery. Zane swiftly secured the door behind them with the golden key, once they were safely in the hall's kitchen.

Kyle sat on the floor, adjusting himself. He found that this time seemed much harder than the last. His body felt extremely heavy and uncomfortable.

'Take your time. We have spent much time over there, so the difference will seem greater.'

Zane sounded so wise and his voice much deeper at that moment.

Kyle moved his shoulders and neck to reclaim his body, still attempting to rush the recovery.

'While you sit, I shall explain. I'll prepare you a drink and a snack.' He reached for the kitchen items. 'While we were around playing with energies, other energies were sensing our presence. The dark energies were seeking you!'

'Me?' Kyle felt weakened, but his mind was certainly sharp.

'Well you see Kyle – you are the one that is needed to save our world and they feel that. You are a threat! If they can

340

either destroy you or contain you themselves for their benefit, then they will. I must advise you that if they themselves hold you, they can tempt you to move onto their side. By their side – I mean a dark side that constantly attempts to take the good from our world. As a result – our world affects this world. If the bad energies consume our world, then so too will it create chaos in the Earthly world.'

Kyle felt the pressure and didn't enjoy what he was hearing. Zane noted his worried expression without surprise.

'So long as you are here on your Earthly plane, you are safe. While I protect you here - when you come over to my side of life – I must protect you even more. Those on our side will also protect you as best they can. There are many protectors over there for you. The perfect example today was seeing Clazadon. He is one of our greatest protectors. He obviously sensed the approach of the darker energies and came to our service. This is his role as part of a great team. We battle together to keep the bad energies under control... This can only be contained by us alone for a limited time. You are our final piece, but you need more time to prepare for this event.'

'I will be at war alongside your great protectors?' Kyle checked.

'I'm afraid this is your life mission. If you don't join us then we are all at major risk of the dual worlds at constant war and sufferings.'

Kyle felt the real pressure, despite already knowing about his purpose from previous discussions. It just became a very real situation after this event.

'The most important thing is to remember your great purpose in the most amazing way. You cannot do this alone, just as *we* cannot. We are a team.'

Kyle felt as if he had heard this a few times now, but things had just moved up a notch in severity.

Zane looked up and noticed something approaching the kitchen area. A great light appeared through the kitchen window, allowing a figure to move through the glass and land on the floor. Just as Kyle recognised the figure to be an Eagle, a flash of light knocked him to the ground.

Zane sighed with the recognition of the healing friend. He felt partly grateful and relieved yet partly interrupted.

The Eagle looked up at Zane, then moved out through the glass just as a ghost would be seen in movies to move through doors.

Kyle woke a short time afterwards to a calm and normal scene in the hall's kitchen, with a mug of tea and some biscuits sat on a plate in front of him.

'It's all fine Kyle. You received some healing. It was obviously needed —as the Eagle will sense it.'

Kyle was shaking his head to what seemed to be reality.

'You have been through a tremendous amount today, so this is a good thing.'

Everything felt normal and calm now.

'Let us replenish our energy for a few moments.'

They both sat with their refreshments, mostly in silence and calm. Kyle was relaxed about his circumstances and grew excited gradually once again about the entire adventure.

It wasn't long before they were on their feet, talking about training plans the following week.

THIRTY TWO

Life appeared to be normal once again. Nothing unusual had occurred during the next few days, allowing Kyle a time to recover fully from the recent experiences.

There was much more family time this week, with a couple of birthday celebrations. The siblings were growing up quickly and apparently – suddenly.

Karen was visiting often and her father became closer friends with Kyle's Dad. There appeared to be a lot of social events, building relations.

As time moved further along, Kyle felt fully rested and replenished. His energy was building up to high levels, making him feel slightly restless and unfulfilled.

Although things felt comfortably normal for Kyle as of late, he couldn't help but desire another visit to Zane's world. He wanted to train further, since the possibilities over there seemed so endless. He knew battles were rising, but at this point he knew he was a safe apprentice in a world of magic.

It wouldn't be long before his next lesson, but before-hand he tried to distract himself with long bike rides to quiet fields so that he could secretly train. His parents took note of his bike rides and 'sweaty-looking' returns. They fed him plenty, noticing his healthy physique. They watched on, impressed with his confidence growth.

Kyle was certainly growing both physically and mentally.

The next lesson was intensified by Kyle's keen desire to progress. Zane knew that the excitement was over training in his world, but had concerns for his safety.

'I'm not sure it's all together safe to take you there so soon after the last event Kyle.'

'But that is the place that needs my help.'

'We can replicate things here. The only difference is that it's more subtle here.'

'How will I know how it feels over there if I don't practice over there though?'

'Ah Kyle, I was concerned you would grow some addiction to that world. I need you to remember that this is your home. There is still plenty of time.'

Kyle's body language said everything. He leant forward – his hands expressing his words...

As they spoke, some familiar crackles sounded in the hall.

A figure began to appear again. This time Kyle was excited to see the shape of Clara manifest before his bright eyes.

Fear of this usual/unusual occurrence had been eradicated. It appeared to be the norm for Kyle now.

Clara formed swiftly in front of them both, stopping all conversations. She spoke with her usual captivating voice.

'Kyle. You are keen to enter the other world. This is a healthy sign that you are willing to work and assist us. You must however respect your master's words. His decisions always hold reason.'

Kyle looked on with his mouth slightly open. Aware of this, he swiftly closed his mouth and stood up straight. She continued to speak.

'I wanted to express dear and continued gratitude for your youthful energy and willingness to move forward. You have certainly come very far in your training. Patience is an immense strength in this instance. I have prepared a space for you in the other world, which is contained from the senses of others. A bit like a field with a great and powerful force-field surrounding it.' She turned to Zane. 'Will this be satisfactory for some continual training Master?'

Zane smiled knowingly. 'That is wonderful Clara. I thank you.'

Before any further words were exchanged, Clara dispersed into air. Kyle was always amazed by her disappearing act more so than her sudden appearance. He turned to Zane, realising he may have been trying to dictate to his instructor. 'I'm sorry Sir. I will go with any training that you feel is right for me at this time.'

Zane smiled at the results Clara left with him.

'Okay Kyle, I know you are keen to get back into it. You only see the happy, fun side of it at the moment, but there is a lot of intense seriousness that goes along with your task. This is why we are going steady.'

Kyle looked disheartened.

'Please, let's sit for a while. I need to explain something to you that I haven't gone through as yet.'

They both sat on the floor attentively.

'Okay, so it's important for me to teach you about the way of things and why things are the way they are.'

Kyle raised his eyebrows, realising his interest since things have always been slightly secretive right from the start.

'So, you know you've been picked and how the leaflet arrived with you... That was important for you to know. It found you with energy. As you've experienced the way energy works between and within all of us, it has a way of finding itself working in ways that appear mysterious.'

Kyle nodded, partly knowing what his master was saying.

'Now I'd like to go further back to the time when peace and calm was the only thing that existed in the other world. It didn't seem possible that any other type of energy other than *love* could exist over there, until the two original leaders started noticing too much negativity occurring over on Earth. The two leaders at the time were Clara and Trion. Now of course you have met Clara a few times now. Trion was just as wonderful as Clara at one time. He still has an opportunity to revert back to being wonderful again should he choose to. The trust would need to be regained in a big way however.'

Kyle's eyes were wide like a younger child listening to a parent telling him a bedtime story. Zane smiled within at his innocence.

'So the two great leaders wanted to influence the people on the Earth to overcome the dark energies and the negativities. Their original idea was to encourage peace and love for one another. Clara continued to discretely work in wonderful ways. Trion started out well, but found himself slowly becoming closer to negative energy. Clara noticed how he

347

grew attracted to all of the bad things that went on, on Earth. He wanted to join in during great wars and influence the minds of many to continue the darkness of hurting one another. Many of us tried to stop him, but his desire and intention was too great.

Eventually he grew addicted and Clara had to attempt to intervene. She spoke strongly with him about the need to step back and remember who he truly was and his real purpose. She hoped that she could get 'into' his mind and make him realise the errors of his ways. It appeared that it was too late to change him now. Addiction became a very unhealthy thing. There was a great battle between the two of them. Because they are both very powerful leaders, their energy is of great levels. This is where great power needs a responsible being.' Zane took a moment to gather his breath for further words.

'So anyway, their great battle brought on a huge lightning strike. At least that is how it would appear to the human eyes. Trion was then banished to our world *only* – not only by Clara but by a combination of many great energies joining forces to aid in the name of good.'

Kyle appeared to be following well. 'So Trion is the negativity that has been influencing all the bad things that have happened on Earth?'

'That's the general gist kid.' Zane hoped his words weren't condescending and quickly continued. 'So since he has been banished he's been influencing the energy lives in the other world instead. Clara and our largest forces in love and peace, have been containing him and his companions well until now,

348

but he appears to be influencing greater forces lately and he's getting harder to contain.'

'So how did you know you needed me? Or someone *like* me?'

'Well, in our world, Clara connects with universal energies. She meditates in the most calm and wonderful ways. Once she focussed her meditation on how to conquer the great Trion. She received a message to create a leaflet from our world and allow the energy to find its owner, who would in turn be discovered as the one who would be able to help. She informed me of the need for me to create this leaflet and begin the works to find the chosen one. After quite a long time nothing happened and we all began to lose hope, but Clara was reminded to keep faith when she decided to meditate on this subject again. So, you see, with the faith and a bit more time, the leaflet eventually came to land on your doorstep. Because you needed some help with self-protection and confidence, you would respond to the leaflet. The greater energies knew that. It was all part of the overall plan. Then of course, I had to keep visiting this hall in wait of your first amazing visit. I had to make it look convincing in my initial story. I couldn't appear too keen to teach you. It wouldn't be good to be too strangely welcoming and excited to teach you. I needed to look as if I wasn't overly interested in teaching you. You were required to do the pursuing so that I could sense your strong desire to train. The rest is history.'

Kyle enjoyed the story and had settled into a comfortable position despite the hardness of the hall floor. He felt at home with it all and felt the need to hear more.

Zane noted his behaviour.

'I'm afraid there's not a lot more to tell, as you know the rest of it. Everything else is about experience and building on it to prepare you for a great battle. The Trion group – if that's what we should call it, isn't an easy force to deal with. You are not quite ready for the severity of the battle yet. This is why I am forced to protect you further.'

'So what happens when all of this is over? I assume that we win this battle – if I am the selected one to solve the problem?'

Zane was shocked at the mature set of questions.

'Wow, well we have just been given the answer to the battle, so expect that you are the cure. I am uncertain of what happens afterwards other than a hope for a reset of things – resetting it all to a time of peace once again. It has been some time though since all of this began. In your time it would have been long before you were born.'

'So longer than fifteen or sixteen years?'

'Oh yes. This time is nothing in our world. This isn't even a mere second. That's the concept you may struggle with.'

Kyle's expression demonstrated the same struggle with his thoughts.

'It is a good time for you to learn what you can though, Kyle, as the best learning years are in your youth. Although, saying that, we can learn at any age. In fact we never stop learning, whether we recognise this or not.'

Kyle nodded with acknowledgement.

'One thing to add Kyle, before we end this discussion – is that although you may a lot of pressure with all of this... The important thing to remember is that you are never alone. The secret to life is that you've never been alone and you never will be. The beauty of this battle is that you are most definitely not alone. You are simply the final piece to our jigsaw.'

Kyle didn't feel so special knowing that he was only another piece of a jigsaw.

'Do you know the meaning of humility Kyle?'

Kyle shook his head but rocked it side to side as if he may have a little knowledge.

'Well, this is what we must all hold. It is about being humble. We are all just as important as the next person. I know I spoke of this before. We all have a great purpose, but some just aren't clear. Many live without realising their purpose, as it can happen so subtly.'

'Okay.'

'So, remember we are all the same. Keep your mind strong, but remain level headed.'

'Okay.' Kyle looked to the side, showing his uncertainty. He didn't know what other words to use.

Zane stood slowly.

'Right then my student, let us get some training done. Clara has kindly set the little sample place up for us, so let's go through that lovely door again.'

Kyle felt excited, regaining the same initial feeling he had upon arrival. Zane could feel the energy increase.

Everything was slowly coming together with the information Kyle needed to gather gradually.

They went through the door that brought them to the other world. Zane appeared to be studying the views in all directions on this occasion. A new path of silver colour moved off to the right. Zane knew to move onto it - Kyle only one footstep behind, curious of the new route.

The silver path brought them to a shimmering wall. It appeared to be a solid, silver wall that shimmered so brightly in the light.

'Are you ready?' Zane prompted.

Kyle didn't know what he was meant to be prepared for, but watched on.

Zane walked into the wall, disappearing into it. Zane was nowhere to be seen, leaving the assumption that he was at the other side this wall.

Kyle looked three hundred and sixty degrees around him, studying his whereabouts and checking for potential signs of any other people or animals. He knew he had to walk into that shimmering, silver wall. A deep breath was taken in bravery, as he closed his eyes and pushed his body through a barrier of a tremendous silky-feeling. When the feeling ended he opened his eyes to witness Zane standing in a place slightly different to the usual golden path and its surroundings.

'Well done Kyle. The wall brings a wonderful feeling doesn't it?'

He looked back to see the shimmering wall behind him.

'It felt like walking through silk. Not that I've ever walked through silk before!'

Zane smiled.

Kyle studied his new surroundings. The area seemed brighter and didn't appear to have any boundaries other than the seemingly small silver wall behind him.

It was as if they had walked into a world of their own. Zane noticed Kyle's curiosity, so gave him time to focus on the surroundings.

'Have a good look around Kyle. This is a safe place, created by Clara, as you know. She would have reserved space and then sealed it with her protective barriers of energy, so that nobody can sense *yours*.'

Kyle wondered how such a thing could be created. He looked around, noticing the pretty features of light. Sparkles of silver spread across the floor and the blue of the sky was amazingly bright, yet easy on the eyes. Trees sat sparingly, but looking extremely large.

'Remember my lessons on how to replenish your energy with the trees?'

'Yes Sir.' Kyle responded, but gazed on at the beauty.

'This world is one of just pure splendour. At least, when it is completely at peace.'

Kyle couldn't imagine anyone wishing to disturb the wonderful world he viewed with awe.

'Pay attention to your feelings now Kyle. What do you feel?'

Kyle realised he was extremely light.

'Well my first feeling is that I'm very light. I feel free and happy.'

'That's great! I want you to know that you can create yourself in many different ways. I don't want to get all serious and ruin this feeling you have, but with the darker life forms that have been building, they are disadvantaged to you. They don't realise this, but they will be slower and heavier in feeling. This means that speed is your advantage when we eventually face them.'

Kyle came to the reality of his purpose and felt extremely nervous.

'Kyle, please remain calm. We are free and safe in this area, but your energy has the potential to reach far. I'm just not certain how far. So keep calm and understand that I will be teaching you everything I can to arm you with the necessary skills and knowledge. By the end of our main practice times, you will know your abilities.'

Zane felt Kyle's nervousness change to a more exciting feeling. 'Well done, I can feel your change to a positive attitude.'

Kyle looked at Zane with a frown, desperate to understand more about his feelings.

'Okay, I can see that we need to understand the energies a little more. So feelings are felt in this world. If you think and feel something, then it is powerfully projected. So, if you are thinking with nervous thoughts and reactions then others here will feel it – even the plants and trees and all of the animals and creatures around you. As I said before, all of this information is the same for the Earth, but it is very subtle to the point that no-one tends to notice. The other point is that most people on the Earthly plains are so distracted by television and entertainment systems – that most have forgotten the general purpose of everything.'

Kyle looked very interested at this point.

'What I am teaching you may seem pointless when you go home, but trust me, it is a better life, and having this information, you will create much more in your life generally. One word of warning is to say that you need to watch your thoughts and feelings. So, imagine you fall out with a friend. Your friend will feel upset and sad... perhaps angry. You could potentially be having the same feelings. This would actually project out – whether you intentionally meant to affect others or not. There will be what you call an 'atmosphere' between you and your friend. Your feelings will rub off on others around you. Negative energy attracts negative energy. So you will generally attract all negative things to you the more negative you think and feel. So things like anger, jealousy, aggression...' Zane checked Kyle's expression for his understanding. 'So you see, if you are the opposite and happy, peaceful and thinking good things to create good things, then life is much more prosperous in more ways than people realise.'

Kyle frowned again.

'So, these negative people here – in this world are projecting all things nasty and negative?'

'Basically, yes. We need positive energy to defeat their negativity. You have a very strong energy and it just needs directing in order to make it powerfully productive.'

Kyle frowned again. 'So I was selected for my energy levels?'

'Well, you also have the basic foundation – like a blank canvas with a lot of potential. You have a strong mind, strong body and the ability to adapt extremely well.'

Kyle smiled. The thought of having great abilities made him feel even more confident about himself.

'This can also be very beneficial on your Earth. I mean, look at all of the changes you have made in your normal life since you have been guided. I know we have touched on some of what I am talking about since the beginning, but it is good to elaborate.'

Kyle looked side to side, taking in the view and soaking in all that had been said. His life had certainly changed, and now he stood in a very unusual world, adapting well to the surroundings.

'So, we need to practice with the sword and feelings today.'

Kyle felt the change of focus immediately and stood to attention for more instruction.

'So, when you witnessed the brief battle in your previous visit, you will have seen me go for my sword.'

Kyle nodded and waited for more information.

'So, I noticed you have your crystal activated. That will be relevant in a minute. I need to focus on your sword to start with. I have your sword here.' Zane pulled a sword from what appeared to be from his back area. It sat comfortably in its sheath.'

'Wow. I didn't know you were holding swords.'

'It will all make more sense in a moment. Take the sword by the handle like this.' Zane demonstrated the correct way to take the sword from him.

Kyle noticed a small handle at the side of the sheath and held it in an upright position, close to him. Zane told him to relax and watch for a moment.

Zane activated a personal crystal and then tapped the side of his belt. The tap appeared to cause the manifestation of his sword. A long handle first began to 'grow', followed by the silver, shiny metal appearance of the blade, inch by inch until it was fully formed and very real to the naked eye.

'So you see, I revealed my sword that was already there, but just needed a 'call'.

Kyle was a bit confused, but mostly understood the concept. 'Okay, so watch the reverse.' Zane held the handle of his sword again and it slowly dispersed in reverse order, eventually disappearing all together from the handle part in his hand.

'Does it feel as if it isn't there when it looks as if it's gone?' Kyle wished to know how.

'Well, let us see young Kyle!' Zane moved closer. 'Now let's attach your sword to you.' He pulled out a belt and fitted it to his waistline. 'Now watch how I do this.'

Kyle monitored every move. He knew it was important to know how to attach the sword onto his belt securely.

It was done within a short few minutes.

'Okay, so your crystal is activated.'

'Yes Sir?'

'So, now as you requested your invisibility during your adventure with the drunken young lady, you wish your sword to become invisible. It is easier to visualise that particular part whilst holding it.' Zane grunted. 'So to summarise, it is

357

visualisation and word that manifests things. The beauty is you can always reverse your manifestations in this world. In this case, the sword is already here, so you're reversing the visualisation.'

Kyle was stunned to know of Zane's knowledge of his experience with the night club and the intoxicated lady.

He shook his head, remembering previous words about protecting him.

Zane noticed the distraction.

'Focus Kyle. You know I watch over you, so just relax about that.

Kyle breathed deep and focussed on the present situation.

'Sorry... but the sword wasn't my manifestation.' Kyle was slightly confused. 'It was a gift from you.'

'You inadvertently manifested it by desiring it initially some time back, but particularly as you wanted to train and learn, it all became part of what is happening now.'

Kyle wasn't sure what to think, but decided to brush his confusion away and focus on the task of reversing the manifestation of the sword.

As he attempted the disappearance of the sword, they both heard crackling noises.

'That's good Kyle. The crackling noises are like static. It's any change in energy. This is a good start. Remember how we heard the crackling noises when Clara came to visit us in the hall?'

Kyle realised how crazy this entire experience was and stopped everything.

'This is just weird Sir. I'm finding it all a bit strange. If I was to tell anyone about any of this, they would say I have some serious mental problem.'

Zane's face looked concerned.

'Oh Kyle, you need to remember how far you've come. Don't suddenly look upon all of this from a bird's eye view and think it's all just a little too mad. Look at it from the perspective of the new and exciting experiences with all of the potentials ahead. It's so amazing how much you have learnt. Don't talk yourself into anything bad.'

Kyle remembered the effects of the negative thinking and tried to regain his thoughts in a better way.

'I'm sorry Sir. I suppose it's all too weird at the moment. I'm trying to think it through the way you say.'

'Let us take a break Kyle. I had a feeling it would all be a bit much.'

The sword remained comfortably on Kyle's well-placed belt as Zane encouraged them to walk for a while.

They came to a beautiful, sparkling lake. It flowed so peacefully and had a heavy amount of silver speckles like glitter.

'Watch this.' Zane walked over to the lake and submerged into it, splashing the glittery water into the air. He walked out, looking completely dry.

'How.......?' Zane wasn't sure Kyle could handle any more strange experiences, but hoped this one would be worth it..

'Give it a go.'

Kyle walked over, entering the water-like substance with his feet as if walking slowing into the sea. What he assumed was some kind of water – felt like an immense flow of warmth. Although his feet were the only parts of him in there, his entire body felt warmed. He knew this 'water' was very different but didn't question it. He walked deeper and felt a warm tingling that made him feel extremely invigorated. Zane watched on with a smile. As Kyle enjoyed the experience that he couldn't understand, a figure emerged by the side of Zane. Clara had made her way into the area, not wishing for Kyle to notice her.

'Is he struggling with the new experiences?' She spoke extremely softly.

'It's all a bit overwhelming I think.' Zane replied as if the circumstances were daily occurrences.

They noticed Kyle throwing the sparkly water about, enjoying the experience.

'He looks contented now.' Clara observed.

'I know... he'll be okay.'

Clara placed a hand on Zane's shoulder and slowly disappeared into the atmosphere.

Kyle chuckled with complete joy of the experience. Everything felt vibrant and comfortable.

Zane allowed him to take as much time as he desired, but noticed Kyle as he began walking towards him. Upon approach, Kyle was walking more upright, with a broad smile on his face. A question emerged from his mouth:

'What is that silver stuff? It isn't water, right?'

'Well Kyle, it's a cleansing place. It's where many go to replenish and allow all emotions to be cleansed and refreshed. So, how do you feel after that?'

'I feel amazing! I'm willing to carry on with the training now.'
'Well I think you need a rest for today. I'm just keeping your mind and body protected.'

Kyle didn't wish to stop, since now his determination levels coupled with his inquisitive mind. He took it upon himself to reach down to the sword by his side. Zane watched as it disappeared perfectly.

'Well done Kyle!' Zane smiled. 'So, let's say you passed this level in training. We can move to the next level next time. Okay?'

Kyle appeared content with the compromise.

They walked to the silver curtain of 'shimmer' and walked straight through it, momentarily enjoying the feeling of silk on their skin.

It was only a short walk along the golden path before they reached the section of the hidden kitchen door.

They walked through the door into the training hall at the other side. Kyle slumped on the floor with the sudden heaviness of his 'Earthly-feeling' body.

Zane watched over him and made the normal cup of tea. Kyle began to recover faster than the previous time, as he recognised the sensations and knew how to deal with them.

'I'm sorry you have to go through that horrible feeling, but it does get easier with practice.'

Kyle sat upright and looked more comfortable after just a few, short minutes.

'So... that river revives people did you say?' Kyle reached over for the drink offered to him.

'Yes. It's a place people go to replenish and clear all of the rubbish out of the body... in fact there are a few of them about, but some have been made toxic by those who have tried to destroy them.'

'Is that the enemy trying to destroy them?'

'Yes. They are trying to weaken us since they don't have anything to build their hatred and anger levels up, other than having more hatred and anger.'

Kyle felt his fear levels build up slightly again.

'Please Kyle, remember not to fear them. You will be greater in power once we have finished with you!' Zane tried to bring some humour in to ease the pressure.

Kyle was noticeably thinking.

'So, does everyone own a crystal from your world?'

Zane raised his eyebrows.

'Well, yes. It enhances everything over there. It is very much a world that is full of crystal. I will show you a great place as an example when we next visit.'

Kyle pondered again.

'So, when we complete this... erm... mission, does that mean you won't have to guard the door anymore?'

'That's a good question oh great student.' Zane made light of things again. 'I am a protector, but it will be a different level of protection once we have defeated all of the bad from our world. You realise that your confidence has changed and that you know you can do this with us?'

Kyle sat, looking up at his strong master. 'I guess so.'

'Well, when you ask a question that involves the words "when we complete this mission" instead of "if we complete

this mission", then I know you have confidence in this whole process.'
They both smiled in silence.

They both slowly removed their sword belts and relaxed with a conversation about the healing "water".

THIRTY THREE

Kyle threw himself back into a fresh week, deciding to spend a lot more time with Karen. The classes throughout Monday were much easier with each other's company.

Kyle could see that Frank felt slightly left out, so tried to involve him as much as possible. It felt good to have such love around one another.

The Physical Education lesson was a disappointment to the teachers as they watched a frustratingly slow run by Kyle. It was important to regain the low profile. Kyle acted it all out wonderfully well, making his run appear to be a great effort at a slower pace. The teachers didn't wish to give up on his potential however, assuming he was tired or attempting to conceal himself for fear of being in the spotlight.

The other students weren't impressed, which pleased Kyle as he wanted a peaceful time at school.

Karen secretly desired more popularity for him in order for her own pride levels to rise. Kyle could sense her slight disappointment, but knew it would be good for them overall given time to settle.

Kyle found a greater interest in English, which he was beginning to excel in. At least using his normal ability, there was nothing he had-to hide.

Mark, an old school friend sat next to him during this lesson as of late. He was a steady-minded fellow who offered a good level of grounding for Kyle.

Later in the day, Kyle felt bad about not spending enough time with Frank again, so asked him if he would like to practice some training together after school. Frank jumped at the chance, looking forward to some time with his friend.

Kyle enjoyed the time practicing against Frank's boxing skills. They trained in Kyle's back garden.
Frank would attempt to gain contact with his punches, while Kyle enjoyed practicing his defence, by blocking or ducking and weaving. It was fun for the both of them and each moment allowed more bonding time as well as improved reflexes and general skills.
Kyle liked to add an occasional leg-trip, which Frank grew used to and managed to avoid over time.

Later that evening Kyle sat on his bed feeling content with things. Friends were plentiful and a relationship was blooming.
He looked down at his crystal and thought about all of the abilities it brought – and how different his life had become over recent times.
Out of curiosity, he sat on his carpet floor, noticing the time. It was nine o'clock in the evening, and the knowledge that everyone would be expected to remain quiet and in their own little worlds, guaranteeing him some peace and quiet.
He recreated the meditation scene he experienced previously. He activated his crystal and sat, relaxing in the same way.

As before, he began disappearing into a world of strange and miss-matched dreams that didn't make any sense. Although he didn't really know what he was doing, it was easy to go along with it all.

Something seemed to wake him with a jolt, just as if an internal alarm had gone off. In his initial alertness, his first instinct was to look at the time. He dismissed it in his mind for the first few seconds and glanced away. His mind was obviously relaxed. Then the sudden realisation of the actual time needed confirming, so he shot a second glance at his nearby clock. It was now actually eleven o'clock at night. Adrenaline hit his body once he realised he had been meditating for around two hours. He slowly stood to look out of his bedroom door, to notice most of the family had gone to bed. The usual signs of doors closed and lights off were very apparent. Still surprised at the time that had passed by in such a flash, he wondered what his mind was experiencing during the two hours. He decided to creep downstairs and study the house for any family members who were late going to bed, but couldn't find any. Everything sat silently across the entire house.

A feeling of buzzing energy was within him. He felt like going for a long run or training hard in some shape or form. As it was quiet, he went through the internal door of the house into the garage, which was empty enough to move around quite easily. He slowly began to move and throw some punches and kicks in the open space. At first it was relaxed and slow, but once he warmed up he went at intense speed. He felt as if he was moving as fast as a film would be witnessed when it was in the 'fast-forward' mode. Although it felt like that, he didn't believe it was *that* fast, so he decided to pick up his mobile phone and set it down on a step facing upward to capture his movement on video. He started slowly once again and built it up to the super-speed he felt he was doing.

Building up a gradual sweat, he stopped to view his recording. He was smiling to see his slow warm-up movements, but grew interested when seeing himself increase in speed to a point where the movements were literally invisible. He knew that fast moments on phone cameras weren't always captured, but after watching it over and over again a few times, he grew intrigued over his actual speed. It would have been nice if Frank was still present to witness his actions. He felt unusually fast and nimble, yet his movements felt more powerful than ever. The meditation was thought of as some kind of enhancement, but he couldn't confirm this without speaking with Zane.

He was used-to unusual things occurring in his life since the start of the Martial Arts lessons, but he felt more comfortable with some kind of explanation behind them. It was hard to relax fully now, which was a tricky sensation given that he really should be going to sleep at this point in time.

He walked restlessly around the house, keeping total silence as not to wake anyone. Minimal lighting retained the calm feeling.

The next morning, Kyle found himself waking up on the lounge sofa, not remembering settling there but somehow gratefully managing to get some sleep. He crept upstairs to the bathroom before anyone else stirred. Passing his bedroom door, he spotted his untouched bed, thinking positively about how there was at least no added bed-making chore before starting the day.

The day began and everyone gathered frantically to leave through the front door as per usual. Kyle was keen to test his new-found speed of movements but kept his patience. The thought of an even faster running ability, reminded him of his need for restraint.

Karen met him at the main school gates and noticed his rugged appearance.

'Nice look. You going for the cool, unkempt style?'

Kyle didn't know exactly what she meant by her question.

'Did I do my hair right?' He brushed his hand through his hair to check at the same time.

'I guess it looks like you rushed.'

'Oh.' He recalled the late night, not knowing exactly when he'd fallen asleep.

He felt slightly self-conscious and took note of everyone's critical eye every time he passed someone.

The assembly was first in the morning, with queues everywhere and a lot of back ground chattering.

In the large hall, the teacher selected for a talk on career ideas spoke of ambition and drive.
They mentioned athletics and how some people didn't put in the right amount of effort and not matching their potential. Kyle felt as if the speech was created directly for him. He checked about for any eyes watching him. Everyone appeared to be focussed forward like well controlled robots. Kyle felt uncomfortable as the teacher continued to speak of potential and noting that many students don't put in enough effort.
One of the Physical Education tutors stood and appeared to take over, as if a relay of tutoring was planned. The students continued to sit still and forward. Kyle felt as if he was the only one with an individual mind, but perhaps the only one feeling as if the speech was created specifically for him. Karen glanced over at him, wondering what he was thinking. He gave a convincing smile to comfort her.

On the way out of the hall, Karen decided to ask some relevant questions.
'So how come you don't put the same effort into your running? People were so amazed by your running ability when they timed you. Now you are kind of half the speed. It's like you don't care, but we all want to see you do amazing. I don't get it.'

Kyle felt adrenaline run through him, as he'd never had any *real* form of altercation with Karen. It was difficult to figure out an answer when such secrecy needed to be retained. He had to think on his feet quickly as this was totally unexpected.

'Well I think it was just a lucky day when I first did that super speed sprint. Even *I* don't get it.'

Karen frowned disappointingly.

'That doesn't seem right. I think you're trying to avoid all of the attention. What's wrong with having an amazing ability? I reckon you're holding back to avoid a scene. You should be proud of it.'

Kyle gulped without intending. The nerves kicked in. He wondered if secret agents felt the same about keeping secrets. Visions of movies where people couldn't tell their partners about their real jobs popped into his mind. There was only one answer he could give.

'Okay, I tell you what. Next time I'll put the same level of effort into it.'

Karen smiled. 'Good. You should.'

They were both silent during the entire walk to the first classroom.

They both sat, looking at one another, feeling a slight tension. Kyle wanted so much to tell Karen the truth. Hiding things from her felt extremely wrong, but there was no choice.

At the end of the school day, Kyle asked his brother Paul to go with him to the running track on the school grounds without explanation, just requesting some assistance. They both climbed over a metal side-gate at the least conspicuous location. Nobody appeared to be aware of them running across the grass to the running track.

'Okay Paul. I need you to time me from this line to the next one... The one hundred meter sprint. I need you to tell me when to go and I need you to be accurate with the time I cross that line at the end.'

Paul looked at him with little interest.

'Why? Are you trying to impress your girl?'

'I am but I'm not. I'm too fast, so trying to tone it down to something reasonable. I need to be able to run it in just over ten seconds.'

'Why do you need to slow your running down?'

Kyle just wanted an easy time of practice.

'Are you gonna help me or not? If not then I can just time myself. It's just easier with your help.'

'Alright, alright. Jeepers.'

Kyle saw that as confirmation of his help.

'I just need you to keep this quiet okay?'

Paul frowned with no response, looking down at his mobile phone to find his stop watch feature.

Kyle sprinted several times without any crystal enhancements. His speed averaged just over thirteen seconds. He knew Karen would suspect that those speeds were without effort.

He activated the crystal under his breath, leaving no suspicion with his brother.

Several runs occurred at an excessive speed, leaving Paul a little bit stunned. The first few were clocked at six seconds or just over. Kyle knew he was performing with extreme speed and needed to judge something slower but believable.

Paul was confused, as he noted his brother's leg pace lengthen but his speed reduce.

Kyle continuously checked Paul's timings and moved back to the start-line for another attempt.

Paul asked on occasion if he was growing tired of the running, but Kyle simply shook his head and returned to the start line.

The times were now averaging eleven seconds with deliberate pacing. Kyle shouted that it was getting better, leaving Paul confused about how that could possibly be an improved time.

Kyle ran and counted ten seconds with a very accurate pace, which Paul confirmed. He ran it several times again, all hitting just over the ten second mark. Paul was growing bored of the ten-second races that Kyle performed over and over. Kyle was practicing the same pace until he knew he could do it perfectly, ready for the physical education lesson.

Paul started to ask questions, making Kyle feel slightly nervous again.

'Have we finished here now?' Paul was preparing to ask more.

'I think so. I've got it on the nose of ten seconds which was what I was roughly aiming for. I would prefer exactly eleven seconds if I'm honest.'

'Why prepare for ten or eleven seconds when you know...'

Kyle stopped him in his tracks.

'I want to start at that level. Please don't tell anyone I can go faster or they'll get me running for everything. Running isn't my scene.'

'So why train like this then?' Paul frowned hard.

'Please don't say anything to anyone. I just wanted to be fast but not too fast.'

'You're getting weird these days.' Paul regretted the words.

'Don't worry brother - things will get back to normal soon. I'm just trying to impress my girl at the right level you know? Not too much, but just enough.'

'Ah man, the things you do for girls. I'm trying to impress a girl at school with this new haircut. Apparently it's the new thing but I hate it.'

Kyle noted his hairstyle and realised he hadn't been paying much attention to his poor brother.

'Ah, it suits you though... Hey thanks for helping me today. I know it seems stupid but you won't believe how much it'll get a few people off my back and win my girl.'

Paul wanted to know more, but Kyle gently pushed him on the back to encourage their movements in the general direction towards the gate. 'Let's get back. I've learnt the perfect running pace to get me through.'

Paul and Kyle picked up to a jogging pace and found the gate to climb over.

THIRTY FOUR

Kyle now felt prepared for everything that lay ahead for the rest of the week.

He visited Zane for the next eventful occurrence.
They both went into the parallel world cautiously this time.
Kyle followed Zane quietly down the golden path.
'Now, did I tell you, you can place a force field around you?'
'I can't remember Sir.'
'Well, just visualise a bubble of white with your mind, starting small in the middle of your chest, building up to a large bubble of white all around you, like a huge ball around you. Close your eyes and try.'
'Okay.'
After Kyle's visualisation, he opened his eyes to see Zane waving his finger in funny ways.
'Sorry, I'm just helping you manifest it. Making sure it's definitely there since it's your first attempt.'
'Oh, okay.' Kyle wasn't convinced of it, since he couldn't see a difference.
Zane smiled and walked on, assuming Kyle's footsteps behind. As they walked, Zane explained further.
'The force fields don't make you invisible, but they stop the bad energies from getting to you. It also stops any bad feelings you have from getting out. I hope that makes sense. You wouldn't be able to perform in battle with it on though. It's just for a peaceful time.'

'Oh, okay, but how come we didn't use that before?' He felt cheeky with the question, but his curiosity was strong.

'I needed you to play with energy first so that you could actually build enough to create one. It has been a gradual process.'

Kyle didn't quite understand the reasons, but had no choice but to go with it.

'Without the build-up of energy before today, you wouldn't have even been able to begin to visualise the force field.'

Kyle didn't realise he had been building energy gradually.

'Your energy has been building gradually. At least with the force field you are a lot less detectable by the negative energy.'

They walked on and turned a corner after quite a while of walking straight ahead. The walk felt long, but it was a wonderful scene, which distracted Kyle enough to dismiss the distance. There were skies of beautiful blue throughout, but the occasional appearance of moons of various types and shades; Rainbows of different heights and thicknesses; Mountains and hills of various shades of greens and greys. Some had golden pathways winding through them, right up to the top. Birds of unusual breeds moved through the air with contented gliding actions. There were bushes and trees throughout that held the usual emerald green colour. Little rustles told Kyle that there were other creatures hiding – perhaps animals similar to Earth's life. It was certainly an addictive place to visit.

They found a pathway that moved up to a gradient, taking them up a hill. The golden path appeared to gradually mould into a silver colour. Some trees and bushes were becoming denser, with the path thinning. Grass was thicker and brighter. There appeared to be a feeling of intense energy and life as they climbed higher.

'Okay, catch your breath for a moment.' Zane looked back to give the instructions.

Kyle stood and realised he did actually need to take a few deeper breaths to recover from the gradual climb.

'Okay, you're ready.' Zane walked forward, moving some branches and leaves out of their faces.

The trees and general plant-life now surrounded them and became thick and heavy ahead.

'Can we walk through this?' Kyle grew slightly concerned about their destination.

'Keep light Kyle. Remember the tree lesson? We're almost there.'

They continued for a few more minutes and then stopped in front of three extremely large trees.

Zane pointed downward, making Kyle realise they must have peaked at the top of the hill.

He looked down, following Zane's finger, only to be amazed at the sight before his eyes.

Before him was a crater of glimmering, clear crystal the size of large rocks. The crystals covered the size of a crater, large enough to have had an asteroid or similar item hit it.

Zane recognised his thoughts.

'You're not far off your idea Kyle. It is vast. This is where much of our power comes from. We come here to gather power and energy for ourselves.'

'Power? Is this another battery charging place?'

Zane smiled at his comment.

'Well, we just need a boost every now and then, just the same as you would need to sleep to replenish your energy.'

'You don't sleep?'

'Only if I stay on Earthly planes for too long, as I change form and become the same state as you are.'

Kyle looked very confused. 'Oh right.'

'You don't have to worry about that. This is good for you to see though. The crystal space is where our energy is replenished intensely. It's another place that is getting attacked in an attempt to deplete us. We don't come here daily but when we need it, we truly need it.'

As they looked at each other's expressions, a loud screeching noise came from the other side of the huge crater space.

Kyle looked for any fear in Zane after hearing the noise, but he smiled to demonstrate calm.

'That is our only protector of this crystal space. You will see him in a moment. He has been injured many times in attempts to save this space. He has fought well and many have assisted him, but it is getting harder.'

Kyle looked over at the empty sky and the land filled with bright crystal but couldn't see anyone.

Zane smiled at his curiosity and knew he'd be interested in the surprise.

A small dot in the distance grew in the sky to appear as a shape that appeared to keep changing form. As this flying 'object' grew closer, its form seemed to go from an Eagle-like shape, to a Dragon shape, to a half-human/half-bird shape. It grew closer and landed with Eagle style claws only a few meters in front of Zane and Kyle. He had a very human, muscular body with a huge set of wings coming from his back. His face was very different. He was most certainly not human, but it was difficult to identify his looks when comparing him to anything Kyle has ever seen.

He appeared to have more hair on his body and face than a human would have. The hair was almost fox-like in colour – a golden or orange feature to it. His facial features were lion-like in the mouth and nose area, but his eyes were extremely harsh and bright looking. His eyes matched his hair, as they were a vivid golden-orange. His eyes were in fact his most striking feature, as they were piercing and quite frightening. Upon closer study as he walked closer, Kyle noticed harsh scars across his face. He had obviously been in many battles as the evidence sat in deep cut marks over the nose and head areas. Kyle studied his features further to notice his human-like ears and eyebrows. He was a beautiful creature but one that you knew you wouldn't like to cross in battle. Zane looked small in front of him, but he reached his arm out to offer a greeting as if matching his stature.

Kyle watched on in amazement and admiration for such a strong "being" standing before him.

Zane looked over at Kyle. 'This is Ryston. He is a great protector of our crystal space.'

Ryston offered a large, powerful hand to Kyle.

Their hands met in a gentle greeting, with much relief to Kyle for the gentle and considerate grip.

There were no words exchanged. Zane looked over at the powerful being and they appeared to understand one another.

Ryston simply lifted with one movement of his wings. It all appeared so effortless. His figure darted off into the distance in less than a couple of seconds. Kyle stood with complete amazement.

'The negative energies must be very strong to fight with such a person!' The realisation of the power involved made Kyle crumble inside.

'Don't fear young Kyle. Ryston knows that your power is even greater than his. It is only *you* who doesn't realise this yet. Trust me. You will see!'

Kyle grew in confidence hearing such amazing words.

'Really? I have more power than that muscular character?'

'It may surprise you, but, yes. You will see, just as I said.'

Kyle looked in different directions, feeling lost in this particular place, but excited at the same time.

'Okay Sir, I trust you, but it's hard to imagine my small body competing with Ryston.'

'Well Ryston is on your side, but your strength is within you my friend. You will see. It's not about muscles, it's about energy.'

Kyle noticed Zane's repetitive words, so decided to hold a bit of patience.

'That's it Kyle. I feel the change in you. Now let me show you the crystals a little closer.'

They walked down rubble of rock and stone. Kyle felt unsteady with his ankles and kept a good eye on his foot placements.

It became smoother, with very small stones all merging together until they all worked their way into a completely smooth stone. Kyle looked down and noticed the thick, yet almost transparent rock beneath his feet.

'That is pure crystal now Kyle.'

Kyle felt a cool sensation work through his feet and up into his legs.

'It feels refreshing.'

'Perfect description Kyle.' Zane continued to walk with Kyle in tow.

Kyle felt cooler but extremely good.

They walked deeper into the crystals, some shapes were sharp and dangerous-looking from Kyle's observation.

Zane stopped suddenly.

'Okay, stand just here and feel light from above and below… So feel the clear crystal light from your feet and the warmth of the golden sun from above. Close your eyes and go with how you *feel*. To look with your eyes will ruin the sensation.'

Kyle moved over to the spot Zane was referring to and stood still, following instructions perfectly. Kyle visualised the light from below and above and literally felt his visualisation in action. It was a very vibrant and tingly feeling moving through his entire body. The light from below made him feel extremely light while the golden light from above made him feel incredibly powerful. His entire body felt refreshed, strong and even more invincible than he ever thought he could feel.

He drifted away with a mind that was almost free of thought. The only expression was the focus on the sensations of his body.

Zane spoke with calm and quiet, but seemed slightly distant. 'Now, keep your eyes closed for a moment. Don't open them until I say, okay? Just relax and trust me.'

Kyle didn't respond with his voice but felt as if he had with his mind.

A gust of wonderful refreshing air seemed to move into Kyle's body from the back of him, filling him with a lighter feel.

'Okay, now then I want you to retain that state of mind and body, but gradually open your eyes and look forward only at this moment.'

Kyle complied and found the view ahead amazing. Swirls of gold and silver flew in front of his eyes, as if he could literally see the movement of wind in the air.

'Can you see the air moving?' Zane was seeking the wellbeing of Kyle more so than looking for confirmation of what was seen.

'I can!' Kyle remained still as if not wishing to ruin the moment.

'Okay, then take a steady look around whilst keeping the same feeling.'

'Okay.'

Kyle looked around cautiously, noting the continuation of the colourful air swirling around. He realised it didn't take much effort to keep the same feeling he had, as it was almost as if it was supporting him!

Zane noted his head and eye movements.

'Okay Kyle, now I noticed you've only gone side-to-side, so now I want you to very carefully look at your feet... but most importantly - keep that feeling!'

Kyle didn't respond, but slowly moved his head downward. At first he didn't realise what he was seeing, but with a few seconds, a small amount of shock jolted him.

'Keep the feeling Kyle!'

Kyle struggled to keep the same feeling once he realised his feet were a few inches from the ground. After hearing Zane's reminder he quickly reverted to the sight ahead, noting the swirls of beautiful colours. He put the sensations and colours together in his mind, which strangely felt right for the action he witnessed. He couldn't make sense of why it made sense, but it did!

Zane looked upward, feeling proud of his student's accomplishment.

Kyle began to feel amazingly good and realised the exciting part of all that was happening. He started to giggle slightly, releasing his joyous emotions.

'Okay Kyle, so you appear to have mastered the retaining of the feeling. Now I need you to keep that same feeling and close your eyes again. This time, fling your arms back and push your chest forward as you did recently.'

Kyle followed his instructions immediately and felt air blowing past his chest, but kept his eyes closed.

'Now when you feel brave enough, bend your knees backwards.'

Kyle bent his knees gradually with slight nervousness.

'Okay, now move your arms and legs about and feel the wind direction change.'

Kyle complied, noting Zane's voice volume changing.

'So Kyle, keep the same feeling, but open your eyes gradually.'

He opened his eyes fairly slowly, noticing he had a different scene before him.   The air was still swirling with golds and silvers, but he had gone adrift and noticed slightly different tones of silvers and greys on the ground.

'Can you still hear me Kyle?'

'Yes!' Kyle turned to look for Zane and noticed he was at least two hundred meters away.

He panicked slightly, wondering how to control his direction.

'Play with your movements Kyle! Move your arms, keeping your chest forward. Experiment! You are safe. Ryston is not too far away, ensuring you won't suddenly fall.'

Kyle took a deep breath, trying to keep calm.

'Have fun Kyle! It's fun and exciting. There is nothing to fear!'

Zane's voice echoed around the vast space.

Kyle looked about and noticed Ryston's huge wings floating in the distance, as if he was treading water.

He took another deep breath and tried to control his *underlying* fear.

'Keep excited Kyle! It works better that way. All of the joyous emotions will keep you strong and light.'

He tried to move around, using his arms like the flaps on the wings of planes.

'That's it!'

Kyle looked up to see the nice blue sky and bright sun, encouraging him to enjoy the moment. He smiled with excitement, moving around and growing accustomed to the directions he could move in. He found his chest would propel him forward and the further back he moved his legs, the faster he would be moving through the air.

'Wow!' Kyle was now beginning to enjoy the control of it.

Zane smiled. 'Well done Kyle.' He stood watching on protectively for quite a few minutes. Ryston was most definitely watching for any mishaps, looking very powerful in the background.

'Okay Kyle, I need you to try to get closer to me now.'

Zane was surprised to see Kyle adapting very quickly to the directional control back in his direction. He soon arrived only a meter in front of him without any flaw.

'Well done Kyle. You truly have done extremely well with adapting.'

Kyle smiled with extreme excitement.

'I now need you to ensure your legs are straight, followed by your body standing tall.' Zane observed his complying actions. 'Great. Now, imagine you have magnets at the bottom of your shoes and it is connecting you to the magnets on the ground.'

Kyle visualised this and within a split second his feet were literally grounded. He caught his breath and noticed the swirls and wind had disappeared from his eyes. His initial feeling was pure disappointment, like a child having a toy taken away from him.

Zane's eyes opened wide.

'Kyle, you can wish the same at any point here. The crystals only enhanced the initial attempt. You will be able to do this anywhere in this world if you keep the visualisation strong. You will be stronger on the ground however. The flight is a wonderful feeling and amazing for any kind of escapism or replenishment.

Kyle looked around his feet and noticed the feeling of grounding to re-capture how things should normally feel.

Zane turned back to Ryston and gave a farewell nod.

Ryston remained in a vertical position, looking on with great strength.

'Come on Kyle. We need to get you back.'

Kyle followed him like a lost puppy back up to the peak of the hill and down the other side, feeling slightly wobbly on his legs.

They reached the path that eventually brought them back to the golden path, which Kyle assumed was the main route to everywhere.

They walked while Zane offered some further words of teaching. Kyle felt that he was growing accustomed to this lifestyle.

They reached the door between the two worlds and walked through. Kyle felt the weight of it all hitting him again, but this time it was even easier than the last.

'Well done Kyle.' Zane was comically preparing a rejuvenating drink of tea yet again as soon as they arrived back to the kitchen.

'So, do you feel any different this time after your interesting experience?' Zane looked on with a smile, whilst stirring the mugs.

As Kyle found himself quickly recovering, he stood to feel taller and wider.

'I feel as if I've grown.'

'Now that is a good description. I love your honest descriptions.'

'Would the crystal place make me feel bigger and stronger then?'

'It will make you feel like that yes – a great sense of energy.'

'Wow.'

'So, you might feel like you have excess energy to use up. Just use it on a run home after this, or maybe some exercises in your room... just some ideas. You'll *feel* what I mean later.'

'This world feels so limited compared to yours.'

Zane's smile dropped slightly.

'Kyle, both worlds are extremely special and each have their own advantages and disadvantages. The good thing is that everyone will experience similar things but without realising it. In both worlds, everything is energy, it's just that it is a lot more obvious in the one I'm accustomed to. The Earth's energy is subtle, but if you find it then you will have a great time creating your future life. There is a lot you don't know about my world, it also has limitations, but you won't find that out until a lot later.'

'But you can fly in your world. That only happens in my dreams!'

'Ha-Ha! Trust me, there are things that we can only dream of doing in our world.'

Kyle was slightly confused but knew the subject wasn't completely open, so didn't pursue it.

'It's time for you to have your replenishing tea and then head back to your folks before they worry.' He handed Kyle the tea.

'Now then, remember not to be tempted by your enhanced skills over here. You really don't want to be tested on in some kind of facility. We need you more than you know!'

Kyle felt honoured and full of purpose.

They drank their tea relaxing in their safe environment.

Kyle left to find his way back home quickly, feeling full of bubbly energy.

Kyle's wonderful feeling continued throughout the week. He could understand the warnings given by Zane on controlling his abilities. It was decided that he should keep the crystal inactive to avoid any further energy-boosting actions.

The training continued every week as normal and life at school was uneventful.

Kyle occasionally caught sight of himself in the mirror, recognising his natural physical growth, wondering how big he would grow to be before he was fully formed. He noticed an extra inch or two in height above other classmates his own age. Karen appeared to be falling behind in height, which they found funny between each another when reaching for a kiss or holding hands.

At home Kyle was the tallest of all of his brothers and extremely close to his father's height.

As all of the brothers grew older, Jack decided to move in with a slightly older friend, despite still being very young. He managed to settle into his career very quickly, earning enough cash from work to pay for a reasonable car.

Kyle felt as if everything from his family youth was gradually changing. He wasn't planning on leaving home or his education as soon as Jack had, but knew his final school time wasn't too far away. This all made him wonder about time frames and school exams coupled with the pressure of Zane's training.

With some comforting reminders of living his youth, he managed to relax and just go with the flow of life.

THIRTY FIVE

Training was getting more interesting as it moved along. Kyle was getting stronger and learning a lot of elaborate techniques which would work extremely well in his daily life as well. Within the parallel world, Kyle was playing with energy a lot more and learning how to adapt the same techniques with added abilities and forces.

He worked with his visualisation and manifestation of things. The sword work was improving to extreme levels of competence. Kyle enjoyed manifesting the sword on his belt and then making it disappear. He practiced the force field protection and started making meditation a regular occurrence when he had some private time.

The movements he drilled into his mind over and over every day became natural. Kicks; punches; defence tactics... He brought the crystal energy into everything to learn his maximum abilities.

He began to feel a bit like a super human machine.

The parallel world was becoming more and more familiar to him, with understanding of how things worked and the 'lightness' of the parallel world, yet much remained a wonder and mystery to him.

His mind was able to remain focussed and healthy without too much confusion, just wanting to understand more and more.

Kyle noticed that the healing Eagle hadn't passed through his life for some time now, which made him realise his coping mechanisms were becoming much stronger. He did occasionally spot a large bird in the corner of his eye, and knowing he was being cared for and monitored, brought him a lot of comfort.

Months had passed and Kyle was getting closer to his next birthday. At almost sixteen years of age, he was now looking very much like a young man. His build was tall and lean, with a very strong, muscular appearance. Even if he didn't know a defence art, others would not have wished to tackle such a stature. This was certainly an advantage over any enemies. Karen's ex-boyfriend for example - crossed Kyle's path on numerous occasions at school and around the local residential area. It was noticeable that Kyle was avoided by anyone from his past time of being bullied. This didn't change Kyle's outlook on things however – he remained kind and humble, avoiding any altercations.

At the most recent lesson, Zane was going through a new idea with Kyle in the parallel world. He was proud of how far he had come, but worrying about his near complete preparation for what lay ahead.

'You have come a long way, young Kyle. The original version of you needed our help so much. It was clear that you were this little rabbit, frightened of the headlights.'

Kyle stood in front of him with a great grin, waiting for instruction during this fresh training session. He felt so much gratitude for everything and was very willing to assist in the mission.

Zane moved straight into what he had in mind for this training session.

'Okay, so we have been working on many levels, attacking things with energy from a distance. I want to enhance that since we have been building our energy training gradually... So, remember our attack towards the stones or rocks from a distance?'

'I do Sir.'

'Okay, so let's practice this again briefly, but the idea here is to actually watch the energy leaving me.'

Zane stopped to create another little wall of stones and rocks. Kyle wondered if Zane was repeating the old lesson of knocking the wall of stones and rocks over.

'Don't worry Kyle. I haven't gone mad. I just want you to observe this time. Last time was actually practicing the attack from a distance. This time I want you to actually see the energy leaving me. Watch the energy from my palm. Study and capture its movements. Okay?'

'Okay Sir.'

Zane visualised the small wall he had built and directed an attack with an open palm.

Kyle watched intently and noted a silver, white light leaving his palm briefly.

'Okay, Kyle, watch again... this time really follow the energy leaving my hand. See if you can literally see the movement of the energy.

Kyle watched again and noted the energy leaving his palm and landing on the stones. This time, the stones smashed into hundreds of little pieces.

'Did you see the energy Kyle?'

'I did Sir.'

'Okay, so I sent the attack with a high intention of causing some stones to break into pieces. This is how powerful energy is. It is in fact much more powerful than that.'

Kyle stood, waiting for further words from Zane.

'We can use energy to harm and we can use energy to heal.'

Kyle recognised the direction of the lesson.

'I need you to be aware that the alternative energy is also strong with this. When the inevitable time comes where the battle begins, I need you to understand the importance of the force field you will place around yourself. There will be times of attack that you won't be prepared for. Okay?'

'Yes Sir.' Kyle was feeling slightly nervous about such a battle, but reminded himself of his purpose.

'So there are three parts to this lesson. The first is the power of energy – or at least how much *we* can use. The second is to be aware that the same power can be used against us. Now however, I want us to move to something a little more gentle, but equally important. Let's just say it is a bit like First Aid. This is the third part.'

Kyle stood with full concentration.

'Right, so now you know you can use your energy for attack, protection, manipulation of shapes and visibility... even flying! We are now going to use this harnessing of energy for a kind and gentle approach.'

Zane picked a plant from the ground beside the pathway. The plant looked as if it was beginning to decompose at an accelerated speed.

'Okay, so in this world and yours... there is a lot of suffering. A lot of it is pure nature, so it can't be helped. Animals killing animals; people harming animals and one another; the air is very much alive yet we are breathing that into ourselves, so even that goes through a process ... I am now harming this poor plant deliberately. Can you see it dying?'

Kyle felt sadness with the words and wondered why Zane would demonstrate something so cruel.

Zane picked up on the feelings and smiled at the result he desired.

'Now then, I can see your dislike of my actions, yet many of us over here and on Earth are harming all life forms. When you harm another, you are actually harming yourself, as we are actually all one rolled into separate parts. Now, I'm sorry for repeating any knowledge I've already given you.'

'Okay?' Kyle still didn't know why he was receiving a sad lesson.

'Right Kyle, watch this.'

Zane placed his palm over the roots of the plant and closed his eyes. A gentle light left his palm, which visibly moved through the roots and up to the tips of the green leaves.

The light penetrated every part of the plant and brought it to a good, healthy and strong looking plant once again. In fact the plant looked healthier than it did before Zane pulled it from the ground.

He then placed it on the ground, roots first and placed his hand on the soil. The plant appeared to be feeling the ground with the roots and sucked itself back into the soil, looking lush and vibrant.

'Wow!' Kyle was amazed at the actions.

'You like that?'

Kyle grinned widely. 'Oh yes! That has made me feel very happy.'

'Well that is fantastic, as I wanted you to feel the sadness of the suffering but see what we can do to help lives.'

Kyle looked directly into Zane's eyes.

'How do you do that?'

'Well you need to change your intention from harming something into the opposite, which is to heal.'

Kyle's eyebrows raised. 'That plant looked alive!'

'Like I said Kyle... Everything is alive. Even the air is alive. Your thoughts and feelings are alive. That is why others can sense you when you are here.'

'Weird.'

'You will understand as time goes on. This can take years for some and a lifetime for others. Your experience is beyond most on the Earth.'

Kyle smiled showing his teeth this time.

'So then why can't we heal everything and everyone at the same time?'

'Ah now then that is another big thing to understand. We all have the power of choice. Now that plant wanted to be healed and I offered it healing. Some people can be sick and be happy to be sick. They believe they are sick and unintentionally intend to continue to be sick. We cannot change people's choices. Some prefer to be unhappy, or don't look to change their ways to be happy.'

'Why would people prefer to be ill or unhappy?'

'Well everyone has their reasons. With some it is a vicious cycle that they can't leave; or they can't see the woods for the trees; or they don't believe they can heal. Some even want to be unwell or unhappy because they attract the attention they are seeking. Everyone desires to attract some sort of attention to themselves, even if it is the attention of wishing to be treated as someone who is unwell. Now that probably sounds very strange to those who desire good health. Basically we can only do what we can do. When people or plants or animals seek to be healed, then they are the ones that react very well to the healing. Unfortunately the natural life on Earth has a life span, so there will be times when their energy must leave the physical plane.'

Kyle found that this was the hardest thing he had-to learn since beginning this entire circumstance.

'I know this is a lot to take in, but as long as you get the idea of people making their own choices. If people don't respond to your healing actions, then it is their choice. It may be sad for you to see, but this is where we have no control over others. Does that make sense?'

'I guess so.' Kyle frowned.

'Right Kyle, so the intention here is to be gentle and have the desire to help and heal with lots of love.'

Zane pulled another plant for the practice.

'Oh no! What if I can't do this? Would I harm the plant?' Kyle clamped his hands together not wishing to make any errors.

'Okay Kyle, I know this takes confidence. If you can't do this then I will take over and heal the plant, okay?'

Kyle felt more at ease and dropped his hands by his side.

Zane talked him through the concept and watched Kyle's attempt, preparing to intervene for any rescue attempts.

There were small sparks of life on the ends of the roots, but it wasn't travelling up from there. Zane encouraged and inspired his thoughts further.

The gentle light from Kyle's hand enhanced gradually.

Zane could see progress, knowing this would take time.

After only a few minutes, Kyle suddenly caught on to the idea and shot the energy straight through the plant with a sudden burst!

Zane stood beaming from ear to ear with excitement.

'Yes Kyle! That is exactly how you do it!'

Kyle literally jumped for joy.

Zane began to elaborate:

'Right, so that is how you direct your energy when you see someone harmed in anyway. This occurs on the Earth but in a more subtle way, although for some it is strong... especially if it is often practiced. Over here you can literally see the energy going into the plant, person or animal... Or even other things, since everything is energy.'

Zane and Kyle practiced on many lifeforms for a considerable length of time and recognised growing energy in things such as trees, stones, rocks and water.

'Kyle!' Zane stopped randomly during the practice session. 'I feel you are almost ready! The healing section was the final thing I needed to teach you. We have gone through so much and I know you have been practicing intensely for such a long time now. I just need you to witness a little more.'
Kyle felt nervous about what was to come.
'Does this mean I'm ready to complete my mission?'
'I feel you are extremely close. I need you to witness a battle that I will be partaking in, just so that you can see what is involved. It is important to bring you in phase by phase until you are familiar with everything I need you to be familiar with. I can offer much more information if you are willing to go through a meditation again, so that I can exchange some information?'
Kyle knew this would be necessary and began to sit down to start the meditation.
'I think we would be safer to relax in the hall.'
Kyle stood before he settled. 'Of course Sir.'

The walk back to the hall felt sad for Kyle, as he knew things were going to become a more serious affair very soon. The reality of training leading up to what was about to happen, began to bring an unexpected level of anxiety to Kyle.

Zane could sense his feelings as they walked and he was not surprised. It was only to be expected.

They moved into the hall and regained their energies with a drink and rest.

'We could do this another time if you prefer? You have had a very busy session today.'

Kyle took a breath. 'Oh it's okay. I feel I need to face this now.'

'I know it's all been fun up to now Kyle, but the main phase will not take long at all and then your life will return to normal.'

Kyle felt sadness fill him, leaving Zane to recognise how much they have grown together.

'Everything will be okay. Just go with the flow.'

Kyle looked about, expecting some healing from his Eagle friend.

'Don't worry Kyle. Your Eagle knows when you are likely to need help. At the moment you are still managing to keep your emotions in a good state. It is only natural for you to feel this way. Don't allow yourself to depend on the Eagle for every emotion you feel.'

Kyle could never get used to Zane's mind reading, but he never felt threatened by it. Zane was only ever bringing comfort to his thoughts.

After plenty of recovery time, they both moved to the main space within the hall and sat opposite one another.

Zane became aware of the time factor for Kyle returning home to his parents, so promised a swift meditation.

They both relaxed in their space and activated their crystals. Kyle fell into a semi-dream state and witnessed a scene before him.

Lots of dark, flowing fog swirled in front of his eyes. Tall soldiers with silver swords were fighting valiantly against what seemed to be an invisible enemy. The dark fog occasionally formed into harsh looking figures with deep set eyes and scarred features. The tall soldiers fighting the dark fog were obviously the good soldiers, trying to uphold the love and peace but had no choice but to fight to contain the bad. They struck with their swords and threw light from their palms, hoping to push good energy into the darkness.

It was a tough battle. The men tired easily with the effort, so the formation moved frequently.

Some of the fog diminished, whilst other sections appeared to spread. It appeared as a never ending battle.

Some taller men moved in from behind and brought with them some fresh energy. They boosted some white light from their palms and held glimmering shields in front of them. Swords still swung in all directions, cutting through much of the grey colour. It was noticeable that with constant attacking came reward, as it gave little chance of the grey clouds to spread. The air cleared fairly quickly at this point and the remaining dark fog was contained by surrounding soldiers. Formations of light worked around the fog, a bit like a bright white rope being tied around it to strangle any remaining darkness.

Kyle jolted back into a clear and awakened state with Zane looking towards him as if waiting for a reaction.

They both sat there, looking at one another for a moment.

'So that is the kind of battle I will be involved in?' Kyle's words were slightly croaky as if he had just woken from a night's sleep.

'It is. As you can see, there is a team of us. Can you see how we managed to contain them and surround them? It takes a while, but it's about trying to stop them from spreading. A bit like a fire, they are able to grow in force. We don't have that ability other than to build our energy within ourselves and direct it... You know how we practiced pushing the energy from our palms to attack; heal; change our visibility; change our weight to become lighter or heavier... or to protect ourselves?'

'Yes Sir.'

'Well, they don't have as many of those abilities, but as I say, they can spread themselves like wildfire. If we can contain and restrain them then we are winning. So far we have contained the parts that attempt to grow, but it's getting harder, as they are getting stronger. Trion tends to stand back in the distance, but he is our greatest threat, as he is as powerful as Clara. They are both capable of such great strengths. If you imagine holding a great power and either using it for good or for bad...'

Kyle raised his eyebrows, not knowing how to respond. Zane continued however.

'If Clara and Trion get into battle singularly, then this could cause a great energy imbalance for both our world and the Earth. It is too great a risk. We aren't sure if Trion is considering this. If a battle between them occurs, then we don't know the future.'

'So, when do we have to do this battle?' Kyle asked with great confidence.

Zane was happy to hear the bravery in Kyle's tone of voice. 'Our side wishes to get together whenever you are ready. Obviously it needs to be at a time when your school and family won't be worried about where you are.'

'So a weekend day perhaps?' Kyle took in a deep breath of air. 'Will a day be enough? What if something happens to me?'

'Kyle, you are part of a strong team and I have seen how strong and confident you have become. We need your energy, youth and new-found wisdom combined with your Earthly strengths. You are the one our energies sought out. You will make it back so long as you practice manipulating energy the way we have trained.'

There was silence for a few moments as Kyle recognised this challenge. He felt nervous again with the pressure.

Zane slowly stood, encouraging them both to stand. 'Look Kyle. Take your time, practice what you know at home. Come to see me when you know you are ready or if you need more training or information. You can take several weeks or several months, it really doesn't matter. You need to be ready and know when the time is right.'

A thought struck Kyle. 'How will I know how to fight in your team when everyone looks as if they have a system?'

Zane smiled, looking very happy about hearing the question. 'That is the key Kyle. We don't want to train you into rules and systems. The beauty of you is that you will have your own ideas, which will completely throw the enemy. They are growing used to our formations and ideas. There is nothing fresh or shocking coming from us anymore. It is getting harder to fool them.'

Kyle frowned, worried that his ideas wouldn't be as good as those that have come from practice and wisdom.

Zane once again noticed his thoughts.

'Trust me Kyle... In fact, trust all of us - as we all look forward to you joining us in the great battle.'

Kyle knew he needed time to absorb the entire idea.

'Okay Sir. I think I will go home and figure out when is best to do this.'

Zane noticed a slight 'wobble' in Kyle's speech.

'Take as much time as you need. You need to digest the idea and know when your bravery and energy levels are ready.'

Zane placed a gentle hand on the back of Kyle's back and guided him to the main doors.

'You have already done us a great service Kyle. Don't forget how far you have come for yourself as well. If you wish not to partake in this event then I am certain that everyone will understand. It is quite a big ask, so if you find it is causing too much concern in your mind, then we shall all understand if you pull back.'

Kyle looked back at Zane's relaxed features.

'I *will* be doing this task. It sounds as if you're all depending on me, so I have to. Not only that, but you have saved my life from torment and taught me how to take control of things. Without your training I would still be pushed around even today.'

Zane gave a sympathetic smile.

'Well, you get some time to think about things and let me know when you are ready.'

Kyle reached for the main door handle.

'I won't leave it too long.'

With that, Zane gave a gentle pat on his back and stepped back into the dark and mysterious corner of the hall.

Kyle walked through the door without looking back and walked steadily home in the remaining part of the day's light.

THIRTY SIX

Over the course of the next few days Kyle experienced a few vivid and odd dreams about battles of various types. During the day he even worried about them and craved the feeling of a normal life. He couldn't help but wonder how things would be if he had chosen the boxing lessons instead. He favoured the thought of learning to defend himself without the pressures of putting his skills into saving an entire world... or two!

After a few days of resentment and the experience of slight fear, he decided that perhaps the whole "waiting game" would only make his situation worse.

The weekend was due and he had no plans set before him anyway. It was a strong decision that he would face his fears and take part in the peak of what he was set out to do.

Friday evening was drawing in and he felt he needed to inform Zane in order to have preparations laid out.

Kyle walked over to the hall to greet a very stern and strongly postured Zane standing in front of him.

'We are very grateful that you have made this decision Kyle.' They both stood looking at one another, knowing what all of this meant.

Kyle appeared to be making the rules now - and was surprised to hear his own voice dictating the plan.

'I'll be here at eight o'clock in the morning.'

'So be it.' Zane remained serious and looked respectful.

Kyle frowned with awkwardness and stepped backwards, spun and began walking home, not sure if that was the conversation he should have left with. He felt strong however and decided to keep walking, despite feeling Zane's eyes watching him.

Everything felt tense and peculiar, but Kyle knew that he was cared for. It was right to feel this way pending a battle that could potentially solve many problems.

The following day came swiftly and Kyle had barely slept a wink. He felt drowsy, but it was too late to pull out of something he had committed himself to and he knew that Zane would have communicated to everyone on his side.

He slipped into comfortable, sporty clothing and slowly made his way downstairs to prepare a large, energy boosting breakfast.

Everyone in his family was fast asleep, or at least resting. Worried thoughts about never seeing his family again crossed his mind. Even after all of the training and experiences, he still doubted himself and the event he was about to take part in.

Although his hunger levels were extremely low, he forced himself to eat as much as he could.

He heard someone moving around upstairs, so tried to eat quicker in order to leave the house before having any interference with his plans.

A deep voice suddenly spoke, making him panic and almost drop his bowl.

'How come you're up so early?'

The obvious words from his father shouldn't have frightened him.

'Oh, I want to go and do some training with Frank.' Kyle was surprised at his swift, invented response.

'This early?' His father studied Kyle's features. 'You look like you could do with a few more hours.'

'Oh we planned it ages ago. We wanted to have the whole day doing some... training.'

His Dad noted the hesitation in his voice.

'Your usual training?'

Kyle felt an interrogation coming on.

'Well, yeah.'

'Does this training involve girls? Are you going to be at Frank's house?'

Although Kyle expected questions as soon as this conversation started, he enjoyed the feeling of being cared for by his father. It reminded him of a normal life and the reasons to ensure a safe return home.

'Kyle?' His father continued the investigatory questions whilst reaching over to get the morning coffee going.

A comforting thought came to Kyle, bringing a smile to his face.

'Yes Dad. Don't worry, I'll be back for dinner.'

'Well your Mum and I were hoping to take you all out for dinner. Make sure you're back for five o'clock.'

Kyle felt his blood rushing to his feet, uncertain of the duration of the battle.

'Okay Sir.' He answered promptly to avoid any suspicion.

'Sir?' You never call me Sir... And if you did, you certainly wouldn't say it with such a stern tone.'

'Sorry, I don't know where that came from. Ha!'

Kyle's Dad frowned. 'Are you sure you're awake enough yet? Maybe try one of these strong coffees.'

Kyle felt warm again with his father's care.

They shared an invigorating coffee together, enjoying a gradual awakening. Nobody else appeared to be rising from their beds, which allowed some personal time. Kyle realised how rare this moment was and how magical this time was with his father. There was so much focus on training and school that family life seemed to miss a lot of Kyle's attention. He realised how much he missed the feeling of bonding with his father.

Kyle savoured the moment.

The time had come for Kyle to leave for the hall. Luckily the rest of the family were beginning to rise from their night's sleep, allowing Kyle a perfectly timed exit. He felt that the father/son moment gave him the emotional strength he needed for the task ahead. He wished he could have spoken of it, but even if he was permitted, it would have been too far-fetched for his father to believe.

Kyle walked down the pathway, not being able to avoid worrying, one of them wondering if he would be returning up the same path at the end of his ordeal.

Others were continuing on with their normal lives, getting dressed for a weekend. An element of jealousy filled his emotions.

Zane greeted him at the door with a caring expression, noting Kyle's pale and worried features.

He wore a strong fitted garment that appeared to be almost warrior-like. He wore very baggy black trousers with a matching black top that looked as if it was wrapped around his core for strength and stability. His sword sat comfortably on his belt.

'I'm so pleased you came, Kyle. I know this must be a weight on your mind, but I promise I will be by your side the entire time.'

Kyle didn't respond with words, but gave a very slight smile.

Zane gestured for Kyle to move into the hall. They walked reluctantly to the end by the kitchen, knowing the route they were taking.

'Kyle, please be assured that should we fail, you will still walk away.'

'We will not fail!' Kyle's voice was different, much stronger than even *he* expected to hear with his own ears, but he certainly meant it.

Zane looked over to note a firm expression on Kyle's face.

He knew he meant business and he was certainly focussed on the task.

'Okay then Kyle. Let's do this!'

Kyle moved forward whilst attaching his belt and manifesting his sword.

They both reached the door to the other world and opened it with the manifested golden key.

The door opened with bright light filling the entire hall space. This light was so powerful that Kyle had to shield his eyes initially until he reached the golden path. He looked back to notice the door had closed behind them. Zane checked to confirm the same.

The place appeared too perfect to visualise any war, making Kyle feel more at ease initially. He looked over to note a very serious expression on Zane's face.

'Now, Kyle...' Zane was obviously ready to warn him. 'I am about to call our team over, Okay? With the battle, I want you to stay near me and just fight with your sword as you would against an attacker. If you can focus on love... which is very difficult during such times... but if you *can* focus on love... then fight with energy from your palms as we practiced with the rocks. Place your force-field on when you need to rest or catch your breath... move back if you do this.'

Kyle nodded, but knew instinctively what was needed of him.

'We will have a moment of gathering and preparing, then we shall be calling the dark energy over...' Zane took a deep breath. 'Once they begin to arrive, be prepared and give it all of your might. Okay?'

Kyle looked over with worrying eyes. 'Okay.'

'Be strong Kyle. Before you know it, it will be over, but for now, just give it the same focus you have during training.

Okay?' Zane wanted to ensure Kyle was ready for this before continuing.

'Yes, Sir. I am ready.' Kyle's eyebrows moved downward, giving a stronger and braver look.

Zane noted the change and signalled them to walk forward. As they walked, Kyle noticed Zane was beginning to close his eyes. Kyle watched, concerned. Zane's forehead appeared to give off white streaks of what looked like electrical currents.

Kyle's eyes opened wide at the strange sight, while Zane's eyes remained tightly closed.

Kyle heard some decisive footsteps from ahead, so spun his head to view some light figures walking towards them. Their walking noises didn't appear to match their strong, yet light-looking bodies. Among the human-shaped people walked some very strong and large looking animals. Some looked dragon-like and others looked like huge tigers with extremely long claws, which gave a clanging noise on the ground when Kyle's ears focussed on them.

Zane opened his eyes to witness the great sight of a strong army growing closer. 'Those are our friends Kyle. They are of white, bright and colourful energies. Feel their power.'

Kyle instantly felt a burst of power fill him. It certainly helped his mind to know he was in good hands.

As the human shaped figures moved closer, Kyle felt extremely small by comparison. He remembered how much taller people seemed to be in this world. As a result of their added height, they were also very much wider.

They grew closer and Kyle noticed their features. One had a very large forehead, but with quite a few scars over it. Another had very large eyes, which consumed most of his features. Another was a very slim, tall lady with long hair that glistened with gold. Some had flecks of the same white electrical current as he Kyle had witnessed on Zane, moving outwardly.

All of the animals appeared to have strikingly bright, golden eyes with a hint of orange.

Kyle wondered if he would be able to focus on the battle with such unusual sights to take in all around him.

Zane looked over at Kyle then glanced over at the rest of the team.

'This is our final piece!' Zane shouted with the most booming, deep voice. It was almost surreal.

Kyle didn't at first acknowledge that the words were focused on him, until the team began to approach, introducing themselves.

Animals moved around Kyle and sat near his legs, as if settling down at home. The people came over to touch him on the shoulder or reach out for a kind handshake.

He felt like royalty for quite some time. Most of them didn't speak, but the ones who did gave a wonderful welcome with the most interesting of voices. Some of the voices didn't appear to hit Kyle's eardrum clearly enough. It was almost as if sound from them moved straight into his mind without clarity.

Zane again noted Kyle's expressions.

'Take some time Kyle, but know these are your friends.'

411

Kyle never felt more welcome, and savoured the moment.

After a few moments, there was a noticeable movement in the crowd of 'beings'. Kyle recognised another figure moving towards them. Ryston glided through the air with some tall characters walking below him, all carrying something.

They all grew nearer and a pathway was permitted by the crowd. The new group came close and offered everyone a tall glass of golden liquid, as before at the table on a previous visit.

Zane spoke again.

'Take your preparation drink all.'

This triggered movement by everyone collecting glasses in their hands and drinking liberally.

Zane collected a glass for Kyle.

'It brings good energy and vitality.'

'Thank you.'

The liquid didn't appear real. It slipped down the throat seemingly without having to swallow. This was an odd sensation for Kyle, although an instant glow came about him. He felt bolder and fresh in his energy.

Kyle looked down to notice his glass had disappeared. He looked over at Zane for signs of collection, but everyone's glasses had disappeared! He looked over at one person still drinking to observe and noticed that once completed, the glass simply dissolved in his hand.

'It's okay Kyle.' Zane once again comforted Kyle's worries. 'It is a manifestation that is set to disperse once the purpose of the glass is complete.'

Kyle frowned, wondering if there would be any more surprises on an already different and stressful day. He moved forward with his thoughts, observing all of the new and different characters all around him.

'Let us move forward!' Zane was the obvious leader and walked ahead, encouraging Kyle to stay by his side.

'It is time!' Zane was obviously all set in his mind.

Kyle felt nerves begin to take control, but others were patting his back and shoulders as they moved ahead.

Zane stopped all in his tracks, noting a dark and tall figure manifest ahead.

A voice boomed from the dark figure, hitting everyone's ears.

'So this is what you want?' The voice was deep and more powerful than anything Kyle had ever witnessed.

Zane responded, attempting to match the powerful voice.

'It is not what *we* want! It is what *you* want! We wish for peace. There is time to step down and re-join us in peace.'

The dark energy appeared to grow angry and growled in a frightening tone.

'You cannot control us! We grow before you!'

The dark energy began to grow in size and thickness, a small formation of large, facial features appeared.

'Trion.' A voice whispered behind Kyle.

The dark energy moved backwards as if sucked into a genie bottle sat in the distance, while other grey mists began to move forward towards them.

'Ready!' Zane commanded.

Everyone around Kyle gathered their weapons in their hands, while animals moved ahead of them, offering claws and sharp teeth.

Kyle stepped back slightly, reaching to ensure his sword was ready.

'Settle your mind Kyle and think of it as training. Just fight through the grey mists and retain a focussed mind.'

Zane offered the information whilst keeping his attention ahead. 'Throw your distant attacks forward when you get opportunities. Do what you feel is right.'

Kyle didn't respond, but prepared his mind.

Animals charged forward, their claws turning silver and cutting through the grey mists ahead. The people charged at a running pace, slicing their swords through the mists and attempting to surround the cloud formations that swirled and changed shape constantly.

Kyle felt as if he had no clue in what to do.

Zane looked back at Kyle and shouted, as he moved forward. 'Follow your instincts and do whatever feels right at your own pace. Stay by my side!'

Kyle moved along with Zane, still attempting to relax his mind well enough to draw his sword. Horrible thoughts hit his mind and the grey mist grew closer as if everything was beginning to take over. He panicked and quickly screwed his eyes tight shut, throwing a force-field around himself. The force field allowed a pause in time, giving him a moment to observe his surroundings. He looked to notice the mild bubble of light around him, confirming he was safe.

Swords and claws were moving forward, creating a powerful feeling of strength and force he hadn't felt before. He did momentarily contemplate remaining safely in the bubble of energy until it had all ended, hoping that all he needed to do was remain present until the end. Zane looked back, catching a very brief sight of Kyle's position.

'Stay with me!' Zane's words pulled Kyle back to focus on the current situation.

Kyle looked around, noting the fight was not apparently piercing anyone's body. He reached down and felt the sword by his side. His mind grew slightly braver, building up to the energy of a coiled spring... He was now ready to attempt what he was finally here to do.

He removed the force-field with his mind and swung his sword forward, bracing his body in preparation.

With a long, vocal scream outward, he ran forward with full force, plunging himself into the grey fog, surprising Zane as he passed.

Kyle flung his sword at the mist and fog that he could see, noting the occasional facial feature appear then disappear, giving clues as to where the aim needed to be.

The faces that exposed themselves briefly amongst the fog disappeared as quickly as they appeared, giving angry expressions – sometimes fearful ones as the occasional one weakened.

Kyle attacked continually, not noticing the formation changes amongst the team. It wasn't necessary anyway, but it was certainly powerfully affecting the grey mist as it was becoming more confined.

There was a notable sound of Trion's voice hitting Kyle's mind. It was almost as if he was shouting a long 'Nnnoooo!' into the air.

Kyle felt much more confident in the circumstances and simply continued to fight forward with his sword. Energies were dispersing and a mixture of whites and greys swirled before everyone's eyes.

Zane shouted the occasional command, encouraging everyone to work hard at the attack.

Kyle needed to breathe, so stepped back a few steps and bent down to create the force-field of protection. He took many deep breaths and shook his arms to replenish himself. Zane looked back in concern, but Kyle was fine, he just needed to regain his strength after so much effort already. Within his short rest, he noticed the grey growing above, out of everyone else's focus. It was as if it was deciding to grow upward and outward like a growing mushroom.

Kyle shouted. 'Look up!'

The entire team took note and witnessed the growth, signalling Ryston to lift himself to begin the attack from a greater height. Zane smiled at Kyle with gratitude, but moved swiftly in for the attack again.

Dragon-type shapes of fog were lifting and fighting from a greater height. Slowly the grey and dark mist grew higher despite the good team's recognition and change of attack to attempt to contain it.

'From above!' Kyle shouted his instant thoughts, triggering Ryston to move on top of the huge cloud that was forming. Kyle was surprised at his own words, but noticed how the others were taking note of him. He realised the power of "words" that were becoming apparent, but grew frustrated at the continual growth of the grey mist and cloud.

He built up energy within him and felt himself breathe in with very deeply. His strength appeared to grow intensely. Noting the changes, he wondered if he could increase his strength with each deep breath.

His experiment seemed to be forming into reality, but this distraction took him away from an image he suddenly caught sight of. As he looked on, he noted some of the large animals were being consumed by the dark cloud and fog. They seemed to disappear into the cloud as if they were eaten into invisibility. The team was growing smaller and the dark and grey fog was growing in size and obviously in strength. Kyle panicked and looked around for Zane, finding him with his vision. He was fighting hard and looking weary in strength. The battle was extremely intense for all of the fighters. Some were disappearing into the grey however, leaving Kyle to panic even more so. He realised that this was how the enemy fought. It built its army by consuming all the surrounding energy.

Kyle looked about and wondered why all of the plant life looked very much alive, but also very still and unaffected. This intrigued him, so he stared with great intensity, wondering if the plant life could ever be affected – and if not, why not? Bringing the battle back to view, he couldn't believe he was wasting time thinking about such things while others were literally being consumed by this darkness.

Kyle was about to throw himself back into the battle, when he felt a magnetic pull back towards some of the plant life to the side of him.

'Huh?' Was all he could manage as his strong intention to fight was completely pulled away from him.

Zane briefly looked back again to notice a distracted Kyle.

'Kyle!'

It was a very strange sensation as he was pulled into a calm "emptiness" of the mind. The battle didn't appear to exist in Kyle's mind at this moment. He tried to shake the distraction and straighten his thoughts back into the battle, noting the background voice of Zane shouting towards him, but something else was controlling him.

He suddenly felt a strong hand grasp the top of his arm.

'Kyle! I need you to keep safe with me!' Zane had gripped him with concern for his wellbeing.

With the grab, Kyle came back to his own mind and re-focussed himself.

'Kyle, are you with us?' Zane noticed Kyle's blank expression and worried.

'I … I am.' Kyle realised he was back in his normal mind.

'Please help us. I know it is difficult, but our numbers are dropping. We may need to pull out soon if we are at risk of being completely consumed.'

The entire battle looked as if it was close to a complete loss and Zane sounded desperate.

Kyle looked on to notice only two main people fighting the fog, with the grey and dark appearing stronger and bigger.

A voice behind, sounded familiarly like Trion's.

'You will be with us within moments! Your fight was foolish!'

Zane moved back into the fighting zone and Kyle noticed a flicker of perhaps another one, or two team members somewhere amongst the fog. Most had unfortunately been consumed.

Zane looked back again.

'Kyle! The severity of this battle I cannot express enough! Your Earth will also be affected by the grey and darkness if we do not conquer it now! We are that deep!'

Kyle knew the severity of the situation, but didn't feel fazed. He slipped back into the feeling of being consumed by something far greater. The plant life around him seemed to hold his attention again. He tried very hard to fight against it and move forward back into the battle, but the force was too strong.

He breathed in deeply to gain strength and once again his strength built to a surprising level. His voice boomed. 'Let me fight!'

Zane couldn't look back to see what was occurring, as he knew the numbers were too low to stop.

Kyle couldn't understand this big "pull" of distraction and again attempted to resist it.

He breathed in again and noticed the strength build within him yet again. His body fell on to the ground as if a large

419

magnet had taken control. He gave into it and decided that if this was his ending then there was nothing more he could do to stop it. This invisible force was more powerful than anything he had experienced in all of the training.

He let go and just allowed his mind to accept that something was consuming him and that this was the end.

Although he was trapped, he felt as if he was growing stronger with each breath. Noises in the background were loud with clangs of metal and screams of effort and pain. The feeling of being trapped and consumed was now too much and he appeared to drift into an unconscious state.

THIRTY SEVEN

Police officers were called to an unusual event in the area.
An intense glow had taken the locals by surprise as it seemed
extremely unusual.
A huge ball of light glowed in an open space of land, with
sparks flying from it. To everyone around, it seemed to be
something alien.
Police taped the area off with great concern and little
understanding. Other specialists were due to attend and the
press were moving in fast, collecting their images.

Luckily the land was an unused piece of green space which
had a little purpose, for taking short cuts between the
streets, through a residential area.

The news on television moved onto the subject quickly,
reassuring everyone that this was contained and confined to
this one particular space only.
The police warned everyone to keep back and to keep all
mobile gadgets and devices away for prevention purposes.

The glow appeared to burst outwards, growing larger, and
then smaller as if the action of breathing was occurring.
This was another surprise to all onlookers.
The news features changed to the possibility of this light
being very much alive.

People were beginning to panic, with some deciding to pack necessities and drive off, hoping this was something they could escape with distance.

Others were trying to get as close as possible, some attempting to reach past the police tape in order to touch it. The Police were gaining in numbers as time moved on and their defence increased with guns, batons and shields. They did their best to retain calm in the area but had to shout aggressively at a few of the daring members of the public.

The ball of extreme light gave off more intense sparks, shocking some of the onlookers. Even the police grew increasingly nervous and ducked at the unpredictable sparks. Some retained their focus and shouted at the onlookers to keep back.

Camera men and women were growing in numbers and becoming almost uncontrollable.

The chaos grew with no sign of the glow diminishing.

THIRTY EIGHT

Kyle found himself lying flat on the golden path, paralysed on the ground. He came to full consciousness, but trying to figure out what situation he was in. He assumed that he was captured by the enemy, but no-one was coming to his assistance. Perhaps they were either engrossed, or thought he had decided to play dead!

Putting other people's potential thoughts aside, Kyle decided he needed to calculate in what circumstances he was in. He managed to raise his head, but felt as if the rest of him was strapped completely down. As he looked about, he appeared to be tied down with a white rope that flickered with transparency, as if it was real but not completely solid. It certainly held him down in this position however.

He grunted and tried to move. With this impossible feeling, he looked further ahead and noticed the grey and black fog and cloud had grown to mammoth proportions, filling the sky and moving outward in all directions. There was no sign of Zane or any other team members. Kyle's initial thought was that of failure and that the grey and dark was on its way to consume everything, including himself.

He looked from side to side, noting the plant life was still glowing, but with greater intensity. Small animals were collecting in the plant life and walking closer to the path, also glowing!

The grey and dark coloured energy grew closer, but Kyle still had fight left in him. He screamed to be set free.

'Let me go!' His voice was strained.

As he shouted, a great electrical surge moved through him, making him feel incredibly strong, but still annoyingly trapped to the ground. He looked over at the plants surrounding the path. The light grew even brighter around the one he set focus on.

'Help me!' He couldn't help but feel weird about shouting to a plant.

The plant appeared to take some form of action however. The brightness increased to a blinding light from the one plant and spread to the one near it. Then the light from the two brighter plants shone to the nearest ones again, consuming all of the local plants. The extra light moved to all surrounding plants and moved up the trees, to intensify the light around every living plant. The light then built to fill the sky and all of the birds. The light filled every living plant, small animal and creature in its path, until it beamed so brightly that Kyle couldn't see anything at all. He was forced to close his eyes tightly. He felt a great power filling him, making him feel as if the light building up around him was beginning to fill him in just the same way. This light within him felt so powerful that he could see it within his mind without having to open his eyes to see it. The light was so bright that it filled his eyelids anyway and his initial worry was that his eyes may become damaged by the intensity of it. Kyle was completely uncertain of the present events, but the light began to give him such an overpowering sense of greatness that he knew he could break from the chains of these strange ropes. His body suddenly felt electrified and uncontrollably strong. He moved his arms with great confidence, breaking the ropes around him. These strange, white ropes snapped with great force, allowing Kyle to stand with a different feeling about him.   He stood immediately with his arms slightly raised and attempted to open his eyes. The light was just completely white all around him. He looked down to see that his body was consumed entirely by this white light as if his body was no longer solid, but his body still *felt* as if it was there. Although Kyle felt completely blown away by this situation, he held his mind and went with the flow. He thought about the plant and how it spread this light. Perhaps Zane's teachings about everything having energy and everything being alive, was proving to be true and extremely useful in the current situation.

He looked forward and noticed that in the distance was the swirling grey fog and that it merged with the edges of the light that was expanding from him.

The great, grey fog attempted to move forward with great difficulty.

The "Trion" voice came through, making Kyle feel vulnerable and alone in the battle.

'You have lost!' The booming voice penetrated Kyle's entire being, but he didn't let it shatter him.

He knew with his great sense of strength that he had a super source of life shining within him and without him, despite not being able to understand it fully. The very nature of all of life assisting him was now the only thing that made sense. He felt an unusual sense of love, but had an overwhelming feeling of the need to "explode!"

He opened his palms and looked at them beaming with complete light, knowing exactly what to do.

Kyle took the deepest breath he had ever taken inward and belted all of the air, along with all of his energy outward, pushing everything forward that he felt he had within him. As he pushed it forward, he let out the loudest cry of power he could ever have imaged while closing his eyes tight. 'Aaaaaaaarrrrrrrrrrrrrrgh!' His voice was deep and louder than any volume he knew he could ever reach.

His scream was matching the feeling he had pushed out. He felt the powerful surge of energy – like electric – leave his body, through his palms and chest, pushing forward, penetrating anything ahead of him. He literally felt as if he had exploded every part of energy out of himself.

He bent forward, feeling as if his breath had taken everything from him. Opening his eyes, he noticed the light was slightly faded and that electric surges were buzzing from him, making him think about Zane's forehead earlier. He looked up to see that everything appeared to have returned to normal, as if nothing had even occurred. A weakness came upon him with the recognition of his energy being nearly depleted.

A panic came over him again, realising he may have used every part of his existing energy to defeat the dark energy. He looked about again to confirm that all was calm. Any darkness or grey colours had completely diminished from the air. Everything instantly returned to normal around him. The plant life returned to normal and his body looked as physical as it always had been before. He viewed the sky and the distance and all was at peace. A sense of great

426

achievement filled him, followed by worry over the location of his good friends, accompanied by a dizziness and sudden thud to the ground.

Everything stopped and blackness formed.

THIRTY NINE

Red and white swirls spun like a lucid roundabout under Kyle's eyelids. He heard voices enter his ears, but he wasn't capable of responding.

The voices were muffled but recognisable. He assumed he was now trapped between the two worlds in some kind of limbo situation that no one could save him from.

His Dad's voice came to his ears.

'When are you coming back boy?'

Kyle felt he was able to move his lips, but felt paralysed otherwise. He wondered if he was in a coma. His mind was still somehow aware, but unable to function with the rest of him.

Jack's voice now came through. 'Where are you? We're all worried!'

He couldn't understand why he could hear voices from his family and why they seemed to be calling out for him. It was almost as if he was in a dream state but with complete awareness. Thoughts of being on a safe hospital bed after all of the recent events was the most comforting idea.

He listened on to hear other mumbled words, but couldn't quite fathom them out.

There was no awareness of comfort of discomfort with him. His mind just floated in a world of being aware but asleep at the same time.

A jolt made him notice more of the white swirls over the red ones. It was a circus in his head.

The white swirls became very bright, making Kyle more aware of himself. The red swirls disappeared and he realised he could actually open his eyes. As he did, he noticed he was lying on soft, green grass. He reached out and touched the ground with the tips of his fingers to confirm this.

He was firstly surprised that he was still *actually* alive.

As he regained consciousness, he noticed white light all around him. His hands felt around the grass ensuring it was most certainly real, but the white light around him didn't make any sense.

He slowly stood up and cautiously walked forward, coming to an opening of the white light. On the other side of the light he appeared to be surrounded by the sound of chaos. He looked beyond the light, squinting his eyes to make sense of everything.

People were wildly moving around, with the police trying to have some sort of control over them. Kyle looked around to notice fingers pointing towards him and screams of shock and horror. Kyle swiftly ran backwards, almost stumbling over his own legs, moving himself into the middle of the white ball of light again where he felt safer. He looked down at his hands, wondering if the energy was about to build again but it didn't. Everything felt Earthly and normal, as if he had crash landed. He looked around at the white light, trying to make sense of it all.

He shook his head to ensure he was fully conscious and functional. He confirmed himself as perfectly fine. His body felt extremely well rested and vibrant. He somehow knew that this white light surrounding him was a protective barrier of some sort. This comforted him, but he needed to know the details of these new circumstances. His mind turned to Zane and the team that he somehow left behind. It was true that no matter what occurred in the other world, that he would still make it back. The only concern now was that he may have made things very different back on Earth.

A sudden crackle and formation came before his eyes, recognisably as Zane's figure with Clara stood beside him. Kyle took a step back in surprise and wondered if he had called them in his mind.

'Hello Kyle.' Zane gently spoke with clarity.
Kyle shook his head to focus on this *new* reality.
'Did I call you? What happened?' Kyle was confused, but extremely happy to see his friend and Master.
'Don't worry, you're completely fine. We knew you would be confused upon waking.'
'Where am I? Did we win the battle?'
Zane smiled at his innocence.
'You saved us all! Do you remember anything?' Zane studied his eyes for wellbeing.
'I remember fighting the dark with a crazy build up of energy. It was as if I had burst and depleted myself of every last part of me.'

Well that makes perfect sense.' Clara spoke with her extremely soothing voice, while Zane nodded in confirmation.

You took on the force of all living things, combined with your own powerful energy.' Clara continued. 'Then you pushed it outward to consume the entire force that was against us.' Zane looked at Kyle with an intense stare.

We came to congratulate you on your successful mission. Our world has been saved and we can continue on with our normal existence. All of our good people's lives have returned.'

Kyle gulped and needed more information. 'But how did ....?'

Zane didn't give Kyle the chance to complete his question. You were great Kyle. All of the training you did appeared to build up to one great lesson...The lesson that everything is energy and that you were the chosen one who could manifest all energy within *you* to conquer the dark energy. This has also taught *us*, as we weren't certain of how to conquer Trion and his army other than the joining of all forces with you, our final piece.'

Clara smiled in agreement. 'You have taught us so much Kyle, and we thank you.'

Zane interjected: 'All of the little lessons didn't seem to come into play during the battle, but they were all part of the bigger lesson.'

Kyle's mind was beginning to catch up with the present. Well I didn't really know what was happening. I think a greater force was taking control.'

'You were the vessel and mind-set needed for the task. Your instincts and trust took over, which is what works more so in our world.'

Kyle listened with intent, looking back in his mind at the events that had occurred. Everything was now coming together. He remembered being drawn to the energy of the plants and the birds, and everything that lives. He remembered the build-up of energy within him and the feeling of everything consuming him. The sudden realisation of the energy that had built up inside him so much, that became too powerful to contain. It had to be pushed outward at the enemy that was growing near. He realised that everything had occurred exactly as it was meant to. All that lived in their world must have known the task they had and the need for his presence in order to perform it at the right time.

'Wow!' Kyle expressed his confirming knowledge.

Zane and Clara smiled at one another when they recognised his realisation.

'Well done Kyle.' Clara appeared to grow in an orange glowing state.

Kyle instantly recognised the glow as a demonstration of her growth in emotions.

'You have learnt so much Kyle.' Zane said in a calmer voice. 'Don't lose your newly found knowledge, as it works here – on Earth. I know I have said this before, but as everything is energy, things work the same but in an extremely subtle way. Don't ever be disheartened to think the opposite just because your eyes see differently.'

Kyle knew these were close to Zane's final words. He felt this would be a difficult goodbye.

'Kyle, you saved us by defeating the dark energy with the light energy from *all* that lives in our world. Now we can live in peace in our world and assist so wonderfully with your Earthly energies once again, hoping to encourage the same for the people here.'

Kyle grew excited about the new hope and possible changes. He then took his thoughts to the people in Zane's world.

'What happened to everyone else in your world? I saw them losing in the battle. Did any survive?'

'We were all rescued by your energy, so we were able to reform and heal. In fact Trion is healing with all the good energy now. He will be reformed to remember the good in him. We are all friends once again. Trion is seeing his errors and releasing all of the bad that he was accidentally drawn to. We are monitoring him however to ensure he remains in our loving energy. As bad as it all seemed it is only love and healing that he requires.'

Kyle raised his eyebrows with the great news. He looked at the grass on the ground and needed more answers.

'How did I get *here* though Sir? It's like I dropped from the sky.'

'After calculating all that had occurred, I found you lying on the ground with pretty much no energy remaining. You needed instant healing, so I called for Clara and between us we healed you. From Earth, we could hear the voices of your family... as they were calling out to you in fear. I had to bring you back here quickly.'

'My family?' He paused in thought. 'So that is why I heard their voices? How would they know I was in any danger?'

'This white ball of light is being witnessed by everyone on Earth at this present time. It is causing a lot of fear. Your family need to know you are safe. You have the ability to hear their thoughts and words with your enhanced hearing at this moment in time. This is the same as us hearing your thoughts.'

Kyle worried about everyone seeing them and the white light around them.

'This would certainly bring a lot of attention to us!'

'Don't worry, we need to erase all memories of this event otherwise there will be widespread panic across the Earth.'

'You can do that?'

'There is so much we can manifest and undo. We can't mess with things too much however. This was a necessary action after such severe events.'

There was a pause in all words and thoughts for a short while. Kyle realised there was a lot he didn't understand about the parallel world.

Zane wanted to give further reassurance.

'You are healed and restored to normality. The light here is formed for your recovery. It is on the land where we manifested the hall for our training.'

Kyle gulped. 'You manifested the hall?'

'Well, I exaggerate slightly with that, as the structure of the hall was already here. It was falling apart with lack of care or use, so I just re-created it to be safe and useable again. We needed somewhere to train you here on Earth without the influence of others.'

'So how did the door to *your* world end up in their?'

'Now that was something Clara and I created. Humans can't just "walk" into our world, so we needed a wall that could transform you as you walked through it. The crystal enhanced your energy to match our energy at the same time.'

Kyle would have preferred a scientific explanation but knew he most likely wouldn't comprehend it anyway. Thinking about the crystal's function was already something beyond *his* capability.

A new reality hit Kyle's mind. The fact that things were complete between the two worlds meant the "mission" was over and that their companies will be parting.

'Will I see you again Sir?' A sad feeling filled him.

'You will see me, but not in the same way. I will be with you whenever you call upon me. You have been gifted with your life now, where you can create your own manifestations.'

Zane felt that many questions were going to be coming from Kyle, but he knew he needed to allow his thoughts to settle into some sense as time went on.

'We need to go now Kyle, to allow your return home to your family. You will know your way from here. Go well Kyle.'

Before Kyle had time to speak in return, he noticed the recognisable wings that flew directly towards him.

Kyle woke within a few short moments, knowing that his Eagle friend had healed him.

He didn't realise he needed further healing, but appreciated the help anyway.

Feeling wonderful and refreshed, he wondered if he would remain conscious this time.

He remembered everything that had occurred and noticed that he was sat in the same bubble of white light. Now that he was fully aware and feeling much clearer in his mind, he wondered about how much attention this white light had attracted and how he could escape without being spotted. Voices from all directions reminded him of the strange scene surrounding him. He wondered how he could escape this area without being noticed this time. Walking towards the edges of the light from all possible directions, there was a spot that appeared empty of people. It steered directly to a large tree. He noticed that the majority of the people were at the opposite side. A sudden memory of how the energy of plant life saved him came to the forefront of his mind. Perhaps this one tree could be his final saviour and the distraction he needed.

He looked out, coming to the edge of the surrounding light, hoping no one would be focussing on this particular zone. Luckily the coast appeared to be clear. People were walking up and down, but with precision timing he could get to the tree. There was a clear moment, so Kyle made a speedy run

o the tree and leant against it, pretending he had been there
all along. One person walked from the distance, smiling
strangely. Kyle hoped and prayed that the smile wasn't a
"knowing" one.

He slowly walked over to join the rest of the crowd, looking
over at the glow from their perspective.

Mm, I suppose it does look rather out of place.' He
muttered under his breath, not worrying about others
hearing him.

There was a lot of talking and concerned shouting.
Kyle realised how this was affecting people's minds in a bad
way. Some were extremely fearful, while others were overly
excited. People were shouting at the police and pushing
through to capture the image.

Camera crews were talking excitedly with mention of the
army due to attend.

Kyle remembered Zane's words of the people not being
ready for such events and he could see this was true.

If anything unusual ever occurred on Earth, it was always
contained. This glow of obvious light just wouldn't be
concealable. He hoped Zane or Clara were able to do as they
promised.

He turned to focus on his whereabouts and realised he was
in the same spot as the hall area, just as Zane had stated.
The start of his walk home began.

As he walked away from the scene steadily he heard a large
group of the people groaning and sighing. Kyle turned to
note that the huge white glow had disappeared out of sight,

leaving a normal view of police tape; grass; an old building structure and a few odd trees.

Kyle was shocked to see the hall looking very old and rickety. He tried to recall if it looked that old during the training, or if Zane had caused it to revert back to the original structure before his manipulation.

The police took swift note of the disappearance of the white glow and shouted their advice to the people. Logical words were heard - to go home and get back to their normal lives. Kyle continued to walk, occasionally taking a glance back at the scene. Some people were determined to hang around just in case anything else may occur, but most eventually moved on - left to ponder over the event.

All *images* of the huge white glow had mysteriously disappeared. People's pictures on the phones and cameras simply showed scenes of the green land, with no hint of the "alien" light. The live news was the only evidence of this event ever occurring. In people's minds it was something that was simply inexplicable.

Kyle gained pace and arrived home within a short few minutes.

As soon as he walked in the door, his parents ran over.

'Oh, Kyle! Thank goodness you're back!' His mother shouted.

'Why what's wrong?' Kyle attempted to demonstrate innocence.

'That hall you usually go to for training has just been consumed in this really unusual, bright light! Where the heck have you been? We've been worried sick!'

Kyle grinned. 'Oh, I heard about that. I was just out training with my friend, but I didn't go to the hall.'

His parents stood tall and sighed, releasing their tensions.

The household relaxed slightly and the television revealed the conclusion of unexplainable events remaining unexplainable.

The night came and everyone was nervously hoping for an uneventful night after the local scare.

Kyle lay awake for a few moments, wondering if everything that occurred had actually happened since it was all too strange to have any truth in it.

As he relaxed on the bed, the distinctively recognisable crackles filled his room.

'No, not at home...' he whispered.

Clara manifested in his room before his eyes.

'Kyle, this is the last time I shall visit, as we promised a normal life for you now. I just wanted to let you know that we shall be leaving no trace of any knowledge of that light ever existing. All memory of the white glow will be removed from people's minds as it is all too much for them. I thought I would let you know so that you're on a level with their adjusted memory.'

Kyle nodded with wide eyes and raised eyebrows.

'Enjoy your life!'

Kyle nodded again with no words, as Clara once again dispersed into thin air.

EPILOGUE

Kyle walked to school with a new hope of great times. It wouldn't be long before his school days were over and he hadn't even contemplated his future.

As he walked, he looked down at the inactive crystal. It was the only evidence of previous events. The hall appeared to be out of use, and there were no mysterious doors to walk through.

His mystical friends hadn't visited since the closure of the battle, but Kyle was mostly comforted by the thought of a normal life.

He hadn't experimented with any enhanced abilities since, and wasn't even sure if they still existed.

The biggest lesson learnt by everything that had occurred, was the magic of family and close friends. He knew he had taken his wonderful upbringing for granted previously, so he now clutched onto his time with everyone.

Kyle even favoured school and contemplated staying on for further education.

As he walked, there were many younger students pacing up and down. One younger student looked very scrawny and weak, walking on his own. Some bigger kids were running past him, knocking the bag from his shoulder.

Kyle felt sorry for him and thought back to the days he had similar circumstances.

He was tempted to walk over and give some advice, but the school bell made the decision for him.

Kyle picked up his pace, reaching the main doors. Many other students were rushing by his side, all pushing through. There was a squeal and thud in the distance, causing most students to look over at a scene.

Time appeared to stop for Kyle as he viewed the weak and scrawny-looking student getting pushed to the ground.

Many barged past Kyle, rushing to their class to avoid any detention for lateness.

Kyle watched on at the poor, bullied kid climbing back up to his feet and couldn't bear to see him suffer.

He ran over and helped him with his bag and to help steady the boy.

'Hello there. You can't let others push you around like that.'

The boy looked up at Kyle with frightened eyes, so spoke further to calm him.

'Don't worry, I'm not here to hurt you. We had better not be late for class.'

The boy looked slightly nervous but walked on silently.

'I used to be bullied just the same until I found lessons in self-defence. How do you fancy some lessons from me?'

The younger boy looked at Kyle's features as if looking for honesty. After a studying his face for a while, he answered with a weak 'yes.'

They walked up the main path toward another set of main doors. Kyle felt good about the offer of help and wondered where it would lead. His knowledge would be passed down with kindness as it was to him.

He felt an unusual warm breeze hit the side of him as they walked, forcing him to look around for a cause of the draft. A large tree was in view, holding a branch that moved with obvious weight.

Kyle frowned and stared intently. A large bird sat, looking on.

Kyle recognised the features of the Eagle and smiled.

He spoke in his mind. 'Still watching over me, huh, buddy?'

A thought came to Kyle just as if it had been placed directly into his brain.

This was the thought of knowing that everything was happening just as it was meant to.

THE END

Printed in Great Britain
by Amazon